PIRATES OF LOBSTER COVE

Pirates of Lobster Cove logo, title art, cover art design
& *Lobster Cove crossclaws* logo
by Sir Richard Wentworth
www.rwentworth.blogspot.com

Pirates of Lobster Cove / S.E. Toon
ISBN-13: 978-0-9896297-0-6 (pbk.)
ISBN-10: 09896229708 (pbk.)

Summary: 14 year old Tyler Byrne discovers a pirate in the present day and a mystical book which can change time and our memory of it. After undead pirates are accidentally unleashed Tyler and his seaside friends must trust in their loyalty to one another to save the world.
1. Young Adult—Fiction. 2. Paranormal--Fiction 3. Pirates—Fiction 4. Zombies—Fiction 5. Nautical—Folklore 6.New England—Fiction I. Title

PIRATES

of

LOBSTER COVE

A Novel by

S. E. Toon

HUBBUB

PUBLISHING

For my family who read to me,
read what I wrote,
encouraged me,
challenged me,
shared my memories,
and above all else, believed in my words.

For endless summers spent,
all those who shared them,
and the many more to come.

.

For you, dear readers, young and old,
for without you all of this would be folly.

For Rich, *Pirates* illustrator,
for embracing the novel's
briny heart and in turn, his own.

PIRATES
OF LOBSTER COVE

Chapter 1

AHOY!

*I*t was during the summer of my fourteenth year when I first rubbed elbows with legend. There he was in all of his pirate glory, stopping before my cottage porch. The man clutched the guardrail to remove his sandblasted leather boot emptying whatever sand or pebble that was irritating his good leg. He slipped the boot back on and tucked his pant leg inside its lavish cuff. The boot's ample leather slouched down his calf in a jaunty, well, piratey way. When he stood up and pulled out a red handkerchief to wipe the early morning humidity from his brow, our eyes met for a moment. The stranger at my front stoop stared at me through the screen.

'Billybones,' I thought. I didn't dare utter the nickname that came to me as I stood there transfixed by every childhood fear I ever had of pirates. I just mouthed the name as he loomed before me.

BillyBones was a sight to see. His lanky form stood a crooked six foot four. He was thin but in no way frail. His bare forearms revealed a taut musculature, rippled like suspension bridge wire wrapped with tan skin. A coat of faded red hair was in full effect. He looked English, or what I assumed an Englishman would look like from my grandfather's tales of WWII, the *big* one. He always commented how threadbare their uniforms were and how gaunt and battle-worn they looked, but to *"beat'm, you'd have to kill'm"*. That was tough, BillyBones tough.

The rest of his appearance also fit the pirate profile. His pants faded brown canvas that hung heavy on his form. His shirt billowed in the salty air where the white gauze hadn't clung to his perspiration. A large buckled belt tied the two together, a walking stick slung beneath like a sword. His face possibly forged in the heat of a hundred summers was sculpted in sun burnt highlights and dull brown hollows that looked more like smudges of dirt than tan. In contrast, his eyes shone sea blue, eyes that knew history, eyes with tales to tell.

"Mornin', kid." the stranger muttered in an exhale as he adjusted the bag slung on his back. It was a statement not a greeting. His eyes lingered for a moment, sizing me up like a wild animal that had stumbled into a clearing only to find the threat of campers. Sensing a safe haven, his look softened ever so slightly and he turned from me, the doe-eyed boy behind the porch screen, and turned his gaze to the path that went from the shoreline towards the center of town.

"I'm a see'n ya, I'm a walkin." He paused a moment in thought. "Morning . . . good mornin," he muttered to himself. He swung his favored leg out in front of himself to walk away and then turned back to me. Making a double check of his safety level he gave me a slight nod of his unshaven chin. With a squint of his one good eye he shielded from the early sunlight he turned up the path. Perhaps it was a wink. The connection was unspoken but very much real. He knew me and I may have just met a pirate.

Before I tell you what happened next and the adventure that unfurled that summer, I need to fill you in on the world where my small circle of friends and I were transplanted every summer. To us, summer was the Cove, Lobster Cove on the map, but it was *"Lobstah Cove"* to us.

There were snowbirds, locals and daytrippers. Snowbirds would fly into town in June as soon as hometown schools closed and stayed in the Cove right through Labor Day. My friends and I were said birds. We did enough time on the Cove so we were welcomed like migrant geese crossing an early spring sky. Locals found themselves trapped in the Cove year 'round, through the vicious Nor'Easter snowstorms and coastal flooding that would ensue off-season. They were mostly blue collar workers in the fishing industry who worked hard and long through the best months of the year only to find downtime between plowing gigs in the misery that can be winter on the Atlantic coast.

So what is a daytripper you ask? They were the time shares and weekend warriors that congested our fair fishing village just long enough to wear out their welcome. They came from Albuquerque to Zaire from Memorial Day to Labor Day. They pronounced Lobster Cove devoid of any discerning accent leaving a week later with the best New England accent that they could muster. *'Lopstahhh!'*

The term "Lopstah" became a slur of sorts like "Arrr!" must be to a pirate. When daytrippers would try to get all chummy and butcher our local-speak with phrases like, "So, how are the

Lobstahhh biting?!", we would just roll our eyes and bite our lips. *'Go home, 'tripper! Lopstahs don't bite; you do!'* we wanted to say.

We knew better. They spoke with cash. The adults, no matter how much the daytrippers looked down their nose at them, refrained as well. They realized that these people were their bread and butter during the short summer months.

Half-awake locals would head to the docks about the same time each morning as my first pirate sighting. They would carry lunch buckets or brown-bag leftovers. Many had beer bellies covered by soiled t-shirts for Red Sox Championships or last year's NASCAR winners, their glory and color as faded like these shore men's memories of youth.

They worked hard and they played hard: up before first light and catching last call in the neon-lit confines of locals-only watering holes. At another time and place Billybones would impart to me, "Good men, lobstah men, workin' with what God gave'm. Can never have a bad drink with a lobstah man," he mused, sounding nothing like a daytripper.

"Ye worst day drinkin' with a lobsterman is league's better than drinkin' top shelf with a landlubber."

I had to take Billybones word on that. The one time I tasted alcohol it tasted like paint thinner. I assumed the difference between shelves was similar to Mountain Dew and the generic drink at the Cove Market, a beverage so poor in taste, they didn't even bother to give it a catchy name, just Lemon-Lime Drink.

First looking upon him I knew that he wasn't a daytripper or a snowbird. You sensed he was older than the bleached docks at the harbor though he looked barely fifty. He was of old blood, as local as the coastline itself. He could say "Lopstahhh" any time he chose and no one would ever challenge that he didn't belong.

Billybones shuffled his way up the street, lame but strong in stride when two of the aforementioned lobstermen crossed his path. The men instinctually knew not to look the man directly in the eyes. They passed, heads bowed slightly, almost reverently. They were a good three paces past before they even dared look back. They huddled together like school boys passing notes in class, fearing of being caught by teacher. One man whispered to the other. BillyBones stopped. The men cowered and stopped in turn. The assumed pirate adjusted his duffel bag and continued towards town. The two men waited a few strides before walking further. Billybones was alpha dog and no curs in the Cove would contest it.

My first vision of the pirate faded into the morning haze. I sat transfixed on the porch. Was it real or remnants of a dream? I needed to know. I sprung to my feet and bounded out of the breezeway to find someone awake who could confirm my pirate sighting.

The golden hue of first light cast a warm sepia tone on the kitchen walls. The toaster popped up similarly tinged slices of bread. *'The toaster!'* That would mean Mom must be about. And as luck would have it, she came around the corner from the pantry with a jar of flour and a wire mesh basket of eggs. *'Alas, a witness!'*

Failing to find words, I grabbed my mother by the arm and dragged her into the porch, almost breaking an egg in the process.

"Tyler Lewis Byrne! What in heaven has gotten into you"

She whispered in hopes of keeping my brother asleep. I escorted her briskly to the porch and pointed repetitively like a mute. She followed my finger and looked up the road to the crest of the hill leading to town. The outline of BillyBones could still be seen in the distance through the glare of the sun. I swallowed, more of a gulp, and found my voice.

"Look Ma..." I whispered in a tone even quieter than my mother's. What if the stranger heard my accusation all the way up the road? I pictured him turning on his heel and looking back with plundering intent.

"...a pirate... see'm?" I asked as if merely asking would question my very own sanity.

There must be a place where they put delusional kids who see things. Perhaps only adults know of the existence of such institutions. They only talked of the place when they were not within earshot of a child.

'Haven't seen the youngest around these parts in a while, dear?' 'Well, one thing led to another and he had to... go away. Saw pirates, the poor thing.'

Admitting the vision to my mother might usher in a fate as fearsome as the potential pirate at my door. If she didn't see him, then it would surely be a one-way ticket to the booby hatch.

My mother squinted at the figure at the top of the hill, tilted her head a bit to focus and then let out an exasperated sigh. Then she did something that made my heart stop. She opened the front door screen and waved. With a lilting tone she called to him.

"Ahoy!"

It all happened before I could pull her back inside to protect her from whatever wrath was yet to come. *'Ahoy?! You might as well go Arrr, Ma!'* my inner voice shrieked. The man turned, gave us a curious glance then managed a halfhearted wave as he turned back to the road. My mouth fell open. We dodged a bullet.

Mother closed the screen and went back to preparing breakfast.

"Him? He's the curator at the new nautical museum opening in the square. A mister. . . Smythe I believe." Her air of familiarity was unsettling. She looked at me with a mother's eyes aware, all too what a short time of this childlike innocence was left.

Stopping her morning chores, she giggled, "A pirate? Of course, a pirate." Her amused voice was louder than before and was enough to rustle my older brother Ryan from cutting *Zs* on the living room couch.

"Maaa? Wh'd ya say," he muttered half-awake under a rubble of sheets. I looked desperately at my mother silently pleading, *'Noooo!'*

"I said pirate dear, imagine that! Tyler thought he saw a pirate." My inner voice lamented, *'O man, here it comes...'* Ryan's head popped up from under the sheets like a maniacal teenage jack-in-the-box. He was all cow-licked hair, pimples and smiles.

My 16 year old poor-excuse-for-a-brother paused a second so that his slow mind could load up with verbal ammunition. The sound and smell of sizzling bacon filled the cottage as both the strips of pork and I was grilled.

"A pirate ya' say? Sure it wasn't the Easter Bunny, twerp? I hear that Santa Claus vacations here this time of year. He's got that whole beard and boots thing going on too. Sure it wasn't the jolly old elf? Snap!"

He rolled back into the sheets in a fit of uncontrollable laughter.

The morning all but faded from memory. I spent the rest of the day awash in daydream questioning whether or not I had even seen the supposed pirate at all. The man I named BillyBones became a half-real, half-imagined figment of my imagination.

It wasn't until after dark that the moment played back in my mind, sharper and more vivid than it did in the hazy morning light. I was alone in my bed, tucked snugly into the eaves on the second floor of our cottage. The repetition of the tide lulled me to dreamland. I saw his figure fade into the distance as my mother turned away from the door. Then, just as I started to turn to follow her to the kitchen, I looked back. BillyBones face appeared not three feet before me on the other side of the screen, smelling of *Old Spice* and chum.

'So, yer thought ya' mighta' seen a Pirate, do ya Lubby??', he spewed, one eye blazing blue in my direction, one hazed over, not quite looking my way. His jagged teeth grimaced a sickly yellow. *"Well, did ya or didn't ya!,"* he hollered, his spittle spraying against the screen door like sea foam. *"Well, well, boy... stranger things have happened... and will!"*

Suddenly there's the tip of a sword, a flash of steel, a spray of crimson. The blade tears through the screen just shy of my right ear. I heard the rapier blade sing, its warmth cutting air.

I awoke, rushed to the upstairs window and looked down on the road below. It was basked in pockets of streetlight. From the shadows I heard a footfall, then drag, footfall, drag. I looked further up the road to see the profile of BillyBones in the distance disappearing past the road's far horizon.

Writing it all off as a bad dream, the result of one too many slices of pepperoni pizza, I turned back to the comfort of my bed. Resting on my pillow lay a sheered lock of my hair, a halo of crimson pin dots encircling it.

I then went to the linen closet to change my sheets.

S.E. Toon

Chapter 2

THE BOBBERS

Shark, the Cyrkle yelled. I laughed back at my friends and splashed about as if I had been bit, my head bobbing in and out of the surface of the waves. Splashing is a dinner bell for sharks. Still, I had no fear. Having seen a real life pirate only a day before, it was going to take more than their warnings to instill the fear of God in me.

Oh yeah, I used the "S" word, sharks, dreaded man eaters of the deep. To cross the bobbers was to enter shark net territory. Shark sightings were rare in the Cove. Still, if you dared cross the bobbers you felt as if you were venturing into an untamed sea where any man not protected by a cage would be called lunch. Sandy would rattle off statistics of shark attacks on the East Coast or a list of indigenous sharks that could be lurking in the area, hoping to deter. It was the ultimate *safe* dare.

The bobbers were a string of orange floats that ran horizontally along the coastline fifty yards out indicating the drop off to the open ocean. If you crossed the bobbers during daylight hours, the lifeguards would whistle their cheeks sore. Nothing ticked off a lifeguard more than having to get wet. They would rather perch on their lookout chair slicked down with tanning oil, white sun block striping their nose and flirt the day away with potential summer hookups. Only an occasional eye was kept on the beach.

Once we were on dry land, the lifeguards would ban us from the beach. Being banned was kick ass. We'd stretch our hands out in front of us and shake them at the guards and laugh, "Fear, Fee⁻yuuh!"

Now the lifeguards had good reason to warn us about the bobbers. First, it was a long way for them to swim if any of us actually started to drown. Also, the potential for a rip current grabbing us was more likely where the shallow floor ended. It was also the perimeter of the shark nets on the other side.

After you crossed the bobbers the undercurrent became toe⁻numbing cold, even in August. Occasionally the icy current was veined with warm water. That was when our bodies would go on full alert; every sense sharpened for that tropical flow was the sharks' calling card. Eyes scanned the waves for fins, the water against your skin hugged you tight and the salt in the water put an added bite into the air.

This gathering started with my need to tell my best of friends about my pirate sighting. I had to reveal BillyBones as the pirate he was for the safety of all Lobster Cove.

Something needed to be done and quick. I could not achieve the task at hand without the help of The Cyrkle. John Lennon coined the name for a band in the 1960s. We thought it sounded Gaelic, cryptic, and cool as we were on our best days. A plan needed to be established then implemented posthaste, the goal, to ferret out the pirate of Lobster Cove, the dreaded pirate Smythe, aka Billybones.

The Cyrkle comprised of Sandy Womack, the resident drama queen and bookworm, Bess Duvall, a tomboy's tomboy, and last but certainly not least, Francis "Frankie" Gambino, my trusty compatriot Gatto, Italian for cat.

I set the rendezvous point. They knew that it was something big, big and important.

"The bobbers!" exclaimed Gatto. "Whatddya do, kill somebody?" Gathering together at the bobbers would ensure that no one could overhear our conversation. It was the location of choice of the Cyrkle for all matters high regard.

I like nicknames like Gatto. A nickname in modern society is the equivalent of a title in days of yore. You weren't merely King Macadamia or Pope Pop n' Fresh, you were respectfully referred to as King Macadamia the Merciless or Pope Pop n' Fresh the Benevolent. Today they would have monikers like King Nada and Pope Benny, both honorable, both righteous. So goes Gatto, if Gatto lived long ago he would be referred to as Francis the Lion-hearted. By the end of this summer he will have earned the title.

At first, the nickname Gatto came from his uncanny way he cheated death. Like his namesake, he had nine lives. At the beginning of this summer he was on life three.

The end of his first life was a mystery to us as young children. It had something to do with his birth, tentative first months and his mother's tears. All we knew was that Gatto was 'damn lucky to be here' because his mother frequently warned him whenever he was remotely in danger. Her voice would peal through the screen door of their porch.

"For the love of St. Pete! Francis Anthony Gambino! If I told you once, I told you a million times, stop it! You know you're damn lucky to be here, don't push it!".

Every summer, pushing it became our favorite pastime. It was more than just the thrill of the risk; it was about testing the patience of Mama Gambino and Gatto's guardian angel. We swam past the bobbers at the beach, cannon-balled off of the high ledge of the jetty, shot tennis balls out of a makeshift cannon, anything to set off his mom. We'd time how long it took for her to remind Gatto of his lost life. Summers are long on the Cove, you find fun where you can.

We weren't daring, we just liked to appear so. Every stunt was performed with the utmost regard for safety. Take the homemade rocket launcher, Gatto's invention, it sounded dangerous as all get out but was fortified with precautions. The tennis ball can was secured on a cinder block anchored with duck tape lit with a match attached to the end of a yardstick. One of The Cyrkle stood poised with the gun nozzle of a garden hose at the ready. We weren't stupid.

Gatto's second life was snuffed out just the summer before. It went out in a blaze of glory.

The Fourth of July weekend in any coastline tourist community is a celebration of everything American. Every stoop and railing is festooned in our nation's colors. The marches of John

Phillip Sousa drift in the air intertwined with whispers of *Kokomo,
Hot, Hot, Hot* and rump-shaking dance beats blaring from boom
boxes. The lapping surf, the occasional racket of firecrackers and
the laughter of the young and old join the medley. Every patio has
barb-b-q; charcoal and burnt hot dogs fill the air. Everyone is at
leisure; all is right with the world.

The shore slowly transforms into an American Carnivale.
The sun hangs low; clouds glow in bursts of orange and red.
Freedom is in the offing. At this time the illicit proceedings dial gets
turned up to eleven.

Now, fireworks are illegal in our state but you wouldn't
know it by the evening's proceedings. There are no fewer than six
bunkers of amateur fireworks simultaneously being shot off the
Cove's beachhead alone. Sulfur taints the pleasant scents of late
afternoon revelry. The gathering crowd breaks into swells of "Ooos"
and "Ahhs".

These aren't every day, 'look, honey, what I smuggled out of
South Carolina during my last golf outing' brand of fireworks. These
are 'You need a permit, a fire truck at the ready and at what time
would you like the Boston Pops to break into the *1812 Overture* type
of fireworks.

The proceedings are four straight hours of unsupervised
mayhem. It is adult recess with no fear of timeouts. Ramparts and
fountains of ill-directed color shower from the trenches on the
beach. Fishing boats join the fury with their own displays shooting
from their top decks. Looking through the smoke you could see the
distant glowing balls of bonfires littering the shoreline. More

fireworks blossomed in miniature in the far distance. The night is on fire.

On the last summer of Gatto's second life, a group of us local kids decided that the view wasn't good enough behind the safe confines of the concrete seawall. That wouldn't do at all. We had to climb down to the rock and sand of the beach to get closer to the action, we had to push it.

To our credit we were in a group. There was safety in numbers. The Cyrkle plays it safe, right? Wrong, not that night.

Why the following occurred is still up for debate. It could have been the beer-goggled lack of judgment of the yahoos shooting off artillery grade fireworks at high tide. It could have been a freak act of Nature like an East Coast version of the Santa Anna Winds. Perhaps Fate the Dealer was sending the message to Gatto that he's been gambling at his table of life a bit too long. Whatever the cause, folly or fate, what went down that night still plays in my memory in slow motion.

This all occurs in less than twenty seconds. One firework, instead of going skyward, burst forth in a horizontal trajectory, only inches from the sand. Its direction moved from the water's edge toward the seawall with us, the Cyrkle, stuck in-between. We all dove from its path, that is, everyone except Gatto. As if aware of our counter move, the white-hot comet made impact against a rock that protruded from the shore like the molar of some ancient animal skull, and burst into four separate projectiles fanning across the entire perimeter of the beach.

Instinctually, I dropped flat and rolled into the safety of the sand. I would have burrowed to China if I had time. Others grabbed one another, forcing themselves to the ground. We were all safe; that firework had Gatto's name on it.

I remember Gatto's eyes, brown, awe-filled, and puppy dog wide. He fell to his knees as if the pearly gates themselves were opening to him. I could see the reflection of the orb growing wider until it eclipsed his pupils. I didn't have the time to open my mouth, never mind call out.

Then there was sizzle, darkness and silence.

That accounts for the snuffing out of Gatto's second life but what happened in the minutes that followed astonished me more, binding Gatto and myself as friends for life. The accident called up something in him that, frankly, I had never possessed.

I thought back to when my mother would try to rattle some religion into me. Whenever I was the least bit blasphemous she say, "Who do you call when you are at your most troubled, what is the name you call out? God, that's who".

I would look back at her and shake my head. "No, I holler Ma!"

Gatto didn't set off the *Ma* alarm that night. He deftly peeled the loose firework from his cheek. It fell to the ground shattering into embers. Cupping his eye like an EMT at an accident site, he stared through the haze for the first adult that came into view. He said in unsettling rational voice, "It burns."

The neighborhood panicked for him, grabbing him up by the arm and carrying him to safety like a fallen soldier. Once inside the nearest seaside estate, Gatto remained cool as a cucumber giving his caretakers information when asked. "Can't open it", he instructed, the pressure building moment by moment. "Hot." "Blurry." "Ice."

Only when danger was a good distance past him, when the hysterical adults gave him a moment alone, did he cry. He never told me this, but I knew he did; he had to. If a flaming ball of consequence attempted to blind me I surely would have.

Gatto's coolness under fire and Angel Gabriel's intervention scorched a badge of courage across his young face. He was Rocky Balboa in miniature; his stocky twelve-year-old Italian features highlighted with a plum of a shiner around his left eye.

They took him to his family cottage to rest. I finally battled through the distraught crowd to see him. Opening the door, I got a good, long look at his face. *'Too close!'* my inner voice stammered.

We looked at each other... well, I looked, he half-squinted, half-winced. I held back the quiver of my concern. I hollered, "Adrianne!!" in the best Sylvester Stallone imitation I could muster, cracking a forced smile. A trembling grin replaced Gatto's wince-squint.

At that moment our friendship was forged; a bond tested during the months ahead. This summer would take Gatto's third life. He would be the Robin to my Batman, the Poncho to my Quixote, and that summer, the Black Bart to my Captain Blood. In truth, the roles should be reversed.

———

"Ark-ney on your utt-bay" Gatto called out as if sharks didn't know pig Latin. My confrontation with belly and teeth started at the break of dawn. We met out at the edge of the nets so that I could spill the whole pirate exposé. Gatto came decked out in a pair of surfer shorts, his baby Buddha of a belly creeping up over the waistband. Sandy wore denim cutoffs and a bikini top that even at her young age was starting to fill out. Topping it off, she wore a rubber swim cap with floppy flowers on top. It was the kind an elderly grandmother might wear, but she made it work. Bess wore cargo shorts and a camouflage tank top over her swimsuit. She rarely ever swam in her swimsuit alone, especially when there were boys around. It wasn't that she felt ashamed that she wasn't maturing as fast as her glamour girlfriend; the clothes just seemed to defy the rough and tumble in her. She knew that soon enough her femininity couldn't be cloaked in baggy pants and Tony Hawk T shirts and on that day she would no longer be just one of the guys. Pheromones would start flying and the horn dogs would start hovering and nothing would be the same. She loathed that reality and wished she could stay fourteen forever.

On the other hand, adulthood could not come quicker for me. I hated being the scrawny victim of a growth shoot. My face barely donned any peach fuzz. My voice would slip back and forth between high and low registers. I would coax it lower with an annoying honking sound that I tended to make whenever I was goofing around.

I came to the beach wearing a mom-bought pair of swim trunks that would blow up like a puffer fish whenever I hit the water. I would have to submerge the material into the water letting out a farting sound to the amusement of all but myself. I compensated for the clown trunks with a tie-dye shirt from the local surf shop that I purchased with three weeks of allowance money. The words 'Levitate the Cove' sprawled across the front in big block letters. It made a statement of spiritual proportions. The coolness of the shirt seemed to offset the dorkiness of the trunks.

I took them up on the safe dare and crossed underneath the bobbers.

Sandy's eyes caught something flittering through a mirage on the lip of the coastline, cutting the smooth of the water, leaving a ripple of a wake. She proceeded to let out a scream fit for a cheesy horror movie as she waved me in. She usually had more words to describe a situation than the rest of us combined but at that moment, she could think of only one.

"Shark, shark, ssshark!"

Sandy loved drama in her life but not this kind.

Sandy's world was pink. She would rather pine away the hours between the covers of a tabloid magazine, kissing glossy photos of the latest hunk-of-the-week. I found a magazine of hers once where she drew x's for eyes, moustaches and devil horns over the hotties competing for her hunk's affections. That discovery gave me great insight into the girly world of Miss Womack.

She read those tabloids cover to cover as well as anything else she could get her hands on; cereal boxes, automobile maintenance manuals, dictionaries and everything on the school extra credit list. This habit became a great advantage to the Cyrkle whenever our ambitions reached beyond our smarts.

Much of what Sandy read was not appropriate for her age. More than once she was grounded for having a racy "chick lit" book stashed away in her underwear drawer. It would be many a night she would stay up late, a satin kerchief diffusing the bedroom light, lost in the mature fantasy world of rogues, dukes, mid-day dalliances, chilled cosmopolitans and Brazilian waxes.

Sandy's strength was the lethal contradiction of her attractiveness, her smarts and her age. The vastness of her knowledge would always catch people off guard due to her beach bunny exterior. She was always one to correct someone regardless of his or her age. Pithy remarks would then be backed up with annotated references to note the source of her attained knowledge.

Still everyone loved Sandy. Even when I was very young and didn't like girls, convinced that they could indeed infect us with cooties, she was the one exception. The boys in town would never share it, but they were all at one time or another head over heels about Sandy. With a flip of her yellow, flaxen hair she could make you feel all squishy inside. She knew of her gift early in life which conveniently made her exempt from the infantile displays of daring-do that initiated the rest of us in the Cyrkle. After all, she was Sandy Womack, it was beyond her.

————

The two girls were now screaming in unison, usual for Sandy, unheard of for Bess.

"I don't like sharks, got it?" Bess said back on shore putting an end to any more needling. "Damn grinning, no neck bastards! I'm not kidding Ty, ba-dum, ba-dum, ba-dum, ba-dum, kick it in high gear and try not to splash around like a seal while you're doing it," Bess coached from the safe side of the bobbers.

If Sandy was the brains of the outfit, Bess was the brawn. She was an exotic mix of Latino and American Indian which made her stand out amongst the other vanilla girls in town. The copper of her skin was lean muscle, not the marshmallow softness of Sandy. She could out-skateboard anyone in her age group including the boys. She was never more gallant than when she rode.

The world of the tweeners in Lobster Cove moved at 15 miles per hour. To not be on a board was to have your youth pass you by on four wheels low to the ground. For The Cyrkle, skateboarding was our mode of transportation. The evenings would be accompanied with the sound of peeping frogs, whiteheads crashing on distant rocks and the chatter of our composite rubber wheels coasting in and out of the streetlights.

The skateboard was the great equalizer between us and the teens. We were no longer children but not quite young adults. We were still clear-skinned and cautious with a daring that a prime hill and some clever banking could fill. Teenagers were acne-ridden, fearless to a fault and were the most likely demographic to be found dead on a concrete jersey barrier after clocking eighty miles per hour on some hot August night. At our young age of fourteen, we didn't know how well off we had it.

Not so was the case with Bess. If the guys had to do it, so did she. You didn't even have to dare her. Outside of her quick flashes of jealousy over Sandy always being fawned over, she rarely gave us a glimpse of her girly side. When challenged, she was in her element and she excelled. It was in those moments when she was her most beautiful.

It was Bess' first rail ride that showed us just how much moxie this tough little keg of dynamite had in her. Rail riding had several prerequisites. First, the ability to go aerial, at least a foot high over the pavement with your board tucked flat against your sneakers. Second, board-to-eye coordination to fly out over the metal railing and ride it sideways along its edge until you lost momentum. Third, the timing to dismount the same way you got on, reaching for the sky, defying gravity. Most important, you needed speed; speed that eats pre-teens for lunch.

Mayhem was inevitable. There was no trick that wasn't paid for in flesh. It took a bit more from Bess than from the boys but, to her credit, many of the boys would quit before mastering such a challenging maneuver. Bess never quit.

When the older skaters egged her on to try the rail I thought she had met her match. She accepted the challenge. I knew it would start badly but I had to let Bess be Bess. After an endless foray of spills when she was first getting street-legs, I would skate over to help her up. She would look up at me, daggers for eyes. She always had something to prove and she had to go it alone for it to count. Here was a girl almost half my size who was "armed to the teeth" as my Mom would say. I wish I had half her warrior spirit.

She took the course in; skating swiftly, sizing up the obstacles. She was a small girl and when it came to riding a board, what she lacked in inert velocity she compensated with technique. This run asked for both velocity and for prowess. Bess was only armed with skills.

She was able to levitate her board with the best of them but her first approach to the rail proved to not have enough gas to make the ascent. Her board hit the rail square on the wheels, catapulting Bess head first onto the pavement.

Spectators tried hard to seem disinterested, letting out quiet groans as the blacktop fed. When she stood up her cheeks were decorated with racing stripes carved by unyielding pebbles. It drew in red like war paint. She spun her board right side up with a swat of her Keds road back around the rail for another run.

The older boys nonchalantly started to gather around to check out the stubborn shortie in their midst.

Looking back, she did everything right. She banked hard as she approached the course, building speed. She straightened, her foot pounding the street as if kick-starting a motorcycle. The rail loomed closer. She jumped high and long. She landed square on the rail. Changing her weight to the board's far edge, she rode the steel like a pro.

Just as the boys prepared to give her a well earned nod, Bess' wheel caught one of the rail's supports during dismount. She pin-wheeled down to the hungry blacktop.

This time there was no pause. She sprung up, her foot snapping the board right side up. Her knees and elbows now matched her cheeks. She approached the ramp with a long curved approach, barreling down towards the throat of the rail. Instead of mounting it, she sped clean past. She banked a curve like a roller derby hellion, pumped her sneakers against the blacktop for speed and scorched towards the rail like a demon possessed. Her board clattered like a locomotive's wheels on icy tracks.

Third time's a charm. Not only did she ride the rail that had denied her twice, she rode it with the far edge of her board bearing down so hard that sparks shot from beneath where metal fought metal.

Her dismount propelled Bess from her board, a free bird. She crouched down to grip the board in mid-air. It was a trick no boy had yet attempted. The rest was just the crust on the humble pie the big boy skaters were served. As she descended she gave her board a spin, rotating it beneath her feet, spinning right side up just in time for her to bite the tar. She landed with a stable *cachunk* followed by a well earned "yeah!" by all who witnessed.

She looked up at the oldest of the boys. There was no smile, no pride, just a focused air of challenge on her face. The duly impressed leader turned away, head hung low and nodding. He dropped his board to the road and kicked off into the night. The others followed suit, giving Bess an occasional fist pump of approval. Bess ruled!

I felt cool that night but only by association. Perhaps I was a catalyst bringing out the coolness in others. I guess that made me cool by default.

That's the way it was with the Cyrkle. The fact that I can tell you the tale of the summer we met Billybones is attributed to the unique coolness of each member, be it Gatto's fearlessness, Sandy's brains, or Bess' bravado. Me, I just went along for the ride... cool.

I looked behind, you guessed it, shark. It was a dark triangle floating over the crest of the surf. Just my luck, my first time out past the bobbers that summer and I'm a dispensable extra in the movie *Jaws*. Although it was heading in my direction, it appeared a good distance away.

The rest of the Cyrkle saw it as well. They were far more anxious about the sighting than I. Gatto coaxed me back to the safe side of the bobbers.

"Be a good ninja, get it in motion, Ty!" Gatto growled quietly as if the shark might hear.

There seemed to be a safe distance between the eating machine and me. Then I saw a shadow in my peripheral vision of something looming silently closer and closer to me, the buffet.

Now the only sharks I had ever seen were during *Shark Week*. With television being my only reference, I was looking at the fin of a Pacific Ocean monster. The ocean has a tricky way of playing with your perspective. You can be floating near coast one minute and be on the edge of rough seas the next. In this case I couldn't tell the proper distance between me and the shark until it was upon me.

There I was, with just feet between me and the shark, but alas, my life wasn't threatened that day. It was a sand shark, the Golden Retriever of sharks, measuring eighteen inches from tip to stern. All I needed to do was float off to one side out of its trajectory and let the shark-pup continue on its way. It wasn't looking for a daily serving of man meat that day, a guppy or two would have suited him fine. To the baby shark, my legs were more like a submerged tree stump, my body the bottom of a dock. It passed me by, gliding to the edge of the net and then gracefully banked around and back out to sea on its eternal quest for smaller fare.

There were two lessons I learned from that event. First, things are not always what they appear. Second, fear, while oft times a butt saver, is not always the proper response. There are times when fear should be checked at the door. So was the case with sand sharks and possibly with modern day pirates.

I crossed back under the bobbers to join my distraught Cyrkle. There were more important things than shark sightings to be addressed. There was business to attend to, important business, pirate business.

"Thought that was scary? Wait until tomorrow, you're all gonna meet a pirate."

"Pirate?," Sandy broke the silence. She kept herself afloat with a dog paddle, her pink painted nails peeking in and out of the water's edge. "Are you out of your mind, Tyler Byrne?" With the bathing cap and paddling, she looked like the youngest resident at a retirement home. She even spoke to me like a senior. "Well, I never! That's it, everybody out of the pool!" She started to paddle to shore.

It was imperative to sell my friends on the whole Billybones thing. My plan wasn't going to be easy and I couldn't do it alone. I told them all about my chance encounter with the man at my door.

"Sandy, listen. Don't you think I know how crazy this all sounds? I knew you'd all give me a ration of poo when I told you, but

I told you anyways. Why would I do that? Why? Because the pirate was real, Sandy."

Bess tried to set me straight. "Welcome to the twenty-first century. The only pirates around these parts are selling bootleg movies in Boston and breaking into secure websites on the web."

Gatto just bobbed around us dipping in and out of the water mockingly singing a pirate shanty from a Disney ride "and a bottle o rum. . . ghosts come out to socialize..."

"Shut it, Gatto!", I snapped. "O.K. I not askin', I'm tellin'".

The rest of the Cyrkle respond yelling a "Fee-yah!", hands shaking in my direction.

"We need to do this thing, the four of us, for the sake of the Cove."

"So let me get this straight. You want us to..."

I cut Gatto off. "Just go with me to his gallery and you all distract him while I snoop around for something, something pirate-esque. "

"Some we find some booty, Moo-ha-ha!" Gatto loved using his evil villain laugh and would put it in conversation whenever he could. This time was as good a time as any.

The rational voice of Bess chimed in. "There are no Yo-Ho-Ho pirates. None. Period. Fineetoe."

"Duh, that's what makes it all so creepy," I replied. "If there are no more pirates, and I would tend to agree with you that there are not, then what is Billybones the pirate doing walking our streets unless..."

Gatto interrupted, "...unless he's like a vampire, or, or, or, the walking dead". He let out another "Moo-ha-ha" before diving underwater, taking none of the proceedings seriously.

"Billybones? You named him??" Sandy giggled. She brought her hand up to her face which disrupted her paddling. She started to sink then regained composure enough to keep her head above water.

"Nice form, Sandy," Bess commented before returning her sarcasm to me. "You really need help, Tyler Byrne, and I don't think Ritalin is going to do the trick. We're talking major pharmaceuticals here, maybe shock treatment."

"A waste of electricity, he's a hopeless case," Sandy added.

"We just need to find a clue. Clues lead to facts and facts will bring out the truth, the truth being that Billybones is a pirate."

"What would be a pirate clue anyways?" asked Gatto, now floating on his back.

"Eye patch!" Sandy enthusiastically answered as if on a game show.

"Peg leg!" Bess joined in.

"Arrr, a Jolly Roger, now we're talkin'" Gatto added.

"I am so out of here" Bess announced as she started for shore, the others followed close behind. I needed her to buy in to this whole Billybones business. She was our backbone. Where she led, the others would follow. Plus, if my hunch was right and we were dealing with a real flesh and blood pirate here, I would need her strength.

"O.K.! Alright! Go girly girl, go! But when we prove that there is a living and breathing pirate right here in Lobster Cove , when we get caught up in some high sea adventures and save the day, when you read all about us in the papers, won't you just be pissed that you didn't come along for the ride!?"

Gatto like the sound of that, he was in. "Scooby doo..." he barked as he again submerged like a manatee.

"Aww nuts, supposed to rain tomorrow anyways, why not?" Bess exhaled. Yes, she was in.

"This better not get messy," Sandy huffed as dog paddled away.

"Tomorrow, noon, town square. Be there. . ." I called out to them.

"... or be square!" Gatto concluded, mocking me but at the same time by my side.

We didn't meet again that night to roam the streets on our boards. I headed home for some needed rest. Trying to retreat to my bedroom I found The Scratchers passing around a suicide punch in my mother's kitchen. The punch consisted of every liquid in our fridge, added one at a time between swigs until it was so foul that the next in line would gak from drinking it.

The Scratchers was the gang name for my older brother's crew of ne'er-do-wells. They all dressed with baseball caps cocked to one side and backwards, oversized t-shirts or basketball tanks draped over willowy chests, pants slung halfway down their legs revealing *K-Mart* boxers. The look was supposed to be dope, instead it just looked like they hadn't quite mastered the fine art of dressing themselves.

They roamed the empty streets of Lobster, bass beats thumping through tinny speakers, idling down Main Street in their parent's LeBaron. With his trusty friend Jose beside him in the suicide seat Ryan would shout the most profane rhymes. His crew would join in, all the while a *Yankee Candle* air freshener dangled from the rear view mirror. Crouched down in their seats, arms dangling out of open windows, they were posers of the first order.

The name of Ryan's gang was meant to give them street cred. You might think it referred to the technique that hip hop DJs used. If that was the case you would have had to give the crew their 'props' with a head nod and a 'Word.' The name however wasn't a 'shout out' to 'mad skills' behind the 'steel wheels'.

I didn't have the heart to tell him he meant Scrapers, those who get into fights or rumbles. A scrape brings up images of switchblades, leather jackets and hair greased back with pomade. A scratch is what happens when you pat a cat that doesn't want to be. Getting in a scrape sounds rough and ready; getting a scratch... not so much.

I retreated upstairs leaving the motley Scratchers downstairs to amuse each other without me present for easy laughs.

Belly up, I followed the shifting shadows of the occasional passing cars that washed across my bedroom walls. My Cyrkle-mates played some message tag for a while, poking fun at tomorrow's escapade. Jokes were made at my expense but never cruel. That was alright, they were onboard.

While a slew of 'what ifs' swam through my mind keeping me from much needed sleep. I could hear the pirate's words play over and over in my head. "wha'cha waitin' fer, *boy!*" emphasis on boy. My greatest fear, the one I needed most to put aside most, was if I was right and Billybones was a pirate as old as time, then what for Pete's sake could I do to protect the Cove? As he pointed out in spittle, I was just a boy.

Then an unsettling feeling came over me that there was something in the dark corner of my room, watching and waiting. This was not an under-the-bed beast or a closet monster. This was as real as Billybones on my porch stairs. I could smell its stink as it burned my nostrils.

Eyes fluttered closed. Something in the darkest pitch shifted. A maniacal grin shone from the darkest corner of my room then faded to black. The night visitor shifted its weight and resumed its vigil. I wrote it off as the product of an overactive imagination, swallowed my fear and tried to sleep, without success.

Chapter 3

THE RUSTY ANCHOR

*M*orning hung heavy, a veil of gray clouds rolled over a half-lit sun. Bess was once again correct; her forecast held true. The occasional showers and imminent squalls of the heeby-jeebies proved a fitting background for the day's proceedings.

The Rusty Anchor loomed over town square, its boarded windows closed lids of a sleeping giant. The two-story building had always been dilapidated for as long as memory served. It was a boat hangar abandoned long ago for locations closer to the harbor. It was boarded up and left for dead for as long as I had been alive.

High School ne'er-do-wells used to pry their way in. They entered from the barricaded back door so police wouldn't detect them. Inside the darkened husk, they would party until dawn. That was before an infusion of bats, possums, raccoons and the like mounted a turf war over the property. The threat of rabies took the high off the beer buzz and it wasn't long until the property was no longer inhabited by man.

Being a seaside town situated below sea level, Lobster Cove had its fair share of flooding. That would mean each year the empty building would fill with salty brine. It would just sit there in the dark; a stagnant pool growing black with a green beard sprawling up the walls. The growth let out a terrible stench intensified during the summer months until it bled clear through the layers of plywood and plastic tarps that were nailed across the doors and windows.

Now the dormant building had been awakened. It cleaned up well. Salt-bleached boards had been sanded down allowing their aged patina to show through. Everything possessed a distressed but well kept look. Two large windows were installed at either side of the store front fashioned as gigantic boat portals complete with brass latches that held its thick glass in place. What was once a large sliding door that forever in my memory was sealed closed by rusty padlocks was now a massive teak door that rose twice as high as a normal house door and whose doorframe was rounded on the top. The door was oiled a dark cherry with a sheen impervious to New England weather. An oversized handle with a thumb lock shone in polished brass that matched the window accents. The curved upper third of the door was ornamented with antique colored glass that gave the appearance of the bottom of soda bottles. If you tried to look inside through them all you would see was a twinkle of light or passing shadows of movement. The firing process of the glass had produced bubbles throughout. When you looked though the glass; everything inside appeared to be under water.

The Cyrkle met at the center of town at high noon. I was there to confront this new addition to the town square face to face. The others came merely to placate me.

The portals of The Rusty Anchor stared us down, glazed eyes daring us on.

"I'm not going in that place, ick!" exclaimed Sandy who would not be fooled by the building's facelift. She could only imagine what lurked within. She knew the nasty funk that permeated that dilapidated boathouse couldn't be eradicated with a mere slop of house paint.

"Kinda looks like a galleon ship, that's cool," quipped Gatto. He could always find the trivial in everything. "Makes sense that Captain Crunch lives here,"

"Are we gonna do this thing or what!" Bess grumbled. She would rather catch some storm waves with her boogie board than stand in the drizzle with the three of us far less daring souls as we mustered up the courage to go pirate hunting.

I got them this far, now I had to spur them into action. "Follow my lead. We'll just go in and browse. I need each of you to spread out and divert BillyBones' ... Smthe's attention from me. That will give me time to find... something."

"Heck, you don't even know what you're looking for, do you? Bess was right, what a loser I was. Sandy was in agreement making an L with one of her French-tipped fingers.

"H, E, double hockey sticks, I'll know it when I see it, let's go," I couldn't tell them how I felt drawn to this place, how something was beckoning me.

The sky clouded in again, mimicking a full moon night. Sporadic flashes of heat lightning flashed in the distance, rumbles echoed in the distant harbor.

"Let's get in before the sky comes down," I shouted over the rainfall. The Cyrkle reluctantly shuffled toward the entrance. The weather turned from drizzle to downpour and we high-tailed it to the protective awning of the former boathouse.

Sandy took little bunny sniffs of the air. "No yuk," she whispered, surprised. We were pressed together against the doorway of the building.

"Are we ready?" I reached out for the oversized handle of the massive door.

Gatto considered that what I had been saying and started rambling. "What if he has a sword? All pirates have swords, right? And know how to use them. If you're right and he is a pirate, then he has a sword. I think pirating a pirate would be reason enough to use it! Am I right or am I right?"

"Then you'd better stay on his good side then," I replied.

"He isn't, he doesn't, we aren't, so he won't!" exhaled Bess who already had enough of this so-called adventure. "Can we get it in tow, I'm getting soaked."

"Remember, spread out! Engage! Make him forget that I'm even in the room."

"What-ever," Sandy sighed with a valley-girl accent.

My thumb pushed down on the door latch. It was so heavy I thought it would take two hands' strength to depress. The lock gave way, releasing with a loud click.

Then the door opened like the last breath of a dying man, a discharge of dry air and lost hope. There were no door creaks. There should've been creaking, like in the creature double feature on Saturday afternoons. There were always foreboding castles with massive doors and ominous creaking. Instead the heavy door just swung open effortlessly, proving far more unsettling.

The Rusty Anchor was a depository for all which Mother Ocean had discarded. One side of the Gallery comprised of bin after bin of ornamental seashells, coral, sea glass and assorted floats. Lobster traps, plastic lobsters, plastic crabs, plastic fish, netting, and other tourist trap fodder littered row after row of tables. Frog bands composed of seashells and googley eyes prepared to start a fanfare to commemorate our arrival. A handmade sign indicated that they were on sale *2 fer a fin.*

The opposing wall was a library of antique books that reached three stories high and went the length of the large hall. The weathered spines containing centuries of nautical lure and myth loomed over us. Throughout the gallery there were displays of historical artifacts, some complete with annotations, others, works in progress. Captured behind the display's glass were barnacle-encrusted anchors and navigational tools. Frail parchment documents and charts accompanied them, each telling the tales of the remains.

The center of the store was the most spectacular. The entire length of the former hangar was fabricated to look like an actual ship. There were large planks that traversed from the bowed banisters forming the main deck. Where the deck ended the banisters formed the sides of the ship. Rope was draped as rigging and knotted to tie downs on the rails. Recesses that once housed cannons, called gunwales, were constructed in detail. The side arched into a bowsprit, the front point of a ship. A raised section served as the captain's deck and looked out over the entire replica.

It took us a moment to take it all in. In the center rose a thick mainsail mast that reached to the top of the cathedral ceiling. At the roof's pinnacle, veiled in darkness, was a crow's nest, a circular barrel used as a lookout. Sailors would be stationed there to detect land or impending danger. Roped ladders and tied back sailcloth streamed from main mast to crossbar. The wind from the storm outside caused them to billow ever so slightly in the dim light.

In unison we all took one step forward into the gallery answered by the ringing of a bell. There were two strikes. It was not the high-pitched chime you might hear when you enter or exit a store, a ding that seems to resound, *"five and five is ten, come back again now y'here."* This was not a ring; it was a deep, resonating peal. It meant business and not of the commerce variety.

A voice, its gravel toughened by time and trial, beckoned from the dark recesses of the massive hall. "Ring my bell in jest 'n you owe a drink to the rest!" We heard a loud swallow and the sound of something shifting amidst the menagerie of nautical memory. We could not see who addressed us but I knew who it was. That was the narrator of last night's dreams.

Always one for a comeback, Gatto replied, "I, I'll have a root beer??"

"I never jest." The voice addressed Gatto slowly. "Never!"

Gatto took a step back into the rain at the other side of the doorway. There was the sound of an electrical switch clicking on. Pockets of amber light flickered alive revealing the great hall in more detail. Multi-color glass floats shone from all corners, a deep-sea diver's suit with a fishbowl-style helmet dangled from one eave like a man long since hanged. Spider webs and blankets of dust glistened in the glare of the gas lamps that ran down the center of the hall. They let out a hiss as they flickered above, breaking the uncomfortable silence.

Again the voice rang out, this time, far less foreboding. "Welcome a'board, ye land lubbers, come in, come in! What are ye, a little wet behind the ears?" His voice let out a chortle seeing us dripping in his foyer. "Well, I guess y'are, come, come." Then with all the bravado of a drunken circus ringleader, our host exclaimed, "Welcome to The Rusty Anchor, Ye Olde Nautical Gallery and Curio Shoppe, William Reginald Smythe, proprietor, at your service!"

The gas lamps arced brighter; their light filling the room to reveal Mr. Smythe standing before us in all his pirateness. Gatto took another step back, again tolling the bell. Smythe stared over at Gatto with his one good eye. His head tilted like a predator detecting a scurry in the underbrush. Cupping one hand to his ear he inquired, "So, are ya buyin?!" His hands motioned to us with magical deftness. The rest of us parted to one side or another, putting Gatto in plain sight.

"Well? Are ya... boy!" His cane hit the wooden floor making a loud crack accenting the *boy*.

Again the hall was filled with a chilling silence, the hiss of gaslight, a fuse growing ever so short.

Smythe let out a hearty laugh at our expense as he popped the cork of a crystal decanter he had in front of him. He was behind a large desk that would be used for surveying maps on an actual ship. "Well, don' mind if I do." He grabbed his tot, a small pewter mug that hung from a chain around his neck, and poured from the vessel a long shot. He paused as if making a silent toast and then with one quick motion downed the liquor. After an appreciative wince, he addressed us again.

"Go on, mosey about! That's what ye came here fer, ain't it? Ah, that's what this here place is all about... finding treasure."

He hobbled towards us pointing with the amber head of his walking cane. "Right thar at starboard is what we called a five 'n' dime in th' day. That should fit yer' budgets might nicely."

His cane pointed out a cavalcade of treats from yesteryear. There were whiskey barrels cut in half filled with penny candy and cheap novelties. One table had an endless assortment of candy, root beer barrels, Squirrel Nut Zippers, candy necklaces, Sweet-Hearts, Smarties, you name it, filled the barrels to the brim. On another table there were barrels of little rubber sharks, cheesy sunglasses, explosive party streamers and the like.

Gatto's curiosity got the better of him. He immediately started rummaging through his pockets to see just how much of the dirt-cheap candy he could hoard. Sandy ever so cautiously walked over to another table where there were crates of nautical clothing and other regalia. There were sailor caps, handkerchiefs and various outdated cabana wear. She started matching pieces together with her own unique sense of style. Bess followed warily behind. A crate of miscellaneous seaside treasures caught her eye. The crate was cluttered with nautilus shells, Japanese glass floats and dried-out ornamental puffer fish.

The latter caught her attention and she picked up a string attached to one of the dried-out fish. It rose from the crate, spinning slowly on its tether; the spikes that covered its round body were as ominous as when it was alive.

Smythe saw the fascination in her eyes and approached with a deft shuffle step until he was so close to her that she could feel his rum-fouled breath climbing the back of her neck. She turned startled and found herself mere inches from his unshaven face.

"In Japanese folklore, my sweet, it is said that jilted lovers would proclaim undying devotion by going to the shores to dine on fugu."

The golden shimmer of the lights above cast a long shadow over her. Bess refused to flinch and responded with a jaded, "Yeah, so? Some hot tamale dumps some sap and he gets all weepy and gets the munchies. What's the big deal, what's a fugu?"

Smythe swallowed a half grin, enamored by the young girl's brashness. "That, ye spunky lass...", he reached out and stopped the fish's rotation, one of its quills biting into his finger but unable to pierce the leathery skin. "... is a fugu fish. Without being prepared with the expertise of a master chef, the eating of its flesh would prove fatal." With a flick of his finger he set the carcass back in motion. "Sionara!"

"They could die?" Bess muttered before she had time to muster up bravado.

S.E. Toon

The shadow of death was always near Bess. She lost her mother at a young age. She couldn't admit to her father that she had no recollection of the woman he showed her in faded color instant photographs every holiday.

Even last year, her one attempt at bonding with an animal turned morbidly awry. An annual agricultural fair would bring droves of daytrippers, carneys and horse dung to the Cove each summer. At the fair Bess bought herself a hermit crab. It was painted with a ying-yang symbol and hibiscus flowers making it appear to have a surfboard on its back. Not much in terms of a pet, you might assume, but perfect for Bess, a girl who had little tolerance for the cute and cuddly. Like her, it was hard-shelled. She bestowed upon it the name Nboquishakwana, "with a silent n", she reminded everyone, and took it home promising to make that crustacean a home.

Her bonding with 'Bo-Q' was short lived. It could have been the fact that when she took it home from the fair it only had seven of its original eight legs. It could have been because the care and feeding of such creatures is a delicate art at best. Whatever the reason, Bo-Q did not make it through the weekend.

As far as Bess was concerned, it was Gatto's fault. Being his jovial self he was at her house goofing with the crab. He got his finger too close and Bo-Q clamped down on his little finger. Now imagine having a clothes pin clamped down on your pinky. Gatto pulled his hand away with Bo-Q still attached. With the snap of his wrist, he sent the crab careening into the kitchen wall. Her legs grew still.

The funeral was at nightfall with only Bess in attendance. We all knew where her secret burial site was but none of us talked to her about it. Gatto couldn't even look at her in the eyes for a week. I was sure she would quit the Cyrkle afterwards. Slowly but surely she came around. We weren't crabs, but we came in a good second in her heart.

Bess looked eye to eye with Smythe, their noses almost touching. "They would chance dying because of their love for someone... heavy."

"Very. The toxin of the fugu could take the life of anyone who dared partake, sushi roulette so to speak." A disarming glint came from Smythe's good eye. The face that a moment ago was threatening, softened, giving him a grandfatherly air. "Ain't it just like life? You could get killed by a bus as you're crossing the street but ye still be a walkin?'. Never ye worry now, lass. Chow down I say, life be overrated." Bess didn't get what Smythe was going on about, but it she liked the attitude. She let out a small grin.

He turned and made a shuffle step towards Sandy. "And what treasure have you unearthed, child?" She had found an antique French sailor's cap made of dark navy wool with a ribbon of red attached by a brass button. She wore it slightly askew to one side with her usual flair. "Very Garbo." Smythe commented, referring to the legendary star of the silent screen.

"I vant to be alone," replied Sandy with a foreign accent mimicking the actress. She gave Smythe a sly wink indicating that she understood his cultural reference even at her young age.

His eyes locked with hers." Smart as a whip you are! Like that scandalous queen of the silver screen, many women dressed as men to sail the seas, be it for country or riches. They were both sailors and the scourge of the sea." Sandy reached up to remove the cap. Smythe reached up and stopped her hand with surprising gentleness. "Don't you be worrin' , little lady, there be nothin' manly about the way you be wearin' that." Always a sucker for a compliment, no matter how inappropriate, Sandy looked away from Smythe, feigning bashfulness. Her attention was then drawn to her own reflection in a faded antique mirror against the wall. She readjusted the cap.

Again there was a pause, a longer this time. It was a pause that could bring into question just where the heck I was and what mischief I was getting into. I looked wide-eyed at Gatto, silently shaking my fist at him from across the large hall. It was his turn to divert the pirate in question and he was blowing it.

Smythe looked over at Gatto without paying much attention and then started to turn with his good leg back towards his desk on the elevated captain's deck.

Gatto broke the silence. "You... you mean there were girl... pirates?" My heart stopped. He used the P word. The last thing we needed was to have Billybones going all piratey on our butts.

Thanks to Gatto, the word was out. I waited. "Here it comes..." I thought as I continued to snoop around the back end of the building expecting to be caught at any moment.

Smythe turned on his good heel to face Gatto. He broke into a smile of nicotine-stained teeth and a flash of gold. "Aye pirates", he seemed to relish the word as it rolled off his tongue. "The most merciless of sorts. They be just crewmates, ye see, 'til their identities be disclosed. A female creature amidst a horde of scallywags, sure enough, all hell would break loose. Thar be one of three results; a good jolly rogerin', mutiny or..."

Bess interrupted, "Yeah, yeah. . . or the plank. I get it. I saw that movie." She turned to Sandy and Gatto, "Don't know about you but I'm getting tired of this old windbag."

Smythe swallowed his smile, let out a contemplative exhale and shuffled back to the desk at the middle of the deck. He poured another long shot into his tot.

"Down th' hatch!" He swallowed the shot, wiping his mouth with the ample material of his jacket sleeve, then turned back to the three standing before him. An intensity burned deep within the man. As it built, the ceiling lights dimmed in response.

"The plank be fer fairy tales, ye mischievous sprites. Them books of yours don't tell the truth 'cause the truth ain't pretty. Ye want the truth? Pirate justice was not about life or death but rather about a life worse than death."

I watched from behind as my friends huddled around him, captivated by the man's delivery. The girls sat Indian-style against the large wooden planks of the deck. Gatto placed a hardy candy into his mouth and hopped on top of a large, whiskey keg. All eyes were on the storyteller.

"We're talking pirate comeuppance here. Be advised; this be not fer the faint of heart. The plank, it be fer' landlubbers who can barely dog paddle." Sandy let out an audible gulp. "They would go off the side, sure to be on the menu fer' a rogue shark, chomp, chomp and a geyser o' blood 'n that would be that. But fer an experienced man of the sea, a man with his wits about him, the plank would just be another in a series of bad days, another mere inconvenience in a series of endless misdeeds and retributions. A pirate not too taken to his grog might hide against the hull of the ship 'til dusk and then ambush under cover of darkness. Another tactic might be taking on the very ocean itself with a raft made up of driftwood and an inner compass of experience telling ye where dry land lies. Fer a real pirate, the plank was a cakewalk!"

As I searched for pirate evidence, I looked over at the rest of the Cyrkle. They were taking a liking to Smythe. His voice quieted as he continued his tale.

"The true revenge of the high seas was called the keelhaul. It was pirate torture of the highest echelon. Picture this: the accused, the poor bloke who has been condemned to this most gruesome of fates, would have each of his arms and legs tied off, all in opposing directions. The ropes would be threaded through a pulley assembly and tied off onto the belayin' pins. Two more ropes were then attached to the victim's legs, weighed down and thrown off the port side and retrieved at the stern as the current passed them underneath. They were then raised and secured on more pulleys making the two ropes parallel stripes along the length of the hull of the ship."

Smythe took a moment to draw yet another shot from the crystal vessel. "The captain of the ship would then pronounce sentence on the scurvy dog or sea hag. Four crewmates would man each of the ropes, joist the condemned off the deck of the ship and, with the victim prostrate over the stern, proceed to drag'm under water the length of the ship's hull."

My friends gasped. Smythe downed yet another shot for a dramatic pause. "Now, if yer lungs were strong enough, ye might be able to hold your breath long enough to survive. That's if you have enough salt to keep from screamin'. Why you might ask, why would a big ol' pirate be a screamin'?"

He leaned towards his attentive audience. "Now here's the rub. The hull of a ship is home to hordes of barnacles, each sharp and hungry, ready to tear at constrained flesh. You could make it without choking, many did. Then again, many did and wish they hadn't.

"because... life is overrated," stuttered Bess, a sound of frailty coming from her lips. Smythe winked at the attentive girl.

"In the case of a keelhaul son o' bitch, you'd better believe it. If you made it to the other side n' back onto the deck, the ordeal had just begun. They would then take your body, a' bleeding and a' twitchin' and place you into a gibbet, a casket of metal bars. The gibbet would then be hoisted up the mainmast where you would dry out in the open sea air. Now barnacles... you see, they be just ripe with germs and all get out. If you made it as far as the gibbet your only hope was that thirst would take your life before the inevitable infections would infest your withering body." Smythe let out a breath of chilling admiration, "Now that's what I call pirate vengeance!"

My friends let out a "Yuk" in unison.

"So boys and girls, what is the moral of our little story this blustery New England day? Anybody, hmmm?" Another too long silence. I would be found out for sure. "Don't go screwin' around with pirates, catch my drift, maties?"

The whole time Smythe wove his tale, I cautiously foraged through crate after crate, table after table of his artifacts. I was looking for something, anything. It's tough to find something when you don't know what you are looking for.

I resigned to the failure of my siege. I had become diverted by the man's tale as well. I was listening to his keelhaul story when my eyes came upon an ornate roll top desk resting at the base of a raised poop deck in the back of the mock ship.

It was old, a piece of junk if you didn't know any better. A veil of dust covered the slats of its wooden door, proof that it had rested undisturbed for many a day. I walked towards it, casually spying the desk through the corner of my eye. My hand slid to the latch and I tried to lift the roll top back; locked. Of course it's locked. There was surely something within, something Smythe, aka Billybones the Pirate, wanted hidden.

I went down on one knee as if to tie the laces of my high tops. I tried one drawer after another; no give. Still, I was determined. Whatever I was looking for was inside waiting to be discovered, waiting for me to let its secret out.

I stood back up, resigned that outside of taking a crowbar to the desk, I would be denied the truth within. Smythe had just finished his graphic telling of the keelhaul.

"Ay, life be overrated, ye see!" I stepped back, my hand sliding across the edge of the desk like a handrail.

He has to be a pirate. Who else tells stories of such depravity to a child? A pirate, that's who. A pirate incognito wouldn't just leave clues to his identity lying around. He would keep it under lock and...

There was the sound; a high wooden, "kpop!" and a small drawer lined with red felt popped open from the ornate molding of the desk. Inside was a small skeleton key.

"Pay dirt!" my inner voice proclaimed, not questioning for a moment where such an antiquated phrase came from. I looked around. It seemed that no one else heard the door open. I deftly pulled the key from its hiding place and tried it in the lock at the base of the roll top desk door.

"Brrappt!!" The door sprung open, the door's wooden slats retracted into the desk like a lizard's tongue. All eyes were now upon me save for the milky poor-excuse-for-an-eye that was recessed in Smythe's left eye socket. I quickly went to nonchalantly close the lid as if no one would notice.

As it closed, a large book fell from its inner shelf, dislodged from the shaking of my nervous hand as I went to pull the door back down.

It was only for an instant, but I swear that I could see the image of a specter grinning up at me, its ghostly grin wrapped around the surface of the book. The roll top started to close but failed to muffle the clap of the book making contact with the desk's counter.

S.E. Toon

Billybones turned to face me.

Deep inside the confines of that ancient desk, a skull smiled its eternal grin.

Chapter 4

LUBBERS

*B*rrappt! The desk's top rolled back. "Clink!" it locked. "Kpop!" and the secret drawer closed with the key within. All else was silent in the gallery save for the hiss of gaslight and Smythe's heavy breathing.

"Yo ho! Now what do we 'ave here, ye 'lubbers? Be it a mutineer in our midst? He turned his one-eyed gaze back at his enraptured audience. "What do ye say? Plank or keelhaul?" Spit spewed from his half-grin, hungry to avenge the invasion of privacy.

The rest of the Cyrkle were thoroughly entertained by Smythe's ranting thinking it was all for show. They didn't just have the skull of death wink at them. I knew Smythe was a pirate and he meant business.

"Keelhaul, keelhaul, keelhaul" the Cyrkle chanted. While I was snooping about I listened to his description of said punishment and was not keen on being the *haulee*.

A corner of the frayed black cloth the book was wrapped in protruded from the jam of the roll top. "It's now or never." I grabbed the tongue of cloth, gently coaxed it out of the locked compartment. It gave a couple of inches before the weight of the book against the boards within anchored it inside.

"Nay, the keelhaul is far too noble a fate fer a landlubber such as he," he mused with a piratey swagger.

I stared out at my friends in desperation. Their eyes were all transfixed on Smythe, the ringleader and the circus he had conjured. On cue they started shouting out, "Plank, plank, plank!"

I did my best to play along. My head slowly bowed to the floor in mock shame. With my head lowered I could see the corner of cloth peeking out the desk.

It was tattered, fragile enough that the black threads that comprised it crumbled in my hands. They were faded black, almost a bruised blue. The innermost portion of the cloth had a white pattern; two circles filled in white connected to each other forming a figure eight. There was one jagged black line dissecting the two.

While I played the repentant prisoner, my mind quickly filled in the rest of the hidden image. What I was looking at was actually the fractured joint of a bone; one of two bones crossed and above them, hiding in the shadows of the desk's hull, a skull. The book was wrapped with a jolly roger; the universal sign of, bingo, pirates!

"We're dealing with a real-life pirate here!" I snapped my head back up and stared right back at Smythe, correction, now pirate Billybones. In response to the dare of my glare, he took a shuffle step to the edge of the mock ship all th while keeping his good eye locked on mine.

"Plank, plank, plank!" My friends ignorant taunting echoed in the rafters.

Billybones kicked over a long weathered board with his good leg and slid the length of the board into a slot in the side of the hull. The plank protruded out over the shadowy edge of the massive hall. The rest of the Cyrkle rushed to the railing to look out into the darkness to see what was in wait.

With agility contrary to his infirmity, Billybones hopped over the side and gave the board that hung five feet from the gallery floor a good shake. Then with the strike of his boot he dislodged a large square of flooring that was below the edge of the board. It was a good ten feet square. With a poke of his cane he moved the flooring aside revealing a bottomless chasm that was hidden beneath. A repugnant odor discharged from the darkness below.

Billybones' good eye shone bright in the golden flicker. "The plank it shall be! Git on up, lubber!"

"You've got to be kidding??," I replied.

"Boy!", Billybones bellowed pointing his cane right at Gatto all the while keeping his steely glare locked on me. "Tell'm, boy!"

Gatto sheepishly parroted the pirate's introduction. "You, ah, he never kids," Gatto realized that this was no longer a game. The change in timber of the proceedings silenced my friend's chants.

I mustered previously unknown bravery. I knew I was dealing with a pirate. Pirates are all about daring-do. My only defense would be to call his bluff.

Standing up to a bully is the only way to disarm him. In doing so you may set yourself up for the walloping of your life. Aren't pirates in essence bullies with a flair for fashion? My options were limited, acquiesce or stand down.

I walked out from behind the desk and stood him.

"Get on up then." He motioned with a swipe of his cane. I stood on the base of the board. The length of the plank stretched out into the shadowy corner of the hall. Billybones put a firm lock on my arms and with a mere two swipes of rope firmly tied my hands behind my back. I tried to keep a confrontational eye on him to keep the animal in him at bay. He was more annoyed than challenged. I was looked away to face the expanse of the plank. With a poke of his cane in the small of my back he coaxed me down the length of the board.

The hole in the floor reeked of all that was long dead. The dark recesses of the hole teemed with putrefied animation. The bottom of the hole undulated like the tongue of a dying man. I would be a sacrifice to whatever lurked below, the elixir that would give this abomination restored life. The chasm below prepared to swallow.

In an attempt to halt my procession to the end of the board The Cyrkle began chanting again, only this time the words were, "No, No, No." It started as a whisper, growing louder with each word until it was all out yelling. Gatto silenced the others by raising his hand as if in a classroom and pleaded, "Please, dude, no, we mean no disrespect."

"Ah, I see there's loyalty among thieves, eh boy! You paid fer all that sugar booty ye be tote'n?" Gatto gulped, guilty of a five-fingered discount of the penny candy that caused the pockets of his cargo pants to bellow. "Y' wanna join yer friend, do ya? Then I suggest ya shut yer trap unless talked to, got that? All of you." His eyes dared all three of my friends.

I looked down into the thirsty pit below and swallowed my fear.

"What's down there, Smythe?"

"Your destiny the way yer heading, lubber. Prepare to meet yours." His cane then swung out and caught me between the ankles. I lost my balance and fell to my knees. The board bowed beneath me. Only one knee caught the board; the other dangled, an enticing treat for whatever lurked below.

The girls resumed their chants. Sandy's voice grew in hysteria with each successive "No" until it was a scream.

With my arms tied behind my back I was unable to straddle the board. As I fell. I remembered the summer before when I jumped off the wrong side of the jetty, a tangle of seaweed and kelp wrapped around my arms and legs like a drown maiden pulling me down to her watery grave. I had to keep it together or surely the slimy tangle would tighten. I would make it back to the surface if I just chilled.

Just as gravity won and I started to fall into the pit, Gatto sprang into action. He hopped up on one of the rum casks and hurled himself overboard. Hitting the floor in a tuck and roll fashion, candy root beer barrels spewed from his pockets. They scattered across the gallery floor like marbles. Gatto jumped to his feet and grabbed the rope that kept the hatch cover levitating just off the floor. He tugged the line with both hands. The ratchet released, the rope whirred through the joist's pulleys sending the cover crashing to the floor.

Billybones took a swipe at Gatto with his cane catching only air. I was in free fall. Swinging out on the rope, Gatto gave the hatch cover a kick with both of his clodhopper boots. The candies beneath the board helped roll the heavy cover back over the pit. My shoulder landed square on top the cover, jostling it closed. Gatto gave me a wink. "Too close," I thought. I think that a lot when I'm teamed up with Gatto.

The shadow of Billybones hung overhead. Gatto gave me his hand, pulling to my feet. We crouched down low in preparation for whatever the pirate would dole out next.

Instead of the threat coming from above, it came from whatever harbored beneath the floorboards. It was more felt than heard. Something from underneath the hatch cover was pushing up; some *thing* wanted out.

All hell broke loose. The pressure of its struggle fluctuated, moving from one end of the gallery to the next. I straddled the cover just to keep it from upending itself. Gatto jumped on adding his generous weight to the struggle. Some of his candies fell inside the whole as we struggled and we felt the scurry of a feeding frenzy below. A lace from one of Gatto's boots got sucked underneath and went taunt causing Gatto to lose his footing.

Sandy's shrieks no longer formed words. Bess put her hand over Sandy's mouth to muzzle her. Holding back a holler herself, Bess commanded, "Stop! Enough! Now!". Her tone meant as much business as Billybones . "No! No!" then out of nowhere, "HEEL!"

The craziest thing happened, whatever it was, did. The turmoil within the pit receded. The tension released on Gatto's shoe. He fell backwards on top of me. As I lifted Gatto up, Billybones closed the hatch with another swift kick of his boot heel. It sealed itself with a wet sucking sound. The lights above arced again, banishing the long shadows to the dark recesses of the gallery.

Billybones looked at the lot of us and let out a barrel-laugh that caused the tot around his neck to clatter against the chains around his neck. "Alas, yer do jus' fine." He extended his large callused hand out to me. Gatto accepted and he was brought to his feet effortlessly. Billybones proffered, "Th' door be always open to ye. May it bring ye calm harbors in ye stormy season of youth!"

Billybones was gone save for the pirate-speak. Before us was Reginald Smythe, not Billybones. Where did the scourge of the sea that wanted a piece of my hide go? Before us was the gentile shopkeeper; a lamb who may or not be a fox in pirate's clothes.

The girls were still breathing heavy, looked at each other's distressed state, and broke into titters of nervous laughter. It was as if they just rode the highest peak of an amusement park ride. Problem with roller coasters is it's not the big hill that *gets ya*, it's the one immediately following that catches you unawares and gives you a fright.

I refused the supposed shopkeeper's assistance and took a step back. He tilted his head and cast his good eye my way. "Come now, we all be maties here."

His arm wrapped around Gatto, giving him a rough but friendly hug. I stepped forward for fear my friend's was again in danger. Gatto's wince changed to a smile when Smythe messed up Gatto's hair in a playful manner. Having once again averted peril, a wash of hero's pride came over Gatto. "Ta-dah!", he exclaimed like a magician who had just made a death defying reveal.

"Never trust a pirate" I thought, keeping my distance. "Good one, Gatto." I took a step towards him. In the corner of my eye I saw the could–be pirate instinctually move his hand to the side of his belt. "Bet he has a knife, or worse, a pistol tucked away back there", I worried as I gave my friend a high five. Gatto robustly returned the slap.

"We'd best be going." I muttered.

"See ya," added Gatto as he peeled his shoulder from Smythe's clutches.

"Wouldn't wanna be ya," I mumbled turning my back on him.

Gatto and I climbed a rope ladder, up the side of the ship's façade to join the girls on deck.

"*Heel*, where'd you come up with that," I asked Bess. She just shrugged.

"How'd you like my ninja moves, Sandy?" boasted Gatto.

"There are no ninjas here, only sad, old men playing pirate," she replied trying to regain her aloof composure after losing it only moments before.

As we turned to the door Bess addressed our less than hospitable host and taunted him. "So, do you put on a show every time a customer comes in here or do you save it just to scare the bejesus out of kids, Big Man?" If I'm not mistaken, taunting is right up there high on the list of what not to do to a pirate.

Smythe aka Billybones chuckled at her brashness. With an agile jump he swung on the joist rope and landed back on the deck with his good leg. He shuffled over to his crystal carafe of rum and poured another shot into his tot.

"What show?" he replied downing the shot.

"Outta here" she exhaled.

I led The Cyrkle out of the gallery, making for the door with deliberate steps. Even with my back turned, I could still feel Smythe stare.

We were all but out of the gallery when Billybones called out me to with a reference to a long dead movie actor who starred in swashbuckler films, Yo ho, Errol Flynn, a minute."

Gatto turned around, all too happy to again join the company of the man who only moments before served him as lunch to the Creature from the Black Lagoon. "Not you!," the shopkeeper/pirate barked, dismissing Gatto. "Aye you, Stretch, a word if ya please."

I stopped at the gallery's foyer and turned to him. His forefinger beckoned me. I cautiously walked back to the deck. He leaned on the very desk I had just broken into.

"Closer now, I'm not gonna bite." I took one step nearer. "Yer an inquisitive cur; I'll give ya that!" He looked me over, sizing me up. "As you see, I'm settin' up shop. Could use a…" He slapped at his lame side. " leg up on the proceedings if ye get my drift." He chuckled at his attempt at humor. "You bein' a young lad with a summer to waste might be in need of some scratch. I would be inclined to spot you some coin in exchange fer' some sweat. Wha' cha' say, matie? Join me crew, under the table, of course."

I pondered the man's offer. He needed help, it was a miracle that he had come so far with the compromise of his leg and his eye. I needed money, they just don't give out ice cream for free at the scoop. Most importantly, I needed a reason to be in the gallery so I could continue my investigation.

Then again, he could be luring me back here without the protection of my friends to finish off what he had started. "Never trust a pirate, especially this pirate," my inner voice warned. Still I read once that you keep your friends close and your enemies closer. Still, I couldn't decide so I gave him no reply.

"Look, ya still spooked. Talk it over with your ma 'n' get back to me. Be here 'bout high tide on the morrow if ye be of interest." With the same hand he just called me over with, he now shooed me away. "Now off with ya, matie."

I returned to my friends at the door and I opened the door to the storm. Sunlight tried hard to break through to no evail.

The would-be pirate called out to me once again. "From this day forth, remember, there be reasons some things are kept under lock n' key... *matie!*" He gave the word the same derogatory tone as he did the word *boy*. He dangled a skeleton key attached to one of the gold chains draped around his neck and broke into laughter. The gold caps on his teeth glared bright in the phosphorescent light, a beacon in the murky gallery.

Even after closing the door to the Anchor behind us we could still hear his laughter. We ran across the town square through the rain. I knew why he was laughing. He knew I'd be back, we'd all be back. Hidden inside the Rusty Anchor was the only proof of Smythe's piracy, my only chance of bringing him to justice. He was my destiny, fate in desperate need of an eye patch.

Chapter 5

SWABBIE

I bathed in the sleep of the just, the shroud of sleep held no dark foreboding. No bleached skulls grinned at me as if in on some celestial joke I was the brunt of. Before retiring I made the decision to take Smythe up on his offer. In that instant, a pact was made that kept all ill at bay.

I needed to win Billybones trust. I refused to be intimidated by him. I would be his lackey, his prodigy, the son he never had. While I didn't possess definitive evidence of the man's piratosity, that one glimpse of that pirate flag was all I needed to set me on my quest.

The Jolly Roger was the name given for the colors flown by pirates when they were in attack mode. Like everything that a pirate did, its purpose was to instill the fear of the devil in everyone. The name derived from the nickname of the devil himself, Old Roger as he was called in days of yore. The jolly came from the evil grin pasted on the black field of the flag. I can testify from personal experience, there was nothing jolly about seeing that face of bone.

Summers on Lobster Cove were bathed in a haze of sun, sand and surf that mimicked paradise but slowly wore into tedium.

There were far worse things to do with an idle summer afternoon than being knee deep in mystery. Surely one clue would lead to another. The truth behind Billybones would be revealed. I would be his undoing.

I lean towards the dramatic. It couldn't just be a middle-aged seaman passing my cottage stoop that morning. That would be too ordinary for the likes of me. I had to see a pirate. There was no peg leg, no eye patch, no parrot perched on the shoulder, nothing but a wash of sea salt on his weary skin. But I saw Billybones, a pirate with a past that stretches across the centuries. At least I didn't live a boring life.

My flourishes of speculation weren't without merit. He had a limp and a slow eye, not quite the peg and patch, but mere coincidence? Do I have to remind you that he had a replica of a pirate ship constructed inside his gallery? There wasn't an exotic feathered friend for hundreds of miles, but you have to remember that we are talking real life here, not an exhibit at the Polynesian Village.

It was the dawn of a new century and with it, a new age of piracy. Data files replaced doubloons; hostile corporate takeovers, the new broad siding. In this brave, new world all pirates had eye correction surgery, artificial limbs better than the timber God gave them, and dental health plans.

It would be two weeks into my apprenticeship before Smythe would show his true colors.

He proved himself quite the taskmaster, the tasks he doled out were continual and arduous. Upon arriving in the morning there would be piles of heavy burlap sacks at the delivery gate at the back of the store. I was instructed to carry each of these sacks, weighing close to fifty pounds each, across the expanse of the massive hall to the front. I did this ad nauseam without the help of a two-wheel truck. After the last sack was moved, there were wooden crates along the front wall of the store that would conversely be moved to the receiving dock at the back of the building. By the end of these tasks, my arms ached to the point where raising one's hand seemed taxing.

The afternoon's chores were just as relentless. My job would be to shelve an endless array of antique books in the bookcases that covered an entire wall of the gallery stretching to the rafters. Due to the delicate nature of these rare manuscripts, I was allowed to shelve only one book at a time. I climbed up and down a rickety wooden ladder equipped with rollers on its feet. It reached straight up to the roof. I spent the duration of the afternoon climbing, dangling precariously, placing book after book in its proper location. At the end of the day, my legs fatigue mirrored that of my arms.

Now it wasn't all slave labor at the Rusty Anchor. In between the tedium of my tasks, he would interrupt to impart tales of local shipwrecks and other seafaring lore pertaining to whatever artifact he was preparing for exhibition. We were kindred souls in that we both shared a dramatic flair. His words painted the atmosphere of each piece's time and place. I could hear the lost vessels creak in time with the surf and I smell the gunpowder as he described each battle.

As the days wore on, Smythe's gruff exterior softened ever so slightly. At the end of my first week of servitude, Mr. Smythe awarded me with my first "under the table" payment. I stashed the envelope in one of my cargo pants countless pockets.

Along with the cash he awarded me with one of his aged books. It wasn't as large as the tomb that lurked inside the locked roll top, but it was plenty thick. In his flamboyant style, he picked the book up from his map reading desk and blew a cloud of dust from its cover. Then with a snap of his wrist he tossed it my way. It landed heavy in my tired arms.

"Err ya go, swabbie!"

In my hands was a copy of *Ashley's Book of Knots*. I flipped through its dog-eared pages, hundreds upon hundreds of pen and ink illustrations of knots passed before my eyes. It was hard to imagine that the old salts at the harbor side had mastered them all.

In the modern world, the necessity of being a master knotter wasn't quite as essential as it was down at the docks. It's not as if a computer programmer could save a system from going down by tying a *marklingspike* with two pieces of Ethernet cable, but if you lived by the sea, and by that I mean sustained your living by harvesting the ocean, not merely having an estate on the waterfront; knots mattered. From securing a dingy to hoisting one's daily catch, mastering knots was an essential skill. Knot work made you a living; knowing the correct knot just might save your life.

Smythe then presented me with two long snakes of heavy gauge rope. With a magician's flourish, another set of ropes appeared. We spent the better part of that afternoon continuing a tradition that had been handed down from generation to generation as long as man had taken to the sea.

He started me off with a simple slipknot. I stared intently at Smyth's stubby hands as they deftly wove the ropes secure. I studied each over and under, aping each motion. My first attempt was feeble at best but Smythe was patient and through repetition, my skills improved. Working at the gallery wasn't a Boy Scout Jamboree, but the knotting sessions made the day pass by quickly.

While I enjoyed this newfound skill, I kept in the forefront of my mind why I really was at the Rusty Anchor. In these moments Smythe and I bonded, building a trust I hoped one day to exploit.

From that day forward, the time I would normally spend daydreaming were consumed by knotting. Break time between tasks at the gallery were yet another opportunity to get the nod from Smythe on my progress. Once he had given me the nod, he'd disclose another knot. I even took to taking the book home with my practice rope to practice. At first I was overwhelmed with the world of knots between its covers but slowly came to understand them as variations on a much smaller set of core patterns.

The other members of the Cyrkle weren't as enthused about my sudden fascination with all things knots. My work at the gallery cut into our hang time. Occasionally they stopped by the gallery to hear Smythe tell a tale and to cop some free candy but the novelty of his presence in the town had waned. When I was off work I was often too beat up to cruise the back streets of the Cove on my skateboard with them.

When we did get together, I would try to demonstrate some of the knots my young hands had mastered. I was in the middle of a rope trick when my friends collectively lost it.

"What gives!" an exasperated Gatto blurted out in the middle of my trick.

"Well, you see, I tied the knot good and tight, see? Now, pull the rope ever so lightly and voila, it disappeared."

"No, Houdini, what gives with you!" he replied.

"Too busy playing pirate?" Bess added.

"You think I'm playing at the 'Anchor? That's hard work. You didn't seem to be all bent out of shape when I bought you all a round of sundaes the other night with the cash I earn."

"From your little pirate play dates?" Sandy added. "News flash! Pirates aren't cool."

"Well, they are," Gatto replied. "But they ain't, cause they ain't no mo. Get it my delusional bucko?" Gatto was always amused by his attempts at humor. He was his own best audience.

The consensus of the group after their first run in with Smythe was that he was an eccentric, albeit scary, dude but there was no pirate proof.

"The man's a wackadoodle!" Sandy chirped. It was one of those expressions that only Sandy could pull off without sounding stupid.

"There is no proof because there can't be any proof. There no more pirates!" Bess yelled.

"Hello!? Wackadoodle." Sandy reiterated.

I reassured them that my working at the gallery was part of the master plan. I would get Smythe to trust me alone in the gallery, and once I was alone, I would open the desk and retrieve the flag.

"O.K.! If he's a "wackadoodle" and not a pirate, why the skull and crossbones, huh?" I retorted.

"It's a museum, duh," replied Sandy her a bratty gum-snap.

"Why then is this wackadoodle in pirate clothes hiding it, duh right back at you, Sandy."

Gatto finished my twisted logic. "Unless. . . Arr!, he's a pirate." He then looked down at the unknotted rope in my hands. "Hey, that did disappear, didn't it? How'd ya do that?"

Bess, as is usually the case, had the last word. "What... ever, Tyler, get on with it and be quick about it. This is getting real old, real fast." She let me off the hook. "Last to the scoop buys... again."

That night was a postcard of summer on the Cove; bathed in ice cream, jimmies, and skateboard stunts. We spent the night as if we had never seen the likes of Billybones before. My brother and his scratchers mocked me with a barrage of "Ahoy me Buckos" while wearing soda cup lids as eye patches. We counted with a chant of "Fee-yah!" and a unison flipping of the loser symbol, our fingers forming an "L" on our foreheads. It was an innocence that would become a fleeting memory as the season wore on.

Halfway into my third week at the Rusty Anchor I finally had an opportunity to reveal the true identity of Mr. Smythe. Busy playing Donkey Kong with the barrels and crates, going up and down ladders for no apparent reason, I spied a preoccupied Smythe busy at his map desk. He opened a drawer and pulled out a checkbook and slid it into the inner pocket of his vest.

In a hurried motion he pulled at the chain that was attached to his pocket watch snapping the timepiece into his hand. His callused thumb popped its cover open. Smythe squinted at it with his one good eye then snapped the timepiece closed and locked the desk with a skeleton key that dangled like a medallion from one of the chains draped over his chest. A skeleton key is a universal, one that opens a host of locks.

"There be business to be attended to, young Starbuck!" he barked referring to Moby Dick, not the coffee shop. "Thirty-five, forty minutes, tops. Think you can handle that, swabbie?"

He gave me one of those assessment stares, one eye dead on, one aiming slightly to the heavens. It was the same look that he gave me when we first met. It was as if with that one look he could detect the slightest hint of bad intent. I passed the test. He saw the same boy he did that morning on the cottage stoop. He gave me a wink of confidence and then with his jagged gallop headed for the front door. The door closed behind him, a heavy thud echoed in the rafters, then silence.

I stood there, dumbstruck by my stroke of luck. Today was the day and I was ready. I took in the vastness of the gallery; I was alone with history. Hundreds of years of nautical misadventure bore down on me from all sides. Dwarfed by the implications of my impending discovery, I walked ever so slowly to the roll top desk. Each step filled with trepidation, each weighted with destiny.

I played the moment over and over in my mind in preparation. Get the key, open the desk, find the flag and... and what? I bit my lower lip to keep myself from panicking as my hollow footfalls neared the roll top desk.

The desk was situated in the back end of the shop just where the golden hue of gas light faded to shadow. It was on the captain's deck a good five feet above the main deck. I climbed the stairs to it as if I was creeping up on a sleeping dragon. I had the strange sensation I was being watched but continued unafraid.

The desk lay before me, the curved slats of its top on guard. I felt along the underside of the desk's molding for the hidden button I had accidentally tripped upon the week before. My hand blindly followed the contour of the rail until it stumbled upon a recessed groove. Pushing down on it I heard the familiar wooden, *knockkk* echo in the vacated hall. The small velvet lined compartment opened revealing the desk's key.

It was a skeleton key akin to the one Smythe wore around his neck. Its jagged teeth mimicked the one plastered on the flag within. I reached into the secret drawer as if it would snap shut at any instant lopping off my fingers at the quick. I snatched up the key with my white knuckled hand, accepting its challenge.

The key's teeth slid gently into the wrought iron lock imbedded in the ornate wood detail of the desk. I twisted the key, aged tumblers turned within. The desk was a massive jack in the box, at any moment the ribbed top could roll back, a maniacal pirate clown would spring forth to grab at me and pull me kicking and screaming into the dark recesses of the desk.

Frrappt, the roll top racketed up in one quick motion startling me as much as it did the first time. No hungry grinning ghoul ready to pounce, no grim reaper in white-face, no creature from beneath the floorboards, and most importantly, no grinning flag wrapped around a book.

'Smythe was on to me, I knew it!' My mind raced. I built his trust by doing his will during the past few weeks. I thought I had won him over but he must have been playing me. I was just a pawn in his game of pirate charades.

What was left inside of the desk was a quill, an inkwell and the book once shrouded in the Jolly Roger. It was a massive volume, three feet high, eight inches thick, so large it barely fit inside. Its binding was moss green leather, weathered and cracked along the spine. The page edges were a tarnished gold. The book was so heavy it took two hands to turn it upright.

As I lifted the book from the desktop I saw lingering shreds of black. They were all that remained of the missing flag. At least the Jolly Roger wasn't a fabrication of my fertile imagination. I swept the stray threads into a handkerchief that I used to wipe my brow during Smythe's arduous tasks, folded it carefully and secured the valuable pirate evidence into my short's pocket.

It wasn't much as far as evidence goes, but it was something. The threads proved that the flag existed. I was one step closer to pirate proof.

I started formulating a theory on the piratosity of Smythe. The man in question, shall we call him Billybones, knows I am onto him. To use a piratey turn of phrase, by hook or by crook, I would root him out. The flag I uncovered confirmed my suspicions, so the alleged pirate needed to find a new hiding place for the incriminating evidence. Using my logic, the lack of the flag in the desk confirmed his guilt.

My snooping time was running short. I needed to stop my obsessive ramblings and cover my tracks before Smythe returned. Picking the book up in an attempt to fit it back into the desk, it became cold to my touch. My hand stuck to it like a moist hand on an aluminum ice cube tray. The arc lights dimmed overhead as I turned the book over, revealing its cover.

The book was bound shut by leather straps. Along the outside edge the strips met and were tied into an intricate knot, unlike any I had seen within the pages of Ashley's. It twisted itself into a maze of binds the size of a pinecone.

Covered more with frost than of dust, I rubbed at the cover with the palm of my fist until the letters could be read. The cover was embossed with gold leaf lettering. In bold, gothic letters was the word, *Manifest.* I then unearthed the smaller letters below, *and Captain's Log.* Beneath the title, embossed into the tarnished leather was a skull and two crossed bones.

My face began to mimic the skull's expression. This was what I was searching for, what was meant to be found. To once again use a nautical reference, I had Billybones hook, line, and sinker.

What I had frozen to my hands had to be of value with that massive tangle of knots keeping its covers shut. Perhaps it was the Billybones' pirate diary, a confessional of all the treacheries and ill-found gains. Perhaps inside was a treasure map pressed between its pages that would lead me to riches beyond the comprehension of mortal men. One thing it was for certain, it was proof of Smythe's link to all things pirate.

'Smythe!' I whispered trying to hold down my panic. Time sped past and he was due to return at any moment.

I ran with the book to my backpack and tried to stuff it in. The bag was dwarfed by the size of the book. I pulled out my copy of *Ashley's* and tried again. The Manifest was not going to be smuggled out of the gallery.

Looking down at my book of knots, an idea came to me. I took both books back to the desk in to decipher the infernal knot. It was unlike anything I had seen during my short tutelage. Flipping page by page, the dizzying assortment of knots convinced me that this was a task better suited for another day.

I was about to close the book when one knot caught my eye, page 269, fig. 14, Thieves Knot; how appropriate a name considering my intent. I studied the inked illustration intently; looking back and forth, again and again between the leather knot and my *Ashley's*. The example was far more difficult than any other knot I had yet attempted.

I was hungry to pry open the book. If I just attempted to unravel the knot there would be no way I could reassemble it so Smythe would remain unaware of my intrusion. I pulled gently at one of the dangling strands when I heard the distant shuffle step of Smythe coming up the wooden boardwalk that led to the front of the gallery.

I sprang into action, quickly flipping The Manifest face down in the desk and *frrapptt* slid the roll top back down, *knockkk*, slipped the key back in the lock returning the skeleton key to its hiding place just as Smythe opened the heavy teak door.

"How'd ya fare... boy?" Smythe grumbled.

"Same ol' same ol', Billyb..." I replied, catching myself before calling him by his pirate name. "... mister, mister Smythe, sir." He paused a moment giving me the hairy eyeball, then shook off my clumsy delivery as me just being me.

He looked over the day's work yet to be completed. "Lagging behind today, I see. What's the matter? Weight of responsibility too much fer ya?"

"Just taking a five sir, which is...over. Back on the clock, sir!"

"Just made me a business arrangement that will mean more what-not comin' in the 'morn. You'd better get a hop to, Swabbie or you'll never catch up."

I spent the latter part of the afternoon, moving sacks then crates from side to side while Smythe worked at the map table. I kept looking back at him as I traversed back and forth across the gallery. He was lost in his work, barely acknowledging my presence. He was quiet, too quiet.

'He knows! The villainous pirate's got me pegged. He's now probably mulling over my demise, be it plank, keelhawl or a good old-fashioned hangin', of the jib arm.'

Finally breaking the silence, Smythe rose from his paperwork to grab a mid-afternoon eye opener of Nelson's Blood from the decanter of rum he kept at the corner of the desk.

"Got yer sea legs yet? Can you handle another afternoon? Guessin' ye can, ya didn't burn the place down when I was out. It's your call." He tipped his tot and let out a satisfied wince.

I was starting to haul one of the crates across the main deck when he asked. The excitement at having another crack at The Manifest caught me off guard. I fumbled with my grip of the crate, juggling it, then resecuring my hands around it before it could hit the floor.

"Take care, swabbie! You're playing with history."

"Yes sir, and, yes sir, I have no problem... helming the ship again."

Again he tilted his head back to take a good look at me, then turned away to pour another tot. "Big things under foot, my boy, big things."

How true his words were. He seemed unaware that I intended on being his undoing. It was my vow. If he had any suspicion, he wouldn't allow me free rein of the gallery.

I was just a Thieves Knot away from the truth. Who knew what revelations awaited me beneath the bindings of the ancient archive? I played it all casual as I whittled away the afternoon. I couldn't wait until I could head home and prepare, one loop at a time.

I did not sleep that that evening. It wasn't a case of the nervous Nellies nor rotten-toothed pirates and grinning cadavers lurking in the shadows. They wouldn't have dared confront me that evening; I was on a mission.

I constructed a fortress of pillows and bed linens. After I sped home that afternoon from the gallery, I swiped the camping lantern from the utility shed in the back of our cottage to hang inside the fort. Its roof peaked like a pup tent with a sheet draped over a rope securely tied with half hitches to each bedpost. The lamp illuminated the inside of my safe haven, silhouettes of me cross-legged under the sheet projected across the far wall of my bedroom. From the outside hallway, I appeared fast asleep. Inside, I had never been more awake.

I labored over every aspect of my plan of attack. I took out the sheet of paper I attempted to draw the knot on and studied it closely. It was a rough blueprint of the knot's many layers.

My *Ashley's* was spread out over my bed like a map. I started doing some of the knots I had already learned, just to get in the zone, then turned to page 269, the page that revealed the secret of the Thieves Knot.

This knot is what you would call a safety knot. It is used to protect you from people who had eyes on your valuables. It couldn't protect you from theft; all you needed to do was sever the rope and a thieving you go. But if you untied it then attempted to cover your trail, this knot you tell you out.

How the knot protected the user was two-fold. First, it was a very secure knot that would not give any slack. If one tried to loosen its grasp, it would actually ratchet up tighter on what it was made to secure.

Its other attribute was unique. Anyone could undo the knot without difficulty. It however was extremely difficult to tie again in the same configuration. *Ashley's*, a book long out of print, was one of the few texts to disclose all of the seventy-two variations on the knot. It also had a section that instructed the reader on how to read a knot you chose to undo.

At best, reconstructing the knot was a crapshoot. *Ashley's* warned up front that mastery of these variations was impossible since many of the knots looked practically the same from one another. When the knot was untied by its creator, the thief's errors could be identified and he would know that he had a thief in his midst.

I was not one to steal. I was a do goody good to the core. So the whole idea of pirating a pirate did not sit well with me. I had no choice in the matter; I needed to take on Billybones for the sake of the Cove.

I spent hour after hour huddled in my dark practicing variation after variation of the confounded knot. 48... 56... 67; until they all became a blur. Still, I studied intently; occasionally splashing my face with the bottled water I had smuggled to my room along with the lamp.

In the wee hours before dawn, sleep got the best of me. My hands grew limp in the midst of knot 72. My eyes fluttered behind closed lids. In this dream state I could still see my hands tying the final knot. It was a complex array, under this loop, around the outside and back again. As the knot became more difficult, my hands continued in spite of my indecision. I was completing the knot but not of my own volition.

There was a steady pressure against the outside of my hands. With a shake of my head I looked down. It was as if I could see through my hands, straight to the bone. I tried to pull my arms away and felt resistance. Before me saw was a pair of disembodied skeletal arms over mine, drifting in and out of sight in wisps of smoke. The bony fingers coaxed my own through the last loop. Then they were released, the visage turn to ink. Red marks rose from where my hands were held. I pulled my arms up close to me and stared down at the completed knot.

In the far corner of my room, the chalky face of the specter was illuminated by the glow of the lantern. As I nodded off I swore I could see it, nodding and smiling at the newly initiated thief of Lobster Cove.

Chapter 6

PLUNDER

I was awoken by the first shards of dawn bathing my room in an orange haze, the previous night's visitation, nothing more than a bad dream. Before me on the bed was the lantern, its battery dead, and a completed thieves knot, variation 69. I nodded smugly. I had secured my fate.

If saving this village meant that I needed to be a thief, so be it. No late night aberrations were going to deter me. 'Let's do this thing!' a confident and unshaken voice proclaimed inside of me.

I suffered through my brother's morning taunts with undaunted chill. Ryan could sense the change in me as well. He blathered on; pirate this, pirate that, but refrained from roughhouse. He knew if I retaliated that morning, he would be the worse for it. I had no time for his shenanigans; I had a pirate to plunder.

Upstairs I dressed for my first day of thievery. I went to pull on my favorite Levitate t-shirt. When I put it on, the fit was uncomfortably tight. The armbands strained against newly developed biceps. Weeks of slaving at the Anchor had pumped me up. I checked them out in the mirror, giving my reflection a flex.

"Quite the set of Popeye's ya got there mate," the voice added.

If I were going to be the thief of Lobster Cove, I might as well start acting like it. A sly grin came across the face in the mirror as an idea came to me. I stormed into my brother's room and swiped his identical shirt that was a medium men's as opposed to my boys 18. His shirts would drape from my shoulders like a nightshirt but this morning, I filled it out quite well. I grabbed the neck tag that revealed the size of my shirt, tore it out, and then placed it in the drawer where my brother's shirt had been.

"Ain't dryer shrinkage a bitch?," the voice chuckled as I marched out of Ryan's room. I was enjoying the new feeling this otherworldly voice encouraged.

With my trusty book of knots stuffed into my backpack, I headed downstairs. Ryan was washing dishes as punishment for, well, being Ryan. He was finished with the breakfast dishes when I passed through the kitchen. I swung my hand through the soapsuds fast enough to spray my brother. While he the soap suds burned his eyes, I swiped the remaining slices of bacon cooling on a paper towel by his plate,wrapped them in the napkin, and with one quick motion stashed them in my jacket pocket.

Be the thief.

Ryan wound-up to attempt a swing. Our eyes locked. He knew that I would not back down, not that morning or any time going forward. He lowered his arm and struggled to come up with a quick retort. The lame retort, "Twinkie!" trailed behind me as I bound through the breezeway door. I paid him no mind. It was no time to get into an altercation with the likes of my brother. I had bigger fish to fry.

As I walked through the center of town to the gallery, the morning haze burned off revealing relentless humidity. I began to sweat just thinking about the day ahead. Did I really have what it would take to bring down a pirate the likes of Smythe?

My morning shift at the Rusty Anchor was uneventful, an endless parade of boxes and sacks. The tasks were far less debilitating than during the previous two weeks. Hours passed, I moved on to shelving Smythe's frail out of print archives as he tended to his bookkeeping. Occasionally he would check my progress, raising his head from his paperwork, peering at me with his good eye.

I got a break from my chores mid-morning. I hopped onto one of the crates and munched on the liberated bacon and watched my intended victim. He was still as rugged as they come, but that morning, watching him crouched over his paperwork, there was a frailty to him. He hobbled from one display to another tending to each rusted artifact and faded parchment as if caring for infants in a nursery. His attention to detail was meticulous. Each display was transformed into a panorama of nautical history.

"We be tale tellin' animals, that's what we be." Smythe proclaimed putting the final touch on his latest creation. "Save for fancy opposable thumbs and the gift of gab, we be no better than a turd-throwin' bilge monkey. "

Only twice during the day did any potential customers peeked their heads inside the gallery; most entered out of mere curiosity, others with hopes of using the bathroom.

"The head be for the paid or the payin', which you be, ye o' full bladder?'" Smythe would bark to the desperate. When a bona fide customer did arrive, the shop keep would warm up a bit and escort them through his menagerie. Such efforts would reap the sale of some five and dime tourist trap junk, a few postcards, and some penny candy.

I wondered how long he could keep his storefront open without the occasional sale of some of his pricey items such as a tide clock or replica figurehead. The latter, was a sculpture, primarily of women, that adorned the bow of a ship back in the day. Smythe had quite an assortment of miniatures hanging from the gallery walls displayed for customers that never came.

The wash of sentiment waned, my newfound cocky demeanor returned. "No matter," the thief voice commented snidely. "The more business he needs to drum up, the more he'll hit the pavement which will translate into more looting time for us, mate!"

Tearing at the last strip of bacon like a hungry dog, I looked down at the broken man who had taken me under his wing. 'Just look at him', the thief inside scoffed. "So, who's the pirate now? Him?," Pity turned to disgust. "Naw! It be you, alas, the thief of Lobstah Cove." I swallowed a smile.

Smythe finally left for his business errands just after lunch with no apparent inklings of my plundering intent. I was his entrusted swabbie with the keys to his kingdom.

It was time for me to get to work, thieving pirate work.

I approached the desk, my trusty *Ashley's* tucked firmly under one arm; a young scoundrel on a mission. With the hidden switch beneath the desk's edging no longer a secret, I deftly opened the compartment revealing the skeleton key. *knockkk!* I put the key in the roll top's latch, *frrapptt!* The sounds of the receding slats of the cover trumpeted to an empty hall. Before me lay the ancient text, still dusted with age. It was no longer shrouded with the Jolly Roger, only some tattered black threads remained as evidence of the flag's existence. I gathered them up and put them in my pocket; exhibit one in my case to convict the Pirate Smythe.

Heavy leather straps secured the book on all sides. A bulbous knot the size of a stickball held guard. It was the one obstacle left between the truth and me; the dreaded thieves knot, variation unknown.

I went to the task at hand with the intensity of a munitions expert attempting to deactivate a bomb. 'Tick, tick, tick, the red wire or the blue?' One choice, victory, the other *kaplooey!* If only my fate was that black and white. Only Smythe would know if my choice was wrong. I would be left none the wiser until his pirate soul deemed it time to avenge my act of betrayal.

I examined each fold and loop of the knot before me looking for a clue to its identity. I carefully compared the knot constricted around the Manifest with each of the 68 illustrations narrowing the choices down to two. 'Red... blue... victory...*kablooey?*' After long deliberation, I decided on the last of the inversions, thieve's knot #69.

I crouched before The Manifest moving my head from the copy of Ashley's to the knot like a pendulum. After some deliberation I chose the correct string. The string pulled freely from the knot, the puzzle began unraveling itself until it was nothing but a pile of weathered, leather cord.

The Manifest was an aged memory; its heavy cover as fragile as autumn leaves. I opened it, feeling the weight of its cover trying to pull itself from the body of the book. Hidden inside were countless yellowed pages stained with moldy streaks of sepia. The inked text was done in an ornate calligraphy, all fancy-like with loops and swirls. The letters were accented with smeared blotches from when the quill could not quite tame the ink. The pages seemed as frail and ragged as the cover, but were as pliable as animal hide. I held the book so tightly in my hands. It was as if my effort was all that kept it intact.

Though the gold emboss on the cover proclaimed, *Manifest and Captain's Log*, there were no bills of lading to be found within. Nor were there any concise dates of entry or detailed nautical cartography. It read more like a storybook than a factual log of journal entries.

What a tale unfolded within. As I turned one leathery page after another a grand adventure unfolded. The chapter that I perused was written from the perspective of a nefarious yet unnamed ship's captain. Yes there were pirates. more pirates than you could shake a cutlass at. Not a page went by that didn't have a swash buckle here or an '*Arrr*" there. They were tales riddled with action, blood and adversities to be won over without a trace of mercy. Any retribution I imagined Smythe would perpetrate against me for my present act of pillaging paled in comparison to the atrocities between the covers of that book.

I couldn't put it down. The content was so engrossing; I could smell the salty spray of a gale off the starboard side, the acrid stench of newly fallen blood drying in the noonday sun. I literally could not pry my hands from its cover. It's words had a death grip on me, each the last testament of a dying man; words needed to be heard or lost forever.

I knew the urgency of the task at hand. I only needed to find a reference to Smythe the pirate and squirrel away the evidence. Time wasted away, still, no piratical proof.

That afternoon, sitting alone on the empty deck of the Rusty Anchor, I was transported into the world of do or die. I could take the time to capture every *'thee'* and *'thou'*, every flourish, every bastardization of the Queen's English, but you would soon be lost in all the folderol. In order for you to grasp the intensity of what was transcribed, I will now tell you as best I can my first adventure within the pages of The Manifest.

In this passage, the author, a pirate of the first order, writes of a seafaring battle against a newly constructed galleon captained by a man whom he had the pleasure of ambushing less than a year before. The pirate's plunder that day was the pristine ship he now helmed. The details of the opposing ship's allegiance, be it to country or commerce, wasn't specified. What was imparted was how infuriated the ship's Commodore was at the pirates who usurped his first vessel. Before The Commodore, obscuring the horizon line were those very same pirates. Their colors grinned proudly over the Commodore's former vessel, the ship the pirates now called home.

That afternoon, the bad blood between the pirate and the Commodore's men took the form of a relentless succession of ramparts. More pirates were bailing water than answering fire. The leader of the pirates, henceforth referred to as Billybones, called out the order to tack away from the commodore's assault and sail out of range until they could ambush the do-goody-goods under the cover of night. It was a standard maneuver in the pirate captain's manual. A nighttime ambush would suit them fine.

Billybones' ship was far less fortified than his oppressor's. His lack of cannons and ammunition, however, made his ship far lighter. Given an opportune sea breeze, the pirate ship would surely speed them to safe harbor.

The pirates took to their stations, wading through a brine-soaked deck. Luck came in the form of a Northeast gale wind. They effortlessly cut through the surf until they were out of range of the Commodore's wrath. As quickly as it came, the wind died down, sails fell limp, and boatswains rushed to pull up the slack, preparing to capture the wind's next breath.

Billybones brought a brass spyglass to his eye, checking if his adversary had noticed his present dilemma. He could see the other ship's captain. He donned a large hat; ample cloth dyed a royal blue. It was accented with gold braiding and festooned with a huge white tuft of plumage sprouting from the top. Billybones possessed a liking of gold chains and the like but even for the most foppish of his sea faring brethren, the Commodore was a bit over the top. Billybones guffawed over the preposterous spectacle he spied.

Peering into the lens, Billybones saw that the Commodore was irate at the pirate ship's counter. He yelled orders to his shipmates who could only give up a useless shrug in response. Taking the situation into his own hands, he rolled a cannon up into its bay. He hurried his crew to prep cannons, knowing that in a moment, the pirate ship, his *first* ship, would be out of reach.

Billybones lowered the scope from his eye and bellowed to his men.

"Hold yer stations, you stalwart bastards!"

One of the young and green members of the crew, startled by the captain's outburst, let go of the rigging whose slack he was taking in. A large swoop of wind returned taking the rope with it. It flapped wildly overhead as the crew scattered preparing for attack. The rouge rope whirred through the triple purchase, a large wooden assembly of pulleys, again finding the tension between the main sail and the wind. It swooped down coiling itself around the main mast. The other end whipped around and like a viper, wrapped itself around Billybones' leg, pinning him against the railing of the lookout.

"All hell, me timber!" he called out looking down at the rope as slowly sawed his leg with each swell of the wind. His first mate saw his leader pinned against the mast and leapt to his aid.

Brandishing a shiv he had hidden on his person, the first mate rushed to his captain's aid. "Say th' word, I'll cut the line fer sure!"

The ship had resumed its advantageous tack. To sever the line would make them easy targets for the commodore's bombast.

"If there be any cutting, it be ya throat. Steady the course, ye dogfish!", Billybones barked with an authoritative howl that masked his pain.

On the opposing ship, cannons were at the ready. The commodore had his sword raised, poised to give the command to fire. Billybones knew time was not their ally.

"Clear th' deck. Man yer posts! Forward ho or I swear I'll off every last one a ye."

Billybones' crewmates fell into position. His words were no hollow threat. Every one of his men knew that the pirate strapped against the sinking ship had gumption enough to sever his own entrapped appendage from his torso if need be. He would be just as able to take it and beat each and every one of them to death with it. That was Billybones tough.

Cannon fire rang off of the starboard bow. Billybones listened to the deafening quiet between the blasts and the inevitable impact. "chillin' as a January downpour, tense as rolling bones fer bounty," he muttered in a voice only he could hear. He figured it was his life or the ship's.

In the mind of a pirate loyal to his crew, the decision was made for you the day you took the pirate's oath. A tried and true pirate would just as easily offer up his own life as take that of his enemy.

The ballast was the first to go, crashing down upon the deck. Then a direct hit to the captain's station shook where Billybones still stood strapped to the deck by the unyielding rigging. The fiery ball ricocheted from the point of impact losing most of its volition. It was still enough to shatter Billybones' kneecap.

His howl of agony turned into a battle cry.

"Let th' fires of a thousand hells rain upon 'm!"

The impact was enough to splinter the post that held Billybones captive. Without the support of his leg, he fell to the slick deck. He took a board from the decimated piling, secured it along the length of his leg creating a makeshift splint. Swallowing white-hot pain, he put what remained of his knee back into position and strapped the loose rigging securely around an undamaged post to recapture the billow of the sail. He stood up on his good leg to address his crew. His other leg bent in a most unnatural angle.

"This will not stand... not by a long shot!"

The sail bit at the northeast trade winds ushering their ship well past the Commodore's wrath. The crew needed to patch up the Swiss cheese that was their hull and wait until dark.

Once the cannon took the captain's leg, the crew's thoughts turned to revenge, revenge with a capitol "arrr". They would attack under cover of night as they had a hundred times before. The plan was clean and bloody simple.

"Too simple," Billybones mused. He knew what had to be done. "About face, yer scurvy dogs. We got some unfinished business to be attendin' to."

To his crew, the order was madness but none dared refute the captain in word or deed. Even when maimed, tigers had teeth.

The ship reversed tack, tracing its former course back towards their assailants who were just specks on the horizon. They were ordered to remove rather than secure the cannons from their moorings inside the ship's side wells and reposition them at the bow of the ship. That would make their ship vulnerable to even the slightest broadsiding. It was suicide.

The figurehead at the front of the Billybones' ship stared death eyes at its intended prey. The excessive weight at the front of the ship shot spray as it burgeoned through the choppy surf. Progression was sluggish but deadly sure.

The Commodore expected a night ambush. It was how Billybones procured the ship he now captained. He would not fall for the same pirate trick twice. He had his crew return to the daily tasks of deck swabbing and hatch battening in preparation for some late afternoon rest. Then they would be fresh to put an end to the pirate menace. Let it be said it came as quite a surprise when the pirate ship came into view heading straight at them at full sail. By the time the commodore let out a warning whistle, the distance between the two ships was cut in half, close enough for his whistle of alarm to be heard on the deck of the pirate ship.

"Ahh, this will be a hearty plate of revenge; a dish best served... coldhearted." Billybones' muttered to his first mate as his fought the pain charging through his leg. He knew they couldn't trump the galleon ship's firepower. The only chance they had would be through brute force, that, and some good ol' pirate ingenuity. His crew prepared, strapping themselves into position so not to be catapulted from the stern upon impact. At first look, ramming the ship was the mad pirate Billybones' plan. The collision would be the destruction of both vessels. It would not fuse his knee together, it would not save his crew from a briny death; it made no sense.

That was why Billybones was the captain, his bravery matched his smarts.

On the deck of the targeted ship, the Commodore's sword swiped down and cannon fire rang out. The pirate crew did not retaliate. They just held on as cannonballs ate away at their already decimated hull. Following the orders of their captain, they swarmed to the back stern of the ship after the last hit leaving the bastion of cannons and brass monkeys full of ammo secured but unattended at the bow.

The two ships were so close one didn't need a spyglass to register the expressions on a crewmen's face. The next wave of fire pierced the front of the hull and Billybones' ship started taking on water. The men held on strapped against the railing at the back end of the ship.

Another direct hit severed the figurehead at the waist. She tumbled down head first to a salty grave, again, no retaliation. The crew was perched at the back of the ship, predators in wait. Their tattered clothes armored with every imaginable weapon a pirate could possess. The Commodore laughed as he motioned for his crew to finish them off.

Billybones drew his sword, using it as a crutch to stop favoring what remained of his leg. Finding his balance, then raised the sword high over his head. The motley crew came to attention with a rustle of steel blades against gun barrels. Billybones looked out over the sea of grinning faces. Gold and silver caps shone between the rot that was once teeth.

One would think the pirate ship had met its match. The first mate, concerned that his captain might just be suffering madness from the pain, joined him on the upper deck. They greeted each other, elbow to elbow. Billybones winked reassurance; the first mate knew it was not their day to die.

Together, side-by-side, they addressed the crew. "Aye, ye be hungry maties?! One more fer good luck eh?"

Another round of cannon fire rained down upon what remained of the bow. The water started to flood the top deck. Vermin spewed from the bilge hatch. The weight of the cannons began to sink the ship plunging it headfirst into the sea.

Cheers could be heard from the other deck as the pirate ship quickly descended. It sunk quickly, over half the ship submerged within the first minute. Billybones and his first mate stood firm as the waves engulfed them. The rest of the crew still strapped to the back of the stern, awaited their fate.

Suddenly, a gurgling sound emanated from deep within the sinking wreck, like the churning in the stomach of some massive beast. Then, as if spat out, the pirate ship rose back up, stern to the sky, back out of the water. Its descent was so quick that a large pocket of air was caught in the ship's underbelly making the wreck momentarily buoyant.

Billybones and his first mate sprang out from under the surf that so wanted to claim them. They pulled shrouds of seaweed from their jackets. Billybones laughed, manically, "Aha! It's feeding time ya bastards!"

The crew crawled up to the banister of the stern and leapt like penguins off an iceberg. These birds however weren't the nice, tuxedoed variety; these were birds of prey, bullets and blades instead of talons and beaks.

The pirates sprang into action. Grappling hooks attached to ropes bit into the ballast and body of the commodore's ship. The pirate's repelled off of the wreck just as it began its final descent. They infested the other ship in minutes claiming ownership. They laid to waste any who opposed them in a spray of blood and blubbering. All save for the Commodore, who was escorted by the victorious horde to await their captain.

The pirate ship gave one last gasp and then disappeared beneath a blanket of sea foam streaked in red. Billybones was the last to jettison. A rigging line was hurled down by his trusty first mate and he was hoisted to the deck. He straddled the rope like a man with full use of his legs.

Billybones boarded his new acquisition proclaiming victory as his good leg hit the deck. "all fer one n' one fer all n' all fer us!" The crew roared in guttural huzzahs. "an' all that rubbish," 'Bones mumbled, adjusting his splint.

Drawing his sword again for support, Billybones approached his captive. For the second time in a year he was face to face with the Commodore. Billybones reached his hand out to the man's face, the Commodore recoiled, bracing for a strike. Billybones sea-worn hand brushed against the blue fabric of the Commodore's garish brim.

"Nice hat..." he commented all polite as he toppled it from the Commodore's head. He shirked his shoulders, motioning for his men to release the man. Billybones looked down at the hat, back at his captive and nodded. The Commodore hesitantly bent down to retrieve it.

"... I think I'll keep it." Billybones added with an exhale. With one upward motion his sword went from cane to guillotine, severing the man's head with one strike of its razor sharp blade. The man's body fell limp, first to its knees, then to the floor. The Commodore's head rolled across the deck, resting face up. The dead face was aghast; astonished that Billybones didn't play by Queensbury Rules.

With another swipe, the large white plume was lopped from the hat by the bloodied blade. Billybones snatched up the feather in midair and stuck it beneath the outer hatband of his far more pedestrian leather hat. He turned away, waving his hand for the crew to wipe away the mayhem.

Billybones gave the man grace that day. It was a far worst fate to have the commodore return to shore, twice to sea, twice taken, than to die nobly with his crew. To let him go to shore would leave him a shell of a man, but to have his blood stain the deck would transform him into a mythic captain of the high seas.

Reading the tale from the pirate's perspective, these acts of brutal inhumanity were noble deeds. As I witnessed these events through his eyes, the villainous behavior seemed downright justified. Reading from The Manifest took away some of my piratophobia.

I had a newfound understanding about pirates. They were more like carnivores on a nature program on television. You never wanted to tame the beasts. Sure, you fear for the fallen gazelle but you watch even as you cringe. You can't tame what was meant to be wild. After reading from The Manifest, I understood, so go pirates. I still didn't like them, but I got it.

Smythe would be returning from his errands and I would have to stop reading the tales of cannon fire and debauchery. I broke from its spell long enough to check the time. Hours had passed like minutes as I sat engrossed in the world of pirates. Smythe was due back at any moment. If I didn't get The Manifest back into its hiding place right away he would catch me red-handed.

To this day I don't know why I did what I did next. I remember thinking at first that I didn't want to lose my place. A bookmark wouldn't have done the trick. It would be a red flag that someone had violated his privacy. Same went for bending the corner of a page back to mark my place. Still, I didn't want to spend the precious little time I would have in the future thumbing through the thousands of pages to find where I left off.

An idea came to me. I spied a feather quill in one of the desk's cubbies. I could make a simple hash mark on the outer margin of the page where I left off at and all I would need to do to continue reading was fan through the pages until I came across it. Then I could continue with the seafaring adventures next time Smythe left me alone to tend shop.

Time was of the essence. I quickly went to work. Recessed in the upper right corner of the desk was a small circular cover, a well of ink resting within. I pulled out the quill and took a penknife from the adjacent cubby and proceeded to sharpen the feather's point as if I used a quill pen to complete all of my homework assignments.

The same ghostly hand that had shown me the thieves knot the night before again led my hand. I cradled the quill between my fingers, brought its point to the well and siphoned up a touch of ink into the feather's hollow center. I then tapped off the excess ink like a founding father. I brought the pen down over the passage I had read last.

It was at that moment that I perpetrated my second sin, the sin of desecration. I didn't know what a criminal act I was committing when I first brought pen to page. I meant only to make a dash in the white margin when the thief voice inside me coaxed me on. "Your initials! Tag the page! Make it your own! None will be the wiser!"

I went to scrawl my initials, T.B., that was all I meant to write. With more strength than I was providing, the quill's point pierced the page, tearing at the parchment. The letters "T" and "B' did not appear. Instead the inscription, 'Sir Tyler Byrne of Provence', came from the quill in eloquent gothic swirls.

I pulled my hand back for fear the quill would continue if I let it. The crimson ink dried a bruised ash. The area around the letters brandished a reddish hue. The ruddy stained tan of the page pulsated with life. I pulled back. Horror turned to fascination as I stared at the page that seemed to heal itself from my strike, the ink rose from the page, scabbing over.

Transfixed, I wondered, "What do we have here? If this pen can make my chicken scratch look like that, what else can it do? "

"Who knows" the thief voice cajoled, "Think how *Billybones* lost the use of his leg. What an unjust fate, him, a pirate among pirates. What if, we change the story a smidgen? Would that be the end of the world?"

I recalled the tale of the Commodore and the Captain. 'What if the pirate didn't get hit in the leg? Would the pirate be humbled by such luck and go off on his way leaving the slaughter for another day? Was the only options lose the leg or lose the crew? Was it justice for the pirate to go the rest of his life with the weight of his dead leg a constant reminder of the day his luck ran out?

Then an idea came to me, compliments of the thief voice. I could change that one passage in the book so that from this day forth it would read that the cannonball did not hit the pirate, just a little sympathy for the devil, all in good fun. Whatever The Manifest did with my edit would be none of my concern.

"Time's a'wastin'!" the all too eager thief voice reminded. The large quill rested beside the inkwell, its tip still wet with the foul ink. Next to it was a small block bound with leather blotched with ink stains. I flipped the pages back to that passage of the sea battle. I reached for the arcane eraser as if I had used it a million times before. I bore down on the line where the accident unfolded and with a brisk motion shaved off the letters. His fate was reduced to a dust of blackened flakes at the bottom of the page.

My hand shook. I wanted so not to be doing this. I struggled to put my hand by my side but the more I fought, the more violent the shaking. I was losing my battle with the thief.

My hand put down the block and reached for the pen. With a seasoned hand, I tapped the quill into the ink and tapped off the residue with expert precision. As I gave in to the phantom pressure, the trembling in my hand subsided. My hand rose over The Manifest. The point of the feather lowered to the now blank passage and bore into the flesh of the page.

Keep it simple. I saw in my mind's-eye what I intended to write; in the awkward cursive of a fourteen-year-old. I meant to write simply,' The blast hit, the pirate moves from its path and is safe to plunder another day'. The line stayed pretty much as I intended save for it being laid down in the same elaborate script as the rest of the book, a thar and ye thrown in for good measure.

The thief's hand against mine vanished. I dropped the quill as if stung. As I reached over to close the book, to forever hide the page I had maimed when a rustling started deep within the body of the book.

Before my eyes, all of the text on the page following my newly inked passage seemed to wither and to crumble off of the breathing parchment. Each letter dissolved, mutating into new words and phrases that clung onto the living page like ticks.

The only passage I read before closing The Manifest was 'there would be no retort that day, mine ship in need of repair and me battered crew in need of the aliment only the cloak of night and a good snog a rum could offer. We would be awaitin' 'til nightfall.'

It was the classic pirate maneuver that the commodore had prepped for all along. For the pirates to retaliate in such a way would surely be their death.

I slammed the book closed as if that very action would stop the transformation. Pages undulated like the gills on the underbelly of a horseshoe crab; wet and frantic. I tossed the book back into the belly of the desk and with a *frrapptt* and a *knockkk* returned it and the key back to their respective hiding places. The very feet of the desk shuffled along the boards of the deck like the hooves of a frightened filly.

The sound grew, emanating from the wall of books towering three stories over me. Pages flailed violently, a musty dust filled the air. The very boards of the bookcases groaned under stress of the writhing stacks of books.

Then I heard the shuffle-step, clip, shuffle-step, clip. Smythe was returning.

There was the turn of the key followed by the ring of the captain's bell as he entered. Smythe's shadow cast by the late afternoon sun sprawled out across the deck of the gallery as if it was going to swallow me.

Then there was silence, again with that damned silence.

Chapter 7

MANIFEST

*T*he man who would be Billybones entered the room in good spirits. His mood had been coaxed by the liquor I smelt on his breath. He crossed the great hall whistling a ditty. There was a spring in the step of his good leg as he sauntered in.

"What would you do with a drunken sailor..."

The man was oblivious to the fact that he had a thief in his midst. With the sea shanty still on his lips he sat at the map desk. A pewter cup, called a tot, dangled from one of the many chains around Smythe's neck. He reached for the half full decanter of rum resting on the corner of the desk and drew himself a long shot. With a snap of the wrist, he downed it. An appreciative wince stopped the ditty, then the tune resumed as Smythe drew yet another shot; slowly becoming the sailor of note.

After his second shot disappeared between his lips he turned his attention to me. Instead of an inquisition, he thanked me with my pay, a far more handsome amount than he first offered. I stood there silent, steeped in a guilt which came off as innocence for he bat not a lash. I was given the rest of the day off, told to enjoy my financial good fortune. I was wary of this whole good guy Smythe routine. It was a setup surely; at any moment his temperament would break into a more Smythian behavior of doling out a ration of pirate whoop ass. Cautiously I walked out of the gallery expecting a retaliation that never came. I walked home relieved but a little let down that the pirate Smythe could be so easily duped.

As I headed for the door, he extended an invitation for the rest of the Cyrkle to visit.

"A month's work to do an' too few days to be doin' it. See you in the morn... and not alone I hope"

I chose not to meet up with my friends that evening. I needed to process all that I had witnessed. Was it reality or the ramblings of my overactive imagination? Endless questions fueled my fear of being banished to the teenage booby hatch. I needed the night alone to collect my thoughts.

Once at home, I walked through the day as if nothing had happened. Eating dinner with the family was just a formality. I went up to bed early, knowing there was no sleep to be had. The din of tree frogs and crickets were accented by the occasional rumble of heat lightning in the distance. My room remained muggy far after nightfall.

Suddenly a flash of lightning filled the room with white light immediately followed by an ungodly crack of thunder that shook the window frames. It was instantaneous but felt like time slowed between the two. The stench of sulfur was in the air. I could hear the crackling of the electrically charged air between the flash and the boom.

Darkness bled back into my room. As my surroundings receded back into the black, I could see a form in the far corner of my room. It crouched down on all fours. Eyes glowed vermillion. Its features were painted in various hues of black; the only definition was its huddled outline against the white wall which was reduced to dark grey. I could hear it move ever so slightly as it drew in breath. The visage then faded back into night.

Flash sssss Boom followed by a rain of hail against hot pavement. Another assault from on high shook the walls of the room, a rain of plaster dust drift in a wash of white.

Before me was my unwelcome guest. It was old, wet and rotting from the inside out. Crouched, almost cowering in the corner, it reminded me of the monstrous gargoyles one would see on the pinnacles of Gothic churches.

Its repugnant features were difficult for me to recall in the morning. You have to do that sometimes in life. When you witness something so horrendous, you need to block it out for fear of going mad. I had to swallow that memory, if only for the morning, despite the potential for it to devour me from within.

Looking back upon these fractured memories I remember it was not the creature in the corner of the room that had frightened me so, it was what it clutched in its stubby fingers. In the lightening flash I saw not a lit beacon outstretched but the severed head of a man. It was smeared with a tangle of seaweed and blood-drenched hair. Where its eyes had been were sockets; pale and empty holes staring right through me. From its gaping jaw came a voice. It coughed up a backwater of low tide and blood as it struggled for words.. With mad urgency its voice hollered, "No quarter!" Then with a wet slurping sound the jaw closed tight and the visage was again swallowed by the dark.

The world remained restless. There would be no sleep. My eyes had been opened wide. My mind pleaded to forget what my eyes had seen.

In the days that passed, a story had made its way around the Cove that the night guard at the local library had gone off the deep end that very night resulting in a leave of absence. He made a habit of getting in a little shut eye in the middle of his shift. After all, what could really go down at a local public library? Would literary hooligans break in to get their fix of Kerouac and Hunter S. Thompson, would stressed out mothers break in to drop off overdue summer readings books? The man had a cushy job, he knew it, so he'd smuggle in a couple of nips, some girlie magazines and drift off into dreamland while on the dole.

On that night while wooing starlets and hitting the winning run in the World Series of dreams, the man awoke to a thunderous sound of rustling like leaves amidst the wrath of a Nor'easter. It spread in waves emanating from the book stacks. The very nails holding the shelves horizontal screeched under the pressure. Billows of stale yesterdays wafted through the air. Time marched on.

He ran from the building for fear that the walls might be collapsing. He could hear the books breathing foul and furious. It started at one side of the building and spread like wildfire. As he bolted out of the emergency exit setting off its alarm he knew the real reason he was fleeing; the sense that those thousands of books wanted his life. So he ran, ran into the mythos of Lobster Cove.

Days passed, his ramblings came upon deaf ears. Going forward, not a drop of liquor passed his lips. For the sake of his job and its fake police uniform, he refrained from speaking the truth about the goings on that evening. He spent his days in sober isolation; his gravelly voice rarely heard, his withered form seldom seen save for his shifts at the library. It was the fallout of witnessing the truth behind the gauze we call the real world. I now know the truth he suppressed but hadn't the wisdom of years to keep it to myself.

After shaking off the heebie-jeebies of the night before, I played phone tag with my Cyrkle mates. We agreed to meet at the Jimmy's, the hot dog stand at the far end of the beach at noon. It was a Saturday and I wasn't scheduled to work. My day at the gallery came upon deaf ears. I dared not speak of the night that followed.

"Come'on, we're gonna check out Gatto's big fish," Bess insisted as if not to do so would break some sort of friendship code.

"Really?? A big smelly ol' fish?, Sandy whined.

"I'm talking real piratical evidence here." I insisted that certainly a tale of living and breathing books would certainly trump a dead fish any day. I stood corrected. Monster books aside, it is hard to avert the attention of people born and raised in a working fishing village when a big catch is involved.

"This isn't striper we're talking about here, Ty", Bess coaxed me, grabbing my arm and starting to drag me towards the pier. Heads up to all you guys out there, if a girl starts to drag you somewhere and you can't stop her, give in and go with it; otherwise you'll look like some loser being bullied by a girl.

We started for the pier. "It's a tuna, a big honkin' 65 pounder! That's like 260 tins of Chicken of the Sea", Sandy added trying to complement Bess' plea with as much enthusiasm as she could muster.

"Ha! That's you, Tyler Byrne, chicken o' de sea!" I didn't find that very funny since I was very conscious of my slight, yet increasingly more muscular physique. "Le Pollo del Mar", giggled Sandy giving the name calling a surprisingly sexy Latin spin.

I persisted, "Pirate, remember, Arrr, walkin' the plank, rum drinkin' nasty ol' pirate Smythe?"

Bess pulled the friend card, "And you call yourself a..."

"Alright! Fish tale now, pirate tale later. Aye Aye!", I exclaimed with a piratey growl.

"Aiii, Aiii Aiii!!!" squealed Sandy like a fourteen year old Shakira as she skipped to catch up with the rest of us as we marched in the direction of Bluefish Pier. Halfway, we took to our skateboards, making it down to the pier in record time.

There was Gatto in all his glory. He stood at the base of the pier next to a fish that was larger than him. Gatto wrestled with the beast for the better part of an hour. He told us how his muscles, or as he put it, his guns, burned afterwards. It was push and pull, Capt'n Jack having to water the line down for Gatto each time the fish took some slack and made a run for it. The Harbormaster and Gatto's Dad were jawing it up a bit while Gatto just stood on the dock like he won the Olympics. Sandy took some, what she was found of calling *snaps*. She felt it added a European flair to taking pictures; so Sandy. Gatto hammed it up for the camera.

The fish thrashed a bit in the netting it was wrapped in as if the fight was still on. The fish was right. It came in at a certain weight, what I truly can't remember but I do know it was one pound under the limit and his Dad and the captain were being told to throw it back. That seemed crazy for it was bigger than Gatto and was three quarters his weight and that's saying a lot, Gatto being big boned and all.

The harbormaster won and Gatto galumphed over putting on a "Yeah, whatever" attitude even though we knew he was a bit hurt.

It wasn't until I was much older that I learned that they don't bring catch in just to release them. Gatto's Dad set up the whole scenario with the Cap'n to boost the ego of his young son. His Dad was a stand up parent like that; keenly aware that his time with his boy was too short due to the hours he needed to put in to keep food on the table and summers on the cove. I liked Papa Gammy (short for Gambino). He was like me, he watched Gatto's back.

"Governor called?", I called out to him like in the movies when a criminal is going to be executed but in the last instance they call in a stay of execution.

Bess gave him a half hug/half noogie, "Aahh, he's just gonna go out there and get bulked up for you to come for him again!"

Sandy threw a literary reference into the mix. "So Hemingway, so *Young Man and the Sea.*"

"Maybe you'll hit the papers!" added Bess.

That was a strong probability. Lobster Cove was still a small town. While other towns featured police blotters filled with accounts of street violence and domestic disputes, the Cove Courant ran stories on dog parks, clam festivals, and kids catching fish.

"Can I have your autograph??!" Sandy squealed rubbing up against Gatto like a purring cat. She hoped buttering him up would make him feel better about the one that got away. All the attention made Gatto feel all squishy inside.

A grin came across his face. "There is something that the Harbormaster *doesn't* know. Be right back." He ran to the boat and came back with a bucket covered by a sheet of burlap. He marched right past us and around the back of the dock house. With a glint of mischief in his eye, he waved us over. Our curiosity piqued, we followed.

Gatto did one of his diabolical madman laughs as he opened the bag.

"Mooo-ha-ha-ha! Whatever you do, do not put your hands in there." He put on a pair of heavy gloves and then reached into the pail. "Arghh!" he yelled and then broke into laughter as he drew back that burlap to reveal the most disgusting fish I had ever seen.

Sandy went, "Gross". Bess went "Cool". I went "Dude!" in disgust. The word "dude" to Cove kids is the most all purpose word there is. Disgust! Awesome! Gross! Never-mind! Disapprove! Agree!

"Cool!" It always teamed up with an explanation mark. There was only one word to describe *that* fish, Dude!

What Gatto gingerly pulled out of the bag was, lucky for us, a dead sculpin fish. It was a dingy metal grey with matching eyes. A spiked fin ran along its spine, similar prods ran along the webbing of its fins.

"Behold The Sculpin; Fugu Fish of the East Coast." Where the fugu Smythe told us about was poisonous only when killed and eaten, the sculpin was poisonous twenty-four-seven. Its chameleon qualities allowed it to become invisible to its prey and to its enemy until... *Wack!*... too late!

"All those spikes are poisonous stingers and, check this out..." Gatto pushed against the head of the fish. Two clear horns began to protrude from its crown. "... the devil of the sea, each horn a mother lode of venom."

Sandy regained her composure and pointed to the sculpin, then at me, "Devil of the sea..."she giggled, "...meet chicken of the sea. Chicken, devil, devil chicken... buc, buc, ba-cauww!"

I thought to myself, 'That's enough of *Deep Sea Fishing with Gatto Gambino*, now back to *Billybones the Living, Breathing Pirate* already in progress.'

"Ha, ha, laugh it up. Oh, by the way, Smythe *is* a pirate."

"Bess went, "yeah right". Gatto went, "cool". Sandy went, "fer sure?"

I spoke of discovering The Manifest and of the treasure of pirate stories within. A quaver in my voice revealed my embarrassment when I told them how I changed a passage in the creepy book.

"What possessed you??" Bess barked.

I nodded. "precisely."

"I don't mean puking pea soup. I mean, what were you thinking, Dude!"

Sandy disturbed by my confession asked, "Why in the world would you do such a thing? It just doesn't make any sense. I don't like the end of *Sense & Sensibility*. Oh! I have an idea, why don't I have them live happily together forever and ever? That would be... blasphemy, that's what that is." Sandy pointed at me in mock accusation, "You sir, are a blasphemer!"

"You live your life according to the gospel of Jane Austin?" Gatto added being very Darsy. "Didn't think I'd get that reference, did ya?!"

"And just who do you think Jane Austen is?" replied Sandy putting Gatto on notice.

"I'm sure she was one of the great literary voices of our time." He thought for a moment. "... and, of course, the wife of Steve Austen, *The Six Million Dollar Man!*"

"I did that, that's all! Its stupid, I know. Why... duh... don't know. It was like I was being ... being *pushed*. It spooked the hell, yeah, I said it, hell out of me."

"Let me get this straight. You found some dead pirate's diary that you chose, out of free will, to deface because in your twisted little mind you believe the pirate in the book is, ooooooooo, somehow connected to Mr. Smythe; Smythe, the very man who just gave you a summer job? That's how you repay him; breaking and entering, defacing of personal property and... and slander, calling a man a pirate. You should be ashamed of yourself Tyler Byrne."

Bess stared me down. "Do you know what you did? Do you get it? If Smythe, Billybones, whatever his name is, takes a look at that book, he'll know that you've been messing with it and if he's half the pirate that you believe he is, he will have your hide hanging from the yard arm by dawn."

"Arr, we're sunk before we've set sail", chuckled Gatto.

I had to agree, it sounded nuts. I looked at my three confidantes with a blank stare and then down at the dead fish in Gatto's bucket.

It was then that I saw if vacuous eyes roll over to a milky white with a swirling glow of life beneath the membranes. It was the eyes of the thing in my room. It then arched its head up at me. It could have been just Gatto shifting his weight, but the fish appeared reanimated before my eyes.

Its bellow rang in my ears, menacing and wet. "Think you can just walk these streets like nothing has happened? Welcome to the rest of your life bucko! This is the way it's gonna be from now on. Everything's normal and Bam! Hello... in your face. Your every breath is mine, your every waking hour muted by my shadow! Want to take me on? Go for it, you green-gilled fool! Have your little friends come along for the ride, I love witnesses!"

The eyes of the sculpin receded like a soap bubble popped, a repugnant liquid oozing from what was once eyes. With one last twitch its horns were briefly brandished from the crown of its head. I looked up to see my friends staring at me bewildered.

I muttered quietly so no one else on the dock could hear save for The Cyrkle. "When I wrote in the book … it came alive."

There expression went blank as well. There were no more jokes. I don't know if the quiet we shared on the way home stemmed from my friends worry over me or my guilt in surrendering them to the powers that be.

Back at the dock in a discarded bucket next to discarded chum and mangled lobster traps, a dead sculpin smiled.

Chapter 8

PEGLEG

*T*he Cyrkle agreed to take up Smythe's invitation. We agreed to meet when the sun crossed the yardarm, the hour just before the sun lowered in the sky, creating *magic hour*. It was just before sunset; saturated tones of gold painted everything with warm possibility. Shadows stretched long as if fearing the last rays of sunlight. The world was safe; fearless of the impending night. It was a good time for us to confront the dreaded Smythe.

Ever since I left the Anchor I feared Smythe would discover my meddling and retaliate the next time we met. I assumed if we arrived together there would be strength in numbers.

As we entered the dimly lit hall, Smythe paid us no mind. He was busy setting one of his archival displays, positioning a shred of parchment alongside a barnacle-encrusted flintlock. The backdrop of the display was the distressed Jolly Roger that I found shrouding The Manifest. I knew it was the same flag because of the unique tear on the lower right of one of the crossing bones. The flag mocked me from behind the glass case just like The Sculpin, *"Gotcha... boy!"*

Smythe turned to us, giving an all-knowing wink to me with his good eye, as he waved us over to the starboard side of his replica ship. "Ahoy, amities, been waitin' fer you mutinous scallywags. Pull up a keg and take a load off ye dogs." He secured his new display with something stronger than a thieves' knot, lock and key.

Spending as much time at the Anchor as I did, I became accustomed to the cadence of his gait. It was the very heartbeat of the gallery. In thief mode, it served as an alarm, a cat's bell alerting the rat of impending danger around the next corner.

That afternoon was different. There was deftness to his approach, one foot, then another, solid footfalls against aged hardwood. As he got nearer, his footfalls began to break into a repressed jig.

I eyed his cane far across the room, resting against the table leg. By necessity, the staff was always at his side. Now it rest in solitary, clear across the room. Smythe had no need; his limp was gone.

"Gather 'round, ye bilge rats, it be tale tellin' time!"

Gatto high-fived Bess. "This is like gonna go down like Disneyland!", he chuckled as he plopped himself on top of one of the wooden kegs.

"This better be good, I'm missing my stories," Sandy yawned. "What, what! The shows are like chocolate; addictive… and yummy!" she added, playing embarrassed by her grown up passion for the soaps.

The man sauntered over to us. A day before, he couldn't saunter for the life of him. He glanced down at his leg, then back at me, then addressed us all.

'He knew', I panicked inside. That's the tale, the one of the entrusted apprentice and his fall from grace, of treachery and deceit starring… ME!

Smythe looked off into the shadowy corner of the hall, engrossed in a vision. "*I must go down to the sea again, the lonely sea in the sky, with a long mast and a tall ship and the stars to steer her by...*"

Smyth's intonation brought each word to life; each successive stanza a palette of time and place. Coming from a nefarious pirate; the poem was an unexpected thing of beauty.

He waxed poetic on his newly completed display. He told us the tale of a band of cutthroats, victims of the first mistake on the high seas; lying in wait. Survivors were few, victory slipping through doomed fingers, a pirate captain leaving wreckage where there should have been glory. We caught a glimpse into the briny soul of Smythe and we were spellbound.

He reached into his topcoat with the floppy, oversized collar and pulled out a fife. The fife was dwarfed by Smythe's meaty hands as he raised it to his mouth to play. It mystified me that such a sweet sound could emanate from such a salty codger like Smythe. His eye's half-closed as a gentle aire filled the hall with tranquility. Once finished, the instrument disappeared back inside the recesses of his topcoat. He looked back into the distance that first inspired him and let out a sigh.

Breaking free from memory Smythe asked, "Any of you musicians or are all of you just a bunch of miscreants I take ye for?"

Sandy feigned embarrassment and half-heartedly raised her hand. "I was first trained in piano at age 3, became disenchanted and started violin lessons. I presently play first violin in the orchestra at school but my first love..."

"A fiddle, ye say!? How grand! Bring 'er on over next time ye shadow me doorstep and I'll teach ya how to make that puppy sing!"

Smythe kicked up his heels, both of them, and danced a fanciful jig. "Now ye be one lucky one me, lass. Back in the day, when pirates be a' takin' ship or village, none would be spared their devil may care. None save fer minstrels and artisans.

Those who could see beauty in deadwood, hands that could carve visages of such beauty that many a pirate's heart would be lost to them were surely blessed by Poseidon himself."

He stepped closer to Sandy. "Now Orpheus' apprentices, the musicians, they would be spared to soothe the savage lot with a lilt or a ditty after the slaughter. They would play songs of Syrens and slain hearts, of turmoil and treason..." Smthe leaned down before Sandy, looking deep into her enraptured eyes, "...of sinnin' n' grinnin." Smythe was all teeth. He leaned close to her ear and whispered in a lecherous voice, "Music is God's counterpoint for all the sorrows of the world. Ye be very special indeed, missy."

With that he slapped his once bad leg and marched in an authoritative gait back to the map desk. He turned on his heels to face us, his sentimental demeanor receding back from whence it came.

Before us was the surly captain of S.S. Rusty Anchor. "Thar be chores needin' to be done. I'm sure master Ty would appreciate yer elbow grease. Many hands and all that rot!"

He let out a smile, more of a grimace, at Gatto, and poked him in the mid-section with the head of his walking stick. "Hard work do ye good, doughboy, good for the soul."

With a dismissive swagger and the *clip clip* of his massive boots, Smythe inspected Bess. "Fer the likes of you, hoistin' up a main sail would barely be a challenge", he chuckled in admiration. "I'll have to keep my eye on this one."

"Swabbie here will give your marchin' orders. Give me honest sweat 'n a pillagin' the sweets trough fer the lot of you!"

While candy in exchange for child labor wasn't ethical, it was surely an incentive. Within minutes, the other members of the Cyrkle tackled the same regimen that bulked me up during the past two weeks. Up a ladder, down a ladder; hoist this crate, drag this sack, back and forth across the large hall with no rhyme or reason. The routine got old as bodies grew weary. I coaxed them along as best I could with promise of sugary treasure.

The new recruits got used to their tested muscles talking to them. I was able to sit back a spell and keep an eye on the formerly lame pirate. He walked from one display to the next without the hint of a limp in his stride. Even stranger, none of my friends noticed. They should've been as weirded out as I, but they went about their newly appointed tasks as if Smythe's disability never existed.

In "pirate detective" mode, I approached Smythe as he admired one of his displays.

"So, how be the leg, sir?", my phrasing had acquired a piratial lilt when talking to Smythe.

"Which one??", Smythe replied, honestly confused.

"Your leg, *the* leg sir, ye bum leg."

Smythe turned to me. Like everything he ever did, the moment arced towards confrontation. "I might be mistaken' fer a flea bitten vagrant from time to time, and my legs, well, they bein' mine own an all, could be seen as a bum's legs, but as far back as memory serves, me timber's held strong.. nary a care!"

Smythe had the best poker face I've ever come across which was expected from a pirate considering their penchant for dropping cards and coin. Either that or he spoke the truth, at least, the truth as he knew it. The Cyrkle didn't have any recollection of his limp either. What gives?! People just don't drag around a slab of meat masquerading as a leg one day and prance around jig-ready the next. Something was up and it wasn't my subscription to the sane little boy's club.

I spied his walking cane, its amber sphere resting against the end of the map desk. "So, ye got your sea legs, why then the cane, sir?" I poised as if Smythe was on trial.

"What's got into you, boy!?" the healed pirate chortled in exasperation, "me walkin' stick, ye want to be a knowin' about me walkin' stick, do ya... *boy?*"

Gatto heard the *boy* word and knew that there were fireworks ahead. He dropped the sack he was galumphing across the main deck and nudged the girls.

Smythe took two solid steps to the desk and with one swift kick from his formerly atrophied appendage sending the cane was swirling into the air. He swiped at the cane creating such a loud clap in the hall. The dust on the eaves flaked down on us. Its impact caused the cane to now swirl in the air in the opposite direction. "Sometimes ..." His good eye stared me down, the other rolled blindly with milky white indifference. He snatched the cane midair by the hilt. "..., sometimes you be needin' a cane."

Against one of the main sail poles rest a broom just itching for action. Smythe drew his cane out before him until its brass encased point was inches from the sweaty handkerchief strapped around my neck.

My eyes broke his gaze. I looked at the broom, then at Bess, the one on my crew who wouldn't hesitate to break into action.

Pirates of Lobster Cove

"What are ya gonna do... *boy*??" Smythe was very good at being both threatening and mocking at the same time. Instead of freezing in fear, my modus operandi up to this point, I countered his move, stepping back and to the side outstretching my right arm. My hand clutched repetitively at the air waiting for Bess' courage to kick in.

Bess snapped into action, breaking into a tumble roll along the floor, more for show than need, and hopped in front of the broom. She then hurled it vertically to me just as Smythe swung his cane down at me like a switch. My hands clutched the broom handle an instant before Smythe's cane made contact. Its weight strained the far more fragile shaft of the broom handle. I held on tight.

With a hearty stab, I brought the broom up against Smythe's cane, riding its length to the end. The bristle brush head detached and flew across the room, just missing Sandy. Fear grew to rage. Smythe took another swipe. I held fast, the handle began to bow under the pressure. With an experienced swirl of his wrist, Smythe caused the broom handle to twist out of my hand onto the floor. I stood before him, defeated but full of fight.

"Pick it up," Smythe ordered. "Pick it up... *boy*!" Now the Tyler Byrne of two weeks ago would have called, *'ollie ollie, in come free!!!* and it would be game over. The swabbie before him was different, I would refuse to give up. Kick-the-can rules do not apply to pirates or life.

"Come on... old *man*..." I thought it an apt retaliation for *boy*. "... I was born ready!"

"You? Har! You aren't ready for anything... yet!" Smythe spat out each syllable cloaked with meaning. He then took another swipe at me.

"I love it when this happens!" whispered Gatto to Sandy as if they were at a Saturday matinee. Gatto swiped a couple of jawbreakers and, playing her protector, grabbed Sandy and sought protection behind a few of the wooden barrels he haf lugged about only moments before.

"Go get him, Ty!", coached Bess on the sidelines like a tag team partner. "Old man, ole *man*!" I could tell that she was just itchin' to join in the fracas if my luck wore thin.

"Show me wha'cha got... *boy*", Billybones cajoled. For every counter I made he deftly changed the weight on his never more able feet to keep me off balance.

"Clack!"; wood against wood, the two sticks collided perpendicular to one another. "Clack, Clack!" Smythe matched my every move. I tried to fake him out by staring at him while lowering myself in surrender and laying my handle to the floor. I then grabbed the stick, spun around full circle and lunged with all my might. His weapon met mine and he just slid its impact off the tip of the cane.

"Bad form, swabbie!!" yelled Smythe meeting me blow for blow with little effort. With a roll of his wrist, he sent the broom handle to the floor.

"Pick it up!" I grabbed at it and rose only to have him disarm me with the same maneuver. The weapon fell again to the floor, a desperate echo rang throughout the hall. Smythe kicked the stick at my feet with the weight of his boot's ample heel.

"Again!"

"No." My delivery was quiet and seething. The broom handle was strewn in front of my feet, awaiting compliance.

"Go to hell."

"Already got an invite. When I get there, a devil of a party they'll throw fer the likes o' me. Pick... it... up!"

Before I could let him utter the *B* word, I grabbed at the broom handle and, in true Bess fashion, rolled my body left and hopped to my feet to await Smyth's next blow. His swipe just cut air. I hopped backwards and spun around on my heels to give Smythe a worthy retort.

Smythe's last move was a setup. As I turned to him, his cane swung low, making contact with the back of my knees. Partly from the sharp sting of wood on flesh, partly from involuntary reaction, I fell to my knees. He easily deflected my interrupted swing and again dislodged my blade.

"You think this a game?!" Smythe hollered at my friends without breaking his good eye's gaze on me. "Take heed, ye never know whom fate will be testin' next!" With the tip of his cane, he flung the broom handle back to me.

"Once more with gusto!"

He raised his cane, my handle countered his. *Clack!* Another swipe. *Clack! Clack!* Then another, once again Smythe tried to unarm me with a roll of his wrist. This time I mirrored his move. Wood on wood, our wrists trembled as if arm wrestling. I pretended to surrender, my lowered, begging for pity. I flexed my wrists and with all my might braced the handle with both my hands. The motion slid Smythe's cane, tip down, to the floor. He still gripped it fast, mind you, but it was *something*. I had answered his call-out. That holds a lot of *cred* with pirates.

I saw a glint of gold from his back teeth. "Ye learn fast, swabbie." The pirate backed down and I, cautiously, mirrored his move. "Seems ye went from swabbie to boatswain in the blink of me good eye!"

He then put the cane between his arm and his side so that he could clap for me with his meaty hands. They made a heavy, hollow sound with great strength in each impact. My friends joined in until it was actually applause. I prayed it wasn't for an encore.

Negotiating the jawbreaker in his mouth, Gatto slurped, "Does this guy know how to put on a show or what!". He helped Sandy to her feet.

The applause died and my friends called it a day turning to the troths of candy promised them.

Smythe stopped clapping as well. Stepping within inches of me, he leaned in to share a secret. His cane was at his side, his good hand resting on the orb of amber secured to the wooden shaft by talons forged in cast iron. "Sometimes..." Smythe flexed his arm so the top of the cane would separate from the wooden shaft revealing a blade of blinding steel hidden within. "... sometimes you need a cane."

"Har!" His left hand come down on my shoulder as if he had just dropped the punch line of the funniest joke ever. His calloused paw took the wind out of me as it started squeezing at my shoulder blade until I wanted to cry Uncle. It was another Billybones moment in time.

Smythe then put his sights on Gatto who was too busy engaging in a sugar high to end all sugar highs. With one fell swoop of his cane he brought Gatto down to a kneel. Unlike me, there was no fight in Gatto, just a hyper nervousness fueled by candy.

"Wha, wha, wha, What! Yeah, I know, I should have seen that coming."

Smythe's good eye bore down on Gatto while the other just pulsed vainly trying to catch sight of me; an ability long since gone. "Master Ty, no longer are you a lowly swabbie, ye be a boatswain." His hand lowered and the chiseled brass point of his cane poked at Gatto's portly belly until it was lost in its excess. "If my boatswain vouches fer you, ye be the new swabbie. He'll teach you moppin' from moping and how to keep me from moppin' the floor wit ya!" All that Gatto could do was nod repetitively.

Smythe released Gatto into my care. He confirmed my promotion by tossing his walking cane with the concealed knife, to me. I reached out for it with a newly honed skill and planted its tip in the floorboard with authority.

The pride of promotion was hampered by trepidation. If Smythe gave me his potentially lethal cane, then there were far more dangerous things in wait all around me at the Rusty Anchor.

Smythe again started the mandatory clapping. The Cyrkle was farr less jubilant the second time round. "Remember all of ye, heed the boatswain's words! He ne'er be perfect, nothing but the stars be, but he may well keep ya breathing."

"See ya", I called out to Smythe. '*wouldn't wanna be ya*', I mumbled under my breath. Gatto followed me out of the 'Anchor weighed down by candy root beer barrels and atomic fireballs.

Throughout it all, none of the three could recall Smythe's limp. On our way home I insisted on a Cyrkle meeting on the floats at sunrise to sort this pirate stuff out. That early in the morning there would be no one on the beach but dog walkers and a lone fisherman on the jetty to interrupt.

The girls nodded then sped ahead, giggling to one another, most likely about yours truly.

I gave Gatto the fraternal shoulder clap and squeeze that Smythe just inflicted on me. "You? Swabbie material? Cats don't like water do they," I asked.

Gatto came back with, "Whoa, fish fear me.", He then looked at me with admiration. "Boatswain dude, not too shabby, whatever that is it must have to do with all them ninja moves. Dude, you got to be showin' me some of those!"

I had to repeat to Gatto the words I have said time and time again with meditative inflection, "Gatto. Pirates, no ninjas."

We went our own ways to mull over what had just transpired. We left the potential pirate inside the reclusive walls of the Rusty Anchor to perhaps tinker with some of his prized his relics, perhaps reminisce of battles waged and won with silver and flint, perhaps he would consider an eye patch, perhaps he would feed whatever lurked under the floorboards of the gallery or just perhaps he would tap his now nimble two feet to the seaside shanty playing inside his head.

Sky drew dark, all golden promise vanquished. I knew as I fell asleep that the darkness wouldn't leech through to shadow my bed; not that night, not with my newly attained ninja, correction, pirate moves.

Chapter 9

MATIES

Nothing to fear; first I discover a man who may or may not be a pirate here in modern day Lobster Cove. My subsequent investigation unearths an ancient Pirate book; chock full of tales of yore. When that book is pampered with, it alters the destiny of the characters between its covers.

The lunacy doesn't stop there. Some spooky slug has taken residence inside of my bedroom. In addition, some apparition is trying to take the helm of my mind. Let's not even get into the slimy things unseen by human eyes I hear sloshing below the floorboards of the Rusty Anchor. To top it off, no one else has witnessed any of these manifestations but myself, save possibly the crazed custodian at the library. Was that my fate as well; to be another local loon with delusions of pirate infestation? Cuckoo! Cuckoo!

"He looked fine to me, a bit of a hoofer for his age." Sandy mused, thinking of Smythe's dance moves. We were heading for the floats.

The floats were large, twine-covered barges tied together in such a configuration that they made a figure eight. The twine which wrapped the floats for traction was prickly and would hurt the soles of your feet until you got your beach feet. As the season progressed, the bottom of your feet would callous, toughened by beach walks, traversing jetty rocks and sharp shells, and hopping across sun-fried asphalt.

Growing up, I hated the floats. The edges grew beards of rotting seaweed and crawly things. Daring the dive-under was one of the few activities you could do for kicks there, the one thing outside of cannonballs that would make the adult world frown. If one dared swim beneath, you would have to dive beneath tentacles of similar algae that would wrap around your legs, hungry for company.

They were moored about twenty yards into the surf and were manned by lifeguards and swimming instructors from Memorial Day to Labor Day. Still, at sunrise, you were assured privacy. The morning water was cold on the Cove, even in August. We braved it, all except Gatto, who took his kayak, which he paddled to the float and docked to one of its slimy sides. The rest of us sat up on the floats, wet and shivering in the morning air. From the look in their eyes, the Cyrkle were more than a little annoyed.

"Maybe he only limped when you were around. It could be all for show like the plank walk and the sword play?" Bess rationalized.

"I'd just chill and just pull out another stealth move from your bag of whoop-ass! Did he teach you that?" Gatto so wanted so to learn some of the fencing maneuvers I exhibited the day before. He probably dreamt of executing them with nung chucks and a couple of ninja stars thrown in for pizzazz.

Truth was, I didn't know where those moves or my newfound courage came from. Smythe did teach me some knot work and cartography but not a lick of hand-to-hand combat. After only two weeks under his tutelage I had the entire book of knots down. It was as if I been on the sea my whole life. When I wove a knot or swung a lance, it never *felt* like me doing it; phantom puppet strings led me on.

I couldn't share this insight with the rest of the Cyrkle. It was hard enough to get them onboard the whole writhing book of fate and the Smythe limping-then-not-limping-thing. The last thing they needed was another dose of the heebie jeebies.

Sandy delicately spread out her towel over the itchy top of the float that she pretty-pleased Gatto into storing in his kayak. Gatto, one smitten kitten, was glad to oblige. Sitting down cross-legged, she contemplated my blathering, attempting to make sense of it all. "Let me get this right, Mr. Smythe had a limp, even if no one else here remembers; fine. You believe that that when you changed the pirate story in the old book..."

"The Manifest", I corrected her, as if the hungry book might take offence at merely being called 'an old book'.

With a strained smile, Sandy continued, "You altered *The Manifest*... so that the pirate didn't hurt his little leg and this somehow affected Mr. Smythe, excuse me, Billybones..." She held back a giggle, "...by miraculously healing his leg?"

"Can I hear a hallelujah?" Gatto exclaimed raising his arms in true evangelical preacher fashion.

Bess continued where Sandy left off. They were good like that. "So... if this is true... if we change something *else* in the book, something to do with that same pirate... the same thing should happen to this Billybones dude!"

Sandy flipped her hair back proudly, "That my friends is what you would call a scientific principle. You need to replicate your findings, Ty."

Bess issued our plan of attack. "Together, we witness the book, err, *Manifest*, tag it and wait for the hoopla to go down. Question is, what do we write?"

"Wood eye...pegleg, pegleg!, Gatto grinned from ear to ear. Not only did he have the answer, he also wrapped it into one of his favorite silly jokes. "His eye, let's fix that freaky-deaky peeper."

"Then an eye patch-up is what we'll give him!" Sandy agreed. "There has to be something in that *Manifest* thingy referencing that. Pirates were losing eyeballs all over the place back in the day."

"thus the..." , Gatto wrapped his arm around his head so that the palm of his hand would resemble an eye patch as it covered his eye.

Ca-Snap! That was when Bess would point her index finger and let out a clicking sound resembling the empty click of a gun barrel while she winked. It was an effective combination of agreeing with him and poking fun simultaneously.

Ca-Snap! "Got ya there, Gat. Here's how it goes down. Next time the old man goes out on business, boatswain boy, you call us to the 'Anchor. We each got a job to do. Gatto; you're the lookout..."

"Aye aye, eye eye", he called out, again miming an eyepatch.

Ca-Snap! Bess nodded to Gatto then turned to me, "... Ty, you're the locksmith; open the desk, break the knot apart." She then pointed to Sandy, "O.K. Brainiac, you find the passage with the eye pop and I'll mark up the page and..."

"Maybe I should ink the page", I interjected. A part of me, the part with the Thief's voice, ached to open the book again, to taint its pages. The first time it was none of my idea. Perhaps I could have fought off the compulsion but somewhere in a dark place in my soul, I didn't want to... it felt too powerful... too... *good.*

That same evil impulse also knew when to back down and stay hidden. Now was one such time. "I mean, I mean... we should change the book together." I thought of the madness I unleashed when I first wrote in the book. "...then *together* we can share the blame."

"Blame?" Gatto barked, "We'll be his pirate HMO! We're going to give the old coot free surgery. *Billybones* should thank us!"

"If he even remembers... hello? He didn't even remember his gimpy leg."

Sandy got up from her meditative position and folded her pastel beach towel corner to corner with perfect detail. "Well, duh, neither does anyone else, Ty, we're just trying to humor you. If we do this and Billybones' eye heals, we'll agree that we've got ourselves a pirate on our hands. If, most likely, nothing happens, then it's the last any of us hear of pirates from you, got it? Seriously, it's getting real old, real fast."

That hurt a bit coming from Sandy but how could I blame her? I couldn't wait until this thing was over and done. All hell would break loose and my friends would finally believe me.

Little did I know; our opportunity would come as soon as that afternoon. Our course was clear; no matter the outcome. In the distance, storm clouds gathered at sea, shunning the coastline.

It was a typical morning at the gallery, endless hours of lugging and hauling. Smythe took time to help me perfect my knot man's skill. I was at the point where I could weave eight inch wide straps of rope around the main mast, jutting up from the center of the store. These braided knots were used as footholds. I first got the idea for this project while I was making rope bracelets for each of The Cyrkle. Smythe felt the bands would add an air of authenticity to the faux ship and commended me on my initiative.

The reason for the rope bands on the masts wasn't for show but for function. Outside of the triangular rope meshing that ran from the stern to the main mast, there was no other way to access the crow's nest that rested three stories up in the apex of the towering A-frame building. The thief voice told me that the crow's nest was the most secret of places, trumping even the desk with the puzzle locks. I was determined one day to climb to the top of the main mast to investigate. Soon enough its mysteries would be revealed; closer and closer, one intertwined rope band at a time.

Smythe hurried through is morning paperwork taking time to educate me on some of his newer acquisitions. He was light on his two good feet as he navigated from case to case. He dropped anecdotes pertaining to each exhibit we stopped at. As he wove his words, you were there, by his side. I waited for him to make one slip of the tongue that would imply that he was Billybones, the pirate in the tale, and not Smythe, the unlikely shopkeeper. "I went to the skipper, I mean the *captain* went to the skipper...and" *Aha! Gotcha!*

Later that morning he got more ears to hear him recall a tale. Word got around town of his storytelling prowess and every once and again the gallery bell would sound and a group of meandering seniors would enter trying to beat the heat or a bored silly tourist family would peek inside looking for adventure. Smythe was more than ready to entertain. Save for Lobster Cove T-shirts, a bag or two of penny candy and the occasional aged map of the cove, there was little commerce but didn't bother Smythe a bit.

Why should it? From my estimations, it was a pirate lair posing as a retail establishment. It may fool the tourists and the townies but not me. I was just itching to blow the lid off this den of iniquity masquerading as a tourist trap.

We finally came to a new display that had pirate written all over it. A weathered map was the background for several artifacts dredged up just beyond these shores. In the center of the case was a cutlass. Smythe gently removed it, explaining how its weighted hilt gave the user increased control not unlike the head of his walking stick.

The blade had long lost its teeth. Years had dulled it green; crawled up the length of the blade. Ornate barbs of twisted steel protruded from the crustaceous growth covering its hilt. The barbs were designed to protect whoever wielded it from an attacker's blade. Smythe rested the weapon in my palm with a gentleness reserved for handling newborns.

The antique still commanded respect. As if inflicting a warning jab, a barb from the handle's rim bit my hand as I slid it into the handle. 'Great', I thought, 'now this thing's tasted blood' I was sure it wasn't the first time. The handle's weight aided the wrist rolls needed in effective swordplay. I gave it a few swipes with a technique that *felt* like second nature.

"Notice the size, boatswain; shorter than a proper sword, less likely to get caught up in the rafters below deck. Not a hard one to conceal as well!" Smythe brushed back his open coat to reveal a pristine cousin of the cutlass secured against his thigh by a sheath. We shared a smile.

I didn't want to put down the sword. I gave it a final swipe then gingerly placed it back, locking the case.

What if that cutlass was Billybones' hundreds of years ago? If so, why then wasn't Billybones six feet under, covered with the same barnacle rot as the blade?

A man is innocent until proven piratical I had to keep reminding myself. Today would be his judgment day.

The man was downright chipper. "To town I be a goin. Be a good haul come sunset, 'swain!'". He gathered up some papers he had strewn across the map desk and put them into a leather binder. The binder slipped into a sand-blasted leather satchel and readied himself to go. With a quick toss of the keys that I snatched as quickly as he threw them, he head for the door. "If I be late, lock up, early, prepare to be sore come sunset." He buttoned up his jacket covering up whatever arsenal concealed beneath. A tri-corner hat then went on top of his head and he was ready for town. The bell rang behind him.

I called Gatto, who called Sandy, who called Bess, who in turn called me to confirm. The message was clear; Project Hairy Eyeball was on! If you were embarking on a mission to magically reconstitute a pirate's long-dead vision, then it was a pretty darn good codename.

I turned to face the desk, once again face to cover with The Manifest. Waiting for the rest of my crew, I sensed I was being watched. The thousands of books wallpapering the 'Anchor were still. The rustling I heard came from above.

I looked up at the crow's nest shrouded in darkness though it was noon outside. A flurry of cobweb floated down. While batting away the rain of dust and time, I was thankful that I hadn't completed the rope bands reaching up the main mast. Where they would make it easier for me to climb into the crow's nest, it would make it just as easy for something to climb out and down.

The bell of the 'Anchor rang; darkness grew silent as the gallery door opened and I was saved from a one-on-one with what lurched above by the Cyrkle.

"Let's do this thing!" Bess barked forearming the creakless door. The bell let out a harsh clang. The Cyrkle converged upon the Rusty Anchor; the mission for truth begun. With door still ajar a shaft of light illuminated the bow of the ship within. All that fed on darkness retreated. The door closed, behind us; shadows slowly reclaimed their domain.

It was a good plan, a solid plan, but was hesitant having us all descend on the gallery at once. The chance of error increased, the more people involved. There was a distinct possibility they would freak out when that book defied the laws of nature. That might be a problem.

My fear of Billybones gave me pause. While we were busy pillaging through his belongings, he was out there, somewhere, healed leg and all; a cat on the prowl without a bell to sound an alarm. His awkward cadence would always tip me off to his whereabouts. Now he was in stealth mode, able to pounce on us at will.

One thing was certain, you didn't want to get caught stealing from a pirate. He might respect the sheer audacity of our actions, the sheer act of piracy. I had read enough pages of The Manifest to know that the result of betrayal was death, dealt out long and slow.

I was also sure that pirates could smell mutiny as easily as they could fear. If thievery was a high crime, what was the punishment for theft combined with treason? It had to be something that would make keelhauling a joy ride.

My compatriots marched into the shadowy hall. I said "Godspeed" to each, sounding more like Smythe than myself.

"Tick, tick, tick! Time's a wasting. In position people," Bess called out. She pointed to each of us with the beam of her flashlight. We followed her orders. Gatto went back to the door, cracking it just enough so that he could see through, but not enough to brighten the gallery.

"Bum... bum bum bum, Bum... bum bum bum.. doodely doo," Gatto hummed the *Mission Impossible Theme* as he crouched on the floor in wait.

Our destiny lay before us; the map desk waited on the quarter desk. I escorted Sandy to the desk where The Manifest lay in wait. She would be our Evelyn Wood and speed-read the book in search of some eye-gouging passages.

Bess watched our back, canvassing the shadows of the hall. Back and forth behind us, her beam traversed the expanse of the room. Her white light finally rested on the desk.

Knockkk! Frrapptt! The book was released from the confines of the desk. The arc lights grew dim, their constant hiss, now whispering a warning. The beam of Bess' flashlight flickered as if the batteries were losing power. We felt the temperature of the room drop a good twenty degrees.

I reached for the book and removed it from the cabinet. . I could feel sickening warmth, like that of freshly turned compost, emanate from the spine of the book. It struggled against my grasp. It wanted no part of me. I dropped it on the desk top before Sandy.

There was the knot, good old thieves' knot #69, once an impossible act of deciphering, now, no contest for my skills. I remembered every turn of twine in precise detail. Within a minute the ties fell away from the book's binding, defeated.

Sandy sat in the desk's mahogany chair as I struggled to open the cover. It would not give. Sandy reached out to it and the jaw of the book loosened. Along with the frail crackling of old glue and must, I swear I heard the book let out a moist sigh.

With a hint of embarrassment, Sandy pulled out a pair of bedazzled reading glasses from her rhinestone spangled fanny pack and slipped them on.

"Don't laugh! No one word, not a peep," she warned. She needn't worry. She even made granny glasses a fashion statement. As she started turning the pages of the book, she grimaced over their leathery texture.

"Peep!" went Gatto, trying hard to break the tension.

"Where did you leave off, Ty?" Sandy asked.

I tried to help her flip the massive pages of gothic scribbles but the Manifest bucked at my attempts. Sandy, however, could turn the pages freely.

"Keep going, keep going" I instructed. She finally came upon the margin where I meant to jot my initials. In a cursive sprawl were the words, *'Tyronious Jacob Byrne, Quartermaster.'*

All the text that followed my signature rose slightly off the page in dark crimson, the parchment beneath the lettering, bruised. A fine spatter of ink laced the body of the text.

Most alarming, was the words that followed. They were not the ones I had read originally. The outcome of the pirates in the tale had changed. Fate took a darker path. Their ship never changed trajectory. They never assaulted the privateers when least expected. Instead, the ship continued out of the bay in an attempt to return under cover of night, under a new moon sky. History had changed and a pirate tale of victory at sea was never to be.

Sandy turned the page I was reading, then another, and another; hell-bent on finding a passage to change. She felt the same charge rushing through her that I felt when I first perused The Manifest. Every minute or so, she would pause to let out a gasp or a giggle in response to what she was reading.

"This is good stuff! There's a real underlying story of love, loss...", she looked up from her glasses and let out a too mature sigh. "... and passion".

From the doorway Gatto chimed in, "Arrr!... peep!"

Another half hour passed. The only sounds echoing in the gallery were heavy page turns, an exasperated "hurry-up" sigh from Bess and the occasional "Peep!" from Gatto. I tried to read along best I could and began to get caught up in the reconstructed tale only to have Sandy turn the page before the story ran its course.

She stopped reading and began to point repeatedly at the middle of one page. The page quivered at the touch of her manicured nail. Her lips of pale pink lip gloss broke into a smile of success.

"You found it? You found it!" I started to give her a hug but hesitated.

"Aye aye, boatswain!", she replied.

"You mean, Eye eye!" Gatto laughed at the far end of the hall. "Peep!"

The passage was yet another high spirited battle on the high seas. I will try to relate the tale to the best of my recollection. With time, detail and memory wear thin.

It was another crew, another ship, another adversary at the throat. The captain, however, was the same as before... Billybones. His salty way with words and women was apparent with every entry.

On this adventure, he would not be alone at the helm. He shared the lording over of the crew with another as brazen as he. He was ten years his junior, a man of ambition, who had earned his position of first mate through merciless acts of bravery resulting in the overtaking of the ship he now navigated.

They were in the midst of a scuffle with another ship. The First Mate was for attack. Billybones would have opted for more caution. The ship before them was fortified twice fold, twenty four cannons to the pirate ship's twelve. The brash young leader coerced the elder seaman to have them flank the far more fortified ship.

"We might not have the gunnery, but we've got th' guts!", the ensign spat in exclamation. He gave the Captain a hard slap across the shoulders. It was apparent that the two were close. It seemed that the Captain, not one for gregarious behavior, had built a tolerance for such enthusiasm from his mate.

Any other crewman would have been under a cat o nine tails for such familial behavior. Billybones had his cat, a large handled switch with nine tendrils of leather, outfitted with knots, barbs of wire, and drilled coins on each strand. They added a bite to the beatings that tore at the men's skin and soul. The captain would lash out upon any who tried too hard to befriend him.

The ship was short on rations as well as munitions. When the mead got low, the crew could no longer compensate their hunger and pain by getting a good drunk on. Without the false courage of rum, living a pirate's life became unbearable; things start to go awry and quick. The last swallows of rum that could be drained from the remaining kegs would only fuel the crew's allegiance for so long. Eventually it was fish or cut bait and pirates never cut bait. That would go against all they pledged, what separated mere mortals from those with piracy in their blood.

If they did not take on this challenge, mutiny would surely be afoot. Billybones was far too seasoned a pirate to allow mutiny. If they attacked the nearing ship cannon for cannon the result would be death or worse. The only solution was to play the cards dealt with a ravenous gut and sober mind.

The first captain stood up on the banister bordering the quarterdeck and called out to his men. "Twice the firepower but half the fight, ehh??!" He pounded his chest and raised his cutlass to the sky in hopes of shaking the rabble out of unrest.

Billybones stepped forward to address his crew.

"They beat us in number, they beat us in fortifications, they beat us in lead and in powder." He looked at the ship along the horizon with his spyglass in admiration. "Ay, but look at 'er, that's one fine bird they be a helmin' ?" He retracted the spyglass and started tapping it against the mitt of his other hand. "There's only one question I be askin' of you this day. One question and one question only. With th' sky so blue that the ocean meets it without seam, with a breeze from the East that soothes the soul rather than flog it, with a chance of greatness before ye where there once there be squalor, I ask ye, be this a good day in which to die?!"

The crew did not take well to the Captain's inquiry and their grumbling increased as they gnawed at the bit of insubordination. The first mate went elbow to elbow with his captain and challenged the men.

"As I be seein' it, you kin live fer tomorrow, breathing fer sure, but yellow of belly..." The young man struggled for words that could turn his disgruntled crowd around. He let his passion drive his tongue. "... or ye die today a pirate, wearin' ye blood as yer badge, ye very death... a testament to ye courage, to th' legend that knows no grave!"

The mumbles turned from anger to inquiry. The captain and his mate almost had the crowd won over. Billybones grabbed at the rails of the deck looking down over his mangy crew.

"Is todee the dee?!", he hollered, eyes of flinty steel.

The crowd's rumble turned to huzzahs. Billybones drew his sword and pointed it across the bow in the direction of their enemy. The rest of the crew followed suit with whatever weapon they had on their person. The crowd let out a roar of allegiance, again duped into a battle with odds far against them.

The first mate, wild with enthusiasm, pulled a pistol from a sash of red satin tied around his waist and confirmed the vote of the crew with a single shot fired into the air.

The gunshot rang out across the sea echoing a warning to the nearing ship. The fate of the crew was sealed. "So be it then, let us see how well they be fighting against dead men!"

The assault on the privateer's frigate was classic Billybones. The crew turned away from the approaching ship giving the enemy the impression of retreat. Warning shots of victory could be heard as the pirate ship veered away. The pirate flag lowered, the main sails gave slack, the ship's tac away from the privateers slowed. The privateers were now no more than a speck appearing and disappearing between the waves on the horizon line.

On the surface this action was contrary to Billybones' intent. The mock retreat was pirate brilliance. Just as the privateers disappeared from sight the first mate ordered the main sails drawn tight as he banked the ship into the cross wind that was kicking up from the South. Closer to shore the wind was more of a sea breeze that would lull you into complacency but further out to sea, it had muscle that banked the ship hard on one side near the point of capsizing. The entire crew of seventy strong, howling like wolves at the moon, clung to the broadside that was pulling up from the ocean, using their collective weight to right the ship.

It was late afternoon; the sky, cloudless, a blinding reflection of the sun glaring against the ocean waves to the South.

The pirates' keel, now even, harnessed the force of the wind, head towards the privateer's ship full tilt. The glare of the sun bleached their approach; a mirage of white against pale blue. It was a small window of opportunity. With the eldest pirate, Billybones, at the helm, they closed in on the privateers before the glare and haze cleared and their new flank would be detected.

To broadside a ship, never mind one twice your equal, was not for the weak-of-heart. One goes alongside your adversary, as close as your sanity will allow, showing the other side what you were made of. It was a showdown of bravery and bombast, a maneuver for a ship of fools. Luckily, many of the pirates on Billybones' ship were endowed with more guts than brains; broadsiding became a common occurrence. On days when luck needs to outweigh arsenal, a pirate the likes of Billybones shines.

The first mate was possessed with pirate purpose. He ordered some of his men to apply a combination of gunpowder, sulfur, decking stain and wax along the guardrails on the broad side. He flipped open one of the chests on deck, rummaged through it frantically and removed from it a round metal tin. It was a jar of white deck trim used to protect the wooden rails of his ship from the abuse of salt water. He reached his hand in and proceeded to smear the stain across his face. The turpentine base of the paint stung but the man refused to wince.

This masquerade brought the first mate's manic behavior up a notch. He blacked out the hollows of his eyes with charcoal from the downstairs furnace. Drawing one long horizontal line from cheek to cheek, across his lips, and then marking that line vertically with frantic mad lines, he put on his war face. From a distance these markings of a madman created a ghoulish death mask of grotesque proportions. He looked out at his enemy, his massive grin smiling madly.

As they neared the frigate, he jumped back onto the quarterdeck to taunt his adversary. Daylight's last gasps stretched long shadows of across the deck. The first mate took a lantern bringing it next to his garish face, its orange flame illuminating his features for all to see. The heat of the lamp caused the fresh paint to smoke on his face, adding to his menace. He cupped his other hand to his mouth and addressed the ship they were closing in on.

"Ahoy! Let me introduce myself. I be death, yer death to be precise. Damn glad ta meet ya! Your choice is clear; surrender or die!"

The first mate then hurled the lantern against the deck, fireballs from the gun powder jumped in every direction followed by the combustible stain catching a blaze. A band of fire streamed across the top of the bow. More gun powder and firepots exploded in a smoky veil.

Darkness settled in, the sun, extinguished. From the vantage point of the privateer's ship, the first mate was a visage from hell; a disembodied head adrift a blanket of smoke and fire. Here was the Jolly Roger incarnate.

Many seamen were superstitious The first mate knew he only had enough men to combat half of the privateers. His job then was to scare the bejeezuz out of the other half. That would result in only half the cannons manned, half the hand to hand assaults, and after taking in a convert or two during the skirmish, the tables would turn in their favor.

The first mate hopped like a jester amidst the flames, laughing and taunting. His efforts proved effective; the privateer's crew was rattled, many scurrying about, many more leaving their posts unmanned.

This infuriated the Commander of the privateer ship who was an educated man of privilege. You could tell from his finely tailored topcoat, brass buttons polished, red wool faded not by weather and its gold braiding across its applets accenting the medals across his chest earned by allegiance to king and country. This man would not be goaded by the first mate's hocus pocus. If his men lacked the brains God gave them, the Commander would take care of this demon gunner himself.

Billybones' men executed the attack to the letter. Men were assigned to each of the cannons, each paired with a mate at a brass monkey, fixtures that housed cannonballs. Others gathered up the ship's firearms from each of the crewmates. From a hundred hiding places both on the person and squirreled away below deck, chests of armaments were procured. Other men were charged with taking the ship's glassware, shattering it and adding to the mix loose metal bolts and wire to be packed into the cannons as shrapnel, adding to the devastation of impact.

A pallor of soot hung between the two ships. The broadsiding was moments away. Night hugged the coastline and the horizon equally. A new moon hung blankly in the sky leaving two ships to navigate blindly in the pitch.

To the Commander, the attack was personal. It was another in a stream of battles to defeat the pagans that had ruined all that was civil. He had made it his life's work to eradicate this scourge. It was his holy war. He would defend both church and state to the ends of the earth. Now the devil himself taunted his purpose and pursuit. Life would be a small cost to send Satan back to hell.

He ordered his men back to their stations. Many obeyed. Some cowered in the bilge or attempted to free dinghies in an attempt to desert. Others jumped overboard braving the terrors of the open ocean. On the Commander's ship all turned quiet save for the lapping of the surf against the hull, the heckling of the masquerading first mate in the distance and the cries of cowards treading water as they came to realize there are far worse things in the ocean than devils and pirates.

The battle would mean heavy casualties on both sides. When morning came, neither side could consider themselves victors. That didn't matter to the pirate crew. The mad gunner had wound up his horde into such a lather that no grog or rum could quench their thirst; only bloodshed and booty.

The first mate took an oil can used to keep the mechanics of the ship's wheel smooth and free of decay and squirt it about his tricorn hat. With the spark of a flint he put the hat ablaze. Flames and sparks circled his head like a legion of magical sprites, illuminating his face.

He let out a laugh, deep from the bottom of his shoes. He cackled for what seemed like an eternity, his mania echoing in the ears of the young seamen on the privateer's ship. Billybones spied the youngest of the commander's boys, no older than I was when I read this passage. His makeshift uniform fit him loosely, looking more like a child playing dress up with his father's clothes. His eyes lost focus, his lip all aquiver. He was too green to be squaring off with the likes of the devil.

It is moments such as this that define you, tests your mettle. That man-child, out of nervousness or blinded by fear, was the first to set off the cannon fire. With a barrage of fire and smoke, the onslaught had begun. The rest was a blur of black smoke and fire. Clouds of spent gunpowder were briefly lit by orange belches of cannonball fire. A dreadful hiss followed as the balls propelled toward their targets. Then screams could be heard on the Commander's ship. From the mouths the pirates, pain was masked as hollers, unrepentant to the end.

For the Commandeer of the privateer ship the mocking demon was his primary target. As a leader falls, so does the crew, especially in the world of pirates. He kept his sight on the glowing devil face as it darted from side to side barking orders.

The Commandeer stood tall in one of his ship's cannon wells, an easy target for a hungry pirate. He pushed aside one of his frightened gunners to man one of his battalion himself. In a more civil manner than the demon pirate, he shouted commands to his men.

The first mate was aware that he was in the enemy's cross hairs. Instead of ducking for cover he turned around so his backside faced the enemy and dropped his drawers; a profane insult to his attacker. The act caused much outrage through the Commander's crew. He, however, did not flinch. He waved his arms for their silence. A cool sense of resolve came over him. He was intent on sending this visage of hell back from whence he came. He drew an ornate sword from his sash and raised it to the heavens. The chrome sparkled through the black dust. His men were in position, in wait. His blade cuts air. Twelve blasts of cannon fire discharge in unison meant to be the downfall of the pirate ship.

Billybones monitored the action the best he could from the quarterdeck. His spyglass was locked on the Commander.

"Steady... steady... hold... hold", Billybones hollered over the din. He saw the Commander's blade flash. "Damn yer eyes, Fire!" Flint met powder but only one report answered the Commander. Then there was the echo and hiss.

It could have been powder gone damp or the flint failing to spark; seconds mattered. Billybones stepped before the bewildered first mate, grabbing his hat still aflame and used it as a torch to light the cannon's wick. The shrapnel-packed cannon fired. It wasn't locked down and kicked backwards as its deadly contents hurtled towards the privateers. Billybones was trapped in the cannon well as the full weight of the cannon came down on him.

Then came the impact; a blistering hit across the mizzen mast. The wind took the shower of splintered wood and orange embers and swirled them down upon the two pirates. Billybones pushed his first mate behind him, sheltering him from the fallout. The burning rigging danced over their heads. The jolly roger flapped in the wind evading the hungry flames.

Billybones shielded his face with the large expanse of his jacket's cuffs but angry metal still managed to spray across the left side of his face. Rogue beads of gunshot claimed his left eye; the hiss, once a serpent's threat, hollowed out the socket that once held sight.

Billybones was so enraged he ordered his men to hoist the main sails tight in the opposite direction making his ship, which was quickly taking on water, to maneuver itself bow first at the attacking frigate. It made for a far harder target and his ship ramming into another would produce far more damage than twelve cannons could muster. The captain was going to make sure that if victory was not his there would be no witnesses to his downfall.

Sandy found the passage. "Yatzee! Bingo!" she exclaimed. There it was, the passage we needed. All we had to do was change a word or two, sparing the pirate's eye and wait for the fireworks to begin.

Oh, how I wanted to feel that quill in my hand again; ghost writing destiny. I thought I had the pirate in me at bay, but as soon as Sandy opened The Manifest, it rekindled my compulsion. It was like a fever. A part of me wanted to be alone with it; for that moment of transformation to be solely my own. The other part, the part not pirate, knew that was never meant to be. I needed my friends by my side to be witness. Touching The Manifest was not a good thing, but it needed to be done. Only then would they understand what we are up against.

"All clear... peep!", Gatto called out in a hushed yell.

"So Ty, what's next?" Bess asked.

"Come on, we've wasted enough time already," Sandy remarked, which was true. It had taken her close to forty five minutes for her to find the passage. Billybones return was eminent.

My left hand rode along the side of the desk, rubbing it the rail of the roll top affectionately. *'Hello, old friend'*, my thief voice whispered inside. The book started to cringe in an attempt to close itself. I had Sandy pat the book open again as if settling livestock. *'Easy, big fella.'*

I stood beside Sandy at the desk. I took a deep breath to clear my head then drew the quill out from its little cubby. I prepared its point and prepped the inkwell with casual familiarity.

"What should we write?," queried Sandy. "Should it be old school in iambic pentameter?"

"Four score and seven... peep!," Gatto added.

"It's not up to us", I replied. I didn't author the first change. Keep it simple and *it* will do the rest."

"Like a Ouiji board." Bess asked.

"First we need to remove the original passage" With a hurried rub of the erasing stone Sandy removed the passage at the point where cannon fire hits the pirate ship up to where Billybones loses his eye leaving the pirate's victory and celebration intact. The less I changed the better. All reference to the ill-fated bombardment vanished from the page. Words fell from its flesh like flaking scabs.

Then it was Sandy's turn to feel the thrill of manifestation.

"Now, make history!" I encouraged Sandy, the thief voice mirroring my words. Sandy looked up me frantic. She now could hear the voice along with me.

The thirsty point of the feather quill hungrily soaked up the crimson ink and then Sandy's deft touch brought point to page. It tore into the page like a talon to prey. The quill pierced the skin of the page before she could even start writing. She paused in a half-gasp. Then the phrasing came to her. She spoke the words aloud as she wrote.

"... I, the captain of this ship had the forethought to step aside, thus, sparing me the impact of said attack."

Sandy complimented herself as she looked down at the flowery cursive scratched into The Manifest., "Simple, slightly ornate... perfect!"

What we read next had none of the intent of her revision. The letters moved on the page like maggots on mutton, realigning into gothic calligraphy in a maddening spit of ink. Words changed and sentences grew past where I erased and where Sandy wrote.

The thief narrated the words in our heads.

"Ay, with a turn of me head, the Gods spared me the bite of the shot but alas, skirting destiny comes at such a cost. Mine eyes caught glance of my splintered mizzen leaving her dangling in the rigging above like a dead man in a gibbot. All around me was a melee of mast, sail and mayhem. Flames rose from blood stained cloth. The cross mast broke free from the rigging in flames, plummeting towards me, destined to have me join the fallen. I slid through the blood of the slain towards safety. Black soot shielded me from all else. I staggered through this erupting portal that was once a ship; cut free a dingy and headed for the safety of the sea. Behind me, the devil himself cried a tear. Alas, no victory befell us that day, only just God's wrath set upon me for not holding me ground, for using instincts more suited to a privateer than a pirate."

The script continued to sleuth itself off the page and reconstitute itself into new sentences, new stanzas, a new world.

Deep inside, the thief laughed in giddy amusement. Sandy cupped her ear in an attempt block his voice. It only caused it to laugh harder. Tears welled up in her face. We shared the curse of The Manifest. I made a move to console her when Gatto blurted out,

"Peep. Peep! PEEP!! Billybones at thirty paces!"

It took all the might of the three of us to close The Manifest. It convulsed and panted as each page transformed. Once closed, the pages rustled and quivered like fish gills out of water. Bess held it down as I quickly wrapped it in the tattered flag and fumbled with the rope to reconstruct the thieves knot.

"Twenty paces...PEEP!" Gatto hush-yelled.

My many hours of practice paid off and in no time I had the egg sized puzzle of loops and hitches secured around the ancient book. On the count of three Bess and I hurled the wild beast back into the recess of the roll top.

"Ten paces... I'm outta here...PEEP!" Gatto yelped more than chirped and rushed from the door to join us at the desk.

Knockkk! Frrapptt! The desk was closed, locked and the key back into its hidden compartment. The Cyrkle got into position practicing the art of acting casual. It's an essential talent all children hone as they get older. Any parent will tell you that the only thing more terrifying than hearing a group of children tearing your house apart is to hear the dreaded silence of children. The more laid back, the more the potential that something was up, something adults would disapprove of.

We all prepared for Billybones' entrance.

Sandy tried her hardest to keep it together. She grabbed for the nearest book on one of the tables that still needed to be shelved. It was a *Pirates and Buccaneers of New England and the Islands* by nautical historian Edward Rowe Snow. She opened it up to pretend to read when Billybones walked through the door. She clutched its cover tight to keep her hands from shaking.

Bess sat on top of the desk next to Sandy and tried putting her head in her hands as if listening. She tried one pose, then another, until one felt right.

I stood before the desk, my arms pressed firmly against the roll top to prevent it from shaking. I felt it hurling from side to side within.

Out of breath, Gatto slid the last four feet of his dash towards us on the polished boards of the deck and tried to look interested in what Sandy was about to read.

Billybones shadow blotted out the sun peaking through the bottom of the doorframe. We could hear the tumblers in the lock turn and the door opened silently followed by the ring of the oversized captain's bell.

Sandy opened the book to read from a random chapter but the words in the book were morphing as well. What she thought were her hands shaking was actually the vibrations of the book rewriting itself.

"... and all the pirates lived to fight another day... the end." She then used the best weapon in her arsenal, her charm, and waved enthusiastically at Billybones as he walked in. "Hi, hi! Welcome ashore, sir!" giving Billybones a perky salute. Her smile could launch ships and break hearts. Billybones was as susceptible as any other to her beauty. He managed the closest thing to a smile that he could muster.

"Hi, Billy... I mean, I mean, I mean, Mr. Smythe!" followed Gatto trying hard to distract Billybones from the fact that despite the four of them leaning down against it, the roll top desk was trying to *walk* itself across the polished deck..

"My name, swabbie, has not nor ever been William, Billium, Bartholomew or Barabbas. But it is mister to the likes of you... master Gatto? Do we have that straight?" He did not share a smile with Gatto.

Gatto nodded repetitively, not knowing if it was a good thing or a bad thing that a pirate knew his nickname.

"Sorry about the crowd, Mr. Smythe" I chimed in nonchalantly, moving my arm back and forth across the desk as if polishing it. I could feel the spasms of the book inside beginning to wane.

"Just beating the heat, sir. I'm... I'm calling you sir, sir, 'cause... well you just said you like being called sir, sir... and I'm... I'm just leaving," Bess rambled.

Sandy turned the mutating book over in her hands to see the cover. She had to hold on tight, the pages fluttered in resistance. "Did you know Mr. Snow?", she asked with a coy flutter of mascara lashes.

Billybones walked to the adjacent map desk and put down his weathered attaché. "Can't say that we crossed paths, but I assure you, he knew about me." He then waved his hands at the lot of us as if shooing away a flock of sea gulls. "Enough jibber jabber for one day, children. Me and 'swain here have business that needs tending to". There was another of those long pauses that empty halls like the 'Anchor seem to invoke. "Shoo, shoo-fly!" he barked again with an agitated wave of his hands.

We were all thinking the same thing. If we just left, what would prevent the desk from clamoring about the hall like a spooked colt out of its stall? Should we just make a dash for the door, a bonafide pirate at our heels, one with two good legs? How long would we have to run? Forever, I assumed. Pirates have a hell of a lot of fight in them. Cross a pirate and you have an enemy for life.

Bess was the first to go. "See ya!" She jumped from the desk landing squat in a surfer's stance then slowly walking past Billybones to the door.

"Ditto." said Gatto close behind her.

Then I remembered what happened next during the book's manifestation. I had to hurry Sandy and Smythe out of the gallery and quick. "Make ye way sir, I be catchin' up with ye forthwith jus' after I be battening down th' hatches."

Billybones nodded the affirmative and turned to leave. "Time to hit the docks, me lady, not a fine place fer such a delicate flower... fish heads and the like", Billybones replied.

I pushed Sandy along. "Do I gotta?" she cooed. She thought staying would spare me a beating if Smythe discovered we've been messing with his stuff. Sandy handed me the book in her hands. Black dust of fragmented moments in time spilt like bile from inside. Billybones escorted her to the door. He whispered, "Good day, missy" and waved for me to follow.

I made it for the door just before all hell broke loose. I stepped away from the desk. The Manifest's convulsions had abated. The desk made a small skirmish as I released it but nothing that caught the eye of Smythe. On top of the desk, Sandy's book continued to flutter albeit less violently. Smythe already had his eyes on the door. I followed right behind him.

Under the strain a thousand books pulling against their very bindings the wood shelves of the wall stacks began to moan. I followed him out into the safety of a golden afternoon as all records of the present in the gallery were slowly devoured. I swung shut the large wood door as if by doing so I could stop the madness inside from leaching into the world outside.

I head to the docks with Smythe, no words between us. The thief voice laughed so hard that it needed to catch its breath before beginning again. Sandy heard the same as she walked with Bess and Gatto trying to ignore the laughing bag in her head.

"I'm sorry Sandy" I thought to myself.

Smythe looked back at me as if he could hear the cackling as well. He stopped walking, turned and stared at me; looking past my eyes. The laughter stopped, then silence, changing into sobbing; pathetic gasps for mercy.

Then I heard Sandy think deep inside of me, "I know Ty, I know."

"So boy..." Billybones asked with a tone that suggested that he already knew everything that had just happened, "what's on your mind?"

Chapter 10

GAUNTLET

*S*andy wasn't on my mind, she was in it.

"Nuttin," I replied, using a boy's first foray into manly non-speak. Manspeak rule #1; emotions were to be swallowed. They showed your weakness to the pack. Nuttin was certainly somethin', just nuttin' worth sharing. Smythe knew full well what was on my mind. He might even know about the commotion that was ransacking The Rusty Anchor as we walked to the docks.

Billybones gave me a break, with a nod he ended the conversation that never started. As we closed in on the harbor we spoke of nothing of consequence.

"Words oft be wasted breath," he mused. "Now actions, actions speak louder than I do!" If that was the case, I hollered the whole afternoon.

The shipment was same old, same old; crates and barrels, barrels and crates, only this time they were oversized and heavier than before. We needed a forklift to load them into Billybones' makeshift transportation.

The vehicle was actually the truck of a local fish distributor. He was responsible for getting the freshest fish onto the plates of the Cove's clientele. Between deliveries the driver helped Smythe lug the latest barrage of God-knows-what to the gallery. The man looked uncannily like the Morton's fisherman, right down to his tattered yellow rain slicker and scraggly beard. He just sat in the truck's cab chewing on a toothpick, looking out at the harbor. "I love work, kin watch it fer hours." He muttered as I toiled.

The truck smelt like fish long since dead. The stench burrowed into my clothes, melding with my ample sweat. The stench aside, I welcomed the coolness of the refrigerated compartment. It gave a briny relief from the day's labor.

When we returned, the gallery was disheveled but not trashed. The desk was a few feet from where we left it. Scratches were etched across the wide blanks of the deck from its wrestle with The Manifest's conniption. The table stood upright, nothing set off Billybones' curiosity. I positioned the last of the large crates as instructed, and he wished me good day. I dodged a bullet; the beating would be saved for another day.

After the events of the afternoon I could have easily headed home for a nap. Instead I walked the beachfront and toyed with sitting in the shade of the concrete seawall and letting the lapping high tide lull me to sleep. It was nearing a new moon and the high tide would certainly tickle my toes before I slept for too long.

I opted for taking a plunge instead. The water even in mid-summer was the coldest in the area and it shocked me to life as I ran straight into the surf until I was waist high and dove. The salt water replaced the dead fish stink with a smell, equally fishy, but refreshingly alive. I felt the salt sting as it healed my chapped hands. I could feel my body temperature drop.

I dove again, this time down to the ocean floor. I brushed the smooth stones and curtains of kelp, keeping an eye out for my little sea friend. After all I had witnessed during the past week, the more

I believed that the girl in the sea was more than a panic for oxygen by a child who had just shed its water wings. Nothing grabbed at me. I shot back to the surface, rejuvenated,

The Cyrkle met at dusk. Our rendezvous point was The Lucky Lick, one of our favorite hang-outs, located in the center of town. I walked to the community bath house to hose off the salt off my skin. Tucking my shirt through a loop on my backpack I walked towards the town green, letting the sea breeze dry me. The breeze blew hot, massaging my sore shoulders. I thought about what flavor I was going to order at The Lick to have enough scratch to treat my friends. We were all lucky we didn't get caught plundering by Billybones. Everyone at the ice cream stand was lucky to spend summers on the Cove. Life shined like a penny on the sidewalk.

As I approached the stand, Bess and Sandy, whispering to each other, gave me the once over. I was wearing still damp cargo shorts, my backpack and a scraped up pair of tan, *clodhopper* work boots. I dropped my backpack between us and went to put on my t-shirt. I looked at the girls as I started to pull it on over my head.

"Woof!" went Sandy.

"Our little boy's growing up, girl." Bess commented to Sandy in the closest thing to a giggle that she could muster.

I slowly pulled my shirt down. I had done some tightening up under Billybones' employ and the shirt was snug. I had even slit the sleeves to loosen their bind on my biceps. I lifted the shirt for a second giving the girls a flash of my newly developed pectorals.

"Down women... damn!", I joked

Not to be out-staged, Gatto quickly maneuvered himself between me and the girls. "Gun show over, girls, now to the business at hand."

"Dial it down a notch, Gat." I told him from behind out of earshot of the girls. Gatto liked it when I called him Gat. It made him sound more like a lethal weapon than a Portuguese housecat.

The reason I had put the "silencer" on the "Gat" wasn't because I wasn't enjoying the attention. I was always on the geekish side of things, so this metamorphosis was long overdue. The reason I hushed my pal was because I spied a crowd of undesirables congregating on the far side of the Lick.

It was The Scratchers and my brother in all their misfit glory. Shoulders were slouched as if the weight of the world bore down on them. They were here to represent the hood known as Lobstah.

When I say represent, I mean as in "holla!" They were decked out in bleached-white *wife beater* tank tops .Oversized mesh basketball shorts hung low over exposed boxer shorts, pale white butt cracks peeked over the waistbands. They were like the offspring of mole-men, allergic to sunshine and wholesome outdoor activity.

A year earlier I wouldn't have paid them any mind. My only avoidance would be for fear of being associated with them. Ever since I first saw Billybones, my brother made sure that I was the brunt of his constant bullying. He told everyone in town about his wimpy brother's invisible pirate friend.

No one noticed as the stumbled onto the porch, too busy lapping up Tootsie Fruity Explosion and Raspberry Ripple to notice.

I overheard my brother snapping at one of his indistinguishable cohorts,
"So, ya little puke, ya get yer bro to hit the packie, he looks old enough..." Stopping mid-sentence, he looked my way. He tipped his

wrap-around sunglasses down to note that I had been sighted. Shades after the sunset, go figure.

I tried my best to stay out of my brother Ryan's line of sight, countering with Gatto, my back to The Scratchers. Since a large pistachio ice cream cone with jimmies is by no means an adequate form of camouflage, my efforts were all for not. Ryan's eyes met mine. He sported a jack-o-lantern's grin.

"Well, my, my, my, my, my! What do we have here, yo? If it isn't Tyler terrific, pirate killa, in th' house!" He started shuffling towards me, his posse skulking behind.

I turned my back to him pretending to talk to Gatto. "Just start talking, follow my lead", I whispered, trying to avoid a scene.

My brother sensed my retreat and proceeded to call me out. "Whoa, yo-yo!" I did not reply but stopped moving away from him. He knew he had my attention.

Ryan was center stage. On any other day everyone would just ignore them, but that night, all eyes were on The Scratchers. This attention got my brother higher than cheap beer and Parodi cigarillos. He liked the feeling, liked it a lot.

"You got nothin', Capt'n Crunch?" My brother started pacing back and forth across his imaginary stage, flailing his arms straight out before him, aping the rap videos that gave him his fashion savvy.

"No adventures on the high seas, Popeye?!"

"I could make you sing a high C if I wanted," both the thief voice and I mumbled together. One voice chimed in both Sandy's and my head, the other came from my lips.

"You want a piece of this?" Ryan snapped. I tilted my head, cracking my neck like a boxer before a fight.

Sandy glanced over and gave me a sly grin.

What followed was a moment in time that Gatto referred to as *the black hole of silence*. It was moments that sucked the air out of a room. Everyone would become uneasy, not knowing what would happen next. It was the love child of anger and frustration. More often than not it would pass by with no event, but when it came, you could taste it, anything was possible, none of it good.

The entire crowd felt it and held their breath. I twisted the towel, once in frustration, again in anger. Each time I thought of one of my brother's insults it tightened a notch. *Captain Crunch?...* twist, *Popeye?...* twist; it was a watch spring being over-wound.

I slowly turned around to face my brother. "Enough," It was a request, not a plea. My tone was hushed and tolerant.

"Or what... WHAT?!" my brother retorted in a yell laced with laughter. I was the younger brother, the recipient of his endless foray of noogies, wet willies and wedgies. I was born to take it all, without question. It was preposterous that I would stand up to him. If I knew confronting him would feel that good, I would've done it long before.

Ryan tried to win over the crowd, "Yo, what's the name of that sailor dude?? You know, from the song yo??" A malicious smile came over his face as the name came to him. "Yeah, the barnacle guy man!" He started nodding as his body bounced back and forth to the song playing in his head. His arms were all akimbo as he hummed along, "hmm hmm hmm, Barnacle Bill the sailor. So wha cha gonna do Barnacle Ty? Hey boy, hey boy, wha cha gonna do?"

'I think he just called ya boy... boy.' The thief voice growled in my head. *'It's time for some comeuppance!'*

Sandy, her mind hearing the exchange, nodded. She clutched my shoulder with such excitement that her nails dug in. It was *so* not Sandy.

I didn't dignify him with an answer, just stared with the rest of the crowd taking in the performance. Nobody felt the wind change direction or the sudden drop of temperature.

Sandy felt compelled to join in my brother's undoing. *'Good for her'*, the thief voice chimed in once she thought it. She stepped forward and unsnapped the top button of her seersucker gingham blouse and let out a baby powder soft sigh. It worked in all of her romance paperbacks, why not now? All the boys switched their focus from our scuffle to Sandy. As if commenting to herself, she moved her head from side to side letting the cool breeze caress her face. "Ah, that's the first breath of relief we've had all daaay" She put in a slight southern drawl at the end for impact.

Her distraction was a slice in time. I let the tip of my twisted towel dangle into a basin of water that was kept at the steps of the ice cream shop. It was put there for people to clean their sand encrusted feet and for the occasional overheated puppy to drink from.

I cleared my throat. My brother's focused honed back on me. I gave my neck another crack. With a twist of my wrist, the end of the towel back snapped into my waiting hand. I kept staring at my brother, all the while ringing the towel tight, excess water dripped from the towel, a whip salivating, hungry for some action.

A cold blast of air came in from the sea coast sending a chill up the spine of all the onlookers. The Lick was manned entirely by teens so there wasn't an adult around to intervene, to be witnesses. My heartbeat was rapid, my breathing easy; the game was on.

"Well...," both the thief voice and I quietly stated, "I could go like this." I unleashed a whip snap knocking Ryan's backwards-worn hat from his head. He stumbled back a in surprise. I methodically stepped forward, countering his move. With his basketball shorts drawn halfway down his legs, it was easy to keep my brother off balance.

I asked him in the same quiet, distant voice ringing in my ears, "How do you say... snap?" No emphasis, no emotion. From my brother, no answer. "... then snap it is."

"Snap..." Sandy and I spoke the word together. I accented the word with another lash of the wet towel. "...period." This time the towel grazed my brother's cheek. He brought his hand to his face then pulled it back to check for blood. A red streak formed where the tip of the corded towel lit. The strike stung but was nothing compared to the humiliation. Ryan held back a tear.

"Then...," all three of voices, Sandy, the thief, and myself, spoke with all the emotion of a Grand Inquisitor, "*We* could, of course... do this!" I snapped the towel two times in succession, once to the left, once to the right. Ryan lost his balance and fell to his knees.

Sprawled across the porch of The Lick, Ryan was a pitiful mess. I Looked down at his scraped knees and welts across his face and smiled. Sandy's smile mirrored mine. Revenge tasted better than pistachio.

We loomed over Ryan in a vulture stance. His posse stepped back until they were lost in the awestruck crowd.

It should have ended there but my debasement of Ryan had just begun. I eyed a loose slat on the bench that stretched across the front of The Lick. It was splintered in two, broken by the same punks that just abandoned my brother.

"I like where you're going with this," Sandy cooed, reading my intent.

I let out an exhale, bored by the whole exchange. There was so little fight in my brother. Tapping the board in my hand, I contemplated the torture of my fallen brother. I spoke, the voice, no longer mine, sound older and faraway. "It always comes down to this!"

I lunged at my brother, he cowered. With a confident laugh I stomped the loose board with my work boot. It broke free from the bolt securing it, leaving a jagged edge where it splintered free. With a maneuver that would make any pirate proud, I swished the mock cutlass in a figure eight before my foe and then lunged again until its jagged tip brushed ever so slightly against Ryan's quivering Adam's apple.

"Do you yield, sir?" I yawned. My brother swallowed, his neck expanding. The splintered edge cut a warning along his throat, one tear of blood trickled down staining his never cool tank top. Still, no reply.

"Quarter?" the thief voice, now my own, inquired. Ryan fumbled in his pocket and spilled out whatever change he had at our feet.

"Not quarters, you fool!" Sandy reiterated along with me, "Do... you... yield?" The spit coming from my lips was hot enough to burn. The thief voice in both our throats was enraged. I could taste his disgust.

Gatto put his arm on my shoulder. "Chill, dude" and then looked at Sandy like she was some creepy crawly found in the tide pools. "Do I even know you?"

"Lucky for you, my trusty Gat, we do," she said with a wink, patting my back for a job well done.

I shook Gatto's hand off my back but heeded his advice. I threw the board to the ground, pardoning my brother. Sandy and I, heads lowered, walked back to The Cyrkle. We heard the thief grumble, *'Pathetic, the lot of you.'* Before he receded back to whatever netherworld he inhabited until his presence was nothing more than the hum of a radio between channels.

I reached out for Sandy's hand as we turned away from my brother. I looked back for an instant making sure that Ryan wouldn't make for the broken board in an effort to retaliate. What I saw was not my brother, but a beaten cur, licking his wounds.

As quick as the moment flared up, it was extinguished. The cool of the evening disappeared; the night air again grew dank. The Cyrkle followed us away, saying not a word. The rest of the crowd chattered amongst themselves as we passed. One by one, they dispersed, a clique at a time, leaving my brother to hobble home alone in shame.

Let's recap the *piratization* of Lobster Cove. One, had proven itself true. The Cyrkle have seen The Manifest become monster. Two, The Rusty Anchor was converted into a whirlwind of paper and ink. Three, both Sandy and I are turning into the very evil we have sworn to root out. Fourth was still a hunch, something I felt in my bones was true; the world was slowly folding in on itself.

"Tomorrow, you'll see for yourself," I tapped my right eye, Billybones gone-wrong eye. "No worries, I would never let harm

befall any of you. That is my oath. They would witness Billybones'
transformation and they come to see these truths. Finally, pardon
the expression, we would all be on the same page.

Sandy, I'll walk you home, you two, on the 'morrow."

"Aye aye," went Gatto.

Bess just scrunched up her nose in disapproval. "What...
ever."

Bess and Gatto rode their skateboards into the night, Bess
traversed between the streetlights, Gatto puffing close behind. The
clatter of the wheels on the road grew faint as Sandy and I took the
long way home.

The thief voice had brought Sandy and I together in a way
skateboarding or bodysurfing never could. Sandy looked around as
we walked as if she was seeing Lobster Cove for the first time. She
looked back at me. There was a connection that wasn't there the day
before. Our shared experience manipulating The Manifest had given
us vision. It was as if the entire world revolved around us, reacting
to our every step, our every emotion, our every whim.

"Feel it?" the thief voice haunted us again. "*Feel* it?" The
whisper of down on Sandy's arm rose in the electrified air. My arms
had goose-pimples. She smiled at me and I back at her. There was a
hint of mischief in the air.

Now, I liked Sandy enough, every male with blood in his
veins did. Her early maturity made me see her more as a big sister
though we shared the same innocent age. I went through the
pigtail-pulling phase with her, along with frog-showing terms of
affection. While others girls seemed rock-throwing-worthy, Sandy
was off limits.

I never felt *that way* about Sandy, that is, until our walk home that night. It might have been my need to be her protector against Billybones. It could have been the buzz we shared the moment before. Looking back, I think it was that Sandy reached out to hold my hand.

Magic, pure and simple, when her hand met mine, the pirate commentary in our heads stopped. Even when it wasn't speaking to us, we always heard the warm pant of its breathing between our ears. Hand in hand, he was banished; there was reverent silence.

We crossed the town green, the one area in town not overrun with summer homes crammed between marshlands like play pieces on a monopoly board. In the clearing sat Haddad Library. Lights flickered through the stained glass windows though it was long since closed. The sober custodian rushed through the back exit, genuflecting as he ran to the security of his rusty bolts of a pickup. Being grounded by rubber wheels must protect you, as they do with lightning, when the timeline does the watusi. We laughed at his antics, secure that, together, we had nothing to fear.

As we head towards the pathway leading home, we sensed being watched. The path was shrouded by clinging vines of locust trees, a Northeast plant akin to kudzu. As the summer heat fed them, they grew up and then over other plants, slowly strangling the life out of the original occupants.

There was a rustling in the weeds, our silence was disrupted by outside forces. Peeper frogs and crickets made an infernal racket as we made our way down the path. The sea grass seemed alive. This insect chatter was normal for such a humid summer night, but never with such urgency.

Other wildlife followed suit. A gaggle, a flock, a murder, or what have you, of birds joined in the fracas. Caws and squawks rose from the sky drowning out the heightened buzzing of the marsh. The cry of the seagulls, which often times mimicked a human laugh, joined in, one on top of another in disembodied hysteria. A lone loon's howl was thrown in for good measure.

Now birds ordinarily only chirped upon the arrival of the next day's sun. It was as if the limited capacity of their little bird brains couldn't comprehend its return each morning. Every night doomed them to think the rest of their days would be under the cover of nightfall; then came daybreak.

This racket was more than pre-dawn jubulation. It was 'baby chick has fallen from the nest into the birder-cat's yard, urgent and confrontational.

They all rallied behind us, riding in our wake. Closer they came until all we could hear was the flutter of a thousand wings overhead. When we looked through the archway of foliage, we could see black motion between the branches, a living, breathing lace, enveloping us.

The insects rose in pitch with our every step. The human gull laughs stretched out long and low transforming into the howls of feral dogs.

There was no fear in us that night. Sandy and I, hands clasped tight. We increased our pace through the path, fanning the cacophony that pursued us.

I thought of the old wives' tale my mother would tell me whenever I would be caught doing funny faces at the dinner table. "Stop it or your face will stay that way!" From the intensity of our grins that night, Sandy and I should have been doomed to live out our days as models for funhouse clowns.

With no lips parting and no words uttered we spoke to one another, "one... two... and..."

Making a defiant stance, we turned around on three. Our grins reduced to intolerant scowls; no fear.

There was a slight shift in the bog, feathers on the wing. Not a peep, you better believe it!

Our hearts beat like a trip hammer, our breathing, as slow and calculated as a Zen master. Sandy gave my hand a long squeeze taking in the moment. It was more elation than affection. We turned back down the road, not another word was shared between us.

In hindsight, I should've mentioned the things lurking in my bedroom. I was sure she would now have her own share of grotesques to deal with. I wanted to station myself at the foot of her bed like an obedient watchdog. She would do fine I assured myself. No harm would come to her that night. She was ready for whatever awaited her in the dark, for that night, she was fearless.

I went to sleep, beasties at bay, thinking, of all the girls I knew, Sandy was the only one who could get away with wearing a cape.

Chapter 11

FATHOM

I kept the specter in my room at bay. I even tried a couple of quick head turns in its direction, in response, sanguine eyes winced closed in the darkness. End result, a few well deserved hours of quality sack time.

Sandy was not as lucky. We were due at the Rusty Anchor at nine in the morning. When I saw her heel-drag toward the Anchor she looked bone tired and more than a bit spooked out. I was to blame. I introduced her to the maddening revelations that went along with intimate contact with The Manifest.

I'm sorry,' I tried to think-tell her; but no reply.

Off her game, she was still more fetching than any other girl in town on their best day. It was rare to see her so disheveled, eyes puffy from lack of sleep. Her makeup, never taken off the night before, was reduced to faded color, streaked from her tears. She looked average. Average was not in the repertoire of Miss Sandy.

Our plan was to stop Smythe on his way to the shop to confirm his pirate ancestry. The only proof positive was visual confirmation of the man's reconstituted eye.

The Cyrkle arrived groggy, but obediently on time. There was silence between us carried over from the night before. They were still freaked out over the turn of events that evening. I was nervous over what confirming Smythe as a pirate would imply. The only important thing that morning was proving The Manifest had woven its magic.

Not knowing where he slept meant he could come from any direction, so we all played look-out, each one looking at a different part of the square. Where did Billybones stay when he wasn't at the Anchor? None of the locals had put him up for the season and summer rentals were scarce. Who was staying with whom was common knowledge in a tourist, yet no one knew where Smythe hung his hat.

Gatto broke the awkwardness. "That was some mega awesome ninja moves you dropped on the homeboys last night!"

"No ninjas... got it," I snapped back with piratical shortness. My response rubbed Gatto the wrong way.

"Sure, no ninjas... we can be knee deep in pirates, sure, but throw in a little Kung Fu action and... aye aye, cap-i-tan!" He then caught sight of Smythe turning the corner of the post office. "Peep!"

The man was in full pirate regalia from his floppy boots, from his large cuffed jacket to his billowy white shirt gathered with a mesh of golden lacing across the front. His black tri-corner hat tipped forward was the cherry on top. With his road worn demeanor, he'd never be mistaken for a play actor in a historical reenactment. He was the real article, torn from the pages of a Robert Lewis Stevenson novel.

The one thing that betrayed his pirate perfection was a pair of navigator sunglasses. They had large wire frames and mirrored lenses that didn't fit with the rest of his ensemble.

He was mere steps from us. Now that's step-steps remember, not step-drags. Face to face, we could only see our distorted reflection in the smoky surface of the sunglasses. The lenses were impenetrable. This would not do for the task at hand.

Billybones' forehead scrunched quizzically as he cleared the early hour from his throat. "What be this, th' whole crew before th' early bird feeds? I have no need fer the lot of ya til noon... off with the bunch of you!"

'Well, good morning to you. Some pirate had woken up on the wrong side of his pirate bed,' I thought to myself. Sandy smiled. *'So, you are listening?'*

Gatto attempted to get Billybones to lighten up. "Hey there, Mr. Smythe! Do you see that bird out there on the green?" There was a large black bird, slick as oil, its feathers reflecting dark rainbows in the early light. "What you do you suppose that be, sir?"

"Starling," Billybones replied without question.

"Really? Perhaps you need a better look. I was thinking a grackle, I'm sure of it."

"It's a starling, you bilge monkey, let me pass."

Gatto brought his hand up to his forehead shielding his eyes from the harsh morning light. He looked hard and long at the bird pecking away on the town common. "You sure? What I'm seeing here is all grackle."

"Are you a feeb, son? Grackles eat starlings fer breakfast. I've seen grackles as big as men in packs, twenty plus, terrorize housewives and men weak-of -heart. What you have here is a lone starling, who would be breaking its fast if it wasn't fer the lot of you. Now shoo, grackle boy, and let me be!"

There was no removal of his shades which was the desired reaction. We were losing him with no piratical evidence. Something needed to be done and done quickly.

Despite her harried condition, Sandy stepped forward. With a half-hearted shrug of her shoulders, she nudged her way before the accused pirate, close enough to smell his signature stench of day old sweat and gut-rot.

Sandy was the whitest girl ever to summer in a beachfront town. She was fair-skinned and blonde, a hybrid of Scandinavian design. Always stylishly dressed she could make walking the beach with a parasol look hip and trendy. She wore the highest number of sunscreen with a spritz of gold glitter. When the flecks caught the sun, Sandy could sell ice cubes to Eskimos.

She also believed she knew men. She had pulled together her philosophy from months of Cosmo magazine quizzes and Harlequin romances. All men were dogs; a few rabid, a few alpha, but mostly mangy mutts that could be mollified by the simplest diversion. If trained and lathered with attention, they would be loyal; if ignored and abused, they would stray. Men were dogs and she was the ball.

Boys were just eager pups who wanted the ball. Their whole life revolved around the ball. The ball was all. On their road to dog-hood boys could be trained to obey, to live wanting the ball but knowing that they don't always get the ball, in other words, heel. In the world according to Sandy, Billybones should be no different.

Sandy began the tease that worked so well the night before. She unbuttoned the top button giving Billybones a little show. It worked wonders then, why not now?

I noticed the blouse she was wearing was the same as the night before. She must have had one hell of a night with her newly conjured haunts.

'Why didn't you call for me?' I think-talked, no answer.

'That'll be quite enough of that, missy,' Sandy and I heard echo in our heads. It wasn't the thief voice this time, but that of the irritated pirate before us broadcasting live in our bones. A frantic Sandy looked at me. I nervously nodded. She then turned her wide-eyed gaze to the mirrored sunglasses looking at her.

Billybones spoke aloud so all could hear. "Go now, it'll be a day fit fer youth, not the likes of me," and he elaborately bowed before the Cyrkle. We awkwardly bowed back in response.

His bow was low enough for Billybones to catch a glimpse of Sandy's alabaster skin, flesh so white it would make blind men squint. His lecherous side took the bait and he lowered the glasses down the bridge of his nose to get an unfiltered glance.

We all froze mid-bow, staring eye-to-eye with a flesh and blood pirate. Both of his eyes rose to meet ours. There were no ghostly swirls of white in a bruised grey orb. Both of his emerald eyes were blood-shot from the prior night's tot-tipping but otherwise healthy. The resurrected eye seemed to twinkle in the morning light as Billybones slid his glasses back into position.

We all held our breath like a toddler in a tantrum, save for Sandy who let out an *'Eepp'*, which was a cross between a gasp and a swallowed shriek. She fumbled at her blouse, refastening the button. She wished she had even more buttons, enough to cover her whole body from head to toe.

Sandy saw Billybones for the surly pirate that he was. He was a bad dog, a cur who did not understand the command to heel. Sandy was no longer the ball, she was meat. Perhaps the term *heel* referred to such feral animals who knew not the command, rather, defied it. That definition worked for Sandy and she noted to change her man-law to reflect it. This was what meeting a real pirate felt like. It was no joke.

Billybones put a choke chain on his libido, returning to his more sullen self. "Now git a move on, I be not in the mood fer such shenanigans!"

We backed away, parting sides, clearing the sidewalk for him to pass. As he passed Sandy, he rubbed his two index fingers together like sticks starting fire. Without looking in her direction he whispered, *'Tssk tssk!'* to her in a voice only our bones could hear.

With his back to us he called for me, "Swain, hands on deck, it'll be a long day ahead, which you can be sure!"

The Cyrkle dispersed, leaving Billybones the pirate, and me, Tyler the boatswain, to lumber off to the Rusty Anchor. I was left behind to contemplate the implications of Billybones' reconstituted eyeball. I followed him I followed him obediently as a good boatswain should, a good three strides behind, as if I was being escorted to the gallows. 'He knew! I knew he knew.' What would be the punishment, the plank, the dreaded keelhaul , or perhaps a horror my young mind couldn't yet imagine.

'Sorry.' I heard Sandy echo inside. Alas, a truce.

'No, I'm sorry,' I thought-whispered back. We were good.

'Not as sorry as you're gonna be!' the thief voice was awake, chuckling over how Smythe's pirate-hood had shaken us.

Rather than being subjected to the rack or the lick of the cat's tail, my punishment was the skullduggery of lifting the infernal crates and barrels back and forth without rhyme or reason. I wished he finished his pirate outfit with an eye patch so I wouldn't have to see his now healthy eye mock me as I went about my chores.

Smythe the shopkeeper, from this point forth, Billybones the pirate, sat slouched over the map desk, his rum decanter keeping him company. He tipped his tot with frequency despite the morning hour.

The rum began to leech into his spirit. Billybones rose from the desk with his two good legs, though, due to the spirits, they were not quite land worthy. He took hold of the walking stick he recently outgrew, and raised it over his head, encircling the periphery of the gallery in a dizzying spiral.

"Y'know what we 'av here, swain?" I continued my tasks hoping my lack of response would turn his attention back to drink. He slurred louder. "Ar ye deaf, boy? Ye know what this be?!"

I hunched up my shoulders giving him the universal symbol of, 'duhh... I don't know'.

"It be me livelihood, catch my meaning, me mute minion."

Again, no answer neither given nor expected.

"It's what keeps me alive is what..." He struggled for the words; there was no language in his lungs. "... It be me life... n' wherefore whatnot." He poured himself another unnecessary tot. "You... you jus be rememberin' that when you be on your watch, swain!"

I looked about the gallant relic of days gone by crammed into the galley like a ship in a bottle. This inebriated pirate and his most prized possession brought it all to life.

What if The Rusty Anchor and The Manifest that spawned it wasn't only the *livelihood* of Billybones, but of us all? Wouldn't my quest then be to protect the book, and its caretaker?

"Work is not done, swain... not be a long shot!" Billybones rant echoed in the rafters. He stumbled around the desk using its edge as a railing. Suddenly a mop was thrown in my direction. It was aimed at my head but sorely missed the mark due to Billybones' compromised faculties. I caught the mop handle deftly, balancing it in my palm. I gave it a swing a figure eight like a Cossack with a broad sword. I then rested the mop head on the deck and prepared for a good hour of back-breaking swabbing.

Billybones approved of my taking to task but that was not what was on his mind. He brandished his cane. An uncomfortable smile came across his drunken face. A duel was in the offing.

He lowered his cane as quickly as he had brandished it. Shaking his head, Billybones mumbled to himself.

"No, no,no... th' boy needs prepare-in-in, gots t' be ready. He will share not the fate of me blood. He can't be easy pickins when they comes fer him."

With his arms reaching blindly before him, he stumbled his way to a long, glass display case. It cradled a series of full blade swords, blades more suited for jousting than dueling. They were not short-shivved, nor thin for fencing. They were dragon-slaying wide.

Confronting Billybones, I saw the same flinty glint in his eye I witnessed on my porch. This time, the count of good eyes were two. Danger smoldered within them, now with twice the foreboding.

'I'm not afraid of you...' I almost said to the pirate.

He read my thought. Without uttering a word, he replied, *'We'll jus' have to see about that!'*

'Careful,' Sandy plead within me. Blind to my situation, she somewhere, somehow, heard the pirate's voice and sensed danger.

He tossed one of the swords my way. I grabbed for its hilt. It was heavy, offering an uncanny balance to the weapon. I gave it a couple test swipes.. It was perfection in forged steel. Billybones armed himself as well. He gave the blade a few turns of the wrist, the tungsten sang as it cut dead air.

The duel began with simple blade-to blade-clashes. 'Crack!', 'Slap!', 'Snickety-snatch!' Each strike gained with intensity.

Joining the party of voices in my head was the thief voice. *'Let's show the ol' salt what yer made of,'*

Billybones lunged at me, the massive blade crossing horizontally an inch before my mid-section. I jumped back instinctively. The blade took out an oil lamp on the corner of the map table, glass shards sprayed across a circle of flame on the deck that grew around us as the wick ignited the spilt oil.

"'Tis not th' fear!" Billybones interjected between exchanges. Metal met metal, blades edges slid along one another until our fists met hilt to hilt. "'Tis th' power ye give it. With the full strength of his arm his pushed me away. "So y' need to be askin' yer self, am I a feared? If the answer be yes, then what ar' you gonna do about it?"

Angry chrome; each stroke countered until they were again locked together in a standoff. This time I pushed off. It was more of a punch than a fencing technique. My hand was protected by the hilt's jagged edges. The detail of the hilt made for one solid gauntlet. My push caused Billybones, two of the proverbial three sheets to the wind, to lose his footing.

One bushy salt and pepper eyebrow rose. He regained his balance, cocked his blade back, and doled out an overhand swing better suited for a battle axe. I hunkered down, knees bent slightly, betting my agility over his brute force.

Fear did not take my helm that day. I was alive, floating calmly in the eye of the storm. Unlike the black hole of silence, this new feeling was not fueled by anger and frustration, rather, by righteousness and purpose. I was fearless.

This man wasn't going to defeat me just because he was a pirate. If he won, it was because he was the better man that day. He would not prove the victor, not that day. I would prove myself victorious for every person who was a victim of a spitball ambush in study hall, for all the downtrodden victims of teenage cruelty through the age, and most importantly, for the village of Lobster Cove that I was protecting from this piratical threat.

Billybones, now the hulking figure of the Norse god Thor, armed with his mighty hammer, cast me in shadow. My drawn blade would be no defense against his wrath. I dropped my sword and grabbed the map desk's chair. Flames danced around it, crackling spectators to this clash of titans. The flames caught on the shellac of the chair, racing up the legs. They licked at my fingers as I brought the chair over my head for protection.

Billybones' blade came down, splitting the seat of the chair cleanly. I could see his grimace between the slat boards as they splintered away. The supports beneath kept the chair intact and kept Billybones from splitting my skull in two.

His blade became tangled in what was, moments before, a chair. I threw the chairs severed arms to the side and dove for my blade. It rested on the deck in a bed of fire. I grabbed at the blade with both hands. The hilt burned white hot. The smell of crackling flesh rose in the air as I felt the detail work etched in the metal handle tattoo its pattern onto the palms of my hands.

I had no time for the pain or the fear. Refusing tears to fall, I thrust my reclaimed blade up at Billybones who was still struggling to free his blade from the twists of burning wood and wire.

I took aim at his sword's hilt. Billybones was forced to disarm himself. My aim was high and the point of the blade rode above the top end of his hilt.

If Billybones hadn't an eternity of swordfights under his belt, he would have added an arm-hook to his pirate get-up. He pulled his hand away not an instant too soon. My blade cut across his backhand from the wrist to fingers. Every inch up his hand, the blade dug deeper into his flesh. Once at the web between the index and forefinger, the skin was cut asunder. It made his two bloody fingers look abnormally long as he pointed at me.

In surrender, Billybones dropped a short shiv he had just drawn with his other hand. He had procured it from a hiding place somewhere on his body. The pirate pulled out a laced handkerchief from the lapel of his jacket and wrapped the wound tourniquet-tight to slow the ebb of blood.

"Ha!" Billybones let out a hearty laugh of resignation. "Who be the greenie now?" I was still on my knees, my scarlet stained blade aimed skyward. With a deft touch Billybones lowered the point of my blade with his good hand. I just stared at the blood at my feet... *his* blood.

'You'll do jus' fine,' both Billybones and the thief voice said in stereo between my ears. I could hear Sandy's breath, short and weepy, as she cowered in the dark recesses of my mind.

I took offense that Billybones resigned himself to defeat. The fight wasn't over until I said it was. This was my chance to put an end to him once and for all. All I needed to do was lean forward and lunge upwards a second time and his innards would spill out like candy from a piñata.

I just couldn't do it. To slay a drunkard wasn't noble, even if he is a pirate. It would make me no better than him, too, making me no better than a pirate.

I looked up at Billybones and saw something I hadn't before. The look on his soused face was one of pride.

'Ye still fear'm, ya snot!' the thief voice grumbled in disgust, reverting back to his wheezing silence.

"Ya win dis bout, matey," Billybones grimaced as if not taking his life had promoted me from boatswain to first mate. His good hand pulled out from beneath the large cuff of his topcoat. He knelt to help me up and then offered me his hand, the same hand that was almost severed a moment before.

"Truce," He proffered. "D-y-no why men offer the flipper?" Did you know was sloshed into one word. His pulled his good hand out from beneath the large cuff of his topcoat. I extended mine to join his in friendship. Billybones then pulled his back. "Hands are joined and shaken heartily but it isn't in welcome or goodwill, no siree Bob. It be a shakedown. It was common, no, damn well expected, fer a soldier of fortune to be stowin' away a pistol, a shiv, or what have ya, in the bellow of his sleeves. Especially wit' pirates; havin' an ace in hole has more to do with life livin' and life takin' than card playin.'"

He offered his hand again. This time I reached out more cautiously. Our hands locked as if to wrestle, his calloused mitt dwarfing mine. We shook long and hard, his hand, a vise. My shoulder ached from the exchange.

Billybones, inches from me, smiled yellow tombstones and gold caps while we shook hands. His voice again echoed inside, *'Jus' remember, pirates play with a loaded deck!'* His hand freed its grip on mine, and like magic, a small snub-nosed pistol appeared in his palm. He cocked the flint and buried its muzzle between my ribs, "Incidentally, boy, don't bring a knife to a gun fight."

He then disengaged the flint and slid the weapon back up his sleeve. I could hear it lock back in position, in wait for the next hapless victim.

I did not cower. I held tough, waiting for the worst, ready to take whatever he could dole out. If today was going to be the day, so be it. Fearless.

He looked at me not backing down. "Feelin' a bit like a pirate y'self, aren't ya. Betcha do, betcha do!" Billybones remarked.

"When there be pirates afoot, rule one, draw first or die. A handshake be an asinine act when dealing with the likes of a pirate. They all be packin'. Now, if he be your matie, tried and true, loyal to the articles ye both swore on, then you must trust him with yer life. That is the only exception. Then, only one greeting would do which brings us to, rule two, ne'er the hands, opt fer elbows!"

Billybones proceeded to show me the Pirate's Welcome. He offered his hand again. When I reached out to shake it, instead of grasping my hand, he passed it to the left ever so slightly. The two hands did not meet; they passed each other, side by side, as if casing each other out.

"Go on, keep up, greenie, caution be not fear!" He leaned forward and I mirrored his move. The two arms traversed each other until the elbows met. With a flex of his arm, the elbows bumped each other in alliance.

"Y'see? We be watchin' each other's backs now. It's a matter of trust. If ye' have trust in yer crew..." He paused as the years, the centuries, of plunder and pleasure, washed over him in a tide of memory. "...ahhh, then the world be ya oyster, mate!"

He stepped back to inspect me bow to stern. I was no longer a young boy looking for adventure in a small town, I was a young man seasoned for whatever God and his ocean dealt out.

"Ay, yer won fair 'n square. We gots to work on that, fairness just won't cut it 'round here. From landlubber, to swabbie, to boatswain, to a full fledged mate. Bravo! Now back t' work!"

I was in a perfect position to defeat the pirate menace of Lobster Cove. I was now his first mate. I went through the ranks and won Billybones' trust. The guilt I felt over betraying his trust was shadowed by my sense of purpose. I held my fear in check. The less I was afraid of Billybones, the nether pirates camped out in my bedroom, or the voices in my head, the stronger I became. With his trust and my fearlessness, I could just go for my blade and give him a good ol' pirate how-do-you-do next time we rubbed elbows; game over.

I looked over at Billybones as he hurried back to his decanter of rum. He was in great need of drowning whatever was eating at his insides. He was many things; crotchety, assertive, even jovial when it suited him. I had never seen him sullen. Beneath his gruff exterior I sensed a drunken sadness.

While I snuffed out the pockets of fire throughout the gallery with musty blankets I found stored in one of his countless chests. As I smothered the flames, I swore I saw Billybones squeak a tear. He wiped it as soon as it fell and poured another shot in hopes of the liquor's promise of memory loss. I continued cleaning the glass and smoldering debris, all the while trying to sneak another peek. Again, the man grew teary eyed when he caught me watching.

"Aaww!", he wiped away the rumor of tears from his face with the breadth of his sleeve, brass buttons brushing against grey stubble.

"What cha' be lookin' at, mate? See to yer chores, ya need not see me in such a state."

It's not like I could just go back to sorting crates when I had a blubbering pirate on my hands. Here was the man I meant to destroy and I was actually feeling sorry for the lout.

What did he have to feel so bad about anyways? So, I beat him in a fisticuffs, at least it wasn't to the death. Hell, he could have sliced me into Swiss cheese well into that exchange.

He was the luckiest man I ever met. In the course of three days, he was gifted one new leg to stand on and two perceiving peepers. I was also pretty sure that he knew the where-a- bouts of some long lost treasure, with the maps and measures. That's a lot of check marks in the plus column. He should be thanking the high heavens for his good fortune instead of sobbing into a bottle of rum.

He waved me away, noticed my genuine concern, and, me now his mate, called me over. He motioned me to sit by his side, thumping his hand against the chair by his side until I sat. He poured us each a tot, remembered my age and then downed them both himself.

"There are chapters in life that can make stones weep." He drew another tot and raised it towards the crow's nest in a toast. "To the fallen, so many years to the day..." He fell back into his seat as if for a moment his feet failed him. "Damn me eyes! Arr, if I'd only stood fast, held me station like a stalwart captain should, that fateful night might never..." Instead of filling the tot again, he reached for the decanter and drew a long shot right from its neck. "... then me brother might be alive today." Rare pirate tears flowed.

I knew how long ago that fateful day was, three hundred and sixty nine years to be precise. The Manifest had healed the lame and had given the man back the gift of sight but not without a cost. It took what was closest to him, his own flesh and blood. Correction; it wasn't the book; it was merely a conduit, a means to an end. It was our meddling that allowed this tragedy to happen. The blood of the brother of Billybones was on our hands.

I didn't know quite how to console him. I tried a shoulder squeeze, but reconsidered. I decided the best thing to do was give the man some space so not to humiliate him further.

"Finish up. Begone! I needs me time," Billybones slurred, trying hard to regain his composure. He offered me the Pirate's Handshake which I accepted, more out of consolation than fraternity. Then I went for the door to leave Billybones to mull over his newly dealt fate.

I walked the long way across the gallery looking for further confirmations of the events that unfolded all those years before. I was familiar with the narrative of all the displays in cases scattered throughout the gallery. There was one at the far end of the hall that honored the victory I read in The Manifest.

I peered into the case to read the parchment describing the freshly forged history. Instead of detailing the surrender of the pirate ship as a result of the rage of the blinded sea captain, the exhibit referenced a merciless attack on a band of pirates, one of the bloodiest every perpetrated. The skull and crossbones that flew over their heads was still draped in the back of the display. It missed the puzzle piece of material from the bottom right as before. The flag had changed though, the top of the skull, once stark white, was now spattered in sepia, like an old, faded photograph. The carnage of the event was so severe that the viscera that erupted on the deck of the damned pirate ship stained the flag that hung high from the broken main mast.

There was a black dust around the document describing the exhibit. The new type's calligraphy was pristine, their story, dark and stormy. Below was what looked like a mound of dead ants at its feet. If you looked hard enough you could see the random serifs of type that had molted off the page along with their meaning. Some still twitched a dance of death.

None of us look hard enough at the world around us. Everything is dying all around, all the time; the newly plucked morning glory, the freshly manicured lawn, the seaweed drying in the sun after low tide, from the baby blowing out her first birthday candle to the senior coughing out his early-bird special to a waitress; all are passing away and being assigned new purpose and meaning.

The difference here was that these deaths and the sorrows that would follow were not part of the regular chaotic cycle of things. It was because of us, because of our thoughts and actions. The Cyrkle had become angels of death and that beats a pirate, hands down.

S.E. Toon

Chapter 12

BYGONES

We met at the town library just after the sun crossed the yardarm that's three-thirty for you landlubbers. Like the bobbers after dawn, the library in the summer was one of the few places in a seaside town where you were assured privacy.

As I walked through the main entrance heading towards the old wing, I saw Hank, the night watchman sweeping a pile of green sawdust with a push broom erasing the Black fodder of now meaningless type mixed with the sick of an over-excited. Hank wore many hats; janitor, guard, librarian's assistant, whatever the building needed. He was the self-appointed caretaker of Lobster Cove Municipal Library.

Further into the stacks a librarian was on her hands and knees picking up book after book off the floor, stacking them alphabetically to return them to the shelves they fell from the night before. Boards hung precariously in mid-air, supported only by the twisted nails that buckled under the torque of the book's thrashing.

In the old wing the antique shelves were made of hardwood and Yankee craftsmanship. The chronicles of the Cove's past were corralled there, kept in check each time history was rewritten.

Throughout time Lobster Cove had the unfortunate reputation of being combustible. In fact, the old wing was the only original part of the town square. The village had burned to a cinder more times than the town elders could remember. All that was left from the burning of 1922 was the old wing, dating back to pre-revolutionary times. Be it the solid mortar and stone foundation or that Fate passed it by to preserve the village's oldest testaments to its past, it stood fast while the rest of the village was reduced to black soot a full mile around.

The wing was a relic of days gone by. The ceiling was a cathedral arch, stained glass windows reached high on the far wall. They depicted settlers on the beach in jagged pieces of glass and solder. A musty cloud of old paper and dust hung in the air. A long mahogany desk reached lengthwise down the narrow hall. Save for the dim light through the window the halls only illumination was a series of a dozen brass study lamps, each with glowing emerald shades. They ran down the center of the table, each a mirror of the other giving the table the illusion of infinite length.

The dim light was a stark contrast to the neon brightness of the rest of the library. When my eyes adjusted, I saw the other members of The Cyrkle waiting for me at the far end of the mile long desk. Bays of rare books banked each wall, seeming to reach as high as the table seemed long. Sitting down beside my friends, I was keenly aware how small we were in the whole scheme of things.

"Uncle!" Gatto hush-yelled at me remembering his library manners. That was the plea you would make to another child when you were ready to give up a fight. I looked at the other's and they nodded agreement. Billybones was a pirate; a pirate with a capitol "P", this much we knew for sure. On Gatto's face I saw concern, worry on Sandy's and barely-under-the-surface anger on Bess'. All these emotions were the byproducts of fear.

Sandy waved me close and whispered in a voice so soft not even the towers of books that dwarfed us could hear. "He's a pirate?", she questioned. "He's a pirate," she repeated, this time a statement. She took a moment for the reality to sink in. "HE'S A PIRATE," she exclaimed, forgetting to use her inside voice. The shrillness of her panic echoed down the empty corridors.

"Well duh-weee!", Bess snapped. "That's math even Ty's bro can do. That makes him old as sin right? So, thanks to you we're on the bad side of a death-defying pirate with a penchant for bullying kids. Well, thank you, thank you very, very much!"

"*Penchant??*", Gatto quipped.

"Shut up, Gatto. Little Miss Encyclopedia over there isn't the only one here who's cracked open a book.

Gatto had a comeback, he always did, "Book?? What is this book thing from which you speak?"

"Difference here is that one of the books Sandy did open has the ability to change history, and not always for good. Manifest isn't just its title, it's what it does. I proceeded to tell them of my duel, the sadness in the pirate's eyes, and how the slain first mate in the Manifest's story was Billybones' own brother.

It wasn't fate that killed him, it was us with the stroke of a pen.

"Butterflies", Sandy whispered to herself. We looked at her as if we asked her what day of the week it was and she had responded, "flapjacks!"

"*You O.K., Sandy?*" I thought-asked. No answer.

"Everything's connected... butterflies" Her voice grew with nervous energy. "A butterfly flaps its wings on one side of the world and..." She slaps her hand flat on top of the desk, the clap resonating down the caverns of shelves. ".. a tsunami swallows an entire seaside town clear across the globe... butterflies!"

Gatto chuckled, his response to most things. "Sandy, I'm digging the whole Asian mind trip scenario, truly. My inner samurai bows to your inner geisha, but I'm not buying it. It's hard enough to wrap my head around a 200 year old pirate with a penchant for swordplay walking amongst us, never mind killer butterflies." He winked at Bess, "...*penchant*."

Sandy then leaned over to Gatto and put her bubblegum pink polished fingernail to his lips. The yapping puppy hushed. She then took his hand and spread it out on the table as if she were about to read his palm.

"Take a pebble, throw it in the water. The water ripples from the point of impact outwards." Sandy started tracing a small circle in the center of Gatto's hand. In that moment, Sandy could make Gatto believe in Santa Claus. She slowly drew another, then another. "Larger and larger. . ."

"Yeah, larger but weaker and weaker..." Bess interjected, trying to find a flaw in Sandy's reasoning.

"Correct, but remember there are thousands... jamillions of pebbles, rocks, and skimmers. They are all kerplunking all over the world, each in some small way influencing the other."

"What does this have to do with our little pirate problem may I ask?" I inquired.

"The Manifest is one massive KERPLUNK!" She pounded her fist into Gatto's palm before he could pull away. "Forget a pebble, this is Lover's Rock!"

Lover's Rock protruded from the furthermost point of Lobster Cove. It was large enough for five grown men to sit on as if it was a huge stone couch. For hundreds of years, happy loving couples would pose for pictures before it; marriages were even performed with it as an altar. If that rock was unearthed and catapulted into the ocean, its ripple would splash up on distant shores.

"I got it! Gatto yelped, pulling his hand back in pain.

"That is why we have to make a vow, here and now, that we will never... ever... touch that damned book again," Bess proclaimed. With me silently abstaining, the opinion was unanimous.

"No touchy", nodded Sandy.

"Eye eye... seriously, too soon? Then ix-nay on the i-rate tay," joked Gatto.

Ca-chink. Bess flashed her gun move. You in, pirate boy?"

I nodded. It was done. We couldn't do anything about how we had warped the past. What we could do was hold each other accountable for not further weakening the fabric of time. If time was a tapestry of woven memory and meaning, what would happen if the cloth became too tattered to hold itself together? It would most assuredly unravel, and with it, our significance in this world.

We all agreed, we must never use The Manifest again.

To seal our pact, I presented each of my Crykle brethren with a bracelet. Each was woven of white cord and reed, the serpentine pattern akin to the bands that I strapped across the main mast in the Anchor.

"Gross," went Sandy.

"Dude!," went Gatto.

Bess said nothing.

"When they dry, they'll fit to you." I wrapped my knuckles against the mahogany desk like a gavel to make a proclamation. "Let these amulets symbolize the bond between us, the Cyrkle of Lobster Cove..."

"Amulets? They're rope wristbands", Bess grumbled.

"... let these *amulets* symbolize the bond between us, like the Keltic knots of yore they so emulate..."

"An emulating amulet, how fancy!" smirked Sandy.

I cleared my throat, dismissing her disruption. "No beginning, no end, when one strand is weak, the others hold strong." I slipped my bracelet, the others followed suit. "Alas, never afraid, never alone."

"Not too shabby", admitted Bess, giving me a nod.

"Yeah, thanks man", shrugged Gatto.

"And its white, good through Labor Day!" smiled Sandy.

We all longed to get out of the murky confines of the old wing. As we turned to leave, I reached out to shake Gatto's hand. My hand passed his as I moved in to give him salutations Billybones-style.

Instead of playing along, he backed away. I never remember Gatto being mad at me before.

"What's this! No way, dude! We ain't pirates, Ty. We're just a bunch of bored kids looking for some fun. Kinda unfair match, don'cha think, undead pirate against the bunch of us?" His fear had bubbled over to anger. "You just don't get it? You are not a pirate, that's how we got into this mess in the first place!"

"We are in WAY over our heads here so honor the pact! Don't go telling us one thing and doing another because it isn't just your neck you're risking anymore, its all of us," Sandy scolded.

"But you still want to play pirate as much as I do," I thought-back to her, the pirate voice choosing the words. She glared back at me as she crossed her arms tightly.

"Well... yeah, it's fun, for sure, but this is serious." she thought back.

Bess brought her forefinger within biting distance to my face. "The way I see it we've been playing Jenga with history. Jenga is a game comprised of a tower of wooden pegs whose object is for players to remove pegs, one at a time until the tower collapses. "First stick, no more gimp. Second stick, 20-20 vision and a dead man, pull a third stick... kaplooey!"

Gatto stepped between the two girls, one in each arm. "You heard her, we're in pre-kaplooey mode here, so no pirates."

"I got it. I quit, honest. I'll give notice in the morning."

"Give notice... to a pirate? You're hopeless." Sandy left in an exasperated huff, her flip flops slapping madly against the marble floor as she strutted out of the hall.

Gatto and Bess proceeded to leave together. As Bess was leaving, her back to me, she gave me the order, "Give notice, whatever. Do whatever you need to do to keep this creep from hunting us all down one by one. Adios, muchacho!"

"She's sooo bueno!" Gatto smiled as they left together.

They left me no choice. This was the end. My bond with them was stronger than any influence Billybones had over me. I felt more in control of myself than ever. The pirate and the thief fed off my weakness, the Cyrkle, off my strengths; it was an easy choice.

With purpose in my stride I emerged from the shadows of the old wing into stale light. The books exhaled in relief. The perpetrators of last evening's blasphemy had finally left their hallowed hall.

I marched back to the Rusty Anchor to tell Billybones I was no longer in his employ. This would be the second time in twenty-four hours that I would be in his face. Odds were this would go well but I had no choice.

Once at the Rusty Anchor, I swung the front door open with conviction. I was no longer Billybones' whipping boy. Enough is enough!

"Hooligans!" Billybones barked as I entered. He was talking to himself more than addressing me. I expected a "Top of th' morn" so "Hooligans" was a bit unsettling. At least he was back to his irritable self, and not the sad sack pirate I left earlier that day.

The Anchor was pretty much as I had left it. Billybones looked haggard, sipping a bit of the hair-of-the-dog to nurse a well deserved hangover. He was still cleaning up from The Manifest's tantrum. "Should be hung by their thumbs, they should." He turned his general despise of youth to me. " Y'sure ya locked up the night before, mate?" He threw on his coat and prepared to leave the shop.

"Yes, sir, I was right behind you as I am now, remember?"

"I remember you a poor excuse for a shadow." Didn't he remember how I won his favor only hours before? Who was the victor? It was as if the event never occurred, no props at all save for the deferential acknowledgement of my first mate status. But it did happen and I beat him fair and square.

He hastily left the Anchor, ignoring me. I followed, locking the door behind us. I worked on my courage as we walked in silence toward town center. Perhaps it was the false sense of safety I felt being with him in the light of day that gave me the courage to let the following slip past my lips.

"Perhaps it was pirates, sir."

"Hah!, What do you know from pirates, greenie??"

"Just with the ship in the Anchor, the plank and all the... aarrgg!" I replied through a nervous grin. He stopped walking and turned to face me. I offered a pirate's welcome to break the tension. He stared back blankly. "Just a little elbow between... or not... your call, sir."

"So all this amuses you, laughing boy??"

"No one's laughing, sir, I mean yes, No!, I mean no, I mean..." He walked past me into the Lobster Cove General Market. I followed on his heels. "I mean you're a grown man with a jacket with epaulets and a life size replica of a pirate ship in your store's lobby, its not *funny* funny sir, but it is funny, no offense."

I was making things worse. I should have pulled out his cutlass from its hiding place and placed it firmly on my jugular and bore down. Because he was in public, Billybones paid me no mind. I knew inside he was quietly making a note in his pirate to-do list; *1) kill the boy.*

Instead of gutting me right there in the entranceway, Billybones retreated into the store. I followed close behind, tracking him throughout the store. He traversed from aisle to aisle as if to lose me. I finally caught up with him in frozen foods. Dozens of Morton fishermen watched our confrontation through the chilled glass of the freezer case.

Billybones looked from side to side. When the coast was clear of shoppers, he grabbed my arm. "Y'fear, so much I can taste it in th' air!" he quietly growled. Then he let go of me in disgust.

"I don't fear you," I whispered back, meaning every word.

"Ya think the green grocer's gonna come to ya aid if I show me steel? Come on boy, wha cha waitin' fer? There's nobody here to cheer you, nobody to jeer ya. Jus' you n' me, boy, and this huge dump of fear between us." He averted his eyes in disgust and crossed the store to the butcher's shop. Slab upon slab of meat that had already seen the business end of a knife was on display, countless fish rest on shaved ice watching us with lifeless eyes.

I would not be so easily dismissed. "You want funny? Your legs seems fine, your eyes sharp, but wait... your hearing must be shot because I clearly said, I'm not afraid of you." I turned to leave then did an about face. "Oh, and, news flash...a moment... wait for it... I quit!"

Billybones reached out and grabbed one of the displayed stripers and gave the gutted fish a good sniff. He threw it back it the pile, disapproving of its freshness as he did my decision. He opted for a couple of tins of kippered herring and walked back towards the front of the store, passing by me as if I wasn't even in the store.

He talked in hushed tones as he walked. As women passed by pushing grocery carts, he would tip his hat. He smiled his tooth rot if a young child was riding along. "Fear's not a bad thing, mind ya, least ya know yer alive, gots something' to lose. What you got to ask is, who's the master? Will you be the captain or swabbie." He looked me up and down in disgust. "but it seems y' already made up ya mind, eh?"

He reached up to a shelf and pulled out a box of English soda crackers and strolled towards the register. I left the market to watch Billybones check out through the large glass storefront. I smiled as I watched a pirate pay for groceries. A five finger discount was the least a pirate of his legacy should have done.

As Billybones walked out of the market, I stepped in front of him. "To make things clear, I quit, and *I* don't fear *you*. Ffeeaarr! Boogada Boogada! I taunted, wiggling my fingers in the air.

"Are you quite done?" an exasperated Billybones asked.

"Let's get this straight. This morning I beat you." I turned my hands so that my palm faced him. The snakelike imprint of my sword's hilt was blistered on my still tender skin. So in this game, that makes me what, first mate? And that must make you, what... a pirate?? Say it!"

Amused, Billybones leaned towards me. "A pirate? So that's it?? If that's what floats your boat then, a pirate it is!" He smiled wide enough to show gold then swallowed it as quick as it came.

"Then repeat after me, I... Reginald Smythe... are a..."

"We're *all* pirates ya' know... pirates or the pirated, captain, first mate, you say tomato, I say tomahto... paste..." He pounded his fist in his hand. "... as in I'll paste you one if you continue with this inane buffoonery!"

Before I dropped all this pirate business I needed to hear him say the words, 'I am Billybones the pirate!' We're all pirates wasn't anything close to a confession.

"So, admit it, it was you that summoned up those sea goblins that have been keeping me up nights."

"The wha? Summoned?" Billybones snickered, his voice getting louder. "Ya' mean as in conjured? Do pirates conjure? I know they be a rape n' and a pillage'n, draw 'n quarter'in, but conjure'in? You must be confusing me with a warlock." Billybone's took one intimidating step towards me, so close the tip of his boot stepped on the tip of my sandals. "...and you don't want to be doin' that, mate."

At that moment my mother strolled up from the post office. She glanced up at us briefly as she sifted through her coupons on her way to the market. "Hello Mr. Smythe, hi Ty-bo! You boys playing nice?"

"Good to be seen, 'specially by the likes of you, missy," Billybones backed away from his threat and removed his hat to knelt into a bow.

"I just love all that fancy stuff," she blushed. "Some of that should rub off on you, Tyler!"

"I'm doing what I can, ma'am...kids?" My mom sashayed into the market feeling like the prettiest mother in Lobster Cove. Billybones was never short on charm. It was just another of his weapons he carried close to his vest.

Billybones stood back up before me, uncomfortably close. "So what is it, pirate or a warlock?? You need to get your accusations straight before you drivel off at the mouth like that... boy!"

I would have none of his belittling tone. "Pirate", I sneered, calling him out for what he was. The ghoulies in my room reeked of the same low tide as he. Surely they were connected. Difference was, I didn't fear Billybones.

Capt'n Jack bust his way out of the adjacent bait shop bigger than life. He was the quintessential East Coast fisherman, a life size version of the wooden carved statuettes you could find at any coastal gift shop, complete with a corn cob pipe that seemed to always be between his two weathered lips.

I stood in front of Billybones, arms by my sides, hands clutched tight into fists. Jack failed to notice my standoff and took a few boisterous strides towards us.

"So what's the hubbub... bub?"

Billybones rolled his eyes. "Seems like somebody got monsters under his bed, Capt'n."

Jack rubbed his calloused hand through the thicket of white hair that constituted his beard. "Bygones, eh??"

"What!?" I stopped staring at Billybones to looked over at Jack suspiciously as if they were in cahoots.

"How'd ya say, boogada in the bedroom?" Billybones half-heartedly mimicked my jest with his sausage fingers. "Bygones is all."

"Bygones?!" I asked confused.

Capt'n Jack laughed, hacking up phlegm that he spat out into the gutter with precision. He moved his pipe from side to side considering my predicament. "Bygones, schygones! Just shadows of things past is all. Hungry fer life, but toothless goons they be. Not scared of 'm, are ye??", Jack inquired.

Billybones just let out a "Harr!" I said nothing with my upper lip firm.

"Not good, they be likin' that, ya see? Feeds their swollen gullets, it does." He talked of bygones with the same nonchalance one would have talking about the highlights of last evening's Red Sox game. "Envy your every breath 'cause they ain't got none."

"What?" I asked.

"Life! The more you touch upon the world that was once theirs, the more they pester. No fret, kid, they're Bygones, dead as doornails!"

Jack and Billybones shared a chuckle at my expense then bid one another good day. Promises to "bend elbows" over pints was made and the Capt'n left as quick as he came. In a few of his mighty strides he was halfway cross the town square heading East towards the docks, a burlap bag of night crawlers swinging in time with a chantey he whistled.

Again it was Billybones and I alone in a crowd of townsfolk too busy to notice pirates in their midst.

"So, you don't fear *me*, but ya fear *them*? He was daring me to lie. I said not a word but the audible click in my throat as was enough of a confession.

"They are of no consequence. *You* give them teeth! They have purpose. Remember what I tell ya here, to fear is to empower that which has none."

Letting my bravery slip I asked, "Are they... everywhere?"

"Everywhere and nowhere of consequence. The Anchor be filthy with'm but they just cower in the shadows. Ye be not welcome here!" Billybones yelled, causing the people entering the market to look around to see what the commotion was about. I heard a scurry in the alley beside the storefront in response to his words.

"Banish'm, boy! Have'm walk the plank... Vamos! Bye! Gone!! You know what they say?? Let bygones... be bygones?!"

Great! The aged wisdom Billybones was passing down was just a play on words.

"Pay them no mind, they hate that!" Billybones laughed as if the joke was on me. His smile vanished, and he glared down at me all serious. "Here's the deal on the table. Go home. Bye! Gone! If what I've told you doesn't work, don't show up at the 'Anchor. If it does I will expect the lot of you at noon for a final days work."

End of conversation, there was no more talk of pirates, bygones and disembodied voices. We rubbed elbows and we went our separate ways; me, the long way home to put off confronting the drooling shadows in wait and Billybones, to whatever piracy consumed his day when he wasn't terrorizing children.

In my attempt to delay the inevitable I caught up with The Cyrkle at the skateboard park. Gatto and Bess were taking turns at different tricks. Truth be told, Bess was teaching Gatto but in such a way as to not bruise his ego. Each time he caught on to a certain maneuver, Bess would ape his move with far less precision. Gatto in turn would give her a tip and her next run would be flawless.

On the surface you wouldn't think that you needed to handle Gatto with kid gloves. He was the "husky" kid in the neighborhood, a body form that he was just beginning to fill out. In a summer town, being a boy toting a baby Buddha was the equivalent of having a "kick me" sign forever pinned to the back of your shirt. We weren't just his friends, we were *all* his friends. At least on Lobster Cove he had friends and that was all that he needed.

Sandy pitched in to the proceedings by tearing out pages from a notebook she always kept in her courier bag and writing Olympic scores in big letters in lipstick. "The Russian judge gives you a 9!" she shouted after one of Gatto's more complicated runs.

We acted as if nothing had occurred during the past few days. We talked a lot of nothing. We strained smiles and feigned laughter. The whole pirate fiasco had taken the wind out of our sails on what should have been a perfectly lazy summer afternoon. Still, we goofed off well into the evening. It was long after the streetlights came on before we called it a day. None of us relished the idea of spending the night alone.

I walked home in solitary. No birds hooted or halted. The evening held its breath. I thought how my meddling spirit had tainted our summer. I tried to convince myself that it was the thief voice that coaxed me to drag my friends into this nightmare. The bygones robbed me of the warmth and security of home just as I had robbed my friends of an innocence reserved for sun-kissed14 year olds. Someone or something was going to pay.

All was quiet on the home front. My mom was asleep on the living room couch. During the summer, she used the television more to induce sleep than for entertainment. Her face was bathed in the pale blue cast of the television screen. I went through my routine of clearing my throat quietly, causing her eyes to flicker in recognition. I then kissed her cheek and tucked the comforter around her.

She fell into a deep sleep, which meant that my brother was home for the night. If he was still on the prowl, my mother would keep one eye open, fighting off sleep. She didn't have to do that with me, until this summer. If she only knew what I had gotten myself into the past few weeks she would never sleep again.

I started to ascend the stairwell when a heavy sound came from the floor above. My mom rustled and with her eyes still closed slurred, "Tyyy! Whatever are you doing up there making a ruckus all night? You might wake your brother, he's not feeling well ...", She then nodded back to dreamland.

I knew that Ryan was hung over but had no intention on squealing. I didn't have to. My mom might be Betty Crocker, but she wasn't stupid. During our summers at Lobster Cove, my mom kept us on a long leash. It was just long enough for us to hang ourselves with and often times we would, but she believed doing the wrong thing was sometimes the only way boys learned. So my brother was a juvenile delinquent and I was quickly destroying life as we know it... so much for her latch key philosophy.

It was a long walk up the twelve stairs. I knew something was waiting, I could *feel* it in my gut. Each step down the dark hall was answered with a scurry of wet footfalls and nails against plaster. I pictured them getting into position as if to yell, "Happy Birthday!" when I entered.

If Billybones told the truth, I should give the bygones a taste of their own medicine. Under a pirate's employ my daring became as strong as my arms. I tip-toed my last steps toward my bedroom door and stood just outside my room, still as a statue. They communicated their frustration with snorts of backwards talking between their gurgles. I quietly pulled out a flashlight out of my backpack. Armed with the one thing bygones hate, light, I swung the door open.

My room had been turned upside down. All the drawers of my bureau and desk were strewn about the room, their contents scattered. At the head of my bed lay the remains of my pillow. Light blue stripes of the cotton within peeked through the shredded pillow case like tendons beneath an open wound. Wet feathers were matted into a frame around one of my prized possessions, my coveted *Ashley's*. It was just a husked out cover and spine, its pages reduced to confetti that blanketed the floor.

Message sent, It could've been me on that bed. Was everything Billybones told me was a lie? Was I being set up?

Bygones are all bark, no bite. "You give the teeth," he said.

If this was the beasts' last ditch scare tactic, it was a total failure. It fed my vengeance and I spun around to confront them.

My flashlight's beam pointed towards their hiding place like a sword. The far corner of the room became bathed in light.

A look of disbelief stretched across their faces in impossible proportions. Their mouths opened wide, a stench of decomposition fanning its way throughout the room. Caught in the beam they seemed frail and terrified, not at all the statuesque gargoyles that stood sentinel over me. I held back my repulsion over seeing them so close, two muddy clots of kelp and flesh, roughly sculpted to resemble human form, a putrid simulation of life They were proof positive that evil was not an artist.

"Bye!" I shout-whispered so not to wake my mother. The aberrations looked at each other with hollow sockets where proper eyes should be. The red hue glowing deep within dimmed to amber. One called to me in the voice of a drowning man going down for the third time, "You tell me nothing, you little puke!"

I smelt its fear far beneath the flatulance that permeated the room. "Bye! Gone!" I pointed to the door, "Bygone!"

The mute bygone grabbed the other by the scalp and proceeded to tear its head from its body. As the head tore free, wet tendrils dangled from the skull spewing seawater. The mute's arm thrust the disembodied head in my face.

It spoke in a spray of anger, "Fear me... *boy!*"

I didn't flinch. What was once repugnant was now pathetic. They stood before me, toothless tigers. Did I fear? Damn sure I did. But as Billybones said, fear isn't always a bad thing. Power is taken not given. That evening, I decided to be the captain.

I took a step forward rather than the cringe backwards the bygones anticipated. The head of the threatening bygone was thrust back in place. There was a sickening sound as the strands wove themselves back into the torso like earthworms in freshly turned earth.

"Boogada Boogada!" I yelled, putting the flashlight under my chin, casting long shadows against my face. I smiled demonically back at them, the fingers of my free hand flapping beside my head in jest.

I didn't know what I expected next; a puff of smoke, a crack of thunder, the two of them melting into a pool of ooze that would seep into the floorboards? They just appeared one day. I assumed that they would disappear the same way.

"Bye! Gone! Now!!"

I pointed the flashlight back at them to catch sight of them charging forward. Was I the brunt of Billybones' joke, about to be devoured by these monsters? Their arms, thin and skeletal, looked more like the withering limbs of dying trees than that of predators. They reached out at me blindly. A high pitched peal rang out as they rushed me.

I was standing between them and the door. They weren't attacking all fangs and claws, they were fleeing. The sound wasn't anger, it was panic. Their hollow sockets, now red lights extinguished, saw me as the aberration.

Like bats out of hell they head for the door. Writhing fingers grasped at the door handle like tentacles. With a slurping sound, the door swung open. Clutching the sides of the doorframe, their arms flexed, they dragged the rest of their bodies through the door. They passed by me. Up close they seemed more kelp and mud, a pure excuse for flesh. They could never survive the light of day. They would be reduced to dried husks by noon.

"Don't let the door hit your rumps on the way out", I called behind them.

Their thin fingers slithered off the handle, the door swinging closed with a hollow thud. I could hear a moist sloshing as they moved quickly down the hall, away from my room.

My mother called up to us from the living room, "Settle down!"

I had won again, first Billybones, now The Bygones. Once squatted by slugs, my room was once again my own. I owed Billybones big time. Picking up the mess strewn around my room, I looked forward to a well deserved night's sleep.

I dreamt of sunshine and Sandy.

One door closes, another opens. A door creaks, a muffled scream, a drowning laugh, a spiteful door slam and a sleepless night that was not mine.

Chapter 13

CALM

A suprizzah! "That's what he said, a suprize!" I shared with the Cyrkle over mouse- head shaped of pancakes drown in syrup.

"No!" the three scowled in unison.

We huddled around the back table of the All Seasons Diner trying not to disturb the adult patrons. Daytrippers and snowbirds flocked to this summer hot spot for twenty-cent eggs, two-cent home fries with a side of gold-laced foi-gras and whatever else could justify the exorbitant prices they charged. Being locals, they gave us a break. We got the basic eggs or pancakes at a cut rate. Rules were in and out quick, before nine A.M. and no shenanigans. We were getting a bit too vocal for their likings; the hostess feared impending monkey business

I tried my best to convince my friends to come with me to the 'Anchor. "Remember, we all promised to help before all this '*oh my gawd, he's a pirate*' stuff began. We all agreed to make a clean break, right? That said, we can also agree we need to stay on his good side, yes? It's in all of our best interests that we appease him this one last time."

I didn't bring up the fact he had saved me from the lifeless mud heads shacked-up in my bedroom. The last thing they needed to hear was that I was in debt to Billybones. When I was too candid about the spooky goings-on in town it had not played well. I didn't even brag about of my victory over Billybones and things that go bump in the night. I was saving that little gem for when Sandy and I were alone.

I knew what they were thinking about me as they stared down over their breakfasts. They were convinced I was as much of a pirate as Billybones. Heck, I had beaten Billybones at his own game. If I *was* a pirate, I was a damn good one!

"Remember the pact, pirate boy, you promised us. Which are more important, friends or fiends?" Bess hissed.

"Yeah, it's Billybones or your best buds?" Gatto added.

I needed them with me on this. Winning them to my side should be child's play for a pirate of my caliber.

"We owe him this much. You can't say that our summer has been boring, can you? Sure, we could have done without all the time twisting falderal but I digress. He *needs* us. If you saw him today... that gloomy Gus is not the same..."

"Pirate!... is not the same PIRATE!" snapped Sandy pointing at me with a strawberry from her fruit cup impaled on a dessert fork.

"O.K. pirate." It was time to play the guilty murderer card. "Heck, we killed his brother, guys!" The diner hostess looked over at our table preparing to give us the boot. "The least we can do is try to pick up his spirits just this once."

Gatto replied with a squeeze of the syrup bottle before him that made a farting sound as a tide of boysenberry syrup poured onto his apple pancakes combining with raspberry and maple in a nauseous wave of sugar. "Point taken, my deeply disturbed friend, that said..."

Gatto cut the stack with his fork, putting a too large slice of the drenched muck into his mouth. He continued talking, mouth full.

"...Don' cha worry. I'll break him out of his funk, no problemo!"

If it wasn't guilt that won him over, it was his loyalty to me. It mad no difference, he was in.

"Flap, flap, flap, remember?" scolded Sandy.

Gatto choked on the syrup, "Hmmmrf! Enough with *The Attack of the Killer Butterflies.* I get it. Its the same reason you can't time travel. You screw something up in the past..."

Bess finished his sentence "...and it comes back to haunt you in the present. That's what Billybones is, the backlash of somebody else messing with the book."

I leaned over the counter towards Sandy, so close I could have drowned in the tranquil sea of her eyes. "No bookey, just a little piratey. Promise."

"Promise?" Sandy replied as if about something altogether different, something personal between the two of us. I couldn't lie to her so I said nothing.

Gatto wiped his mouth with a wad of paper towels. "The man's havin' a bad day, needs is a little Gatto-fi-ca-tion, that all. Let's just go and say farewell."

"This is going to be a long day", Bess groaned in concession. All in.

We hung out at the beach until noon; all skim boarding and smiles. Then side by side we headed back to town, side by side, to say goodbye to the Rusty Anchor. If we were in this thing, we were in it together, good times and bad. That's what true friends do.

Every part of my life I've over thought things, but not this simple truth. Friendship is of the moment, then forever. You can count your friends on one hand. There was no better proof than The Cyrkle, I didn't even need to use my thumb.

Good or bad, since we first encountered Billybones, our world had changed. Sandy was just beginning to come to terms with it. There was a downside of her awareness. Being wired to thief/pirate radio 24-7 takes its toll. Being watched attentively by drooling creatures, it is hard to look on the bright side of things. It tainted Sandy's demeanor from flighty to solemn. She was still movie-star-stellar but the weight of things showed in her tired, yet perfectly made up eyes.

The others would be brought to speed soon enough. Reimagining the world around you was not something you digest in a morning over flapjacks and chocolate milk. Like the syrup on Gatto's mouse cakes, you had to give the new truths time to sink in.

Inside Billybones lair, we were greeted by the largest wooden crates I had ever seen. They were higher than I was tall at that age and a good twenty feet across. A collage of shipping stickers and international bills of lading were plastered across their sides. No stencils of the words fragile could be seen. These crates were heavy duty.

Billybones haphazardly threw a couple of crowbars at Gatto and myself like they were dueling swords. I caught mine firmly and sure, Gatto got a piece of the other, its forged steel stinging his fingertips. It fumbled from his grasp and clanged to the deck.

"Surprizzah! Now get to it!" The pirate failed to greet us further, just motioned for us to pry the boxes open. Gatto and I both banged and prodded at the wood slats of the crate. We finally got the tip of one bar to bite and slip underneath one of the weakened boards. It took the weight of both of us on one bar to pry the large nails away from the crate. After the first two boards gave way, it became easier going. Another ten minutes past. The four of us wrestled with each box until the tops were freed to reveal the 'surprise' inside.

A waft of must rose from the crates as we peered inside.

"Sails?" Sandy exclaimed. She had visions of treasure for sure; tiaras of royalty, bangles and baubles from ancient times; the accoutrements of princess past. What she helped unearth was just huge bundles of canvas and rope.

These were *serious* sails. They weren't any kind of sails that I had ever seen. They weren't traditional nylon sails for jaunting across the harbor with Buffy and Brad, they were honest to God tall ship sails. They were distressed in appearance but were still prepared for whatever Mother Ocean could throw at them. There were many years still left in the faded stitching that held the canvas intact. They were tough as nails yet light enough to catch even the subtlest changes in sea breeze. There were bordered by large copper grommets ready for action. The rigging to be laced through them was of just as tough.

"I don't squelch on authenticity," grumbled Billybones. I guess when a pirates heart is filled with bitter sadness, suppressing it comes off as ornery. "Well go on, git'm hoisted" as if all we do all day is rig clipper ships. His tone had the threat of 'or else!' in his order, as if he knew we were the ones with his brother's blood on our hands and was looking for any reason to punish us. It was best to follow his orders but had no clue where to begin. The four of us all put our hands in the air at the same time and let out a simultaneous "What-th..."

"Look to your *new* captain, you don't need me no more!"

'*Ah, yes, point taken o boy!*' my inner voice and that of the thief agreed. That must have been my lesson for the day, I don't need Billybones to go forward.

I lowered my hands, they were not my own. The same ghosting that knew how to master quill to paper and how to foil knot 69, knew everything about rigging a ship. I started barking commands, showing each of my friends the proper techniques of strapping rope and hoisting sails.

The narration of Billybones and the argumentative sideline commentary of thief voice bickered back in forth in my head as we labored. Sandy, tuned into the same inner frequency stopped working from time to time to hold her head in her hands. The vise of a migraine clamped down on her.

Occasionally I yelled, "Stop it!" to the open air in hopes of silencing the verbal tug-of-war. Confounded by my outbursts, my crew looked up from their tasks.

"No, not you, keep on!" Billybones winked at me, amused at my struggle but impressed by our progress.

My instructions were short on patience and high in expectation. The Cyrkle, though grew thin on patience. By the time the sun crossed the yard-arm three majestic sails towered over us stretching up into the shadowy eaves of the gallery.

When it came to the actual raising of the sails, I quit barking orders and lent a hand. I grabbed the rigging attached to the main sail and climbed up the bands of rope I had woven around the mast and ascended into cobwebs, past the gaslight, to darkness.

Shimmying up the last eight feet, I reached the crow's nest. From that basket perched on top of the main mast I had heard rustlings during every shift.

I grasped its wicker sides and with a flex of my biceps, rose up enough to swing one leg, then the other, onto the minuscule deck. Inside was the smallest of stools meant for a sentry on duty and an antique bottle for water.

There was one other thing. Beside the long empty bottles was the source of the commotion. Cowering in the corner was a wisp of a bygone, a mere shadow of my former roommates. Its elderly form was bent by years of the earth's pull, its limbs all aquiver from either time or fear. It was more a fearful mutt than a marauder.

I smiled but not maliciously. It looked back at me expecting to be banished. The words, bye and gone did not pass my lips. It closed its eyes, wincing. I decided to let it be.

"No worries" I whispered as I threaded the rope through a three block, a wooden pulley assembly, and threw the lead down to my friends on deck. Its sockets for eyes expanded in amazement that one of the living would pardon its very existence.

I was feeling pretty good about this whole living fearless thing. My world was anew, my eyes aware of all around me. If this was what being a pirate felt like, I knew why so many were drawn to it. I hoisted the sail up and secured the rope with expert knotsmanship.

'Arrr!' I whispered. The wee bygone heard my words and covering its head with its withering fingers and closed its eyes. It feared what my utterance more than its own name. It had seen where my train of thought could lead.

Billybones pulled out an ornate silver whistle, a Boisen Pipe, the used in days of yore to bring crews to attention. He brought it to his lips, his cheeks swelled up like redden puffer fish and he blew. It let out an ear piercing tone. It held high and long, rose five notes higher, held and then down four notes, holding strong until his cheeks deflated. The high pitch accomplished the desired effect. All four of the Cyrkle turned in his direction.

I slipping down the main mast to join the others. We stood at attention, waiting for inspection. The pirate slipped the whistle back under his topcoat to address us. He motioned to Gatto and me to hoist up the remaining two sails. I manned the starboard, Gatto the mizzenmast. Billybones bristled chin nodded and together we pulled at the rigging, hand over hand. The sails bellowed to life, flapping as if they were biting wind on the open sea. The girls applauded.

After a couple more minutes of wrestling cord and cloth, installation was complete. I was proud how much Gatto had learned during our knot sessions.

We stepped back to take in the the ship's majesty. It was beautifully out of place, three stories high and hungry for adventure. It appeared as sea worthy as any ship moored in the harbor which is saying a lot for the lobby of a gallery.

"Now be gone with the lot 'a ya!" Billybones hollered, now that we had out lived our usefulness. His banter was devoid of any humor or mischief that was always present in the old Billybones. Even in his scariest moments there was always a touch of mischief in his demeanor. Despite the pageantry of the sails, there were no smiles for miles.

"Save you, mate," he scowled, making the word *mate* feel too much like *boy*. He waved my friends to the door, I reassured my friends by mirroring his gesture, a charade of the pirate by his side.

Bess rolled her eyes, kicked her skateboard to attention, cradled it in her arms and led the others to the door.

"Shove off, ya scallywogs. Ya scallywaggahs!!" he shouted in the most New England of accents. It was Billybones' way of saying farewell.

Gatto followed on Bess' heels. Sandy followed, head down.

'I'll... we'll be all right,' I thought-whispered to her.

'I believe you.'

When you're thirteen and someone you care for reassures you like that, you want to believe the words are true.

The bell rang, the door closed and I was alone with Billybones. The muddy sentinel above sensed the quiet blanketing the 'Anchor and scurried across the eaves. It knew the only thing worse than one pirate was two pirates and silence.

"Ya takin' me words to heart. I can see it with mine own two eyes." Billybones paced back and forth, his gaze never leaving mine. I was prepared for his every move. "It's in yer walk. An aire of confidence ya have, ... "

He began to close the sentence with a derogatory *boy*, reconsidered and allowed an admirable *mate* to roll off his tongue.

"...mate. Go now 'n don't look back!"

He waved me to the door as he had the rest. I started to walk away, dejected that there wasn't a final clash of blades, a flourish of curse words, or even foul mouthed threats between us.

"Make sure ya swaggah don't curdle into arrogance, my beamish boy. That's how they git ya!"

That kind of talk gives me the heebie-jeebies. *'Just who are they exactly?'* I didn't ask the question I thought. I forgot we were hard-wired together. He looked back at me as if any young, man-of-the-world should know the answer by rote.

"Bygones, Cussers and the like. This world is never as it first seems, every instant has good and bad woven into it. You choose every outcome"

He stopped his piratical meanderings short. "Never you mind, the less you know, the less they can harm. Just mind ya Ps & Qs!"

He didn't answer my question. Who are they exactly? For once I wished he didn't answer every question with such cryptic answers. While we're at it, what are Ps and Qs anyways... periwinkles and quaghogs??

Again, he heard my quizzical inside voice.

"Do we have a skeptic in our midst??"

Not knowing exactly what a skeptic was, I all I could do was shrug my shoulders, the universal symbol of "dunnknow." Billybones always hated when I did that. His brow knitted down, suppressing his frustration.

"Until the other day you know not the world of bygones. Now you are up to your armpits with the buggers. You started to believe and you became aware. Whatever you encounter in your wretched little life will only be empowered by the attributes you assign to them. You fear bygones, bygones are scary! You don't fear them, they are reduced to... sniveling snits! "

He yelled the last two words to the rafters. More feet than two burrowed in the darkness.

"Every ceremony, superstition or talisman is reality to those who believe." I could then hear his voice deep within me.

They all give the power, so freely, and the few of us, aware, we can take it!' This truth was not spoken. The only sound in the gallery was the hiss of gaslight.

Sorrow washed back over him. No steel was brandished, no flint locks cocked; I was free to leave. With one eye on look out, I slowly headed for the door.

Billybones finally let out the pirate sound that all but confirmed my suspicions.

"Arrr, but ye already know that? That's where ya swaggah comes from."

Me, myself and my swagger head for the door, not looking back. I left Billybones in the shadows of his own construction. More than the death of his long lost brother was on his mind. There was much for his pirate mind to ponder, least of all me.

"Don't you listen to the old windbag, young sir." The gravely thief voice rambled as I closed the mahogany door to catch up with my friends. *"Fear keeps you from the lion's gob, it does. Some things warrant fear... even reverence"* His last word dragged on too long for comfort. *'To think otherwise makes you mutton for the minions.'*

I kept walking confidently along, not fazed by his thinly cloaked threats. The thief voice did not take kindly to being so esily dismissed.

"Heed my words, fool!" He reverted back to static on the line.

A soft, thin voice rose through his ever-present wheeze.

'What is all that about, Ty?'

It was Sandy, my poor Sandy.

'I'll meet you at your home within the hour. We'll sort things out. Promise, remember? Think of The Cyrkle, strong together.'

'I'm so tired and creeped out Ty'

'I will set you free, Sandy, believe in me, O.K.? Repeat after me, no worries!'

I could sense the beginnings of a smile teasing the corners of her pursed lips that were trying so hard to maintain a pout. She forced a giggle and answered with a surfer-dude drawl.

'No worries... dude.'

I picked up the pace of my gait as I headed for her cottage. There was a jig in my step; my legs shimmied to a shanty my ears never heard. I had swaggah. All senses were heightened, every pore, alive. The sting of the salt air that filled my lungs was a whole new experience.

Instill fear, don't have it was the moral behind Billybones' tirade. I felt *was* a pirate and it felt, to quote Gatto, booyah! After mastered the fine art of knots and pirates, wooing a fair maiden should be no sweat.

In a matter of minutes I shadowed Sandy's door like Billybones had mine a month before. She was sitting Indian-style on the stoop. Her purse was nestled in her lap assuring that the folds of her billowy sundress would modestly cover what they should. Borrowing Billybones' twinkle of the eye, I gave her a wink.

"Tyyy", she whined like a toddler with scraped knees desperately in need of the healing magic of a boo-boo kiss. I had the magic she needed, pirate magic. Let's not even begin to think about an actual *kiss* kiss. I might have been fearless but the notion of a lip lock with Sandy Womack would bring me to my knees.

I gave her a comforting hug. She held on longer than felt comfortable. Truth, it felt *too* comfortable, I liked it, believe you me, but I wasn't prepared for what may come after. Big pirate I turned out to be.

I sat down and in comforting tones told her the truth of bygones, power, fear and our control over our world. What a pirate's parrot I was! As I blathered the fire behind her rosy hue reignited.

She *got* it. She rubbed her teary eyes dry, frantically reached into her purse, pulled out a compact, and with a flip of her fingers, opened it. She checked her makeup, bringing her pinky up to the corner of her eye to erase a smudge of eyeliner. Then with another quick motion, the compact was closed and returned to her bag. Sandy was ready for action.

"I'm... I'm ready,"

"You believe?"

"I... I believe... you."

She took a deep breath, building her courage.

"... I believe that, that those miserable monsters up there are going get a piece of my mind!"

As she talked, her anger rose.

"Well, what are we waiting for?? Let's go! Let's get medieval on..."

"I'll be right here,"

"Oh."

"Ready?"

Sandy realized banishing bygones was a solitary task. She again drew her compact from her bag, reapplied lipstick, blotted with a tissue, checked the mirror, and with the snap of the compact closing, she was ready.

"Born ready,"

Sandy meant business. She stood up gracefully, brushed down her skirt and then marched through the doorway with galumphing footsteps. I heard her stomp up the stairs. Doors opened, slammed shut. Then I heard the words of incantation I shared with her. Her pissed off voice rose high and shrill. The very glass of her bedroom windows shook with each shouted exclamation.

"Bye! Gone! By! Gone! Bye gone bygones!!!"

What I saw next was only privy to eyes are opened and aware. Sandy's had exorcised them from her house. The bricks that formed the cottage's fireplace started to shake, bulging like the skin of a snake that had just swallowed a mouse. A couple of bricks dislodged from the mouth of the chimney stack and tumbled to the sand strewn street. Ooze spewed from the top and poured like hot tar over the roof. It covered the top of the chimney like lava and collected in pools at the base of the stack. Rather than continue to drip down the pitch of the roof, the mucous defied gravity and moved up the shingles to the pinnacle of the rooftop. It congealed into a couple of mud-headed bygones, far smaller than the lugs that had haunted me. Their features were fetal in proportions, oversized heads, bulging bellies and underdeveloped appendages. They must have been new recruits in the legion. Perhaps their leader thought that was all that was needed to terrorize Sandy.

Something was different with these two. They didn't seem as wrapped up in panic as my bygones had been. They grumbled in wet gulps at each other, more out of inconvenience than fear. One then chortled to the other, pointing at me. Sounds akin to laughter spewed forth from them both.

They descended the chimney, more drooling down its side than scaling it. Gobs of the decomposition that comprised them trailed behind them following like ants to butter until it could again be absorbed by the muds again.

They took towards the shore. Stopped, looked back at me and then tore off in a mock performance of bedlam, in hysterics. I wanted to chase them, to give them *something to laugh about.* It was a phrase my mother would holler at my brother and I when we tried her patience to the breaking point. I saw myself severing them into so many pieces that they could never reconstitute themselves. Instead, I stood steadfast at the front door, waiting on Sandy.

She was no longer trudging, she glided through the doorway as if on air. She opened the door with a curtsy. I applauded her as she had me so many times when we played. She brushed her hands in front of herself as if to remove bygone dust from them.

"Fini!" she exclaimed with a French accent. Her savoir faire had returned, which is French for Sandy. It was a good match for my swaggah. She gave me another too-long hug, letting out a squeal of delight. I knew she too felt the salt in the air for the first time. We both shared the thrill of commandeering life with piratical zeal.

'*Welcome aboard, Sandy!*'

She play-begged for me to walk with her down to Harbor Pointe, an elevated green atop of a cliff overlooking the sea. It was bordered by marshes on one side and the ocean on the other. There was only one path that wove through a maze of thickets and blueberry bushes, the only thing connecting you to the Cove. With senses heightened, she was all too keenly aware of the delicate pastels dimming into night. The point was a perfect place to watch the sunset, among other things.

It was the *other things* I was worried about as we started for the path. Sandy swung her impromptu picnic from side to side as she walked in nervous anticipation. I sensed fear in the wings but it wasn't of squawking and scratching things, but things of the huggy-kissy variety.

Arm in arm, we approached the crossing at the center of town that led to the solitary path. A car turned the corner, moving down the street towards us. The belching and occasional backfire of the Scratchers makeshift low rider approached as we entered the crosswalk. Indistinguishable beats throbbed from inside the car's trunk, a musical victim flailing wildly to be let out.

My brother rode shotgun, being chauffeured by Jose, his main man, numero uno. An unlit cigarette dangled from Jose's bottom lip, his tattooed arm strewn across the edge of the open window. The tattoo was of a sleeping burro with a Mexican hat slouched over its head. He had it inked to cash in a promotion from a restaurant. For being a living billboard, he got a free taco on Taco Mondays. Like the rest of the scratchers, he dreamed big.

We paid them no mind. I smiled, Sandy, not so much. The Scratchers stared ahead without raising an eyebrow. As they crossed the intersection, the racket in the bass speakers stopped and they crossed our path, only the ramble of the car's shaky idle in the air.

I kept smiling, Sandy lost hers entirely. She hadn't yet grasped they were of no consequence when you were the center of your world. They were as inconsequential as bygones.

Once the car reached the end of the block, the stereo again resumed its distorted thrashing. It ground its way in gear with the chirp of worn wheels on hot pavement.

Sandy found her smile again, more joyful than before.

Being ever so gallant, I dropped my hoodie across the crosswalk, spreading my hand before me, allowing for Sandy's safe crossing. Who said chivalry was dead? I was king and she was my queen, correction, make that pirate and piratess. We held reign over all we surveyed and it felt... boojah!

Our walk held no foreboding as in the previous evening. Rather than being on attack, the world held us in its embrace. No brambles conspired to trip us up, no birds perched to assault. The birds chattered their normal pre-evening songs back and forth. Crickets and peep frogs joined in the symphony of life on the Cove. Branches and sea grass swayed in time to the soft gusts of the ocean breeze that delicately played with the curls of Sandy's hair. There was a reverent peacefulness, as if the entire world was performing for our benefit.

Sandy came prepared. No, that's not what I meant. She had packed a large blanket, snacks and soda in a quilted shoulder bag. She proceeded to spread the comforter across the tall grass at the clearing of the point. A banquet of cheese doodles and soda were complimented with more sophisticated snacks of Gouda and brie cheese bordered by whole wheat crackers on a cutting board. That was the extra Sandy touch she brought to everything. She was nothing if not fancy.

We sprawled out on the blanket side by side overlooking the shore as the sun began its descent. Soon enough all we could see were the fading orange highlights on the crests of the waves. Everything else was quickly swallowed by night. With another flourish, Sandy lit a couple of stubby candles that washed us in orange. Harbor Pointe was far enough into the marsh area that the overgrowth blotted out all but star specks of the streetlights. We were alone, together.

We spent the evening entertaining each other. Now don't be like our parents and read anything into that statement. It was silly stuff. I pretended to teach her how to fence, Sandy armed with a cheese knife, myself with a cheese doodle. I played the broken egg trick on her. You get behind someone and pretend to crack an egg on the top of their head and then, by barely touching the person, you simulate the yolk drooling down their back. Sandy giggled.

"Gross!"

She immediately wanted to do the same to me. I tickled her in an attempt to avoid further intimacy. What a boy I was. I might as well have thrown a rock at her while I was at it.

The air turned cool, but not cold. I pulled off my sweater and wrapped it around Sandy to warm her. She cuddled her treasure and breathed deep what I would call B.O. but she cooed was musk. We both lay on our backs on the blanket, staring at the stars. She spoke of her butterflies and I comforted her retelling my triumph over Billybones. I identified fictitious constellations in the sky like the incontinent cow.

"Those stars are the tail, and, that stream of stars there is the..."

She giggled on cue and nestled up closer to me encouraging me to continue my nonsense. I continued with the medium sized dipper who hates being the middle child and never gets any props.

Everything and nothing happened that night. We shared the quiet hum of insects and rhythm of the lapping waves. It was the closest you get to quiet you get living on the shore. The warmth of our bodies kept us at first very much awake.

A squeal of tires could be heard in the distance followed by the faint whoop of a police car snuffing out that evening's shenanigans. We shared a smile knowing well who was to blame.

Being in control of our newly discovered world, we felt safe in each others arms. and allowed the evening's song to lull us to sleep.

Nothing... everything!

S.E. Toon

Chapter 14

MOONCUSSERS

*T*he town was on fire. Let me start again

The town was upside down in panic... no. no. no...

My memory of Lobster Cove was now a curled up photograph of summer painted in fading hues. To behold it, one would need to unfurl the paper. The image would then crumble in your hands, a captured moment lost forever. Nope, one more try.

The once sun-bleached streets were reduced to black and white with a threat of crimson. I awoke to a world gone askew. A fog sprawled thick on the common washing everything in its gauze. In the early morning sky, the moon still shone. It was one of those impossibly large moons that hung in the air like the large bald head of a Titan. A sea breeze had escalated to a gale. My bones ached as swipes of wind cut through skin.

I had slept through the night. Sandy's breathing rose and fell in unison with the lapping waves below, lulling me to dreamland. The wind played with her hair, every now and again a lock would fall on my face like angel's breath.

As the sun made a failing attempt to rise, I drifted back to sleep dreaming her hair wove a cocoon, hugging me close. I was at peace. Under waves, trapped, years before, I felt the same comfort through my seaweed panic. Pirates and dogfish could infest the town that morning and I wouldn't care in the least.

I was half right.

In the distance a foghorn blurted longer than you would hear when a fog bank was hugging the harbor. It rose over the white noise of insect chatter. Its volume drifted in and out, sounding alarm like an air raid siren in a war time newsreel. I so wanted to drift back to my comfort place... *just five more minutes... to only I had a snooze button.* The wind picked up, a shiver of chill shocked me awake.

I was alone, Sandy no longer by my side. Gone too was my sweater. All that was left was the comforter we shared and the moist residue of lip gloss on my cheek. I wiped my cheek, brought my hand to my nose. The scent of Sandy still lingered. I wrapped myself in the comforter, a pale consolation for my dream cocoon and clutched it tight to keep out the brisk slap of the morning air.

I faced the morning clear-headed. There was no calamity in my head, my lady fair was well. The ever present drone of the thief was dormant but ever present in the background. Billybones was also not in the house. I presumed he was sleeping off another tipping jag from the night before.

Stagger-stepping to the cliff that looked over the beach front, I looked out over a thick fog that was rolling towards the shore. It blotted out the horizon.

Going down the sheer side of the cliff was a pathway of sand and stone traversing back and forth across the bank of the shore. Husks of dead sea grass and the compressed sand of centuries of tides held it fast against the sheer of the cliff.

I descended the Pointe on many a safe dare. If you kept your wits about you, using the healthy grass as tethers to keep balance, you could trek down without making the front page of the Cove Courier.

With the comforter wrapped around my shoulders like a cape; I descended down to the churning beach below. My thought was, take a quick morning dip, shock my body awake and face the day. There is nothing like the cold slap of the Atlantic to make you feel alive. My trek down was uneventful save for the last twenty feet or so when the comforter tripped me up and I slid down the remainder of the dune on my backside. The Russian Olympic judge would still have given me an 8.5. I laughed all the way down, not a care in the world.

The beach was wet and flat, the tide, low and angry, pent up with undertow. The beach was devoid of the feeding frenzy of gulls and sandpipers that would commence every time the sea bed was laid bare. There were no flapping feathers making dizzying circles in the sky, no laughs of seagull hunger echoing from the jetty; nothing save for a lone dog.

He ran full tilt across the damp clay on the shore line and back up to the drier dunes, a wake of sand spray behind him. He frantically kept changing direction.

In his maw was a fish head, not the full scaled, easily identifiable kind. It was cleaned to the bone, a damp skull peeking out between the dog's white incisors.

I approached the mutt, crouching down low before him, allowing the charging cur to assume the alpha position, building its confidence to play. The dog stopped, stared at me, and then shot away hoping for pursuit.

I took the bait, flipped off my Vans, my prized surf sneakers, and ran in pursuit.

"Gonna git ya boy, gonna git ya!", I called in play. The dog made a wide arc back towards the shoreline, dropped his treasure in the mud flats, and stared back at me to assess my approach. He was all slobbering smiles and wagging tongue.

Again, I lowered myself, respecting his authority. He broke his stare and brought his muzzle down to snatch up his bony prize but stopped midway. His ears lowered in confusion. He let out a bark, moved his head from side to side and then darted off in dizzying circles away from me.

Standing upright, my focus broke from the spooked dog's frenzy and focused on the sprawl of beachfront before me. The slick bank of moist sand was littered with fish heads and full carcasses of fish, either picked dry to the bone or half devoured. At first, I saw just one or two scattered between clumps of seaweed, rounded stone and litter. I let the comforter drop free as I jogged to the break of the surf. The closer I came to the lip of the coastline, the more the beach revealed itself as a bone yard. There were a thousand remains strewn across the wet sand.

I suddenly stopped in my tracks, before me was a half gutted corpse of what we call a dolphin fish. There are no actual dolphins as far north as Lobster Cove. Dolphinfish actually were fish rather than mammal but shared many characteristics as their namesake, most of all the same streamline form, flippers and size.

The corpse was stretched out at my feet, the protruding Lover's Rock, its anchor. The half-eaten remains were as long as I was tall. What was once was a playful nose was now exposed skull. A long zipper of teeth turned up in a death grin smiling up at me.

Its rib cage was picked dry, in its hollow, smaller sea life fed. Only the tail portion still had any flesh or scale left to identify the body as a fresh kill.

The sun, obscured by clouds, bathed my seclusion in bruised daylight. I was alone, even the dog had disappeared up past the high dunes to the safety of dry land.

It was my investigative nature, not my bravery that spurred me on. I pulled my jersey over my shoulders and rested it on a dry rock. Dodging the scattering of fish carcass and algae, I ran into the breaking waves. The water was brisk and caulk full of brine. Slipping on the slime of the clay bed I was prematurely dunked. I dove into the ocean to shorten the torture of the first bite of cold water. I let out an underwater howl and headed back to the surface, slapped awake by the cold salt. Every sense was heightened.

I cautiously took in all 360 degrees of surf and fog. I could barely see my hands in front of me breaking the water. Eye to eye with the surface of the waves I couldn't see but five feet in front of my stroking arms. I took it on faith that the floats were ahead as they were swallowed by a grey billow of clouds closing in. I swam for the floats resting just before the bobbers. Once I climbed on top of them I would have a better vantage point. I swam until they came into sight, their sides overgrown with a beard of seaweed and whatever muck called the floats home.

I dove under the next wave to swim beneath the float before me. It was connected to the others in a figure eight so when I came up on the other side, I would be corralled by them.

With my eyes open underwater, I saw the sea grow dark as the float started to cross overhead what little sunlight that peeked through the morning gloom was snuffed out. Once I surfaced, the walls of the floats would break the tumult of the tide making it easier for me to climb up.

A murky light before me indicated that I had just cleared the breadth of the float and I arched my body to return to the surface. Suddenly there was a tug at my ankle. Some *thing* constricted around my leg, something warm and strong. It held me underwater. I fought panic, trying to keep my breath; my lungs burned. Another tendril wrapped around my mouth, insisting on compliance.

The more I thrashed to break free, the more my constraints tightened. The first bubbles of surrender began to escape from my mouth. I became lightheaded, my bodys fight weakening until I went limp. Whatever had me in its clutches allowed me to float to the surface just enough for my head to break the surface. I gasped for air like a guppy out of water.

I wanted to break free had no strength. My lungs wanted to cry out but whatever held me fast stifled my call. My body was forced to stay just above surface, silent and still. My captor made me a silent witness.

I surfaced between two floats connected by rusted chains. Forged iron rings attached to each of their sides bound them. The green fur that grew on the links muffled the metallic sound of the chains making contact between waves.

I could see clearly between the connected docks, at least as far as the chowder of fog would allow. On the other side of the floats I saw what appeared to be the oval shells inching towards the shore. They appeared as sea turtles in migration slowly cutting across the surface of the ocean in formation, one after the other, side by side.

They were matted with black decay; one actually seemed to have a pattern to its shell hidden by the foulness.

Something passing overhead blotted out the sky. I heard the tired groan of waterlogged wood. An oar cut into the surf, the wooden surface of a boat lumbered closer to the front of the float that hid me. The boat butted the float's side, then another swipe of an oar corrected its tack and the vessel continued towards shore.

From my vantage point I couldn't see the boat's occupants. They made the sound of penned up animals, rustling against one another, gnashing teeth. A stench that came from the passing boat made low tide smell like Sandy's perfume.

Now aware of the impending danger, I was freed to cower by my own free will. The tendrils that made me mute slipped under the waves unseen. A whoosh of water rose to the surface behind me and I turned round to face my captor but all I saw was a wake heading back out towards the horizon and a hint of scale.

I was left to face whatever lurked on the other side of the floats alone. I kept my eyes forward. The boat passed my vantage point and I could again see the shoreline. It was slowly being swallowed by fog.

What lay before me was danger personified. The turtles riding the tide rose from the surface revealing marauders from the deep. They stood waist high in the water in all their rotting glory. The supposed shells were matted skulls. The patterned one wore a bandanna wrapped tightly around bone. They were picked as clean as the fish on the shore. Barnacles grew on some of the white orbs; jaws held in place by decayed tendons, the hollows of their eye sockets, glowing dull green.

They were pirates, at one time and place. Now they were nothing more than the decayed memories of what a pirate comprises. Shirts and pantaloons were now rotten rags hung on gaunt forms. The swords that dangled from their waists clattered with the hollow sound of metal on bone, what was once skin, now just gelatinous membranes holding them intact.

Four bodies dragged a large rope in servitude. It was attached to the boat of rotting wood. Another four of the undead pirates flanked a figure in the center of the boat. They doted on him, one offering drink from a bladder sack, another holding its spyglass. The skull of the apparent leader was cloaked with a large hat, a semi-circle of royal blue accented with a badge of red ribbon. Sea water poured from the hat as if from a spout. The specter lifted its arm, soaked crimson wool hung heavy on its skeletal frame. It pointed to shore.

Behind the boat more mock turtles and more boats stormed the beach. Even though they were no longer submerged, they still marched forward with a sluggish gait. In the stifled morning light, they glistened like wet leather. As they lumbered into the brighter lit mirage which was the coastal road to Lobster Cove, I witnessed them lose form and evaporate into inky streams of black and green, grotesque etchings of their pirate selves floating on air. No longer anchored by their physical forms, they caught the bleached ocean wind and rode it swiftly towards the center of town.

"Sandy!" *'Sandy!'* Both my outer and inner voice yelled to her. There was no response on shore or in my head.

I floated like a jettisoned buoy parallel to the coastline until the cliff of the Pointe towered in front of me. The dense fog seemed to creep from the water onto the shore and was ascending the wall of stone. I looked behind me to spy any more danger. The coast was clear.

While the Cove was reduced to the bare, white canvas of an unfinished painting, the horizon line of the ocean came back into clear focus. I spied in the distance, a dark blight on the pristine band of aquamarine, the silhouette of a ship... not boat, but a ship. It did not have the bread box shape of the massive tankers one would see from time to time crossing the coastline. It had no resemblance to the commuter boats that would taxi tourists from our coast to the ritzy islands just off shore. Nor was it a warship, at least none from any recent century. There were no hulls of grey metallic brandishing the invincibility of modern technology.

The ship on the horizon was a *ship* ship, big and tall... a jo ho ho and a bottle of rum ship. Four towering masts flapped in the wind and a sculptured figurehead on its bow reached up to the heavens. It was a ship that didn't belong in the here and now.

Fear crept in. Just a little, but then again, a little is all you need. I started swimming to shore with the rigor of an Olympic competitor. As soon as I was shoulder deep I started to run. Breaking free from the ocean I made tracks for my Vans. My shirt, further down the beach, was too close to them. I left it behind and started for the cliff as if the devil was on my heels.

Going down the cliff to the shore was a joyride. Going the other direction, up the cliff, pirate peril or not, was more of a challenge. For every five steps up the rocky dunes, I stumbled two steps backwards. I used my outstretched hands to keep balance and to break my fall when slate steps gave way. Like a mountain goat in the Andes, I ascended the cliff one crevice after another with no regard for gravity. Only once did my feet fail, my knee meeting the unforgiving granite. I could feel a bruise swelling underneath but the pain was less than a barnacle kiss. I finished my ascent unaware of the blood from my knee trickling ever closer to the black and white check of my sneakers.

It wasn't fear that drove me; it was something even more powerful. Looking out over the desolate beach from the top of the Pointe, I knew what it was. It was purpose, comeuppance and Sandy.

"Nanananana ..."

I heard her sing-song in my head. I kept calling her name with my inner voice, but she did not hear or if she did, she did not respond.

"Nanananana-dadadadada-nananana-dadadadadada..."

Sandy was humming the theme to one of her favorite French new wave films, *A Man and a Woman*. The song always sounded like elevator music in my ears but I never possessed the cultural tastes of mademoiselle Sandy.

I used her lilt as a homing beacon as I sprinted down the winding path towards the outskirt of town. I passed brambles that thrashed in the wind, nipping at my bare flesh. They snacked just briefly, leaving a series of bloody pinstripes across my arms. Once I reached the clearing, I slowed my gait.

Before me was the main drag leading out of town and the intersection where Sandy and I witnessed the Scratchers drive-by. The town that stretched out beyond the roadway was *socked in* as the locals would say. A grey/white haze swallowed every detail. The streetlights throughout town all blinked red, dotting the town with nervously pulsating quasars.

I made my way to the intersection when something akin to instinct held me back.

'*Hold it!*'

I stepped back onto the curb. A pickup was barreling towards me. I could only hear it at first, metal grinding metal as the driver shifted the gears like a blind man. As it neared the intersection, it cut through the fog, taking shape. The truck was a weathered relic, its paintjob gnawed away by seasons of hungry salt. The back of the cab was jam packed with plywood two by fours and the like. With a belch of exhaust and a tired backfire it turned left in the intersection onto the roadway heading inland.

I again entered the intersection only to hear a howling to my left, another warning not to take a second step. The sound was the wind was sucking into a funnel behind a silver roadster that shred silently through the fog. Its engine was not in gear and it idled silently at a speed three times the posted limit. I could see though a spider web of broken safety glass a pair of white knuckles clutching the steering wheel. There was no driver at the wheel that I could see. Everything else was a blur.

I tried to shout a warning but the silent bullet plowed into the pickup truck on its blind side. Metal screeched as it creased, the impact collapsing the back cab of the truck, tossing the vehicle off the road in a spiral. Roof, then wheels, then roof, again and again as it kissed the pavement and the soft shoulder. Plywood splinters showered the air.

The roadster skidded in pinwheels, its tires burning donuts across the asphalt. As it circled before me, trunk, then grill, then trunk again, I caught sight of what was once the driver. The face of the man streaked across the shattered glass of the dash, painting in a deep red. As the car continued to spin, the head and arms of the driver were propelled through the open window on the passenger's side. They thrust towards me like a maniacal jack-in-the-box, all lacerations and bulging eyes. Arms flapped akimbo in the wind. As quick as it appeared, the body was sucked back inside by the spinning motion of the car. It crashed back lifeless on the driver's side seat.

The car spun past me, a black trail of filth flapping wildly on the back of the car. As it tore the dark that lurked deep within the fog bank before it, I saw the filth in the funnel of air congeal into the form of one of the marauders. As it hung onto the car like a bronco buster from hell, it let out a gargle that mimicked laughter. Then the car swerved into oblivion.

Finally able to cross the street, I rushed to the overturned pickup to help pull the driver from the wreckage. He was way ahead of me struggling with the latch inside the cab as if the truck was engulfed in flame.

We each pulled at the driver's side door. It was wedged closed. We kept at it until finally, with our efforts in sync, the door gave up the fight and opened enough for me to pry the man free.

Gratitude was not on his lips. Once he fumbled out of the wreck, the injured man not only refused my help, but took a swing at me. He attempted to stand but his leg would not support his weight. From the slouch of his left shoulder it was obvious that a broken arm was one in a long list of his injuries. He protested but I reached out, grabbed him about the waist and with one heave to raise him to his feet. He let out a yell that is creepy to ever hear from a grown man. He smelt of Ben-Gay and bait, the scent of a seasoned fisherman who didn't know when to call it a day.

He scrambled back to the cab, reached inside and pulled out a flashlight and a long filet knife. He looked side to side then at me and then side to side again. Panic was plastered over his face, as if just taking that instant to look at me would seal his doom. He swung the thin razor from side to side.

"Don' cha' know?! Ye daft?! It nar be a fish tale ye been fed. When the moon be full in day now night... ba-ba-ba... That's when the 'cussers come."

I seemed to remember something in rhyme, a schoolyard taunt of sorts, but words wouldn't come. The hobbled fisherman saw my blank expression, left me for hopeless and attempted to walk away. He turned, the knife blade whistling in the air, cutting bleached air. From his stance, he had a leg break to match his arm. He looked around, found his bearings, and then hobbled up the road to points west.

I ran in the direction the pickup was fleeing from. A few blocks up the road I saw cottages peppering the sides of the road. People scrambled to secure their homes. One of them caught sight of my form approaching and cowered. Once they realized I was another human, he continued at the task frantically. Others shook their heads at me, writing me off as some fool running through town without a care while our world was being torn asunder.

The sound of latches locking, the whirr of buzz saws and hammer strikes boarding up windows joined the guttural bellow of the wind. Underneath it all I heard *"Nanananana... dadadadadada..."* My inner voice called out to her... *Sandy, answer me!* no answer. If she was playing hard to get, this was not the time or place.

Sandy's cottage was a few blocks further into the fog. Her father was perched on top of a ladder fortifying the storm shutters on the second floor with wide planks left over from building a deck the year before. The ladder was unsteady, his efforts slow. I rushed over to help.

Mr. Womack was not a member of the Tyler Byrne fan club. He was less than appreciative of my assistance. The town was under siege, his daughter was missing and he had the sneaking suspicion that I was to blame.

He knew well of my infatuation with Sandy. Earlier that summer, he had caught me shimmying down the cottage drainpipe as I snuck from Sandy's bedroom. If he caught me going up it would have been a case of boys will be boys, but I was going down which meant a father's worst fears. It didn't matter if we were just cracking jokes and being thrilled that we were doing something illicit. In Mr. Womack's eyes, my invasion of his castle was tantamount to a shotgun wedding. Now his daughter was gone and there I was, shirtless before him. I get it.

The Cove was the last bastion of innocence in a world seemingly filled with adult dangers and temptations. Outside of the ever present threat of a drowning, there was little for children with their wits about them to fall prey to. I think that's why when a team of lifeguards strung themselves across the beach arm in arm to comb the beach for a drowning victim, the indiscrete nature of the undertow gnawed so deeply within us. It broke the promise of the Cove as a safe haven from all the bad in the world.

Mr. Womack knew the nine-headed hydra of adolescence was just around the corner. Our teen years were just an altercation away. From that point on, everything would be Romeo and Juliet; breathtaking elation and consummate despair.

If teenage rampage was one fear of our parents, natural disasters would be another. When a village hugs the coastline as tight as Lobster Cove, it becomes host to a number of catastrophic occurrences; Nor'easters with winds so strong that they shattered window panes like rock candy, floods that would turn streets into straits, complete with seaweed, jetsam and sea life. It was not uncommon for rounded stones as large as Volkswagens to catapult from the bed of the ocean, past the concrete barricades of the reinforced seawall into the streets and living rooms with an overview of Mother Ocean's tantrum.

Then there were the *unnatural* disasters. Events remembered yet not recalled, like the multiple burnings of the Cove through the years and the haunting of the old wing. What would legend weave into the canvas of time to recall the madness that swarmed around us? Only time would tell.

Natural disasters seemed prophetic, as if torn from the pages of the good book. Unnatural disasters came from another tome, a book bound in bad.

"Byrne! What have you done, damn it. Where's your shirt? Where's my daughter? Don't you know?"

That seemed to be the question of the day. Thing was, I *did* know, just the memory was dusty and dim. I recalled tales told beneath star-studded skies on cool summer nights, my gullibility lulled by the crackle of a driftwood fire.

"Once in an age, when the moon be full,

when day be night, tides rise with fight,

all is caught up in her pull;

Take heed and run, hide your loved one,

in night called day, don't run astray,

this be when 'cussers come"

"c,c,cussers?" I mumbled.

"Damn straight 'cussers! Where is she, Byrne. If they harm a hair on her head, I swear...."

I let go of the ladder leaving him dangling on top. The last thing I needed was to get caught up in a tussle with him while I should be saving Sandy. I was thankful he was armed with a hammer and not a rifle. I sprinted towards the center of town to find Sandy and to avoid airborne hand tools.

I passed more cottages, more panic, more looks of bewilderment as I ran past. I head in the direction everyone else ran from, towards town center.

I reached my porch where I was first introduced to the world of time-bending pirates. The front screen door was unlatched and flapped angrily in the squall. That is never good.

I ran up the steps to check on the safety of my mom. Passing through the screened porch into the kitchen I slipped in a puddle of blood congealing on the Formica squares of the kitchen floor. The kitchen, usually as spic and span as a television commercial, was doused with a spray of red fanning out from the sink to the door.

I called out the word that made everything right, "Maa!"

My call was answered by movement in the living room.

Scenarios raced through my mind tying the absence of my mother with the blood at my feet. The blood pumping in my veins sought blind vengeance. I scanned the kitchen for any makeshift weapon. My mother had put a lock on the knife drawer years before after my brother defaced her newly purchased antique dining table.

The best weapon I could come up with was a barbeque fork left in the sink. Its shaft was long enough for me to keep a distance from my attacker, three sharp prongs, while they would never prove fatal, it would keep the intruder at arm's length.

Bending my knees in a fencing pose, I prepared to attack. There was the shattering of knick knacks toppling from the mantle.

I let out a war cry and attacked. My assailant charged as well, matching me yell for yell.

Gatto stormed through the archway armed with an eggbeater. Its blades rotated as Gatto cranked the handle feverishly. The intersecting circles of metal whirred in circles without threat. Gatto's eyes were mad with fear.

It may have been the first time I ever yelled at Gatto.

"Where is she?? Damn you! What happened!?"

"Dun'know! I, I, I came looking for you, and, and…"

"What?"

"Just noise, lots a feet, yelling, then silence."

Fear for my mother made me weak. I had to get back into control. Chill or be chilled I told myself. At least I wasn't face to face with a mooncusser. Relieved I wasn't defending my life with a utensil used to turn charred hot dogs, I let out a long exhale.

I needed Gatto by my side. The fate of both my mother and Sandy were in the balance. My brother could fend for himself. He was probably sleeping one off safely inside a cell at the Cove police station.

"I, I, I didn't do it, I swear!"

"Yeah, I know, I know."

"What the hell, Ty?"

"Precisely Gat, pirates from hell… they're called 'cussers."

I tried my best I to talk Gatto out of his freaked-out state.

"When I asked you to help me beat up some pirates, this is not quite what I had in mind"

"Not, not funny!"

I half-laughed as I pointed to Gatto's weapon. Gatto never felt stronger than when he was doling out one-liners. Still breathing heavy, Gatto thought of a comeback. He looked down at my weapon of choice.

"I guess you think everybody's a wiener. Where's your shirt, Tarzan?"

When our laughter stopped, we could hear the ensuing panic outside.

"Us against them, it's all about the girls."

"It's *always* all about the girls,"

Gatto winked. I nodded and smiled back.

It was time for action. We looked around the house for anything more lethal than kitchenware. I remembered what might still be hidden in the fireplace. Unlike the 'cusser sing-song that was hazy recollection at best, this memory was crystalline, vivid as the day before me.

When Gatto and I were younger and bored out of our trees, we would grab the fire poker and tongs to joust. They were cast iron and made a heavy clanging sound when they met like the weaponry heard in the black and white movies that played Saturday afternoons on television. Sometimes I would use the copper ash shovel from the matching set to shield Gatto's strikes. When they made contact, again and again, there was a cinematic crash of conflict.

Our matinee melees came to a close during a spirited final bout that took the life of my mother's prized Victorian desk lamp. It had a bulbous body of milk glass that lit from within and a matching glass shade with scalloped edges and painted flowers that glowed comfort. Gatto had me cornered and went for the kill. I defensively dropped to the floor and his swing caught the base of the lamp cleanly. There was the shatter of glass, the sound of our weapons dropping to the living room carpet and my mother's furious footsteps. I took the blame. If I hadn't, another of Gatto's lives would have been snuffed out.

From that day forth, my mother put the stand and the fireplace tools inside the chimney, a copper screen as dense as chain mail keeping them from our clutches. With the cottage now just a summer home, we rarely used the chimney. I couldn't even remember the last time we had dried kindling stacked beside the hearth. Chances were our childhood weapons were still being held captive within.

I knelt down and looked into the charred recesses of the hearth. Pushed in back beneath the flue was the copper stand. It had waited all these years for us to return them to their former glory. Today was the day.

The screen was locked tight. I was far stronger than I was back in the day. I bear-hugged the screens grate that encompassed the inside of the fireplace and pushed the copper frame out. The poker, tongs, shovel and matching ash broom were shoved against the soot covered back wall patiently awaiting their next conquest.

The few times we let Bess join our boy's play, the broom was her weapon of choice. We each grabbed our favorite and hooked the remaining two pieces under our belts in hopes of arming the rest of the Cyrkle when we reunited. These weapons would have to do until we could get to the Rusty Anchor and trade them in for some more undead pirate worthy arms.

"Any port in a storm, old friend." I winked to Gatto. He went to shake my hand, passed it and then rubbed elbows, pirate style.

"Nothing beats a pirate better than a pirate. Let's go kick some butt!"

Shoulder to shoulder, we head towards town. Our vision was through a wash of milk, streaks of squid ink drifting within. The rotten greenish black swirls rode the turbulent tide of the wind past us. Dodging between shadow and light, they took physical form, only for an instant, then back into a sickening froth.

The blinking streetlights were accented by the sounds of incessant racket of car alarms, honking horns and geese. A migration of people rushed from the shore as if someone had shouted, "Shark!"

We started across the town green which was now colored a soot-speckled white, the new fallen snow of a mining town. The inflated moon was all that lit our way. The sun did not shine in Lobster Cove when the mooncussers came.

Gatto and I trekked blindly through an onslaught of the aforementioned 'cussers. They were rotten cores of the ne'er-do-wells of yesteryear. Some floated in an ink state looking for life to taint while others, cloaked in dark shadows, crouched in their lanky forms, waiting to strike the unexpected.

As my memory became more my own, I recalled the meaning of the name 'cussers? Mooncussers. That was it! I recalled reading about them during my apprenticeship with Billybones. That was the moniker given to a rat's nest of criminals that littered the

South Shore coastline during the seventeenth century. They had far less ambition or scruples than your run of the mill pirate. They were rogues on a budget, caring not for handshakes, nor articles. They would befriend only to betray. They possessed no conscience and no quarter.

Why they were infesting our coastal village in a plague of undead still remained a mystery.

It was apparent that mooncussers had no control over how they materialized. It had something to do with the glare of the moon and the cloak of shadow. As ink they moved swiftly through the gusts but as so-called flesh and bone, they lumbered at a crawl.

As Gatto and I neared town center, we had a close call. A tree we crossed offered unwanted shade masking the glare of the moon. Beneath one of the tree's branches vines of tarnished emerald transformed into rotting-flesh and no-blood pirates.

We tag-teamed the *goon*cussers as Gatto referred to them, with an encore our childhood heroics. My poker landed mid-thigh and the gelatinous surface that played as skin gave way with little resistance. A stench of low tide and road kill burned our eyes. The solid head of the poker pierced through, stopped only by the bones that shattered beneath.

Gatto finished his match with a round house punch with the flat side of the shovel across its neck. His strike chimed a loud twang as it leveled the mooncusser. Writhing at our feet, its translucent skin, black seawater and gentrified tendons of kale, wove feverishly with bone to bind the fractures.

"Good news, we can kick 'cusser butt," Gatto mumbled.

"Bad news, their butts can regenerate," I gulped.

My assailant still had some fight in him. Severed arms and legs flailed trying to stand upright without its disconnected torso. In repulsion, Gatto and I started swinging madly down at the poor excuse for a body. Poker, then tongs, poker, tongs, doling out more fractures than it could ever make right.

With our first kill under our belts, we marched confidently towards Cove market steering clear from any further patches of dark. Can it really be a kill if mooncussers aren't technically alive? No need to worry now.

The market loomed before us, its incandescent light casting sickening yellow streaks onto the street. Mooncussers had taken the market in a siege. Smears of shadow passed in front of the shattered glass, snakelike shadows projected into the mist as they slithered through the air. Others crept between the shards of glass to ransack the store patrons from within. Others skulked in the darkness between buildings.

People rushed in and out of the market's entrance like ants across a toppled anthill. Panes of glass had been shattered by the desperate looters moments before we arrived. The shop keep was less concerned with the score of shoplifters than he was of locking the steel security gate.

We were so close to Sandy, her voice came in loud and clear on Tyler Radio. I could hear the lilt in her voice as she hummed.

"Nanananana..."

"Earth to Sandy, earth to Sandy, do you read?"

I pointed past the market to Monument Place, a large public memorial that overlooked Town Center. Gravestone markers and statues commemorating the history of the cove flanked its borders. In the center stood a bandstand, really nothing more than an oversized gazebo. We could see the spiral pinnacle of the structure stretching out over the fog cover. We would find Sandy there.

We began to siege the gazebo, when we both saw of a hapless couple pushing their way out of the market just before the mooncussers bore down. Their heads were bent down by the force of the storm winds. Weighed down with emergency provisions, they retreated as fast as they could. The man juggled 2x4s and firewood preparing to hunker down in their home for the long haul, until this plague no longer darkened their door. The woman was right behind him, juggling bags of groceries. Canned goods bulged against the sides of the grocery bags and loaves of French bread peaked from top of those paper sacks. Between her fingers she clutched the handles of two plastic gallons of milk. They tugged back and forth against her grip, fighting her efforts to keep stride with her mate.

When the couple crossed between the market and the bait shop, Gatto and I witnessed our first *get*. Two dark hands reached for the couple from the dark between the buildings. The reach was as long as mooncussers were tall. Fleshless fingers caught their skin like talons, stopping the couple's flight. The hands spun them around to face the alleyway. In an instant, two gossamer swirls of chartreuse swept down from the sky behind the couple like water down a drain. Then the couple vanished from sight, sucked into the same vortex.

Then there was the breaking of boards, a stifled woman's scream, a plea for mercy denied, a struggle, then... nothing. A sickening froth of pink viscose, once milk, trickled out of the silence, pooled on the sidewalk, snaking its way down the storm drain.

The silence in the alley put the chaos around us on mute. All Gatto could see was the dull green glow of mooncussers in wait. My eyes, opened wider by The Manifest, saw bygones peering down at us from the rooftops, red eyes rolling up in their sockets as they chuckled wetly; as I if was the brunt of some cosmic joke they shared.

I wanted to run to the couple. Maybe they were still alive. The thief voice joined the fracas inside my head.

"You know that they aren't, kid."

We crept past the alley towards the gazebo. The mooncussers avoided us, skulking out of the alley in search of easier prey. I felt invincible.

"You know that you aren't."

Despite the naysayer in my head, I believed I could make a difference.

"You know that you can't."

"If not you, then who... boy?" A voice far lower and more menacing than the thief's joined the exchange. It felt good to hear Billybones chime in. I felt stronger than ever.

I moved towards the alley in an attempt to rescue the couple. Gatto brought his hand up to my chest to block me. *"Sandy."* was all he needed to say.

Before us, through the blinding white, we caught sight of Bess. She wove back and forth across Town Center, her skateboard floating on clouds. She swerved one way, then the other to avoid the pea green swirls of sick. Finally she stopped in front of us. The cell phone dangling from her belt loop chimed a robotic version of *Highway to Hell.*

"Been ringing for an hour, my dad's having a conniption." She looked me up and down. "Ok, beefcake, what's with the whole sans shirt look?"

"Long story made short, Sandy gone, mom gone, me shirtless, battling undead pirates with the Gat."

Ca-chick.

Gatto presented Bess with her weapon of choice, the chimney broom.

"Now the *goon*cussers haven't a chance!"

Spying the shovel hanging by my side, she made a gimmie motion for me to hand it over.

"I can do a bit more damage with this baby."

She strapped both of them to her side.

"Don't know about Mama Byrne but Sandy's up at the bandstand, waltzing about in her own little world."

Bess gave me the hairy eyeball as if Sandy and I had been canoodling.

"What have you two been up two? Is this all your doing??"

All I could was raise my shoulders and give her a *dunno* expression.

"Look! I've got to get to her. You two watch over each other. Watch your back, watch your back's back! I'll meet you at the 'Anchor with Sandy as soon as I am able."

"The Anchor??" they asked in unison.

"Look, if what we are dealing with *is* pirates, breathing or not, then they must be hell bent on pillaging. Its what they do! So... what may I ask would be the number one booty in the village?"

"Sandy?" asked Gatto.

"The Manifest! That has to be what they seek. We all know that pirates are all about treasure."

"Crazy for the treasure." agreed Gatto.

"So we should go back to the number one place these goons will ransack??" Bess countered. "Anyone in their right mind would hit their wheels to the pavement and get as far from the 'Anchor as they can."

"It's all about leverage. As long as we got what they want, we keep on breathing", I replied.

She thought it over for a bit, looked to Gatto and myself. *Ca-chick.* Bess was on board. "What are ya waiting for, 'anchors away!"

Gatto and Bess flanked each other, back to back and ran across the green. I saw a swirl of bile compose itself into one of the sea-drenched pirates only to have Gatto strike it down with one strike and Bess pummel it to the ground with the weight of her skateboard. They made a great team.

Then I lost sight of them and I was alone in the mist.

'Nanananana… well fiddle dee-dee, hello monsieur,' Sandy purred with a French accent she had practiced many times on Gatto and I.

I looked up towards the center. She still wasn't in view.

'Someone's being a bad girl, eh, Ty?' the thief voice whispered.

'Follow my voice Sandy, run to me now!' I hollered inside.

Sandy finally thought-spoke back. *'Shush-a-bye baby. I know the boogadee in the shadows, so he holds no power over me. Like you said, 'No harm can come to those who are aware.'*

I ran towards the bandstand. Her voice was getting clearer; I was close.

"You're wrong, dead wrong, babe, just run" I thought to deaf ears.

A veil of clouds draped over the moon, tinting the all encompassing white to grey as the cloud cover passed. Where shadows were cast, the green ribbons that danced in the air took form. The rolling shadow slowly chased across the town center towards the gazebo.

While Sandy was flirting with the specter behind the gazebo, all I could see was her shape, a parasol perched over one shoulder. Her image revealed itself to me then was hidden as she crossed between the bandstand's support beams.

Behind her, one of the blotches of ink took grew legs. She was unaware that a mooncusser had materialized behind her. The circular shape of the gazebo kept it from her sight as she walked I could see in each clearing between the poles, Sandy, then the mooncusser, Sandy, 'cusser.

Ignorant of her danger, Sandy's hum of Muzak continued uninterrupted. Her parasol spun slowly, one direction, then another, in time with the music on her lips.

Beside me, something shifted in the blinding grey. At first I thought it was my friends retreating from a heated scuffle. What pierced through the haze were by no means Gatto and Bess. Barely recognizable, it was the mooncussers Gatto and I went Neanderthal on only moments before.

Their latest manifestation was a blasphemous imitation of life. The victim of my onslaught, the beast whose arms and legs I had severed repetitively, had reformed itself without any respect for humanity. Feet and hands dragged deadweight along the ground as each of the breaks in its appendages now served as new joints. Its arms and legs rose high in the air, then back down, then up again, more spider than man. The trunk of its body lay low to the ground, the sound of gravel grinding what to them sufficed as flesh.

Its companion aped man to better effect, save for its head which Gatto was able to sever cleanly at the spine. Its head rest sideways against sloping shoulders and swung side to side with each step.

Eyes smoldered green hate as they blocked my path to Sandy.

"Mon Cherie?" the specter whispered in Sandy's ear.

"Qui?" Sandy gave her parasol an innocent twirl. She had an audience.

I knew the voice of her visitor. It was the same nasal inflection than ran commentary over my every move the entire summer long. It taught me to master the art of the knot and to desire the pirate's way above all else; it was the thief voice. There he was in the flesh, albeit a poor excuse for it.

He pulled off his hat and crouched into a formal bow before Sandy. It was the same hat I spied at the beach; the pirate thief was the captain of the mooncussers.

She gasped when she first caught sight of him. Beneath the transparency of his skin, his always grinning skull mocked her surprise. He was unlike any bygone she had ever seen in her short career of identifying such things.

"Une very stylish fille... I am a very stylish girl," she snipped with an aloof Holly Golightly attitude. She tried hard not to flinch when she looked into his emerald eyes. She hid the fear that had crippled her earlier.

The thief pirate stood a good foot taller than Sandy. Face to face with him, she was engulfed in his shadow. The gel that comprised his skin, when it caught the haze of the moonlight just right, reflected the metallic silver of fish skin. In the dark, he was all skull and bones.

"You are quite the brave mademoiselle aren't you, my sweet? I must commend you, my cheri."

I don't fear you!" she giggled, trying to believe the words crossing her lips

"Aye! Smarts, spunk and a face that could launch a thousand ships; it's been an age since my men have beheld such beauty."

The two mooncussers flanked me at both sides; keeping me at bay. Swipes of my poker met unresponsive meat and they closed in undeterred.

"Head for daylight! Run, Sandy, run!"

The pirate thief looked back at me in the mist. "A most annoying suitor, don't you think, mon cheri? What you see in that rapscallion is beyond me."

"This idle chatter bores me, sir, so, I fear I will have to bid you Adeiu!"

Nothing, no reaction, nada. "BonJour! Fini! Adeiu! Do you need a translator? Bye, gone, bygone!"

The pirate thief did not panic, far from it. Instead of backing away in a planet and fleeing from her sight, he stepped closer.

The pirate thief held back a laugh. His effort failed and he stepped back and let out a cackle that was amplified beneath the roof of the bandstand. His laugh joined in the melee of horns, sirens and screams that blanketed the square. The echo of his amusement also burned in our brains.

A blanket of clouds drifted from the face of the bloated moon casting a band of shimmering white that crossed the town center as fast as the veil of shadow was drawn. The two mooncussers were short on time.

"Pardon?" the thief tried hard to compose himself, muffling his titter with a lace handkerchief that he pulled from his soggy topcoat. "That's rich! A sense of humor as well; what a treasure you are! Tell me you are touched by the muses and I'll have to take you right here and now!" he laughed.

As moonlight ceased, my captors closed in, undeterred by continued body blows with the poker. Light finally diluted darkness and again they reverted back to ocean ink, swirling between my swings. They caught the northeast wind and soared into the air towards their leader.

The band of light threatened the darkness that shrouded the bandstand. Time now a dwindling commodity, the thief reached out and brought his gloved hand to Sandy's face. In that instant, Sandy realized she wasn't dealing with a bygone.

First he brushed her cheek amorously then proceeded to smother the scream that was rising from her throat. His grip muted her inner broadcast voice as well. The last words heard before her voice was reduced to muffled sobs were, "Ty, sorry..."

Moonlight raced towards the bandstand with me in hot pursuit, The pirate thief sensed the movement of the moon and stepped backwards keeping himself in shadow with Sandy in tow. A white glare basked the bandstand as I reached the top step. I was a lunge away from striking distance.

"Thief! Here I am! It's me you want! Well? Here I am, you chicken-livered bastard of youth! Come get it!"

His glowing green eyes closed tight in amusement, then slowly, he wiped away a tear before addressing me.

"You are priceless, master Ty. What *I* want? What I *want??*" With the hand that wasn't holding Sandy mute, he scratched at his exposed skull, feigning puzzlement. Another smile of his skull teeth, then all expression of amusement left his scaled face. "What I want is everything... kid; your world, on a plate."

With that he wrapped his free arm around Sandy's waist. He could no longer censor her inner sobs. They rose to squeals as she struggled against his iron grip. He nuzzled his skull against her cheek. "This... this little parfait will be a good start!"

The clouds lifted, moonlight cascading free. The thief pirate's transition had begun; arms and legs reverted back to translucent snakes of green oil writhing in the air. He kept moving backwards, riding the line between dark and light. Half solid, half liquid, he was able to wrap himself around Sandy, binding her tight. Her legs and arms kicked as the thief absconded with her, taking them both high into the air. Her parasol fell from her hands and took to the sky, spinning madly to no song in particular.

"You're not very good at this now are ya kid? Adeiu!"

And with that they were gone. It was as if I banished them both like bygones from my world. I swung my weapon in vain into a wind of no consequence. Tears ran down the cheeks where Sandy's soft lips had once lit. My tears crossed her lingering lip gloss, another memory fading.

I looked past the bandstand, out past the tree line. She and her abductor were but black scribbles in the grey haze. All that was left was a lone flip flop, the plastic flower that adorned it, soiled and pruned.

I fell to my knees, letting out a banshee howl as primal as the ocean's roar. It was a conflagration of every emotion a human could feel, all full pitch, all at once. Only the living, upon hearing that sound, could feel that which no words could convey. That complexity of emotion was beyond the likes of bygones and mooncussers.

There was nothing but silence on Ty radio. Sandy was gone, my mother, gone; all on my watch. As the sky cleared, I cursed the sky and, in turns, myself.

I would need help.

'Go back to the 'Anchor' an inner voice pleaded.

Gatto, Bess, even Billybones would help. They must help.

All was gone, but revenge. It would be mine, as time allows.

Chapter 15

CAREEN

*T*he sun came out of hiding as I reached the door to the Anchor. A cacophony of the calamity reverted to the sole cry of a seagull, out of hiding, making lazy loops in the sky. The onslaught behind was me, now reduced to flash images from a fever dream. To think of that morning otherwise, to linger on the carnage I had witnessed, would be enough to drive any sane man mad.

The Rusty Anchor looked no worse for wear. Even after Byrne's renovations, it still looked abandoned. The assault hadn't aged it further. Like a book taboo to read, but impossible to resist, a book passed from one to another until the paperback spine curled outward into a fan, the Anchor was always a little worn around the edges. The Rusty Anchor, like that book, contained a story that shouldn't have begun.

Out of habit, I gave the knocker in the lion's jowl a healthy two knocks before pulling the heavy teak slab open.

It was a full house; sweat and blood locals, lobstermen, tugboat men, fishmongers, shop keeps and the like talked over one another as if their experience was most significant to the crisis at hand. There wasn't a political import or a daytripper in the lot. The spineless had already taken the low road to mainland at first warning, an essential thinning of the herd.

Off in one corner I caught sight of the library custodian who found solice in routine. He had broom in hand and was sweeping the latest fall out of spent letters that once comprised our past. Words were sprawled across the deck's planking, barely a twitch left in them; lifeless and devoid of meaning. The custodian sculpted them into uniform piles, swept them into a dustpan to later give them a proper burial. He applied this meticulous nature to all of the mundane tasks that made up his life. It kept him focused on the here and now, less on the precipice of madness. After the events of the day, his piles were higher and more uniform than ever. He looked up briefly as I entered, winced as he recognized another tormented soul. He then lost himself once again in his sweeping, where it felt safe.

At the center of the hall an unruly mob gathered. They were in the heat of an indecipherable discussion. In the center was Capt'n Jack towering over them all. The men surrounding him were all bent shrimp-like by a lifetime of seaside labors making the Capt'n seem even taller. The crowd, a grumbling sea of head nods and shakes, spoke in guttural shorthand.

In the center of the verbal melee was Gatto trying his hardest to make head or tails out of their ramblings. Gatto tried to fit in. He waited for his turn to bond with the ramshackle congregation of tattooed curmudgeons.

Each man followed his outburst by showing off one his many tattoos burnished into their weathered arms, legs or chest. These were all historical footnotes in varied states of deterioration depending on the year the ink dropped.

Each yarn spoke of the men's kinship with the sea, all blood, sweat and tears. Gatto's memories also hugged the coastline, but

were of playtime, not work, good times, not strife. The only tattoo
that Gatto wore was a sunburn tat, which he burned into his bicep
at the beginning of the summer. To achieve said tattoo, one had to
wake until the beginning of spring after the skin faded in the
sunless winter months. We would all join in; painting a pattern with
water on our skin, sprinkling it with sand, blowing off the access
grains and then baking in the sun until crisp. The skin beneath the
sand clung to the moisture, remaining white. The exposed skin
became the first burn of the season; resulting in a sun tat. The
design would slowly brown closer to the rest of your skin as the
season progressed, but was still discernible straight through Labor
Day.

The first year we burned a tattoo of The Cyrkle, a "C"
surrounded by a circle, on our legs. Intertwined Celtic knots were
out of our skill set. Our parents were less than enthusiastic with the
results which made the tats all the more special.

Gatto improved the process using masking tape instead of
damp sand. The edge between the clam white flesh and burnt skin
was sharp and far more dramatic. He stenciled out the letters TCB
with a lightning bolt crashing through the letters. He got the idea
from reading that Elvis made the words *Taking Care of Business*
his game phrase.

"If it's good enough fer th' King, it's good enough fer me.
Thank you very much!" he told us in a Presley drawl the afternoon
he burned it in.

Gat's tattoo didn't hold a candle to the waves, fins, buxom
ladies and devil horns that adorned the horde that surrounded him.
Still, he wanted to be one of the guys so he lifted up his sleeve,

showing off his artwork. The letters were now smothered by various shades of chocolate tan.

Gatto yelled to be heard over the motley crew.

"Takin' care of business!"

They crowd went silent and stared down at him. I broke up the awkward situation by shout-singing the chorus of a Bachman Turner Overdrive song.

"Everyday! Everyway!!"

I joined my friend in the center of the crowd, went for a handshake, passed his fist and made for his elbow to give my fellow compatriot a proper pirate's greeting.

The slew of ornery faces stared at my offending elbow. Their expression was clear, *'There seems to be a pirate in our midst'* I heard echo in my head. Not exactly the time and place to bring up such suspicions. These locals lived off salt air and brine but they were anything but pirates. To them, pirates, alive or undead, were their sworn enemies.

All the group needed was pitchforks and torches to complete the picture; they, the angry mob, me, the monster. I snapped into Frankenstein mode and proceeded to shield myself from their wrath. I started for the poker draped by my side but its staff was far too short to tussle with the likes of them.

Snapping into action had become as involuntarily as swatting a bee. The custodian methodically swept to the left of me as the crowd closed in. With one quick snatch I swiped the broom from his hand. One swing of the handle against the floor dislodged the mop head from the handle. I had in my hands my weapon of choice as of late.

Hours of practice suited me well. I spun the pole in pinwheel fashion like a Samoan warrior juggling sticks of fire. The crowd backed up. To protect Gatto, guilty by his association with me, I stepped in front of him and crouched down, ready for the mob to ambush me.

Just before the pummeling of us was set to commence, Capt'n Jack held up his hand, holding the crowd at bay. He gave me a sly wink before addressing his fellow seamen.

"Seems this pirate doesn't know his arse from his elbow! Harr! The dee before he was nary scared of his own shadow, don't have the common sense god gave a sea slug."

Capt'n quickly changed the tides of anger. The men's grinding of teeth turned to belly laughs; a far better result than a knife fight or fisticuffs. Jack escorted Gatto and I away from the group, a stalwart arm on each of our shoulders, ushering us deeper into the crowd of distressed neighbors.

"Thanks, Capt'n!" Gatto muttered. "That didn't go well."

"You laid it on a little thick, don't you think, Mr. Jack?" I whispered.

"That's Capt'n to you, ya young whippsnapper!"

He turned us to face him with a twist of his wrist, and shared with us this little gem.

"When you lay your head down to end this day, look in th' mirror, take a good long look. Remember that face lookin' back... an' fear him."

Billybones leaned over the guardrail of the deck and hollered over the din at his uninvited guests.

"You all know wha cha' need to be tendin' to! If ya vow to be keepin' with the articles holds, I'll see you at nightfall err ya be on ya own. Good luck wit that. Now scram, the lot of ya!" The crowd, no longer focused on my pirate *faux pas*, started for the door in a begrudged crawl.

I looked out over the exodus of people, then back at Billybones.

"Capt'n! Have you, has anyone seen..."

Before my lips formed the first words I had ever uttered, a voice rose over the clamor, echoing in the rafters enough to shake cobwebs from its shadowy eaves.

"What's got into you, Reggie? For the love of all that's good n' green, get a hold of yourself!"

It was my mother, safe and sound. She scolded Billybones with a tone I was very familiar with, it was her you're-in-the-doghouse voice.

"What has gotten into you? Let it be, you said it, the kids are the key."

"Maaaaa! Hello?" I hollered up with my newfound lower register. My matured voice caught her off guard and she smiled a smile only a mother can smile when she sees yet another landmark event in her offspring's life.

Pushing her forefinger between the many chains draped across Billybones' chest, she poked him as she continued.

"One moment, hold yer thought, not finished wit you yet."

She caught sight of me and her gruff tone sweetened.

"Ty-bear!!" she called out.

I cut through the crowd to her. The boy in me rushed into her arms, happy to find her warm, very much alive. She had no injuries or wounds that I could see, certainly none that would explain the blood I discovered. I began to tear up.

"What's going on??" I muttered, my mouth muffled by the hollow of her shoulder as she held me tight.

"Confounded 'cussers," grumbled Billybones beside us. The adult in me grew self conscious of all this emotional Ty-bear stuff and I pulled back, still held her tight, but at arm's length. I wasn't going to lose her a second time.

"It's the mooncussers dear, remember?" as if the occurrences of the last four hours were as ordinary as opening presents on Christmas morning.

"Yeah, I kind of got the gist of that while I was slaughtering the breathless goons on my way here, Ma."

"You've become pretty darn good at that I've heard." She flushed with pride and turned to Billybones to give him a sly wink.

"Reg, I have you to thank for that."

Billybones took in the compliment with a half-nod.

Gatto stepped onto the deck and stood beside me to gleam some of the 'cusser killer recognition.

"Good to see you breathing and stuff, Mrs. Byrne."

"Why thank you, Anthony, it's good to see you... breathin, and stuff. My mother's maternal smile was powdered with more sugar than a homemade donut. She gave Gatto a hug.

"Now, come close. You need to hear this as well. The mooncussers, do you *really* remember them, Ty-bear?" she asked, all quiet and serious. It was a mildewed memory, a tale told from generation to generation that hadn't any anchor in my reality. I never experienced them firsthand. They seemed unreal. Mooncussers possessed the same mythical properties as any of the series of events in Lobster Cove through the years that reduced meaning and hearths to rubble.

"It's kind of fuzzy."

"Do you remember the party I threw for you on your fourth birthday?"

She stroked the side of my head as she spoke. Her voice was calm and serious like a sideline doctor checking a football player for a concussion.

"Do I! You made a cake in the shape of a dragon... smoke even came out its snout and the knife I used to cut it was shaped like a lance. It was awesome."

Gatto joined in my excitement. "We all made armor out of tin foil and cardboard. That was like the best party ever, Mrs. B!"

Her patting stopped abruptly.

"That, gentlemen, is a real memory... a *crystal* memory, so real you can taste it. Mooncussers, on the other hand, are a memory not quite in focus, right? That's a *green* memory. One is your true reality, felt and ripe with meaning, something that actually happened to you in one place and time. The other is just patchwork of what once was, moments recalled, no resonance, no truth."

"How do you know the difference?" Gatto asked.

"It takes practice to differentiate between the two, but you'll get the hang of it. Listen to your heart and not your head."

"So mooncussers aren't *really* real," I asked.

"Oh, they're real enough, mate..." grumbled Billybones as he studied his sleeve of intertwining tattoos climbing like vines up his arm. "They just weren't as *real* yesterday as they are today... much as I can tell." He returned to the story unfolding on his arm. The features on his face were scrunched up as he tried to decipher their hidden meaning.

Gatto pulled up his sleeve and looked at his own fading tattoo. "Just what is it are you looking for, Billy... I mean, mister Smythe?"

"A clue, young swabbie!" replied Billybones slapping his arm and looking back at it as if he was contemplating quantum physics.

"Trust the flesh, it never lies."

He moved his finger over the vines of sea foam and ships in combat. I spied a white skull on a flapping flag hoisted up one mast. As he flexed his arm, the flag appeared to flap in the wind. Below the waves, a chest rest half-buried on the ocean floor. Bordering the illustrations were nautical coordinates, compass flowers and other cryptic symbols.

What I was looking at was a series of historical footnotes. The overlapping tattoos were in various stages of disintegration as if time itself toiled to erase any remnants of reality's past. All the townspeople in the gallery had variations of similar tattoos, each based on their individual experiences. When they gathered together after each of the many Cove cataclysms, they were able to reconstruct a semblance of the truth through the commonality of the art they wore. This assemblage of weathered appendages was all that remained of the town's true past, fading meanings to memories long lost.

"Flesh is tough, more resilient than words. The written word be but a fragile thing." Billybones mused as the crowd exited.

Bess fought against the tide of locals who spewed from the Anchor's door way. She used the nose of her skateboard as a battering ram, splitting the crowd as she trudged forward. With a well positioned elbow here and a head but there, she was able to navigate through the crowd. Spilling out the other side of the crowd, Bess stood before us in the freshly emptied hall.

"Storm's clear. We're out of here or what! The less time we spend between these walls the better"" Bess didn't like the whole vibe of the Anchor even when it gave her shelter from mooncussers. Bess talked a good game but she was chock full of convoluted feelings, fear among them.

"She's a deep puddle," Gatto once marked.

She couldn't band together with us without first knowing her family was fine. After dropping Gatto at the gallery, she had made her way back home. Bess came from good stock and her family was as self-sufficient as her. They bunkered down, waiting for the storm on mooncussers to pass.

"Ty, you made it, with yer Ma to boot, good man!" Bess exclaimed.

"Come sweetie, we need to talk." My mother cooed.

"Where's Sand?" Bess asked not knowing her best friend's fate.

My mother told her the difference between green and crystal memory, how our present day was merely a composite of infinite rewrites and the unknown fate of her best friend.

Bess pointed over to the roll top desk that was leaning to one side, its lid reduced to kindling.

"So, you know about..."

"The Manifest, yes, dear Bess, we all do."

"Who *all?*!"

"All the townsfolk who were just here, to start, and apparently mooncussers and..."

"... and you just let us hang here all summer? Why didn't you just let us play with oily rags and matches? And you call yourself a..."

My mother's tone lost all of its maternal lilt.

"Listen, little miss toughie-tough, you are not too old for me not to put you over my knee for an old-fashioned hide tanning. Don't think for a minute that I won't do it. Do...not... test... me!"

Just as quick as her stern temperament flared up from the saccharine, my mother's expression changed to a dangerous mix of the two; all smiles and short blades.

"Sorry, sweetie, it's just that you have to know just what you are dealing with, comprende?"

Billybones broke the two spitfires up.

"Leave her be, Anne, she's not the ruffian she touts herself up to be. Fer one, she fears the book, as well we all do. If it wasn't for some *real* scofflaws meddling about, we would all be keeping our distance from that infernal device."

He settled into the captain's chair beside the dilapidated roll top. The Manifest rested beside him intact, pages breathing like gills. Billybones proceeded to tell us of the evening's proceedings, events that brought mooncussers gnawing at our heels.

"Ne'er-do-wells, the lot of them!, he cursed as his account of the night before began.

It had been a long night at ol' Rusty. He had drifted off into the ether of demon rum when, by the time his eyes had opened, night had fallen. Stumbling to his feet, Billybones locked up for the night.

Taking a drunkard's walk down the barren street, he sensed unrest. He turned back to look at the darkened shop. One of the major traits of a pirate is acting with his gut. If the tales of The Manifest were true and Billybones was the pirate on the page, his instincts served him well. His rum-soaked gut called alarm and Billybones listened. Turning on wobbly heels, he returned to the Anchor for a little look-see.

He heard the scramble of vermin as he approached the teak portal. He peered into its thick glass on the top of the door. Inside, dim lights danced like fireflies. Billybones was certain all lights were out when he locked up. The tinkle of empty glass bottles as they spun on the spit deck within followed by titters of hushed laughter could be heard coming from the other side of the gallery's portal. Bygones watched from the rafters and mimicked intruders like agitated howler monkeys.

Interlopers!! Billybones thought, not spoke. The intrusion was more sobering than a hot cup of joe. He was about to put an abrupt ending to the evening's foolhardy proceedings. Navigating his compromised legs, he sped to the back of the building to give his uninvited visitors an *un*-welcoming.

Jimmying the back window was easy enough. Climbing inside undetected in his condition was more of a feat. Drawing his blade strapped to his side, he walking cat-like in the dark, his steel blade leading the way.

He crept between the stacks of barrels and crates until he saw a group of inebriated teens huddling over his decimated roll top desk. Each boy had a flashlight, beams moving as erratically as their owners' stagger. The Manifest was open before them, one boy sitting in front of it, nervous quill in hand. His drunken buddies cheered him on.

"Go buddy, go buddy, go, go, go buddy!"

It was then that Billybones heard Him, the thief voice, coaxing the lemming behind the desk.

'Excellent! Now, my beamish boy, end the sentence.'

Billybones needed a more abrupt method of ending the meddling than a cutlass. His hand slipped the sword back into its sheath and reached further down his leg into the top of his ample boot where a firearm waited for such occasions.

'And how do we end sentences?' Him, the thief voice, hissed. The figure behind the desk just looked glassy-eyed at each of his friends. The voice went from hiss to holler.

'We end sentences with a period, you dim-witted dolt!'

The boy raised the quill into the air with dramatic flair to stab the quill into the text.

Billybones raised his piece, his thumb pulled back on the flint lock. Using the boy's insipid grin as a beacon, he aimed into the dark.

The rowdy cheering section slapped at the boy's back, the roughhouse bringing on a wave of drunken nausea that stopped the boy for a moment.

Billybones aim was true; his timing, not so much. Pen met page with a definitive black dot.

"Period!" the boy laughed. It was done; ink etched into the flesh of the page, the deck of time again began reshuffling.

The boys broke into a bout of laughter.

"He said period, haw!"

Just as the word left the boy's mouth there was a flash of gun powder and the stench of sulfur followed immediately by a scream as the bullet pierced its target. Billybones' firepower was as antique as his wardrobe and its ammunition was large and unforgiving. The palm of the boy's hand was pierced by the heavy slug as it burned away flesh and splintered bone. The Manifest, already writhing in the ecstasy of transformation, sucked in the droplets of spilt blood deep into its dry parchment.

What followed was incoherent panic. The drunken louts dragged the injured author across the deck towards the front door. Billybones, amused by the mayhem, let out a laugh, deep and from his belly, where all good instincts resided. His voice silenced the bygone chatter. The disembodied voice of Him fled along with the youths. Billybones reloaded and let out another round in the air, a warning shot over the bow to keep the delinquents from ever entertaining trespass again.

Putting two and two together, I lunged at Billybones. My mother's arm was all that held me from the pirate's throat.

"So, you shot my brother?"

"Can't say for sure, but if I did, I have to say we're even, eh... boy?" Billybones spat with a bitter grin.

Drifting in and out of sweet little schoolmarm and Cruella Deville, my mother tried to calm me down.

"If my own flesh and blood was messing with that thing over there, then he had it coming, bless his heart. He was never strong like you, Ty-Bear. You resisted Him... the thief, isn't that what you call Him? Your brother, I'm afraid to say, was not like you. He had no moral compass."

"Was? Had? Are you saying my brother's dead, Ma?"

"We all die a little after we've touched The Manifest, dear."

"...and now it's within their grasp dang-nam-it!" Billybones spat. "We're playing right into their hands and its all because of your brother and his band of nincompoops! If he be dead, good riddens to'm."

"Just what is it that you are going on about?" Gatto asked.

"Treasure, you fool boy!" my mother snapped back at him as if she had been asked the question for the umpteenth time.

"Treasure, I knew it!" added Bess. "It's always about treasure in the long run."

"The Wydah treasure to be precise, Bellamy's bounty," grumbled Billybones, giving a slap to the shipwreck sprawled across his bicep. He took out a jagged splinter that he was using as a toothpick out of his mouth and used it to prod the tattoo of the sunken ship.

I had heard the name before though its former history and context had been wiped as clean as a blackboard after school. It was the largest pirate treasure ever discovered off the East Coast. My green memory of it was more legend than fact, more Edward Rowe Snow than Jacque Cousteau.

The Wydah in the world that existed until that very morning was discovered off the coast of Cape Cod by the tireless treasure hunter Barry Clifford. His combination of determination, technology and attention to his gut had at last hit pay dirt. He meticulously extracted one treasure at a time from solid blocks of sediment that had preserved each artifact like flies in amber. It was a monumental achievement that spanned a lifetime. Now, with the stroke of a quill, all that toil and its eventual reward had been erased.

"Arrrg!" went Billybones. None of us dared snicker. His tone took away all the cartoonish amusement from the exclamation. His anguish, a combination of maddening frustration and stilted dreams, was nothing to joke about.

"Ya see, only me, me arm..." Billybones started slapping the side of his head. "... and Him... be knowing the truth of the matter. As of today, the Wydah treasure has never been found. It is still lost in the briny deep, three hundred years of time and tide burying it again."

"Which means its up for grabs! Free fer th' takin!" It all became clear. The pirate in me licked his lips.

"...and it means that the pesky mooncussers won't let us be until the treasure is theirs," my mother added as she sorted through a crate of vintage clothing. She pulled out a long-sleeved jersey with broad red and white stripes made of a rugged canvas material, rugged as sailcloth. She threw it over to me to cover my naked chest.

"Put this on, dear, you look like you haven't the brains god gave green apples."

"Aye aye," I answered, not cracking wise. My mom meant business.

"Just what do you think you've been doing all summer long?" she asked as I pulled the shirt on. I checked out my reflection in one of the fisheye mirrors, a half globe of reflective glass framed by the brass hardware of a ship's porthole. All I needed was a bandana strapped across my head to complete the pirate portrait.

My mother, the woman who gave me life, tossed a short blade my way. I grabbed it in mid-air. "Give any one of those burlap sacks over there a stab." There was no more time for Ty-bear.

I went to the stack of 80lb. sacks that were the bane of my existence for the past six weeks and proceeded to gut one like a striper trout. A stream of sand poured down onto the floor like a massive hourglass.

"You've got to be…"

"Just look at you! My little boy's all grown up, how big 'n strong you've become. You can thank Mr. Smythe here for that."

"Weight and repetition makes a weak man strong," Billybones replied.

"You've got to be kidding me?" I hollered. I stabbed another sack, then another, more beach sand spewed across the deck. I took the flat edge of my dagger's blade and wedged it under the lid of one of the wooden crates and worked it around like a crowbar until the lid gave way. A pile of rounded sea rocks of no apparent value was all that weighed the box down. "Unbelievable! Worthless!"

"Not so, dear," my mother corrected me. "If it wasn't for these boxes and these sacks you wouldn't be ready for the day at hand."

"Ye should be grateful you were chosen, you little snot" spat Billybones.

"What about me?" interrupted Gatto. "Tell him, Ty, I got me some sweet ninja moves, tell this moldy pirate what arrr got!"

"Seriously Gatto, no ninjas…not now," I advised him.

Billybones took two heavy steps towards Gatto and looked him up and down as if judging a fisherman's catch. "Do you think you have what it takes, laughing boy. I am not here for your amusement, I am not here for your perusement, I am here to make ya or break ya!"

"Got it, sir," was the only comeback Gatto could think of.

"Even you are less the plump guppy you were the first I laid eyes on ya. You'll do… ye all have to. Gawds save us all," Billybones groaned in an exhale. "an' what about you, missy, are you ready to step up?"

Bess turned her back away just enough so that she showed her disapproval but could hear every word.

"We need to fight fire with fire. Gods know, Bessy, you've got plenty of fire in your belly to go around," My mother exclaimed.

"We need her to mark the book," Billybones exclaimed to me.

"Why her?" I yelled over Bess' reply of "No way!" My hunger to get back at the helm of The Manifest was intense. "I've been there; I've got the whole thing down pat!"

"And look where that's got us," Bess snapped.

"Let'm try," Billybones scoffed as he gently moved my mother to one side making a clear path between The Manifest and myself. "Go on, mate, be the hero, save the day."

My inner pirate salivated. I was almost giddy with glee. In spite of all the horrors The Manifest had unleashed that summer, I was more than ready to return to its pages to taint what was left of our world. Deep within me, the thief voice, Him, purred approval.

I walked cautiously towards the dilapidated desk where the book lay at rest. As I neared the book, its pages rustled awake.

As I reached for its cover, it recoiled. The page's agitation increased making the entire book inch across the tabletop. The rope that bound it closed had already been severed by the previous evening's violation. Only a metal latch kept the book closed. I tried twisting it into the open position but felt resistance. The Manifest refused me entrance.

My frustration grew; I so wanted to feel the power of the quill carving a new future by my hand. With both hands clutching the sides of the book, I even tried the biting edge of my flat blade to pry it open, but to no avail.

The Manifest was alive and full of fight. The book's spine flexed like a muscle, a rabid froth starting to drool from its bindings. Its feverish resistance made me step back from the desk in repulsion.

The Manifest had the power to either make everything right or to bring the world to its knees but it only gave these gifts/curses to the uninitiated. I had my chance and wasted it. I could have made a difference; instead, I stood before the Manifest, powerless.

"It knows you, mate," Billybones spoke softly. "We are all on its list now. You, me..." His eyes looked over to my mother, her head down.

"Mom??"

"We all had our chance, son, some with better resolve than others. I'm not proud of it..." Suddenly her tone changed, I knew she battled its power over us as much as I did, "...but it needed to be done... and I'd do it again... just... differently."

Someone somewhere once said the definition of insanity was doing the same thing over and over again, each time expecting a different result. The same went with tangling with The Manifest. In return for taking the timeline roulette wheel for a spin, you got in return a tad bit of the crazy.

"We never know how our best efforts will affect the world around us, but that's no reason not to try, blind as we be," Billybones assured me with the closest he could come to comfort.

"It's your turn now, dear," my mother said as she reached her hand out to Bess. Instead of grasping my mother's hand, Bess put her skateboard in it as she took a step towards the Manifest. If anyone in Lobster Cove had the sincerity of purpose to make things right, it would be Bess. Plus, her abject hatred for all things pirate would keep her in good stead.

"So what do I do? Just write, i*xnay* on the *iratepay*? Proclaim 'Mooncussers begone'? Do I need to do a bippity-boppity-boo thing afterwards? What, what!?"

"Just read, dear, read between the lines. The relationship between things will show itself to you." my mother coached.

Keeping my jealous pirate self at bay, I tried to coach her.

"This is important. Listen to your heart, not the voices in your head."

Bess looked at me, her eyes widening as she heard Him, the thief king, for the first time.

"Yeah, we all hear'm. He gets more insistent, the closer you become with the book."

Bess took another step closer to the desk. I took a step back to calm the book. It grew still, mimicking an inanimate object. Billybones joined me, also keeping his distance so not to agitate the now dormant Manifest. He whispered in her ear some instructions as he backed away.

"Careen." Was all I could make out. He then patted her on the shoulder, far softer than the ham-handed slaps he would give me. Then Billybones gave Bess the slightest push down into the desk's chair.

Hesitantly she sat before the book. She prepared the table, clearing away the broken slats that were once the roll top.

"If I'm going to do this, I prefer to be alone."

"Git to it, then. Time be like me rum, ne'er you waste a drop. You have 'til nightfall, moppet." Billybones muttered. Honoring her wish, Billybones motioned us away with a swipe of his meaty hands.

Bess was left to contemplate the potential of the moment. Both her hands, white-knuckled, clutched the edge of the destroyed desk. She stared The Manifest down like she was preparing to execute her most complex skateboard trick yet. There was no room for error. The penalty would be harsher than the hungry bite of warm asphalt; ten-fold.

Careen? Doesn't that mean to collide in an oafish manner as in 'I careened across the cafeteria, spilling my milk on the school bully and inciting a food fight'? What else did he whisper in her ear? What cryptic meaning was not privy to my ears?

As we walked away from the Anchor, all I could think was of Bess being enraptured by the allure of The Manifest. It was hard to believe the book even existed, never mind the power it possessed. It was a Captain's Log, it shouldn't have the powers of seduction never mind the ability to rewrite time. It should be navigational charts and rudimentary details of the ship's travels, not a narrative of tales and the promise of hidden bounty.

Billybones went on about the lost Wydah treasure as if it was the be all, end all. What if The Manifest is the treasure in and of itself, not the chests of gold coins and jewels encrusted in brick-hard sediment? What need would an un-dead pirate have for them save their pirate nature insisting treasure at all costs?

The Manifest offered more than a ship's bounty; it offered a new lease on life. Never again would mooncussers have to rely on the alignment of the stars, astronomical tides and full hunter moons to roam free. The promise of The Manifest must trump booty.

Billybones instructed us to say goodbye to our town as we remembered it and meet back at the Anchor at yard arm time. In the safe glare of a summer sun we walked the streets of what remained of Lobster Cove. Gatto went on his own back to his cottage to check in on his mom. We could hear the clanging of her dinner bell, a wrought iron triangle; she had been ringing ever since the mooncussers receded back to the sea.

On the way home, my mother and I checked on Sandy's parents. Her father just stared at me, daggers for eyes, while my mother gave him an update with soothing tones that could lull a crying baby to sleep. She left me in the front yard to enter into a conversation meant for only adult ears. She spoke for a good minute, followed by a series of slow nods. They broke their huddle and looked back at me.

'What?' I yelled with my inner voice, not wanting to bait Sandy's dad into a fight. My mother heard and gave me a wink.

'All in time,' she thought back then looked at Mr. Womack gritting his teeth and added, "If it's any consolation, Ty here's next!"

"What, what?" I said aloud this time. Trust me, I was going to be doing my darnedest to make that happen. Then I'll be face to face with the Pirate Thief and put an end to his undead life. I just didn't want to be bait for some kind of parental conspiracy.

I reluctantly followed my Mom back to our cottage. I loved her, she was my mom, but after so easily disregarding my brother's demise and being in cahoots with Billybones and now The Womacks, I questioned everything. Still, my gut said, go with your mom.

At the front door, I cleared my throat to ask one of the hundred questions swimming in my head. My mother put her forefinger to my lips and shook her head gently. Some moments need no words.

Armed with large yellow gloves, we proceeded to scrub away all evidence of the bloody altercation in the kitchen as if by doing so we could erase the event from our life. Tears mixed with ammonia as we cleaned. When we were finished, the room was lemon fresh and squeaky clean but the taint of its history remained. It would never again be the room filled with warm memories of comfort food and family.

Just as quietly, we went through the cottage to pack together essentials to take back to the Anchor.

"Pack light and with intent."

I heeded her advice. Grunts, socks, shorts, slicker, shirts and a toothbrush, the only frivolous item I stowed away was a dusty cologne bottle of *British Sterling* that I swiped from my father's room. It was for the day when I am face to face with my rescued Sandy.

As we packed silently, I became keenly aware of a growing roar outside of the cottage. Walking out to the screened-in porch, I recognized it as the sound of the tide. It was the breath of an asthmatic giant, deep, wet and troubled.

It wasn't just the crash of waves colliding with the concrete seawall. The real lion outside the door was the undertow. The repetition grew fierce as the afternoon wore on. For every wave that battered the shore came an equally strong rapport from the ocean as it was sucked back in towards the skyline. The water rushed through the rocky New England sea bed in a thunderous exhale. The sound was the drowned applause of thousands of souls lost at sea, all now jubilant that the time had come for their release.

Sea gulls aligned the crest of the jetty, all at attention waiting in motionless reverence for the show to begin.

The ocean was rabid. Walking down to the beach, I witnessed the normally blue seascape transformed into a convulsing bladder of white tripe. Each wave collapsed on another connected by webbed sheets of foam undulating in spasm. Geysers of ocean water and foam rocketed over two stories in height in rapid succession like bleached white fireworks. Rocks and ill-fated sea life were propelled far across the main street pummeling summer homes and Charlie's, the beachside snack stand. Brownish white froths of sea and salt flew in the air well into the village like ghosts made of soiled bed sheets. They collided into the sides of cottages, lamp posts and roadways, one just missing me, exploding in a shower of churned brine at my feet. When a particularly large wave met the resistance of the rocky shores, a strong vibration rushed through the ground. You could feel the tremor in your bones as the earth buckled under the impact.

If there was a pirate ship in the periphery, it was impossible to catch sight of it through the commotion.

More questions. Had Bess broken ink to page and this was the result? If so, how could this angry sea possibly be the solution to all of our troubles?

There was still a good three hours before high tide which meant that the ocean hadn't even yet begun to show its hand. I was glad that was wearing my knee high fisherman boots. The tops where folded down with pirate panache. As my mother neared the Anchor, waves crested over the sea wall, coaxed by gale force winds. A river of salt water created by the run off started down the center of Main Street. The water clipped at our heels as we crossed town center.

Bess sat on the step outside of the Anchor, skateboard by her side. Her hands were cupped against her ears as she tried to block Him out. The thief voice cackled over her failed attempt at silence. She kept her head down as the locals arrived. Each dragged provisions inside. Another wave thump hit home, its shock rattling the thirsty shingles of the Anchor, a puddle building at Bess' feet, rippled.

Gatto's incessant yammering rose over the pirate radio in her head. Looking up, Bess saw Gatto walking along side Capt'n Jack. He was excited to be part of the Capt'n's crew. They rolled old leather-strapped chests past Bess.

"Bess! We need fortification, that's what I told the Capt'n. I got a plan to beat all plans, and get this, he listened!" Gatto boasted as he wrestled his chest into the doorway.

"He's a little waterlogged, that one, but the boy's got potential, I'll give'm that," chuckled Capt'n pulled his chest up with ease despite its girth.

The pastels that the setting sun cast on the scene did not soften the threat of the tide. The running down Main had spread out until the entire road was flooded. Then it began to take on depth. It overtook dry land at such a clip that it had a current of its own. By the time we got to Bess, we were trudging through a foot of water.

"Gooncussers, now a flood. I did wicked awesome," exhaled Bess. Her eyes were wide and sullen, those of a dog who had just pooped the rug. The Manifest had already taken its toll on her.

Billybones poked his head outside to assess the progression. He was in his element. The events of the past day had sobered him into a leader of men.

"Get you up, moppet, you done good. Time's awastin! Get inside, vow to the articles and prepare for a ruckus."

As the copper of the sky faded to grey, time was of the essence. Looking back towards the shore, you could see wisps of piratical black flit between the rockets of ocean spray. The afternoon turned as dark as a moonless night. The mooncussers started for the Anchor under this brief window of darkness. Soon the moon, as large as it was in the morning, would ascend the sky, threatening twilight on the ethereal undead.

"Ya in or yer out?" hollered Billybones and with that he closed the massive cherry door, water already rushing inside the hall. We helped him fortify the door as he barked commands to all who arrived. Walking into the heart of the Anchor, I could hear the pounding of fists against wood and desperate cries of those who did not follow captain's orders to a 't'.

"All hands on deck! Be of service or be served! There be no quarter this eve!" The locals all scrambled to task per Billybones instructions.

Bess' pity-face turned to steel, ready for anything, Manifest be damned.

We heard a crash against the outside of the Anchor, then another, none with the weight of the pummeling tide but each packing similar threat. Something wanted in. There were soggy footsteps walking outside. Every door, window and loose board rattled as the unwanted foraged for a way inside.

The desperate pounding on the doors by the tardy villagers was snuffed out. There were a scurry of footsteps, struggle, sluicing and then silence. Billybones knew their fate but showed not an iota of remorse for any of Cove's fallen. Rules of the articles were cruel but necessary in his world of piratical rule.

We all followed his lead. My mother manned the weapons case, distributing artillery to the locals. I unlocked each of the displays, gathering up daggers and the like, making sure to keep the ones with the surest hilts for Gatto, Bess and myself.

In one far case rest a blunderbuss, a pistol on steroids. It has three barrels of brass, each festooned with trumpet-like bells on each end. When the flint went down, scattershot, it would tear through anything in close range. Instead of squirreling away this beauty, I removed it from its velvet cradle and presented it to our captain, my head lowered, my body crouched in a half bow.

"Arr, that's the spirit, mate. Finally, after all this time; welcome aboard, the night's young, thar be adventure ahead."

I stood at Billybones' side. It was the only way. I would embrace my pirate self and wait for destiny to intervene. Only through my unflinching loyalty to my captain would I ever see Sandy alive again. He would bring me to the pirate thief, this tyrant of the sea, and together we would take him down. Billybones would get his beloved treasure, and I, the girl.

Then while he wallowed in his pirate gluttony, I would avenge the death of my brother Ryan. Blood *is* blood.

Chapter 16

DREADNAUGHT

*I*t's all about articles, the articles of employ to be precise. This is not employment in the modern sense, like bagging a part-time job at the register of the Cove Market. It's a pirate pact, an alliance scripted in blood if broken. Each stalwart local who returned to the Rusty Anchor that stood in line to make such a pledge to Billybones. I was among them.

We didn't consider ourselves pirates, far from it. We had congregated in the gallery to combat the piracy of our village. What better way to fight the enemy than to think like them. By signing the log we agreed to pirate the pirates, yo-ho-ho and a barrel full of vengeful whoop-arse.

Waiting to cast my fate to the wind, I wondered how many of these people in line had a one-on-one with The Manifest. Let me count: Billybones, without a doubt; mom, well duh; Sandy, the Manifest might have well have sprouted arms and legs and snatched her away; Bess, I could already see the ghost of the pirate's call floating in the dark recesses of her eyes where once resided her youthful spunk; and myself, I've been in an ongoing duel for my soul ever since.

Outside, the mooncussers were aching to ransack the Anchor. Claws, curses and clamor were muffled by boards securing all points of entry. Their strength lay in that they could not be vanquished, they would continue until they broke through. Our fortifications held fast against their siege which was not much of a feat. Despite their ghastly exterior, mooncussers were more bark than bite. They were mostly reanimated skeletons with the intestinal fortitude of dried kindling. Their other weakness was the adverse effect of light on their physical form. They could only attack the Rusty Anchor in the shadows. A hunter's moon swallowed the evening sky, its glow keeping the mooncussers at bay.

The ocean swell possessed more teeth than they did. Inside the Anchor, water kept rising as high tide neared. Sea water seeped through the floorboards like blood through a band-aid. Puddles formed in the lower areas of the unlevel floor and grew until the entire floor was engulfed. The water then took on depth, from a film of water you could slosh through to ankle deep all in the passing of an hour.

Billybones looked out over his toiling minions from the dry land of the upper deck smiling all tooth-rot and gold. He was a man smiles averted. When he was prone to shine his once pearly whites, it was with malicious intent. In my own history with the pirate, such a grin preceded trudging worthless cargo about, walking the plank or dueling to the death. Billybones never played nice.

With the smile plastered on his face he orchestrated the chaos around him. What seemed to Bess, Gatto and me as another ill turn of fate compliments of the Manifest, was all well and good to Billybones. We had to trust his pirate intuition to get us out of this latest jam.

When the water neared our knees, the century old floorboards began to buckle from the infusion of salty water.

Antique nails started to give way with shrieks of steel against wood, finally giving up their century long bond. Our footing became unsure as one by one the boards gave way.

My pirate mother stood at the bow of the lower deck looking out over the crew below in the water. She looked back at Billybones and, on his nod, put two fingers up to her mouth and let out an ear-piercing whistle that, no matter how she coached me, I could never master. Everyone halted mid-task and looked up.

She looked back at Billybones, all eyes followed her lead. Billybones swallowed his smile.

"Anchors away!"

Capt'n Jack nodded and in a few of his large strides manned the large wheelhouse that was wrapped with a heavy gauge cable, rope as thick as his wrist. The rope reached down the side of the replica ship and through the floor with authenticity.

The Capt'n's ham hands released the safety peg from the wheelwell and, clutching the wheel, bent down, muscles flexed, he put all of his shoulder into turning the wheel. His first effort proved fruitless. He spat choice salty language into his paws and tried again. Sweat brewed on his brow as he wrestled the wheel. It was a tug of war between him and whatever lurked beneath that refused to give.

Gatto, now Capt'n's self-appointed first mate, stormed up behind the Capt'n to lend a hand. The newly acquired muscles on his husky form were enough additional torque to break the anchor's vise grip on the deep. We could all feel heavy rock shifting deep underwater.

Once unfettered, the wheelhouse turned heavily but without resistance. The lack of tension caught Gatto unbalanced and he fell backwards. Capt'n Jack kept cranking the anchor up while he chuckled. The cable wove around the hub, at first dried rust, then wet, then coated with a green coat of kelp.

A banged-up Gatto took a good crack against the deck on his way down. He held back any tears. That was for boys and there was no place for boys on this ship. He followed Capt'n Jack's lead and laughed his pain into a green memory.

As the tide pool inside rose, the massive facade of a ship shifted. The books in the stacks, still transforming history, rattled and thrashed overhead, an audience in anticipation of the main event.

My mother, Billybones' quarter-master, kept shouting orders at the crew still in the water. Her voice was stern but urgent, the battle between mother versus the pirate in play. The wading locals took heed. They removed dingys and sloops that hung ornamentally on the gallery walls and hoisted them up the side of the ship's hull. The crew on deck tied them securely down. The rising water compromised their best efforts.

The Rusty Anchor, correction, the ship encased inside the said gallery, took on a life of its own. It rocked from side to side slowly breaking free from the floor that moored it. It was a newborn colt, defying gravity for the first time to stand in all of its equine glory. There was a loud crack as the hull severed itself from the floorboards and then the rocking abated. The boat became buoyant, bobbing side to side with the water that encased it.

Everyone bound by the Articles did their part without question. Those still in the rising waters checked each barrel and crate. If they contained provisions or ammunition, they were hoisted onboard. If they were sand or stone, they were toppled to one side.

Working in tandem, the crew on deck took each crate or barrel of valuables and secured them down into the storage of the faux ship.

Faux? Yes. That's French for fake just like Him, the zombie captain who babe-knapped my Sandy. All the commotion and frantic orders seemed nonsensical.

Billybones stood tall behind the ship's wheel and with a holler that even hushed the few remaining marauders scratching outside.

"Forward Ho!"

The ship rocked more from side to side, the colt matured into a bronco-buster.

'Careen,' I thought in response.

I wove through the fracas to Bess who, along with her wing man Gatto were still sledging through the water, stuffing their backpacks with any of the remaining artifacts; shivs, pistolas, round shot... Whatever they could stow away.

Bess reached into her bag and pulled out a book wrapped in a Jolly Roger.

"Ashley's... check!".

I opened up my own backpack and pulled out the other valuable imprint.

"Manifest... check!"

It writhed in my hands like a fish out of water. I forced it back down into the bag and joined my mates in foraging for anything dangerous.

"Careen? It means more than this, doesn't it?"

I jerked my body back and forth in the water, splashing about.

"Cool dance moves, dude!" joked Gatto.

"What did the big man tell you, Bess?"

"Ok! He said look for the word careen. It's when a pirate ship is intentionally beached to scrape crud off the bottom and... what did he say... to fortify it."

"It's the 'Anchor! ol 'Rusty is careened!" Gatto replied, getting all excited by the prospect that we might have an honest to God pirate ship on our hands. "We've been fortifying her all summer!"

We looked at him quizzically.

"What? It's like cars, dude, ships are girls, right? Fortify *her*!"

Bess continued paying Gatto no mind, "He said the hard part isn't getting the boat..."

"Ship", I corrected her.

"What-ever! ... getting the *ship* to dry land isn't the hard part. It's getting *her* back to sea. It would take more than a able bodied crew could muster. They would need a help from, you know, Mother Nature."

"... or Mother Ocean. Nice going, Bess."

The wind thrashed more violently against the exterior of the gallery with more attitude than any mooncusser could muster. The ship, the elephant in the room, rocked side to side with each gust.

"Mission accomplished", gulped Gatto to Bess.

Then another spine-cringing sound, this time wood on wood like the loudest creaking door ever, erupted from the drowned floor in a rush of foaming brine. The three of us looked down to see where the outer hull met the floorboards of the gallery. The ship had risen over a foot revealing the hull continuing past the floorboards. The

Rusty Anchor, once thought to be a real as the papier-mâché volcano scene in the *Congo Cruise* ride at the town fair, was for real.

"All aboard who's comin' aboard!" I whispered.

We rushed to the dangling ropes being used to wrangle up provisions and shimmied up the ropes hand over hand as if in gym class. In a three way tie, we all hurled our selves over the guardrails of the ship to safety.

One of Billybones' prized fortifications was secured on the very bow of the ship where both sides of the hull arched into a point. Billybones had no time for such accoutrements as a figurehead, or, to note, anything French. Instead, he gilded the edge meant to split the sea with a brass band. It was not correct for the time period of the ship, more appropriate for a modern military ship like a dreadnaught or an ice breaker off the Alaskan coastline. This was, however, more than just functional. It was adorned with intricate etching, intertwining patterns of wave and scale, not unlike Billybones' arms. Not only was every marking a warning to all who dared shadow its bow, they were details of memories lost. Hidden in the intricate mosaic were the sightless skulls of crossbones and Maltese crosses like the ones indicating treasure on a map. They read like a bumper sticker that stated, '*if you can read this, you're too damn close*'. Its raspier edge gleamed ready to back up the threat implied.

With another rush of the gale outside, ol 'Rusty heaved, releasing a swell of seaweed into the gallery. The remaining crew not yet on board struggled to stay afloat. The towers of books on either side became unstable, volumes falling from the highest shelves like desperate souls jumping off the Bourne Bridge. The bite of the bow's edge carved through the waterlogged floorboards with ease, uprooting them as the ship lumbered forward.

"All hands on deck!" Billybones hollered, leaning over to my mother who then parroted his orders to the crew on deck. The crew took heed of her every word. The few stragglers still in the ever-deepening water were to be left behind.

With another belch of rising bubbles, the sea water rushed up from the gaping hole beneath port side where ol 'Rusty once lay dormant. Along with it came a silver streak of sea life weaving itself between the brown sheets of seaweed. The swarm of fish jetted back and forth under the water, distraught and agitated.

One of the few remaining waterlogged locals called up to me, pleading for help. His hand reached out in between his paddling to stay afloat. He jerked for a second, panic flushing his face.

"Wolf fish!" he screamed, his mouth stretching so wide his voice was silenced by the salt water that rushed inside. There are few things more unsettling than the tears of a grown man.

Thanks to Gatto we all knew about the nasties of our coast. Along with the devilfish he introduced us to, there were dogfish, the cur of the sea, known to bite many a line and finger; congy eels, known to eat rocks at their most desperate; and most feared of them all, the wolf fish. They were aquatic evil personified, armed with huge talon-like teeth like their brethren in the deepest dark of the ocean. They would bite at anything, even themselves. '*B-b-b-bad to the bone,*' as the song goes. The man before me was lunch meat. Thrashing about in the water, all soft and vulnerable, he was far more tempting than a lump of granite or one's own fin.

Hero or pirate? Pirate? Hero? Hero. I rushed into action, gathering up a line to throw down. Billybones caught sight of my attempt to save the man and shouted,

"Don't you listen to your mother... *boy*? She said lighten the load! We need no dead weight here, you included."

The first fish drew blood, a dinner bell for the rest of the pack to follow. They swarmed like sharks, bit like wolves and feasted with the veracity of piranha. They snapped at the drowning man, each other, themselves, even at the sky as they sprang airborne during the fracas. What remained of the man quickly disappeared into the blood stained water.

I turned away from the carnage; head hung low, and followed my mother's orders to the letter. As I secured line with the longshoremen I tried to convince myself that the man's blood was not on my hands but on those of my captain. One thing was clearer than ever before, I hated pirates and that said, I hated the man I called Billybones.

Paying attention to the tasks at hand was an elixir for my guilty conscience. It was the Tai of the custodian. '*Neat piles, even piles.*' I rolled up my red and white stripes and helped empty out any of the remaining exercise barrels, spilling the sand and stone overboard, lightening the load. It felt like I was burying the recently departed.

'*Stay on task. We need no dead weight here*'.

Another gust from outside rattled the building's foundation. The ship bucked forward and, with a lighter cargo, rose further from the gallery floor. The pier of the main mast harpooned the ceiling of the gallery. Shingles and wood showered on us along with the downpour of rain from the outside.

The withered bygone that had made its home in the crow's nest scurried down the main mast looking for cover. Its mud feet held sure to the mast thanks to the bound rope I had woven around its trunk. When it had made its way down to the main deck, other crewmates shooed it away, trying to stomp it with a boot, a mop or the butt of a musket.

Bess, Gatto and I had found shelter in the bunker that led down to the cargo hold. I tried to do my mother's whistle to call the bygone to safety but no sound game from my fingers.

Bess looked at me as if I had finally lost it by wanting to save such a repulsive thing. "Really? Gross." She then put up two fingers and let out a whistle even louder and higher pitched than my mother's. It stopped the fearful bygone its tracks.

"Mud head! here, now!" she ordered it. The bygone had no choice but to obey and scampered to us before the custodian could swab the deck with him.

Moonlight shone down through the ribcage that was once the roof of the Anchor. Electricity had shorted out reducing the water to black molasses, thick and boiling with carnivorous life.

The sword-edge of ol' Rusty met the sentinel of the Rusty Anchor, the massive door. Its weight halted our progress. As the gallery's tide continued to rise, the edge of the bow carved back and forth against the hardwood to no avail. A lash of wind came down on the hollow shell of the Rusty Anchor causing a downpour of books to join the rainwater as the walls gave way. Still the portal held strong.

Capt'n Jack signaled to the longshoremen. In an instant Big Red and his crew traversed the masts and the rigging, secured lines, freed up sailcloth, then manned stations awaiting further orders.

Longshoremen knew their place, and in doing so, insured their survival.

Everybody knew Big Red; he was a mountain of a man, his face the color of his nickname. He was a lobsterman which when I was younger, I thought was his superhero moniker; Big Red, the Lobster Man; half Man, half lobster, all business! Now older, holding onto the railing at the mouth of the bunker, I hoped that my first impression was correct. We needed a Superman.

I watched them in action hoping to gleam some of their primal expertise. It was skills only experience awarded you. Perhaps, today was my chance. Hungry for knowledge, I watched their every move. The more I retained, the less I would need Billybones, I thought, biting my lip to make sure not to use my inner voice.

Capt'n nodded to Billybones as did my mother. Everything was set.

"Forward, Ho!"

The ship came to life. A Northeast wind shear ripped down from what was once the roof and the sails billowed tight against the rigging. Ol' Rusty found its true strength and surged forward. We had to grasp onto the railings to keep ourselves from toppling over the deck's rails into the wolf fish buffet.

To give the gallery door credit, it held its ground. The rest of the building did not fare so well. The building's frame broke away like matchsticks. The frame around the door finally gave way. With merely a flesh wound to its nut brown veneer, the door fell forward, defeated. The heavy ring in the lion's maw clanged dully as it submerged.

The water once contained inside of the Rusty Anchor spilled into the Town Center like a bonsai tsunami. Ol' Rusty rode its crest to freedom, tearing through what skeletal remains were left of the gallery. The concrete sidewalk that ran in front of the gallery was torn asunder. Main Street, which ran alongside the gallery, had been reduced to a flue of rushing tide water. We lumbered straight into its rapid current.

Billybones spun the ship's wheel sharply; hand over hand, as Capt'n Jack barked new marching orders to his men. They gave the sails slack while the Capt'n moved the cross sails into position. Then with a countdown bellowed through his teeth that still clutched his smoldering pipe, Capt'n Jack had them draw the lines tight, harnessing the wind at its most gnarly.

Ol' Rusty was no longer careened.

'Good job, Bess,' I thought-spoke to Bess.

'Yeah, right,' She replied silently.

I got closer to her so that I was not in Gatto's earshot. My observation was just for us two. I spoke aloud.

"Y'know, I don't know if this helps, but, in time, it gets easier."

I got it. The weight of the world is in the hands of the ones who have held the quill. It was her turn and was a lot to take in.

"Yeah, that's what I'm afraid of."

"There's no need to cry, Bess, we'll get through this."

'Cry?' she thought back at me, a bit miffed. *'Do I look like the word cry is even in my vocabulary?'*

'My bad. It's just that I thought... you know... I heard you,' I thought-spoke back, tapping my bandana-clad head.

"No tears, not even on the inside," Bess grumbled aloud.

That could mean only one thing, if I didn't hear Bess, it must have been Sandy weeping. Sandy was alive! She probably had kept silent for fear of her captor. Whatever message she would project to me would surely be heard by Him as well. Her silence kept her alive.

I heard nothing to indicate that my brother was alive. Rest in peace, bro. You were a major pain in the butt but didn't deserve such a fate as death by pirate, no matter what Mom says. I will avenge you, first the Thief Pirate known as Him, then the murderous Billybones known as Smythe.

Our progression down Main Street was as uneventful as it would be for any pirate clipper ship careening down a formerly dry land thoroughfare. The pavement flaked away like the crust of a fancy pastry. Ol' Rusty trekked toward the beachfront in jerks and starts, the blade of the hull parsing the subterranean boulders this way and that.

It made for a bumpy ride. The three of us, four counting the bygone, huddled together in the opening of a bunker that led down to the holding quarters. We anchored each other; white knuckles on wet wood. All the while I suppressed any expression that could be interpreted as panic.

The shambles of what was once Lobster Cove was illuminated by stark moonlight. The village played across the bow of our ship like scratched footage from an old black and white movie. The Cove Market was a gutted shell, remains of the guiltless crimes of the desperate and the mooncusser feeding frenzy that followed. Every landmark was broken, smoldering and abandoned save one. Only one building towered over the hellscape that once was our town; Haddad Hall, the oldest wing of the library. It held strong century after century of erased tragedy. It towered defiant, its armor, the mortar and stone gathered from the very sea that now attacked.

I stood tall in the mouth of the bunker sharing the hall's indignation. The difference between us was, while all the hall could do was stand as a constant reminder of all that was lost and forgotten, I was flesh and blood and able to make a difference. I could end this cycle of devastation.

An occasional mooncusser could be seen crossing over us, high in the sky; emaciated crows, all oily rags and wings. They were more intent on retreating back to their ghost ship than taunting us further. Riding the inland wind, they disappeared into the dark horizon before us.

Ol' Rusty barreled down Main in hot pursuit. Each jolt and stagger brought us one step closer to revenge.

It's not that I hate the French, I like, nay, love, croissants, and they're French. I even like saying the word... *croissants.* You have to understand while I refused to cower in the bunker; Captain Frenchie had my Sandy in his clutches. I'm sure that *Him,* The Thief Pirate, being half-dead guy, half sea rot, actually had clutches. As Ol' Rusty negotiated sinkholes and uprooted mailboxes, Him was probably pillow-talking innuendos at his captive with a François, slow-jam accent.

While the roads latticing through Lobster Cove were reduced to mud pits that ol 'Rusty cut through with little difficulty, the sea wall up ahead appeared as immovable as Haddad Hall. The wall held back the rage of storm after storm for as many years as I have breathed. Despite its age, mere stress cracks across its battered grey were its only wrinkles. The worst the ocean could muster was a constant gnawing on the ocean side of the concrete slabs. Fractions of inches would flake away at its base as the years passed, nothing a good slap of cement couldn't cure.

Poseidon could hurtle his waves over the wall but never through it. Today, we needed to one up a Greek god. Luckily, ol' Rusty wasn't a wave.

Ocean Street intersected with Main Street. It ended with a large hill that led down to the waterfront. The street was barren. Any locals who had not signed the articles had either long sped out of town or were seeking sanctuary inside Haddad Hall.

Upon Billybones' order ol' Rusty banked right, a turn that would surely topple a less stalwart ship. She tipped precariously to one side. A wave of mud and gravel threatened to board. The ship turned a tight forty-five degrees then lost much of its momentum as it righted itself. We slowed to a crawl at the pinnacle of Ocean Street.

This may have stopped less savvy souls, but this crew had seen it all and possessed all the where-with-all to push forward. My mother surveyed the situation, nodded to Capt'n who, in turn, looked to Billybones. With a finger sliding across his nose, our pirate captain gave the go-ahead.

"To the bow, and then back starboard, the lot of you, pronto!" My mother yelled then ran across deck to repeat the order down in storage. The entire crew, half still negotiating their sea legs, rushed towards the front of the ship. She instructed the burlier men on board to free the cannons from their perch and to wheel them to the bow of the ship. The boards of the hull groaned as gravity battled which direction to sway the ship. The crew hurried to shift the weight of the ship seaward. All was quiet as the ship teetered on the brink.

"Batten down the hatches!"

The men secured the cannons, blocks jammed beneath wheels, and tethers bound tight just as momentum swayed east. The crew stormed back just as ol' Rusty started its decline to the sea. First it was a sluggish crawl, then ol' Rusty moved at a swift clip, building speed, its destination, non-negotiable. Our destiny lay at the other side of the sea wall.

I kept my mates at my back inside the bunker that led down into the belly of the ship. Perched at its mouth, I continued taking mental notes.

Granite, like a pirate betrayed, is unforgiving. Now I'm talking full-blooded pirates here, of the Billybones variety, pirates that if you cut them in half would be pirate to the core. Not like Him, The Thief Pirate, a pirate of convenience, evident by to his allegiance to France and the fact that he cowers under the cloak of darkness, absconding with defenseless girls instead of tangling with adversaries of consequence.

Billybones was stone, an immovable force. So was the sea wall that we were closing in on. The black of the skyline and the grey of the mile long seawall exchanged proportions. In an instant the wall was upon us.

It came upon us like a foregone conclusion. It grew from a small horizontal etching of grey in the distance to a full size barrier insisting on our respect. My Cyrkle-mates held on to one other by the rope bracelets we wore, a far more secure grip than our wet skin. The skittish bygone I had befriended pulled at my red and white striped shirt trying to coax me to come downstairs to take cover. It had seen this all before and he knew that pirate bravery never ended well in the long run. I shook him off me in a way so not to hurt its feelings but would order him down to safety. I strapped my free arm around the nearest mast post and prepared for impact.

The sidewalk was the first to go. The hull tore through the large concrete slabs, all the length and height of your average car. Next stop, the sea wall.

Our first warning was the shriek of the brass blade's edge of the bow buckling upon impact. The concrete twisted away all of the intricate molding's aesthetic. Brass grommets pulled out of the hull as the adornment broke free from the ship's hull. Before it jettisoned, it had inflicted a crease along the slab before us, cracks forming a spider web of weakness.

Sea walls are constructed to protect the land against the brutality of the tide, never the other way around. If we were running aground from the ocean side of the cove, the barrier would have left us in shambles.

The iron rods that helped anchor the wall to the shore bent at the will of our charging ship, slabs of concrete breaking free like random bricks of God's Lego.

I waved my friends down to join my mother below. The wind whipping around our heads denied speech. With one hand clutching the doorframe of the bunker and the other around the waist of my adopted bygone, I held tight as we broke through. Invisible hands pushed my body backwards as if attempting to toss me down the stairwell behind me. Any provisions not secured were hurtled across the slick deck and crashed against starboard side; many items were flung overboard altogether. The heavy iron cannons tested their tethers.

S.E. Toon

I could hear the rush of water below followed my mother's muffled orders below deck. The wall's support rods had pierced the underbelly of the ship. The crew downstairs rushed to bail out the cabin and patch up the fissure.

The real threat was never the sea wall; it was what waited for us on the other side. Clearing what was once a concrete partition, we met the sea head first. The first wave crashed over the railing, spraying the deck with a coat of bilge and foam. Full sails harnessed all the fight the storm proffered. Our downhill volition was quelled by the impact of a second wave that dwarfed the first. The same phantom hands that first tried to throw me back now attempted to pull me from the hatch like an oyster from its shell. I held on with both hands, leaving the bygone to fend for itself. I could hear its wet retreat behind me. With each wave of brown muscle, another attempt was made to hurl me across the deck like so much useless baggage. This tug of war intensified with each consecutive crash.

Billybones, his hands one with the captain's wheel, gave an exaggerated nod to Cap'n Jack who in turn whistled a command to Big Red and his men. With a flex of his bicep, a grimace and a spin of the captain's wheel Billybones played roulette with our lives. Pirates are always good at gambling. They were always the house and the odds were always in their favor. As ol' Rusty banked sharply left towards the rocky shore I prayed his pirate luck hadn't run its course.

ol' Rusty cross masts swung wildly across the breadth of the deck in an attempt to regain the bite of the wind they lost as the ship turned. One of the swinging timbers nearly lopped the head off of one of Red's crew while he negotiated the rigging. It swung so close that the ties of his bandanna flapped in its wake. Years of living on the edge provided the intuition to duck as the timber swung from behind; most impressive. Note to self... duck!

The sails went slack for an instant. They immediately sprang back to life, canvas flapping madly until again they caught the wind now blowing against their other side. The ropes groaned, coiling against the force of the gale.

Our ship was now parallel with the coastline riding across the swell of a high tide. The force of the wind coupled with the rush of the waves doubled ol' Rusty's speed. We traversed the surf at breakneck pace while the ocean fought to push us to shore.

We are in the East Coast. We're not talking about Caribbean beaches of pristine blue water and white sand. We're talking the wrong coast, as they say in California, all broken rock and brine. There was no smooth sailing into our shores. Boaters and surfers alike navigated the waves leery of the jagged stalagmites that lurked just below the brown stew. One wrong move and an incisor of stone would bear down and take a piece out of any ship foolhardy enough to trespass.

Also not in our favor was the fact that we were navigating the ship in a cove, a circular bite taken out of the coastline. It was a safe harbor for those moored between its arms or a whirlpool of destruction, all depending on which way the winds blew. That night the wind blew in all ways wrong.

The Fates showed us no favor. If your intentions were to wait the storm out in the confines of the cove, then you would be chum for dog fish. That was never Billybones' way.

Watching the crew in action from the confines of the bunker, I felt like I was again reading from the pages of The Manifest.

Billybones played before me just as I envisioned him in the tales spun within. Perhaps one day, a young boy in the future would read from that book what went down this night and it would play in his awestruck mind the same way.

If this was just another Manifest tale told, it was far from a happy ending. Billybones stared down the coastline with one eye and winced with the other; the impact of the sea on the right, threat of the stone jetty on the left. Our speed was increasing, the jolts, becoming more threatening. The crew securing the rigging, dangled from side to side of the ropes violently like Punch and Judy mannequins performing in a cyclone.

The ship rode the curl of the larger waves like a surfer at one with the sea. Billybones leaned ol' Rusty into the wave sending us to shore. Then as the wave crashed, losing its hold on us, Capt'n would have his crew tighten the sails and bank the ship back towards the horizon, now just two stripes of black in the distance. With each successive wave the ship gained speed, cutting deeper into the surf pushing ol' Rusty one wave at a time, further out to sea.

Their seasoned maneuvers alone would not be enough to save us. While the ship was making progress pulling away from shore, the outer bank of the cove, Rocky Pointe approached on our starboard side.

To surrender and bank back into the cove would reduce us to a bottle in the ocean, victim to the whim of the pummeling surf. Not quite as violent an ending but an end just the same. We had no choice but to press on.

The northernmost edge of the cove was a ledge of jagged rock as unforgiving as a pirate. Our present trajectory would have us broadside it, tearing our hull out from under us. The inner side of the point was jagged tombstones in a nautical graveyard, each protruding blade of stone awaiting our epitaph.

Beyond that point was the ocean deep. That is where the ghost ship lay in wait. That is where we needed to be.

Billybones held his position countering each swell; Capt'n Jack grabbed each gust for all it had. Another smile washed across Billybones' face followed by a half -laugh, half-cough. As spooky as it was, any time that laugh was heard, it was a good sign. It was the sound of a pirate in the moment.

Billybones looked back at me, summoning me by his side with a furrow of his brow. There were no words. None could be heard over the roar of the ocean.

I looked down the bunker to see the cowering bygone creeping up the stairwell to throw a worried look up at me. I motioned for him to get Gatto, then yelled my command with my inner voice. The bygone heard my words but shook its head, mucus spraying this way and that. He knew that Gatto could not see mudheads. I waved my hand at him in a scolding manner and the bygone ran rat-like down into storage. It returned a moment later running, Bess following him with a confused Gatto in tow.

'The two of you, here, now!' Billybones' voice rang inside my head. Him chuckled at our dilemma with his cowardly thief voice. Pirate radio was back online.

I grabbed Gatto by the arm and bent my head in the direction of Billybones. Gatto shook his head and yelled though I couldn't hear his words. The expression on his face, however, said it all. *'Are you out of your mind?'* Perhaps I was. Embracing your pirate self is nothing short of crazy.

I gave Gatto's arm a firm tug, and in time the impact of the waves, we made a go for the upper deck. We grabbed a post halfway across when a wash of surf knocked us off our feet. Using Billybones' spin of the captain's wheel as our stopwatch, we made another go for the bridge. We grabbed hold of the upper deck's railing just as the next wave sprayed over us.

Once by Billybones side he grabbed Gatto's hands and placed them on the ship's wheel. What was I, chopped liver??

Gatto's hands moved with Billybones'. They were at one with the tide, feeling the strength of the waves resonate in the wheel's wood. Then Billybones removed one of his mitts at a time from the wheel until Gatto was manning the ship by himself. Gatto started to smile and I mean smile wide, a grin of exhilaration or defecation, depending on what won, thrill or fear.

Billybones took out a short shiv and handed it to me, then pulled another from yet another hiding place for himself.

'This is no time for an impromptu duel,' I thought-spoke. Billybones rolled his eyes. He raised his blade and instead of making a go for me, he stabbed at the wooden railing, using the knife to ensure a steady grip. I did the same and stab by stab we marched toward the Capt'n and his crew who were battling the waves on the main deck. He shouted to Jack, the words I could not make out, but afterwards the Capt'n shared the same possessed grin as Billybones. He nodded his soaked white beard in agreement.

The shoreline drew ever closer, mouth open, teeth hungry.

One by one, we all gathered around the wheel well that held the anchor in place. The cable attached to it was tight, the weight of the anchor so heavy it barely wavered in the storm. Big Red and his men tied off ropes to either side of the anchor's cable. I nudged one of the men to let him know that despite my age, I was as adept at knotsmanship as the best of them. We had a good eight ties lassoed securely around the cable from which the anchor hung.

Then Billybones and the Capt'n counted off and gave the anchor some slack. One had to be careful, too much too soon and the anchor would plummet to the bottom of the cove causing the wheel well to spin, taking limbs at will. Slack was given and the wheel stop was again secured. The anchor hung loosely halfway down the hull.

Billybones then looked up at Gatto waving his hands side to side. He yelled, "Rock the Boat, swabbie."

Gatto complied turning the wheel side to side in time with Billybones swinging arms.

"Rock the boat, don't rock the boat baybee, Rock the boat, don't tip da boat over," Gatto sang through the ocean's spray.

We could hear the anchor pound against the side of the hull. Billybones kept motioning to Gatto, the boat thrashing contrary to the pounding of the surf, the anchor's impact stronger, shaking the deck boards beneath our feet. The surf lapping the deck tested our footing.

The Capt'n looked at us holding the eight lines attached to the cable and hollered "Tis' time to pull us out of the mouth of hell, gentlemen!"

"There be no gentlemen here, Capt'n!" barked Big Red.

"That's what I'm counting on!" he replied.

With that, he nodded and we pulled at our ropes, four pulling to the back then letting up lack, then the other four to the front until the dangling anchor no longer struck the hull but swung back and forth alongside it, each time swinging like a pendulum, each time wider, further and faster.

Billybones stabbed his way back to the upper deck chuckling all the way. We could hear the submerged rocks bordering the point grazing the bottom of the hull as ol' Rusty approached the rocky shore.

Billybones pushed Gatto aside, taking the quickest of moments to muss up his hair in an approving manner.

"Hold onto yer hats, ladies!" he laughed as he spun the Captain's wheel with all the force of his body left towards land.

"Let'r rip, Anchors aweigh!" he yelled, echoed again by Capt'n Jack. Simultaneously, the Big Red crew and I let go of our respective lines while the Capt'n released the stop on the wheel well as the swinging anchor swung portside. It anchor swung forward away from the ship like a fishing line, catching the rocky beard that bordered the point just as the rocks beneath wrecked havoc with the hull.

Ol' Rusty banked sharply into the next wave that crashed against its side pulling the anchor cable tight and instead of crashing along the shoreline; the weighted tether swung the ship, backside first, around the horn of the point by the force of the tide.

Capt'n and his crew had no time to waste. They hurried to release the cable before another wave could send us crashing against the shore on the other side of the point. The cable was hot to the touch but with some frantic sawing using whatever blades were at hand, it finally gave way. The cable dived into the rocky shore and the next wave pushed us towards the northern coast.

Billybones steered the ship parallel to the beachfront, then methodically resumed countering one wave at a time inching our vessel towards the open sea.

"Kin always get ya an anchor, can't always git another ship."

The storm abated, the wind subsided, yet still enough of a gust to maintain our charted course. Gatto and Bess got some long needed sack time down under.

I, however, was on a mission. I stationed myself in the crow's nest of the main sail, staring intently at the two bands of black, the ocean and the night sky, looking for a blip in the distance, for signs of the ghost ship of the dreaded Pirate Thief, Him.

I nodded off sometime before dawn, the bygone at my feet, holding watch while I slept. When I awoke there was no land, no gulls, just open water; unknown threats lurking just past every horizon.

Rubbing sand from my eyes, I continued my station, looking out over the abating sunrise for signs of not-quite-life. Then I saw it, looking more like a mirage, a trick of the light; the thinnest line of black peeking out behind the blue band of the ocean. Then there was another, and another; a trio of bare masts of a ship reaching up to the heavens against the burnt sienna of the sky.

Billybones was top notch as far as pirates go. "Mad skills," Gatto commented over a breakfast of hard tac and fruit roll-ups before getting himself some down time.

That said, I still had to kill him. That morning, with the sky clearing and color returning to the face of the world, his demise would have to wait. There were bigger fish to fry, another act of revenge that took precedence. I needed to avenge the living before the dead while there still was time.

While there was still *time*.

Chapter 17

HORNSWOGGLE

Dear God, Be good to me.

The sea is so wide and my boat is so small.

— Breton fishermen's prayer

Lobster Cove hid beneath the portside horizon, a cherished sandcastle washed away by the tide of time. Before us, beyond where surf met sky, the stuff of history, to be written anew in strokes of steel and sweat.

Sunrise burnt away its orange singe to reveal another steamy August day. With the sky clear, the unfettered sun slowly baked unseasoned skin to leather. The sea breeze masked its severity. As it neared noon all of us crewmen had fashioned damp cloths to drape over the back of our necks from our bandanas to keep the fire from rushing down our spines and searing our souls.

It was *hot* hot, but more important, it was daylight. Sunshine would keep the mooncussers at bay allowing us to work under the cover of broad daylight. We needed a plan against our pirate adversaries. We needed a plan and we needed it pronto. We had to act while the sun still shone.

I climbed down from my sentry in the crow's nest of the main sail to state my concern.

"What's the plan, Stan?" I asked my faithful bygone shadowing my every step. It was always underfoot ever since it was befriended. Climbing down the mast was difficult enough without worrying about tripping over its slimy form or punting it overboard. Bygones can read thoughts, at least the thoughts of the manifested. Knowing my ambitions, it was now his duty to deter me.

My master plan was simple; first, save Sandy, and in so doing, save the world from the scourge of piratical wrongfulness, Him and his band of mooncussers. Second, avenge the death of my brother Ryan by killing the man I call Billybones. It would be in that order and I would not rest until this to-do list had been completed.

The bygone slithered down the mast past me and stood at its base. Willowy arms crossed in front of its sludge of a body blocked my way.

"I know this is dangerous business," I told it like a parent talking down to a hysterical child. "There are some things in life you don't get a vote on. Sorry to bring up the whole life thing, but you catch my drift."

Bygones, having been stripped of their own lives, are envious of the living they shadow. It had bonded with me because I was alive and I was the first air breather that hadn't shrunk back in revulsion upon seeing it.

I lifted it up by the shoulders to continue my march towards Billybones. Bygones have weight but no substance, no spine. Just as I moved it aside, this composite of slurry and puss passed between my hands, splattering across the deck where it began to congeal back into a humanoid form.

"Bother!" I exhaled watching it adjust the proportions of its body to and fro until he resembled what had become my pet. Its exaggerated rendition of life was akin to a premature child, all head and little body. "That's your name... Bother." I said as I walked past him. Having been named, the bygone seemed less like an object, more of a *him* than an *it.* "Now if you would quit *bothering* me, I need to have a little face time with the big guy." I left him behind as I climbed to the upper deck.

Billybones peered through his spyglass at the three charcoal lines that peaked out from under the horizon line before us. He called out to Capt'n Jack who was at the helm.

"Give it some slack, men, ne'er be a surprise if they git an eyeful of us." Big Red and the boys complied and the faint mirage of the pirate ship's masts dipped back and forth over the bleached blue band between sea and sky.

I had barely put my checkered Vans on his upper deck when Billybones sensed my presence. Without losing his focus manning the ship, he welcomed me.

"Twas goin' to call for you, mate. Good call, good call, eyes of a sea hawk. We might make a sailor out of you yet."

"What's the plan? You gotta have a plan! You got a plan? I got a plan!" my mind raced trying hard not to broadcast to any interested parties. I fell in line and stood to the side of Billybones to state my case.

"He went for Sandy, he knows I will follow, if its me he wants, then let's give him me... in exchange for Sandy."

"He's a pirate... he wants everything."

Billybones lowered the spyglass, contracted it down to quarter of its size with one snapping sound and slipped it in his breast pocket.

"… don't you?" We were face to face; Billybones looked deep for the pirate behind my eyes.

"I want… revenge," I replied. It wasn't a lie.

I spoke words he could understand. Billybones pondered my proposal. "If he had to choose, he'd take treasure. You'd be an amusement, no doubt… good for a torture or two, tonic fer the troops, but at the end of the day, night for this lot, its treasure he be thinkin' bout as his eyelids close shop."

There are two things a mooncusser holds dear: life and treasure. They had already lost one; they would not let the other go without a fight.

I walked over to one of the boats we had salvaged from the walls of the Rusty Anchor. I banged on its solid hull.

"We'll take this sloop here, the two of us."

"Ketch, not a sloop, a ketch."

Be it a sloop or a ketch, it was a modified-to-the-max dingy to be sure. It was made for two men, had a single triangular sail that a learned hand could use to harness the wind and save oar strokes. Its hull was needle-nosed to cut through opposing current and ride on top of the pounding surf without capsizing.

I pointed over stern side at the horizon.

"*Him*! If he's such a big fish, then we need bigger bait. You said it! He wants treasure and, heck, you're a living, breathing treasure map."

I slapped Billybones' bicep with no fear of retribution. We were on the same side.

"Not only can you lead the way, you know how to get it." I accented the last two words to stroke his ego; I was so full of myself.

Billybones took my foolhardy words to heart. He rubbed at his red brush of beard then walked out of my earshot to Capt'n Jack on the bridge. What followed was a conversation of "Arrs" and "Ahhs", a comparison of ink, and a unified nodding of heads. Billybones marched back to me, each boot fall as solid as the next, and proffered his hand. Hands past and elbows rubbed all knowing.

"Let's go out-pirate a pirate."

Bother anxiously returned with Gatto and Bess close at his heels, my mother close behind. She called from behind for them to return to task below deck.

"This is not your time, children," she scolded.

Billybones popped open an ornate pocket compass. Its bobbing needle gave Billybones his bearings and he snapped the chain it was attached to. The compass swung back into his weathered topcoat.

"No time like the present," he announced.

"Better than no time at all," I retorted, stealing thunder.

Bess pulled at her rope bracelet. "What about all this Cyrkle garbage, Ty, strength in numbers, all for one..."

"... and one for all. This is something I have to do alone."

Gatto corrected us. "Umm, dude! Three Musketeers weren't pirates, they were musketeers"

"... and they weren't ninjas either, Gat. We... I need you here, watching my back and keeping the women safe." I patted Bess on her backpack where she kept all her valuables. She shook my hand away.

"If you go get yourself killed, that's it, no more best friends, buddy boy!" Gatto added. He manned up and took Bess' arm as he left.

The ketch was retrieved by Big Red's crew and prepared to launch. It was already high noon. My mother gave me a hug and slipped a pearl handled shiv into my back pocket.

"Give him one stab for me, son, and make sure to give it a good twist,"

Bother looked on, the hollows where his eyes would have been half-closed in sadness.

We boarded the ketch. I slung my backpack over my shoulder and shimmied down the ropes. Billybones followed, an arsenal of weaponry clattering beneath his clothing. I manned the rudder and Billybones managed the sail. The lapping waves rapidly created distance between us and our ship. It wasn't long until the ketch caught its first hurtle of wind and ol' Rusty was soon another memory swallowed by the horizon.

We sped along at a good clip, Billybones finessing the sail. He would pull the rigging tight, let up some slack and then tightened again, getting every pull the summer wind would offer. We countered our weight with each swell that threatened, cutting alongside the waves then up and over them as the sail filled.

The once three charcoal down-strokes in the eastern skyline were now dark shadows of a once gallant schooner. Each side had two rows of cannons, twenty long between the amble hull and top deck. The back featured a bulbous captain's quarters, the ship's penthouse suite. The bow's figurehead was just a splintered shard, only the faintest suggestion that a feminine visage once toted high in the sky marking their way.

The ghost pirate ship was far less threatening in the harsh light of day. It was a wreck that had forgotten to sink into the sea's netherworld. What was once sails were worm eaten and wind shorn, mere tatters flapping on worn rigging, fluttering as lifeless as the ship's occupants. The outside of the hull was equally abused by time. Boards were buckled, pulling away in shards from its main supports. Still the relic remained belligerently afloat.

Despite its decrepit condition, the ship still held threat. It looked by all accounts abandoned but its gullet held evil just waiting for the sun to lose its shine. When the sun was tampred out like a spent candle, the ship would awaken to feed its pirate lust, feasting on everything honest and good.

Now with the sun high in the sky, the ship lay dormant. Save for the tired timber of the ghost ship groaning with each large crest against its bow, silence ruled. The bay of windows that latticed the port bow showed no glimmer of activity within. As we rode closer it was apparent that each square of glass had been painted opaque from within. Some of the blacked out panes were streaked, clear glass still visible. No shadows danced behind them.

We both knew the ship was a liar, a snare set. With all the telepathic unity the messed-with-Manifest club possessed, were also bestowed with a keen sense of smell. It wasn't a blind man's awareness of the nuance of lavender and the toxicity of ammonia. Our heightened awareness could smell out the undead. That sounds a bit too *Night of the Living Dead*, correction, we became aware of the presence of what was but is no longer. Is that *undead* enough for you? The more the moss of green memory encased it, the deeper the stench. With each memory the stench grew more repugnant than the last. The odor wafting in from the ghost ship darker still; brine and bad news.

We traversed closer to contemplate our broadsiding of the vessel. We were close enough to weigh our options yet a good enough distance to schooner away from a rally of cannon fodder was sighted quickly changing our initial intent.

We made for an unlikely team. I squatted in the back of the ketch navigating while Billybones held court in the center. He paid more attention to a length of rope that he tied into an ornate knot than he did our progress. Every now and again, he would peer out over the ghost ship and mutter a random command.

"Starboard ho! Tac back, mate!"

The more I manned the rudder, the less he felt compelled to interject his commands. That was just fine with me.

I needed his prompts from time to time for I was too busy contemplating my plan. Billybones for Sandy; I get the girl, Him gets the treasure and Billybones gets what's coming to him.

The beauty of it all was that Billybones had agreed to it... hook, line and sinker. Alone on the ghost ship he could more than fend for himself. He was a Swiss Army knife of pirate armaments, always a shiv or a short arms within an arm's length. He could hold his own against 'cussers and cutlass.

Never underestimate the greed of a pirate. It was common knowledge to all who had been *manifested* that the treasure of the Wydah, the largest ever to be lost in these waters, was back to its rightful place; hiding within the coastal shelf of the South Shore. All Billybones and the Pirate Thief needed to do was become confidantes and write up a new Articles between them and the undead crew. By combining their knowledge, green, crystal and present, they could claim the bounty.

Oh yeah, and Sandy and I sail off into the sunset... and, scene.

Pirates dream big. What if they could acquire *all* treasure? Sure, a human pirate map and a green memory bloodhound like Billybones would insure success acquiring the lost Wydah booty, but only The Manifest would give them the power to not only turn back time, but change it. That surely trumps what Billybones brings to the table.

Sure, it was a game of Russian roulette, a gun passed back and forth and fired at one's temple, six chambers with only one packing lead. Spin... click. Spin... click. Spin...BLAM!" If you were already undead then what would be the harm, become *more undead?* What's the worst that could happen? Everything else around joins you in suffering yet never quite dying? Misery, like miserable pirates, loves company.

The Manifest must never be in the possession of Him. As much as I cared for Sandy, it would be a deal breaker. Sitting in that boat in the shadow of the ghost ship I understood why my mother so heartlessly dismissed my Ryan's passing. Albeit unknowing, he crossed a line and paid the price. Some things are bigger than one man.

That was why the cursed book was safety squirreled away among Bess' possessions. She was a proper guardian. Having joined the manifested, she knew its potential. It would take an army of mooncussers to pry that ultimate treasure from her hands. She had armed herself with weapons far more lethal than a chimney shovel and a broom and was itching to use them. There would be hell to pay.

Billybones stared at his most recent knot, looking down at it quizzically.

"Gots yer *Ashley's,* mate?" he stated more than questioned. The outline of the large book protruded against the canvas of my knapsack in a rectangular bulge. As was my habit all summer long, I didn't go anywhere without it.

"Sure thing, captain, or should I call you admiral. I mean, with Capt'n Jack being a captain and all?" I wanted to add Billybones to my choices of name calling but I refrained.

"Not one fer titles, jus fer merit. Hand'r over, I wants to check me knot 69. You remember that monkey's fist, eh mate? Something doesn't seem quite right."

I slipped the backpack off my shoulder and unzipped the bag without apprehension. The inside reeked of the foulest green. The ghost ship was a field of poppies in comparison.

Billybones snatched the bag out of my hands with a bear swipe of his arm and reached inside for the book. It was wrapped in a jolly roger, just as I had at the Rusty Anchor. The book he pulled out was larger and thicker than I remembered, taking up most of the inside of the bag. Then I panicked realizing that the prized book stowed away in Bess' belongings was my page worn copy of *Ashley's Book of Knots*. That would mean that the book in Billybones' hand was...

'*The Manifest!* my inner voice shouted until it was hoarse. Everything in my world shifted for an instant; the expression on Billybones' face, the quake of the tide, even the deck boards of the pirate ship as I broadcast my revelation to the heavens.

The Manifest was a living thing in his hand. It writhed beneath the cloth of the Jolly Roger like an eel in a canvas sack. It took both of his hands to wrestle it back into the safe confines of my backpack.

"Arr, what's this ace ye be hidin' up your sleeve... boy?"

Gambling on a pirate ship was answerable by death and not of the pretty kind. Reasons were plenty. It bred unrest amongst the crew, especially in those who preyed upon those with a lack of skill. Gambling offered a distraction that was contrary to a crew's singularity of purpose. To gamble, one would need something to wager and if you were pegged as a mark, losing time and time again, you would need to get more coin for the table. The end result, the crew would thieve amongst themselves and nothing was more taboo than pirates pirating pirates.

I was being accused of playing a game of chance with our very lives. More important in the eyes of Billybones, now standing up over me, I had broken the covenant of The Articles... *his* articles.

"Ya don't want ya lady faire at all do ya, boy? Ya got more pirate than puritan pumpin' in yer veins, to be sure."

I made guppy half breaths, struggling for words. The knotted rope was snapped back to a thin white line wrapped tight between Billybones hands.

Billybones, also with a loss for words, fumed over what he saw as the ultimate betrayal.

"*You* hornswoggle me?! You hornswoggle *me*! I'll show just how a hornswogglin' goes down if that's the next lesson you need to be learnin'. Perhaps I'll teach you how to plead for your miserable life, you... you sniveling snit... naa... I'll save that for our host."

With that he brought his captain's Boisen Pipe to his mouth and blew one high angry tone out over the lapping surf followed by another tone, an octave lower sounding like a melodic growl. His other hand was placed under his topcoat against his pant leg. I was sure his forefinger was caressing a flint lock.

The ghost ship showed signs of a half-life. The abandoned deck creaked and then I heard the rusty tumbler of a lock turn. A heavy steel door slid aside as the ship's crypt was opened.

Out from beneath the belly of the beast *He* came, The Pirate Thief, slowly floating on air in a regal procession. Over his head he held up a large umbrella, pill-shaped, longer than wide, casting the pirate's upper body in shadow. It was lacquered black with tar protecting him from the sun's rays, allowing his face to maintain a physical form.

His face was a failed attempt at aristocracy. The consistency of his skin was akin to a mooncusser's; a bag of brine and bone. For vanity's sake, the thief had blotted over it a pale makeup, pallor of grey encrusted his face. It would flake away in his face's wrinkles unmasking the pulsating sick beneath. A pencil thin mustache, trained to curl at each end by wax long turned yellow, moved contrary to the breeze. It was more a crustacean's feelers than a proper man's beard.

On top of his head, beneath the gay plumage and ample folds of felt was a real hell toupee. It was a rat trap of blonde and silver, the locks held together by centuries of applications of powder and spit. Two crimson smudges were rubbed on each of his cheeks where the living's blood would blush the skin.

Perched upon his shoulder where any respectable pirate would have a parrot with calico plumage was the remains of a death bird. The vulture skeleton hung its head down in servitude to its lord. It was all bleached bone save its head which also basked in shadow. Its head was all beak and feathers with all the life of road kill. What was once wings rustled as it floated to the deck on top of its master, the sound of bone on bone, a macabre wind chime.

The Pirate Thief stood on the top deck looking down on us. From his waist down, the glare of the afternoon sun unleashed damage. From the lavish buckle of his belt on down, he was all tendrils of black ink twisting and tangling in the wind. He hovered over us, squid legs dangling in mid-air.

The Pirate Thief cleared his throat in and addressed us in a gargle of seawater.

"Ahoy, and what have we here, mon ami?" He pulled out a delicately-laced handkerchief to his nose as if the fresh sea air was as vile to him as his guilt stink was to us.

While I looked up at my public-enemy-number-one, Billybones swung the knotted rope around my leg and pulled tight, efficiently hog tying me.

"Its not just learnin' th' knots, boy, its learnin' how t' use'm," he cackled as I fell against the back of the ketch. He smiled so wide I could see his back molars. "Oh, and note to self... there's no knot 69, greenie, I knew all along."

"The pirate thief", I said in awe, looking up at the massive ship before us, "Him."

"The name's Commandeer LaBouche, Phillippe LaBouche to my allies."

Billybones gave the other pirate a tip of his tricorner hat. "A present, for you, LaBouche, sorry I didn't wrap it."

"Please, Mr. Smythe, we go back too far, you may call me LeBouche. You still haven't lost your spunk, Reginald" he replied raising his hand to his own wide brimmed hat but stopping before giving a reciprocal bow.

The Thief otherwise known as Him called to me from the inside my head so Sandy, Bess, my mom, Billybones... all of the manifested could hear.

'Now you, Romeo, O Romeo, finally my latest acquisition, I just might be your undoing. You may call me Death.'

His reptilian eyes smoldered red save for the faintest black slivers of dilated iris. One eye winked at me with malicious intent.

Then I heard a thud, inside and out... pain, perhaps stars, then darkness.

Before my world faded to black I heard the pirate's salutations, both cautious but consolatory.

"Drinks are on you!" said Billybones.

"I am on the wagon of eternity; have one for me!" LaBouche replied.

"Don't mind if I do." A cork popped, more stars and another thud, my head slamming against the bottom of the boat.

Whenever it was that I finally came to, seconds, hours, days; my world was still cloaked in black. The rot of past evils hung thick in the air, a musty fur that you could taste in your mouth. My quarters were quite close, walls of wooden board only inches from my face and the back of my head. I figured I must have been inside the back walls of steerage. My legs were restrained by leg irons, iron bars pressing against bruised ankles, my arms were bound behind my back by a crack knotsman's work, tight enough to make my shoulder sockets ache. I inched my hands to the back pocket of my cargo pants only to discover that I was thoroughly stripped of any weapons of rescue.

I wanted to call out but my own bandana was pulled between my lips. The only voice I had was on the inside and I knew, just as Sandy did, that LaBouche would hear my every plea. So I stood propped up like luggage in storage; mute.

My eyes, being human as opposed to that of a nocturnal animal such as LaBouche, took a while to adjust to the lack of light. My imagination played tricks, animating black on black. Time passed but still little of my surroundings were painted in.

I was not alone between the walls. Objects in steerage shifted their weight in time with the rocking of the ship. The occasional scurrying of a bilge rat underfoot became less of a panic once I learned human flesh was no contest for brown sugar and grog. There was something else, deep within the walls, far from my night vision. I could hear its staggered breath muffled by the dark. It was larger than vermin and very much alive. Whatever it was, it was trapped like me.

Hours passed like days, finally there was light, just a shard of muted amber only inches from my face. Between the boards, a round knot of wood long ago broke free from the wall. The hole where it once resided was just large enough for one of my eyes to peer through. Everything on the other side of the wall was bathed in a warmer tone of black, shining like daylight to my light deprived eyes.

Then I saw a play of shadows that matched the vibration of weight shifting just beyond the wall. Life, or something just short of it, was only feet from where I was captive. I tried to focus on the far corner of the adjacent wall. The fuzzy shadows bled together but I could make out a seated figure in a chair. Its head rocked forward and back, an arm reached into the air, then back. As the figure leaned forward I could see a long fall of hair. It was a woman.

'*Sandy!*' I thought before I could suppress my inner voice. The shadow quaked and the silhouette of the figure sewing in a rocking chair turned its head my way. She knew better than to answer.

She must have had grown accustomed to sitting there, hours at a time, watching the blue surf through the glass scraped clean of paint, sitting, patiently awaiting rescue. What a knight in shining armor I had turned out to be.

"Mademoiselle Ooo la la!"

The voice was not in my head. It played in the here and was now beside me in the dark. It was the evil triumvirate; pirate, undead and French. I looked back from my peephole to see LaBouche's rotting face inches from my own.

"Thought ya seen a pirate, boy? Stranger things have happened... and will," he laughed, mocking the soundtrack of my nightmares while his mascot pecked at my hair.

"Have ya said bonjour to your bunky, young pirate Byrne?" He took a wooden safety match from the back of his ear just under his putrid wig and struck its sulfur tip across the jagged wallboard. A flame shone blinding orange. LaBouche revealed a lantern in his other hand and proceeded to light its wick. The hands closest to the flames sheared away into ribbons of black, tangled enough to keep the lantern raised high.

In the far end of the eaves of the ship was a large object hanging from the ceiling with a damp woolen cloth draped over it.

"Could you give me a hand with this," LaBouche quipped. "Pardon?" he giggled over my incapacity. After threatening to burn my cheek, LaBouche snuffed out the match on his hand without the slightest expression of pain. After hanging a lamp on one of the many iron hooks that adorned the ceiling, he reached over my head for the cloth that kept my cellmate covered. His green odor stung my eyes.

"Voila!" LaBouche pulled the blanket away with a magician's flair to reveal the debasement it shrouded. Hanging from the ceiling was a rusty cage, large enough for LaBouche's pet that flapped its dead bones beside him. Inside was a boy about my age, give or take a year. He was stuffed into the cage in a crouched position, unable to either sit or stand. His skin was a sallow grey enhanced by the sand and mud that filtered through the floorboards of the top decks and covered everything in steerage with a coat of ash.

Before him was an empty pewter plate decorated by smears of dried blood patterned by hungry hands. The boy startled, stared up at me, then at our captor, then back at the plate before him. There was no recognition in his eyes; nothing else existed in his world but the emptiness at his feet.

I knew him, or who he once was. He was Jose, a Scratcher, my brother's right hand man who always drove him around when Ryan wanted to sit shotgun.

"He is the dam-med." said LaBouche pronouncing the name with two syllables. "Say Bonjour, dammed!" he ordered Jose. "Sacre bleu! Cat got your tongue? Pardon?" he let out another of his unmanly giggles. "After his little run in with The Manifest, this little piggy just couldn't shut his mouth, so I did it for him."

I looked at Jose's mouth, now a misshapen gob without his tongue housed within. His eyes were cigarette burns, dark and recessed from his ongoing pain.

Labouche's laughter stopped. "I severed his tongue and fed it to him. Funny thing is, the ritual silences his inner voice as well! Who knew? Magnifique! I left the remains for him to feast on when he gets a bit peckish. "That's a good boy..." Labouche covered his rouge lips with one of his fancy handkerchiefs as he continued his debauched tittering. "... you've cleaned your plate."

LaBouche then pointed with the tangle of black eels that was his hand at the chest of my brother's former friend. His t-shirt was as soiled and stained as his plate. "Now, poor dammed be in a purgatory of his choosing; hunger wins over humanity. Ah, but he does have a way out. If he eats his own heart, his soul will be lost along with his bloodlust; the road to becoming a bygone begun."

A rush of ink wormed its way under and through Jose's shirt until all the black strands made a unified retreat tearing the shirt from his body.

"*X* marks the spot!" LaBouche whispered from behind lace.

LaBouche's handiwork hurt just to look at. Just below Jose's ribcage was a large Maltese cross carved into his flesh. It was the same wide cross one would see on a treasure map. The flesh that comprised the cross floated separate from the rest of his body over an open wound. It was held in place by crude stitching with cord used to mend sailcloth. The wound was fresh and wet, innards twitched behind the cord, easy access to the life muscle hiding beneath.

"He may resist the hunger, but it will always be there alongside his broken hopes and dreams. When he succumbs, with each bite he'll also digest all opinion and will," LaBouche whispered to me as if I was next. "Being a bygone is a painless way to not live real. Damned if you do, dammed if you don't."

LaBouche patted me on the shoulder with his broom hand of swirling ink. He extinguished the light with another strand, then slithered out of the recess in the back wall as quick as he came.

As darkness again swallowed all definition I could see the dammed's eyes close. His meditation ended in a banshee's wail as he clawed at damnation. I focused back on the room at the other side of the wall, trying my best to block out the sound of gnashing teeth and swallowed tears.

The leg irons had worn my ankles raw as I tried to maneuver my body to gain a better vantage point. Sandy's profile in shadow was not enough to reassure me of her safety. I needed to see her unharmed and safe or as safe as you can be on a ship of undead pirates. I shimmied and squinted, shimmy, squint, each time the hole in the wall offering me a new panorama.

My first view filled me with more fear that I had ever felt. It wasn't fear for my life; I had put that on the line the moment I teamed up with Billybones. It was the fear that I was already too late to save Sandy's.

Against the wall furthest from me was a skeleton hanging from the rafters. A decoupage of tanned skin stretched dry against the bones. It hung from the arms were tied behind the back. The body hung forward, the head tilted up in one last appeasement. A Victorian gown of water-stained satin hung on the husk of a woman who once was.

Was it Sandy? It couldn't have been more than a week since her abduction. How could it be? Still, in a world ripe with mooncussers and bygones, anything was possible. If it wasn't her, then it was a foreshadowing of what was in store for both of us.

With another corkscrew turn to my left, I could see to the left of the decomposed diva a fright of bygones swarming around a post of wood that was as thick as I was long. Chisels, mallets and files were busy whittling away anything that didn't resemble a goddess. It was early in their labors but I could already see a head with a cascade of curls, the contours of a female form, shoulders forward and arms back. A new figurehead for the ghost ship was materializing before my solitary eye.

Another shove to one side and I could feel the irons cut, drawing blood. The pain was worth it for there she was. In the corner of the room haloed by the blackened panels was Sandy, an obedient model in repose. The bygones combined the outstretched desperation of the cadaver for form and the beacon of life in Sandy as their reference for the figurehead's life-like beauty.

The young woman sitting patiently was not the girl of my daydreams. LeBouche had transformed Sandy into a courtesan from yesteryear. She was snugly dressed in velvet to her waist. The bone stays of her bodice had her fill out the dress voluptuously. From her empire waist down was a waterfall of petticoats hoops. Where LaBouche was a sideshow clown, Sandy was romantic perfection; her face, alabaster white, a doll with scarlet accenting her lips and cheeks. She had just walked off the page of the memoir of Marie Antoinette. Sandy's was the face that sailed ships, a face that men died for.

I held my tongue, feeling fortunate to still have one, when a guest came to visit her cabin. I could hear the door open. Bygones scattered every which way, all fighting for the exit. All I could see was Sandy. Her face rose up from her needlework and her face grew paler than the chalk and powder plastered on her visitor.

"Ma Cherie! How you say, how does this day find you, my sweetness?"

Silence echoed back.

"Ah, I look at you and... words escape me. Let me see... the moon, la luna, it pales in comparison."

The amber light reflected on all of the fancy adornments decorating the room. Crystal, silver and beveled mirrors refracted the light making LeBouche waver between real and ethereal, bringing to question whether he was in the room at all or just a manifestation of our collective fear.

"Amour... love, it need not be a fickle thing, you know." His tendrils for arms formed a ball and the gathered fist struck the wall that separated us.

"You, you may love *him...*" Another slam, the impact knocking me away from my view. "... but it be not *love* love, that which stands the test of time. One can learn to love, yes*?* Oui?"

Sandy winced at the mere suggestion of such an abominable pairing. Still, she appeared emotionless. Putting her sewing aside, she looked up as if giving LeBouche her undivided attention. Unable to keep her feelings to herself, Sandy spoke back to him. Each word spoken was tentative and measured, trying not to offend.

"You can love how I look. You can love the scent of my hair. You can love the voice of the strings as I play. You can love whatever memory I keep alive for you, but you can never attest love for anything that does not love you back and dare call it love, sir."

Now it was her turn to be answered by silence.

"I... I mean no offence, mademoiselle. Your words are, well, beyond your years. My time has long ago been spent; to moi, love be but the salutation at the end of correspondence. Alas, love is for the young and the living. I have neither to offer and you deserve nothing less."

He turned to leave. His vulture closed up its bony wings and hung its head lower than usual. I couldn't believe that Sandy actually felt pity for the monster but she called him back.

"Shall I play for you, sir? You say it soothes you somehow." She reached for the ship's fiddle she kept by the side of the rocker, her firearm against the undead around her.

"To be taken away in the arms of Orpheus, to be taken away from all this, ah the sheer bliss... but no, not tonight for I have news to tell... news of amour, yes!"

LeBouche poured Sandy a goblet of what I was sure was not lemonade.

"Relax, child, and listen, there be a courtier in your midst."

Sandy's eyes darted to the knothole I was looking through.

"Not *him*! The boy is history and the sooner he is green to you the better." LeBouche spat, momentarily losing his sickening sweet delivery. "This is your life now, embrace it! He, your soon to be betrothed; he is my quartermaster. Never you fear! He be not mooncusser, bygone or dammed... none of our ilk. He is of the living and alive he is whenever I speak your name, m'lady. Please, take drink for me, I miss it so," LeBouche coaxed. Sandy smartly kept the glass from her lips.

As LeBouche spoke of her suitor's infatuation he stroked the wooden suggestion of Sandy the bygones had slaved over.

"Sins of the flesh are not mine to be had. For me, to love is to ache, the only pain I can *actually* feel. I need a vessel for such desires... to satiate my longing for you, my sweet. So shall be my quartermaster."

One black wisp after another flitted between the carved curls of the figurehead as if the locks were Sandy's.

"We will have you; in that there is no doubt. He is my Cyrano and my Torquemadda, my romancer and inquisitioner. Pray for love, dear one. Rejection can be so bittersweet."

I held my breath hoping that Sandy had the where-with-all to let it go and not continue to spout off about her favorite subject; romance. She tapped her darning needles loudly then put them in her lap in false servitude. Holding back the words she dare not think or speak, she spoke in a whisper.

"Will that be all, sir?"

"Oui."

"Au revoir, monsieur?"

"Au revoir, mademoiselle."

With that he slid away from her sight; thus ended Sandy's worst mystery date ever.

We both waited until we could no longer hear him slithering on deck. All we could hear was the clock in her quarters ticking away the seconds along with the lap of the waves on the other side of painted glass.

Sandy picked up the violin, a fiddle by any other name, but when she played it, it was a violin. She plucked at a string or two, adjusting them as close to in tune as its age and disrepair would allow. Raising the bow the horsehair deftly touched the strings. A lullaby swept through the room, a sound so sweet it cleansed the air of the filth for as long as the melody lingered.

All pirates were a sucker for song, especially some fiddle playing. My inner pirate was no exception. It was true that music soothes the savage beast within. The music she was playing had a different purpose. It was meant as distraction so the two of us could talk.

"Is this how you propose to save me, Ty?"

"Good to see you, too! Please, please don't start..."

"See you, hello? You're tied up, aren't you? Aren't you?? I could fend off these goons better with these needles here, couldn't I?"

"Sandy, no... well yes.. *presently...* but I have a plan."

"And how 's that going for you so far ,plan master Byrne?"

"I, I, I got hornswoggled!"

"What's hornswoggled??"

"I... don't... know, but it was done to me and done good."

"If we don't think and think fast that's the best darn thing that going to happen to you all day."

The whole while the violin played on, Sandy never missing a beat. Her playing grew faster and faster as we argued.

"Do you have anything sharp? You got needles, scissors, a knife?"

"They aren't afraid of knives. I've seen them stab each other for sport."

"I'm tied up, remember? There's a hole. If I can lift my hands high enough..."

"Scissors, I've got scissors. Where's the hole??"

"Follow my voice ! La la la la la... " I started singing along with her playing. The violin was a calliope, spinning faster and faster, a vortex of mad clowns and terrified horse heads.

"La la la la la, cold, la la la, warmer warmer, la la la la, red hot, doc!"

The music stopped.

"Here ?" Sandy asked as she stuck her pink tipped finger into the knothole practically blinding me in the process.

"Watch it! There's something in here with me that would love to nibble on your little digits. Open the scissors, now slip one of the blades in ..."

Just as we began to implement the great escape, we began heard heavy footfalls trouncing towards Sandy's cabin. The stride was slow and confident. Along with the sound of sole leather slapping the deck was the sound of wood being sheared like saw blades against timber. The grind slowed between steps and then sped up again with the gait. The closer the footsteps came, the louder the sound of wood being torn asunder became.

Then nothing; silence paid another visit. Sandy took the scissors out from the knot hole and fumbled to get the fiddle back into position but she was too nervous to get the proper finger placement.

The door knob rattled but the unlocked door did not open.

"Bon jourrr? Phillippe??"

There were three authoritative slams on the door.

"Apres vous! The door's open." Sandy walked to open it. She turned the knob and it swung open revealing her suitor, hands full.

I could hear her gasp but had repositioned myself to cut the ropes free and my face was far from the knothole. I could hear the visitor step inside, all heavy boots and scraping. Sandy's feet shuffled backwards until I heard her fall into the rocker.

I twisted to reposition myself for a view of her visitor. The first thing I saw was his shadow. It was LaBouche in miniature, from the feathered hat to the oversized epaulets on his ill-fitting dress coat. He stepped towards her, almost stumbling in oversized boots. The splintering of wood followed each step.

I again repositioned myself and looked again. All I could see was the table that ran the length of the room, its surface a richly oiled dark wood. Running across its surface was a harried line, a blonde gouge across the tabletop, curls of wood and sawdust lining the path. I followed the damage along the table until the source was in my sight.

It was a hook. Go figure, a man with a hook in a pirate ship? The hook was of polished brass and sparkled sharply in the amber light. The tip ate through the wooden veneer without effort. The business end of the hook was soldered onto a similarly polished sleeve that had a circle of grommets embedded into what I could make out was a human arm. Cords of rigging laced through holes in the metal sleeve and the owner's bruised flesh. His other hand held a map.

"You, you, you're my suitor?" Sandy stuttered recognition.

I slipped in my own blood that flowed from my ankles that had been gnawed at with every turn of my body. My head fell forward into the wall between Sandy, her guest and myself. *Thud!*

Sandy tried hard to draw the phantom's attention from the commotion behind the wall. "That, that, that was just mice, place is just crawling with them. A drink? Pirates like their drink, *pirate!*"

As I got back on my feet, I saw the phantom spread the map across the defaced table. It hit the table with considerable weight, a damp unfurling as the phantom's hook spread it across the wood. Looking at the hook, past where its edge had carved wood, I noticed that the brass was stained with red. The map the hook rested on was an uneven parchment, the back of the illustration still moist from being skinned. Somewhere in the recesses of the ship, Billybones was in great need of a Band-aid.

In spite of the brutal act he had just recently perpetrated, the visitor seemed quite unsure of himself. His good hand rubbed nervously the curve of his hook as if wringing a hand that once dangled there. In Sandy's presence, he was a toothless tiger.

He finally spoke. "Let's dispense with the French, little lady, I've always been a bit of a slow learner. All the ladies in the house like bling, yo!"

The phantom waved his hook in the air as he nodded maliciously at Sandy, insisting on her participation. More annoyed than afraid she complied without an iota of enthusiasm.

"Yo?" I mouthed silently.

The phantom pointed to the map nervously.

"Here, here be the bling." He brought his bloody hook down on Billybones' tattooed collage. "I've got me a new crew and one bitchin' ride. I will get the bling, which means ipso facto... I get you, beach girl... word."

He attempted to cross his arms but his newly attached hook made his signature stance impossible.

He then rushed away from the table out of my sight. I heard his hook tear wood as it cross the wall between us, moving closer.

The knot hole suddenly became all eyeball and anger.

"And, I have very special plans for you, little brother. Arrgg and word to our mother!"

Then with my inner voice, I yelled for all who can hear words unspoken, one word and one word only. The word was Ryan.

Chapter 18

LEVIATHON

"Think you've seen pirates, bro! I'll show you pirates!"

My brother's words echoed through the dark labyrinth of walkways under deck. I could hear the stomping and tripping of Ryan in his over-sized boots as he left Sandy's quarters and went back up the hall into the belly of the ship.

Muffled orders were given, subordinates did his will. Crates of provisions crashed to the floor as the mooncussers burrowed their way towards me. I smelt them closing in long before I felt the boney fingers clutch and grab. Securing purchase, they dragged me topside by my heels like a waterlogged duffel bag.

The blinding darkness lifted. Night had fallen, the sky, up to no good. The sun exited leaving a blanket of grey. A waning full moon replaced the sun. Soon enough, you could see your hand in front of your face.

My brother lacked the savior faire of his pirate captain. His wrong-footed mentality was contrary to the eloquence of his wardrobe. He had exchanged baggy-assed pants and backwards ball caps for pantaloons and plumage; he was once dressed clown-street, now his attire was clown-pirate. He didn't feel right in his new skin either. Ryan awaited me, his boot tapping and his hand nervously buffing his hook to a brilliant sheen. He then gave a lumberjack's swing at the main mast, his hook pelting chips of frustration into the air.

I love my brother, as does my mom. Heck, I was going to battle Billybones to the death just to avenge his life. Yes, he was a pain in the posterior, and yes, his world revolved solely around him, but we shared blood, and it was good blood. The more he acted out, the more the goodness in him struggled with the bad. Being hog tied before him I had to rely on his good side winning out.

Ryan stood before me, the brunt of all jokes. My predicament, however, was far from a laughing matter. I was flanked by three mooncussers on each side. In the black and white world of mooncast, they had regained their physical form. The skeletons, sewn together with seaweed, towered over me. Each mooncusser sported an array of pistols and cutlass that clattered against bare bone as they marched me to the feet of their quartermaster.

The mooncussers were obligated to obey. They were all *on the account* as they say in pirate-speak. They were as devote to The Articles as were the crew of 'ol Rusty were. LeBouche had appointed Ryan his quartermaster. The crew had no other choice but to second it and stand by the decision rank and file. To waver from the will of the ship and its captain's wishes would be tantamount to treason.

There was another even more important reason why they bent to Ryan's will. After Jose's decent into the realm of the bygones, Ryan was the only living pirate on their crew. That fact alone did not invoke loyalty, quite the opposite. It would breed jealousy, foreshadowing a grisly accident in Ryan's near future.

The mooncussers realized that their quartermaster was the only living soul on the ship that hadn't changed The Manifest.

Mooncussers were hard-wired for treasure. The Manifest was the key to all treasures, perhaps the key to unlocking the shackles of their own damnation. Only Ryan could turn that key, so Ryan was appointed quartermaster and his orders obeyed.

My processional in the arms of the mooncussers crossed the stern. I was able to look out over the outside word for the first time in days. The moon sparkled on the crests of a turbulent sea. Waves lapped the upper deck with saliva of foam. The ebony sea was alive, a mesh of thrashing tails and twisting scales.

'*Shark*', I thought-spoke, broadcasting fact, not fear. It was meant as plural, shark, as in; 'we have shark in these parts'. We were awash with a threat of shark. I say threat as one might say; 'a gaggle of geese' or 'a pace of asses'.

It was the most unlikely assortment of aquatic predators ever found in our waters. There were bull sharks, a nasty breed that tends to worm their way inland to breed in fresh water marshes. They are a most dangerous shark. They don't attack because of hunger or to protect their young. They fight because they can, and they do it well. Whatever they encounter, be it a tin can, a school of fish or a baby's arm, it's all the same in their murderous eyes. Don't let their size fool you. Give me *Moby Dick* and a sturdy harpoon over a bull in the shallows any day.

Not that I mean to discredit the great white. A large cloud drifted by deep beneath the dark surface of the ocean; indeed a great white may have come to join the party. They can grow up to three thousand pounds and still manage to lift themselves out of the water when attacking. They have been sighted snatching seals in their jowls from rocky perches, then submerging back into the cover of the waves. That would be a sight to see... just not on that evening.

Along with bulls that should have been hugging the coastline and the ghost of a white, I spotted a hammerhead that by all rights should have been foraging far south of this coast. The problem with hammerheads, outside of the freakish placement of their eyes, is their number. If you see one hammer, you see a hundred. They travel in packs, not a rouge among them.

"Chomp." My brother whispered.

"I walk, but if I live, the girl goes free."

Ryan tipped the foppish hat on his head back up his large, freckled forehead. It was equivalent to corkscrewing a baseball hat backwards.

"I don't negotiate with pirates."

"Have you taken a look in a mirror lately? You should be advertising rum at the Cove packet."

"We are privateers. That means, we call dibs on anything that floats in these parts, by letter of the law."

"A pirate by another other name is still..."

"I... we are not pirates!"

The doors to the captain's quarters overlooking the main deck swung open stopping my brother mid-threat. A freshly powdered Lebouche stood between them, arms outstretched as if in mid-yawn.

"I prefer the title corsair, more an air of pageantry, more *j'ne se que!*."

He sashayed to the railing on the two solid feet the evening had restored. His delicate blouse willowed in the sea breeze.

"Carte blanche is what we have, what's yours, is ours."

An angry voice joined the exchange. It bellowed through the threadbare sails. The very bones housed in mooncusser skin were shaken by its timbre. It was Billybones, tired and surly.

Billybones had been hung high and dry above the mizzenmast in a gibbot cage, a device of high seas torture. Iron bars bent into an outline of human form kept the prisoner within upright. It was an open air coffin. After a stint of no food and drink and prolonged exposure the condemned were left to die. There the body would decompose; a reminder to all the price of treachery. Billybones arms were already blankets of broken scabs where there once was skin. The open air invited a host of parasites to dine on the exposed flesh. On Billybones arms, where the Wydah map once held residence, gnats circled the wounds, landing to feed amongst a swirl of maggots. LeBouche's vulture licked its black tongue as it swept down checking how much fight was still in his eventual meal.

LeBouche left Billybones in the gibbot without a gag. He wanted to treasure every blasphemy that would pass the pirate's lips, every plea, until his last breath.

"Just who... bequeathed ye with yer letters eh, a crown long dethroned, a monarch no longer on this mortal coil? You sir, are a privateer of retired privilege, all 'n all, lower than the lowliest of pirates. You are a mere shadow of a man who holds no claim to his own world."

LeBouche ignored his captive's diatribe.

"Bon jour, monsieur Smythe! A tip o the hat to you, my guest eh?"

LeBouche crouched down on one knee, his arm extended straight by his side in a flamboyant bow. His other hand, instead of clutching his hat, grabbed the back of his head and, with a sickening slurp of brine, his neck pulled away from his body.

His painted lips clenched, bitterly pursed in a kabuki pucker. The stem of his spine peaked out from the lace cuff of his blouse as LeBouche rose his head in front of the rest of his body like a lantern.

"How you say... quartermaster Ryan?..."

"Payback be a bitch... non??" my brother regained his impish smile.

I finally knew the identity of Him. It was the same specter that the bygones mimicked in my room. I recalled from the pages of The Manifest, the tale of a captain betrayed. He was the remnants of man Billybones decapitated after surrender. He stood before us now, bigger than life, hell bent on righting a wrong. If that was his soul motivation Lebouche was indeed more corsair than pirate, Billybones, in turn, less of a victim. He was getting his comeuppance compliments of re-dealt fate.

"Arr, tis you. I regret not a tad. I gave yer men freedom. Never again would they slave under the words of the wealthy, the very people that starved their homelands and banished them to sea. They could decree their own providence and say proudly with their last gasp, I am my own man."

"No king, but a ship's captain, which shadow's longer, eh?"

"Blades do cross the loyal, only those who betray the common will. If that be a pirate, then all free men be so."

LeBouche returned his head to its lofty perch, adjusting its placement like one would fashion a hat's brim. As he primed he continued addressing Billybones who was shaking the bars that bound him.

LeBouche looked up at his caged guest dangling in the wind. "Oui Smythe. My pardon, I see you are the epitome of a free man."

Ryan wiped tears of laughter from his face, practically blinding himself with his hook in the process.

"Yo, yo, yo! Billybone's been served corsair-style!"

Ryan pointed his hook up at his captive and gave the cage a shake.

"That's what my bro calls you, know that? Billybones, haw!"

His laughter stopped as he turned his attention back to me. "Your turn bro, and trust me, your punishment will not be so charitable. Fetch me the plank!"

"And what's my crime? Piracy?? When? Where? Against whom? I am as much a pirate as you are."

"I'm a... a privateer, yo!"

"Are not!"

"Am too!"

Lebouche rose his white gloved hand before him to stop the brotherly squabbling. His vulture swept to his forearm like a hawk, its head bobbing approval of the impending cruelty.

"I am the captain of this ship, its judge and jury." He looked at me, through me, looking for the inner pirate cowering within. "You did pirate The Manifest from my rotting pet Smythe there, but that was more a present to me so for that act, you are absolved. Thank you for your cavalier effort."

His sockets stared hard, as if peering into a crystal ball.

"... There it is, your true crime!"

A smile then stretched across the rouge of his lips, the white pancake on his face creasing into a dozen alabaster grins. Deep in the hollow of my eyes the thief pirate saw my inner pirate.

"When you justified the death of your own brother for a crime you were just as guilty of. Bad, bad pirate. Tssk, tssk."

I hung my head, guilty as charged. Ryan looked at Lebouche and then back at me with hurt in his eyes.

"You, you were *glad* I was dead, bro?"

"Not that simple, we thought you messed with the big book, The Manifest."

"*We?*"

"Mom and I, we though you unleashed all *this* into the world..."

"Ma too? Glad I was dead? Harsh yo!"

LeBouche was stoking Ryan's inner pirate which swelled even without the influence of The Manifest. After mulling over my pirate intent, LeBouche made his ruling.

"Alas, I must admit I consider myself a connoisseur of judicial punishment... and in keeping with the protocol of my ship and its articles, I must support my quartermaster's decree. Walking the plank it shall be. Free his arms and keep your cutlass close. He will walk the plank to his death by the volition of his own two feet."

Ryan obeyed his captain, unlocked the irons from my legs and roughly tore at my binds with his hook.

"Ha! A fair fight, would a pirate ever do that?"

Billybones heckled the decision. "

"Arrg, the plank! That's what yellow-bellied pirates do to their most feared enemies; have'm walk the walk they never could take themselves."

"Enough! He walks to his death. If he defies, he dies."

"What if he dies not, the girl goes free, agreed? And, to make the soup more binding, your quartermaster must take the short walk as well, to prove who the true leader is. This isn't a pirate ship, what's the harm in a little wagerin'?"

"There shall be no godless gambling on my ship" Lebouche protested out of formality. He paused, scratched at his yellowed wig and considered the wager.

"Your wager however does suit me well. One must be tried to be true, the weaker dies in disgrace and to the victor..."

He drew back the curtains of his quarters to reveal Sandy, head down giving the smallest curtsey. She looked up at me for a second as the mooncussers clawed away my remaining binds.

"... a rightful place by my side, the mademoiselle by his."

"That's the spirit, Lebouche! To the victor, goes the spoils"

"I knew my decision would please a pirate such as you, Smythe."

"I am no more a pirate than sleep be to yer waking hours, Phillippe."

"That's LeBouche!

The sea, full of piss and vinegar, gave that ghost ship a stiff jolt. The ship's bell rang without a pull of rope. Billybones cringed at the omen; one would die on this night. All on deck bent down to keep balance. My brother pushed me towards the stern's railing where a long board stretched out over the turbulent sea.

"Its supper time! You! Pirate! Time to take a short walk!"

Billybones had just enough wiggle room inside the confines of the gibbot to pull his compass from its hiding place and toss it down to me.

Without thinking, I stepped forward to catch it. My sudden movement was met with the business ends of mooncusser swords.

Four skulls grinned beneath slime waiting for me to make another ill conceived move.

Billybones called out over my captors.

"When you win and win you will, remember, heroes like cowboys, come from the west."

Lebouche offered his hand to Sandy. She raised her hand to meet his as obediently as the captain's dead bird. They neared the railing overlooking the undead crew on the main deck, bygones served as pages, priming the two's garments as they walked. Each mooncusser gave an obligatory nod as their leader and his escort passed by.

Another flank of mooncussers dragged out the plank and slid half its length over the agitated sea. Encouraged by the cold insistence of four long blades, I took my first step onto the plank. I had been here before. I'm not sure what was scarier, the soup of hungry scales below or staring into the dark unknown of the Anchor's pit. Lebouche crossed beside me. His undead stink coupled with perfume stung my eyes. He turned around, back to the railing, to watch the festivities. Lebouche tilted his head, his glowing sockets staring blankly as they tried to relish my fear as I walked towards what would surely be my death.

As I looked down at the ocean I gave LeBouche no satisfaction, my face remained devoid of any of the elevating panic I struggled to keep at bay. The water beneath raged at full boil. Shark pierced the surface, all teeth and stomachs. Fins circled and collided blindly. As my Vans met the last of the wood, the commotion subsided. The lashing of scale against scale was replaced with a belch from the ocean's floor, a rush of bubbles rising.

All eyes were on me as I prepared to take my final step. They didn't see the shadow beneath the surf take form. Confusion was all that could read on my face. Suddenly something surfaced along the arch of the ship's hull. It was a leg, dark brown and ornery. It shot out of the water, as thick around as the main mast and stretched skyward nearly as high. Then as quick as it emerged, it retreated back into the ocean. With it went a good section of the ship's railing that tore from its moorings.

It was the revenge of the sea, nature turning on us for all of the warping of time that messed up its evolution. It was either that or it was just an extremely bad day to have to walk the plank.

Sandy cringed and fell backwards in her antique heels. With no rail to secure her, she lost balance and fell forward. I dodged the bite of a mooncusser's blade and stepped back up the plank to catch her. My hand met hers and I held her firm as she righted herself.

Lebouche, not having a hero's instinct to save a damsel in distress, saw my sudden movement as a threat against him. Fearing attack, he stepped back in his own inappropriate heels towards where the railing once stood. There was another eruption and another leg tore through the surface of the ocean. The end of this leg wielded an enormous claw, akin to that of a lobster, armored in shell, big enough to block out the moon as it rose from the sea.

Lebouche sockets were on me, he never saw it coming. The claw opened, teeth as jagged as the ocean's shoreline. I pulled Sandy close to me as the shadow closed down. The jaws snapped down on Lebouche's midsection. Instead of the claw dragging him down to a watery, undead grave, it severed him in two, bones crackling like dry reeds on a sandy dune.

The beast's leg slunk back into the water as quick as it came. The mooncussers were shaken by the leveling of their captain. They broke rank and scrambled away on their vulnerable skeleton legs. Bygones hid in the shadows doing what they do best. Each mooncusser and bygone knew its place and fell in line. This was their damnation, an endless stream of days, the hell of infinite repetition without question. With no one of consequence doling out the orders, they were at a loss.

Their leader was now two gelatinous globs, oozing like mercury back towards each other to reconstruct human form. LeBouche's disembodied head slid across the deck as the ship was tossed by sea and serpent. Strands from its neck base writhed like tentacles on the slick deck.

Ryan was in a dilemma. It was through LeBouche's decree that he was in command. With his captain indisposed, he needed to show his crew who the boss was.

"You're not off the hook."

I helped Sandy off the plank in an exaggerated gentlemanly move sure to please Lebouche.

"But the deal stands. I live, I steal Sandy back."

Ryan started rubbing his hook, wringing ghost hands, looking back at LeBouche's head, then back at me. Any French words that spilt from his lips drown in a rush of seaweed.

My brother was near his breaking point.

"It's your decision, bro. Make it! It doesn't matter to Frenchie there. He will just go on forever as whatever that thing reduces him to. What's down there will pick us clean. We're flesh and blood... we die. This is the elimination round. So, I repeat, are you in, bro??"

I give him credit. I was certain he would back down. There are more things in life than just a time-bending book that bring out one's inner pirate. Believing you are loveless may be one. Ryan stopped buffing his hook and brandished it before me. The man before me was no privateer, he was all pirate.

"Deal's a deal, but first, little brother, but the odds must be in favor of the house. Let's make you a *bite* more appetizing."

He lashed out against me, swinging his hook back and forth. Fresh blood flowed from two smiles carved in my chest. Where there was blood, the threat of shark was certain.

"Bon appétit, monstre mer," LeBouche managed between gurgles.

Then a depth charge shook the ship. I heard the surge of storage taking on water below. The strands of filth below LeBouche's chin lost their grip, his head jerked from side to side with the rocking of the ship, a bobber with a bite on its lead.

Two smaller arms silently rose from the water beneath me. I looked curiously down at the rising spires. They where smooth, not covered with a coat of barnacle sharp burrs. Each end had smooth pools of oil swirling. I was eye to eye with a sea monster.

'*Krakin*!', I thought-spoke for all tainted ears to hear. The crash of a wave on the sea wall, even the shore stealing crash of a gnarly storm has a distinctly different growl to that of this sea creature from the deep. It was a rumble of distant thunder as opposed to a lightning flash, thunder clap, one on top of the other. Its threat is not of a wave crashing down but of the undertow sucking the surf back beneath the waves.

When a Krakin... I don't mean to offend that which considers itself a singular beast... when *The Krakin* spews itself up from the rocky depths, blood runs cold. Few have seen such a sight and lived. Those who have are mute to tell what follows. Leave it said that the black etchings of ship attacks do The Krakin no justice. Just remember that the sea monster gilding the edge of pirate maps is real.

"The Krakin." I said out loud.

Billybones corrected me.

"Leviathon." His reference came from the bible tale of Jonah. Leviathon fit. Krakin called up too much Greek mythology and memories of stop motion animation to adequately describe what we were up against. This was indeed a leviathan, *The Leviathon*, it being the one and only, for the beast that crept out of the deep was indeed biblical in proportion.

All the other creatures of the sea swarmed around it. You could not tell where the atrocity ended and the normal scale fish began. Bare trees for arms pierced the surface swatting blindly at the side of the pirate ship. My jaw dropped as a claw as big as the ketch Billybones and I sailed on, surfaced in front of me and quickly went to task severing the ship's rigging. Beneath the water, sea life was its camouflage, an armor of tentacles and razor sharp jaws.

I had mere inches of oak plank in front of my black and white checked toes. I felt the cold tip of Ryan's hook burrow into the small of my back. Its point tore past cloth readying to part skin next.

"A deal's a deal."

"Privateer's honor, yo"

No elbows were exchanged.

I spun around and kicked his arm away and went for his cutlass that dangled from his belt. I grabbed at its hilt just as Ryan brought his hook around attempting a swipe at me with. I placed the dull edge of the cutlass in my teeth to dive head first into the marine life below.

I cut the surface of the water cleanly. Every muscle was clutched tight awaiting jaws and claws.

The life below the surface paid me no mind. Rather than a composite of scales with individual primal desires of mating and mischief, they worked together, moving in unison in response to each of the monster's gyrations. The Leviathon, Levy for short, was more than one singular beast. All the creatures of the sea bound together into one formidable being, all parts of a larger whole.

The nucleus of this monstrosity was in essence a crustacean. The way to kill them is through the shell, either that or to boil'm. As magically invisible as I felt at that moment, The Manifest had not bestowed me with any wizardly powers so I could not set the ocean to a boil. If I had any special powers save thought-speak I certainly wouldn't be entertaining my pirate brother by walking the plank.

Fortified by a thick of fish, Levy swung another of its claws at the bow of the ship. A rush of air bubbles spewed from the sight of the impact. If the ship goes down, my Sandy goes down with it.

The Levy needed to be stopped. I needed to act and fast. I had a cutlass, it had a shell. I could take a stab where it was most vulnerable. All I needed to do was get close to one of the leg joints or better, its face. Billybones barked encouragement from the gibbot cage, swinging side to side against the main mast like a boxing coach from the corner of the ring. The exact words to me were lost between the waves crashing about.

What if I did open up Levy like an oyster on the half shell? What of its fish posse? Would they snap out of their cultish trance, regain their vivacious appetite, put on white plastic bibs with red illustrations of teenage boys printed on them, and with a dollop of butter and a squeeze of lemon, chow down?

Presently Levy's wrath focused on the pirate ship. The ship was taking on water and Sandy was on said ship. The rupture to the hull was just below the devil, the longest expanse of the hull before it arcs towards the bottom. I could see bygones arm in arm patching the breech with their own bodies as mooncussers tended to repairing the boards. Their efforts were to ill effect. The ship was taking on water. If the Levy's attack was allowed to resume, the ship would go down. Time did not allow me to mull over the consequences of my actions.

Decision made, shuck the Levy.

Ascending the monster was far trickier than crossing clay flats at low tide. I used a technique from Billybones' bag of tricks and used my cutlass as a pick axe to secure my progression up its body. The surface of any crustacean is devoid of any signs of life but as I climbed this mountain of claws and muscle, my body close to its surface, I could feel the life within. There was the rush of fluid, then a quiver; a rush of urgency beneath the brown plates that held its gelatinous soul.

I reached the summit of the beast in spite of waves that sought to dismount me. I spread my legs out straddling its shell so that I could free my blade. To my left was the large ridge of its shell, below sprouted one of the many legs that were tearing at the damaged hull.

'*Down and across, feel the blade go snicker snak!*'

Billybones' voice instructed me from within. All I needed to do was get my blade down into the sweet spot between the leg and the main shell and then jump from this mountain of menace allowing my weight to drive the blade inside. I could then ride the circumference of the shell until, to quote LeBouche...'Voila!'

I pulled my cutlass from my side and grabbed its hilt with both hands and lifted it over my head like an Aztec priest performing a ritual sacrifice.

'Down and across, down and across.'

The coloration of Levy's shell played tricks with my eyes. The tortoise shell swirls of brown and black were bruised clouds on a lazy spring day. With your back against a bed of young green grass, you could look up and see horses, castles and giants within the bellowing wisps. Within Levy's marbleized shell I could see smudges of color flaking from its surface like old graffiti on a subway car. The images were stretched almost beyond recognition but I could make out the remains of... a palm tree... possibly a beach umbrella... then waves and a yellow sun... with a smiley face?

'It couldn't be!' I inadvertently thought-out to my crew. My mind raced. How many legs does a crab have? Eight, like a spider. I looked around me from the top of the beast and made an inventory of its appendages. 'Five...six...seven... seven!" It only had seven legs. I then knew why this monster was so pissed off. Problem was it was attacking the wrong ship.

What we had here was not The Leviathan, nor The Krakin. It was the offspring of Bess' temptation under the spell of The Manifest. What did she call it? I started think-speaking out loud.

'Bo-Q? No, there is a silent N. Bequeath? No. Bo-que-java??

'Nboquishakwana!' Bess thought-yelled back, holding back tears. Her voice was broadcast to all authors of the big book. Even the mooncussers heard the name. They all stood on the main deck

looking back and forth at one another, shaken by Bess' nonsensical moniker for her one and only pet. Bo-Q's name did role off the tongue like some sort of incantation.

Mooncussers and bygones, like pirates, were very superstitious. Stories of ancient curses and celestial paybacks were the things of legend and it was those tales the breathed them life. It was the muscle in the ink. In the eyeless sockets of mooncussers and the bygones alike, Bo-Q was surely the product of alchemy.

'It's not like I wrote this to happen, grow up!'" Bess cried out.

Clairvoyant and sarcastic was an annoying mix. What followed was an eventual rainstorm pent up within her during the summer's emotional drought.

'I'm so sorry. I did what you asked. I found the passage... calm seas to rough. Careen, careen! Free the ship from the coast. I, I just wanted that one thing, not treasure, nothin' bad... I just wanted my broken boy back.'

Bess was speaking to herself, unaware that she was broadcasting live. We could all hear, in a moment as fleeting as an eye blink, the soft underbelly of Bess' own shell. Something beneath my feet quaked in response to her voice.

My blade was poised over my head, ready to sever Bo-Q from our world.

'Sorry Bess, this baby's all grow'd up' The two tendrils with the two lifeless eyes rose up in front of me and made a serpentine turn to face me. Then from behind me one of the large front claws pulled away from its assault on the hull and swung over my head to swat me from my perch like a sunbather shooing away a greenhead fly on an August afternoon.

'There has to be another way' Bess pleaded.

The claw swung over my head, a moon cast shadow darkening the pitch around me. As the claw opened, the serrated teeth within shone tarter white as the full moon broke through. Its light illuminated the panic on my face for LeBouche to enjoy.

'*Heel!!'* Bess commanded into ether. Mooncussers stepped back from the ship's railings. The claw stopped a mere foot from squashing my head like a grape. The bastion of sea life surrounding The Bo-Q dispersed. Overcast muted the moon as if the entire world heeded Bess' command.

'*Heel? Is that all you've got??'* I thought yelled with a nervous laugh filtering through. It was enough, it worked. The shell I was riding submerged back into the ink of the ocean with a wake of bubbles, leaving me to tread water on a silent sea. Who knew that Bess was a serpent whisperer?

There was no mistaken that the spooks were spooked. They backed from the shattered rail looking back and forth at one another to confirm that they were not alone. Bess mystical words fanned their flame of fear.

Human skulls do not have a range of emotions. They are always surprised and menacing in the same instant. Any nuance of feeling in a mooncusser was in the transparent bladder of skin that held them together, impossible to decipher unless face to face; even then, a tough read.

Everything else was body language, also a difficult read, for many mooncussers had been broken and reconstituted into beings barely recognizable as human. They stood strong, cowered and shirked as if they had a soul to lose, more a mimicry of life than the real McCoy. It was perhaps a shadow of a memory long ago green; days numbered before the curse of death, delayed, took residence.

When opportunity rears its ugly, and in this case, *really* ugly head, you act, and fast.

"Nboquishakuana be praised!" I proclaimed raising my cutlass out the water while treading water with my other arm. While backing away further and clustering closer together, each mooncusser shielded its eyes with trembling fingers of bone. A drone of sound emanated from the legion. They were a mute bunch but if they had the gift of speech, that tremulous groan would be their word for fear.

I swam back to the ghost ship victorious. Thanks to Bess' intervention, I had won the bet.

"No fair..."

Ryan cleared his throat and attempted to sound strong in front of his crew. "... This will not stand!" he hollered to all who would hear.

The mooncussers did not move.

"Cowards all!" LeBouche spat. His orders held far less weight when he had been reduced to a disembodied head clinging to the deck by desperate tendrils of tendon and seaweed.

"Cut free the lines. This infidel shall not board.

The mooncussers had a new alpha dog in their presence, one who apparently held reign over the sea. With their captain down for the count and their quartermaster no more than an empty suit; they shuffled about without the beacon of loyalty, a rudderless ship.

I was able to ascend the rope attached to the ship's anchor without resistance. As I swung myself over the stern's guardrail unscathed. I caught sight of my brother Ryan stamping his over-sized boots against the deck in a tantrum, very much unlike a pirate. I reached out my unarmed hand and made a repetitive clutching motion with my hand. I wanted my prize.

"Sandy... now." I requested, as if anything could possess a beauty so free. She looked up at me, a glint of hope in her eye.

It wasn't mere infatuation that had driven me to a standoff with my brother. I knew it right then and there. *Love* love will make you do foolish things that are oft interpreted as bravery but are nothing more than foolhardy acts of desperation. *Familial* love, love of country, family, friends, our very earth, breeds courage that is based on the brick and mortar that holds our world together. The end results may be similarly ill-fated as those fueled by amour's intent, but in a knife fight, courage beats girl-crazy every time.

Billybones, weakened by exposure and infection, coached me from his roost high up the main mast, fighting for every breath.

"Power be not given, young Starbuck, it be taken! Destiny's ahead, all sails full. Claim your inheritance; grab the helm with both hands, mate"

I kept my eyes on my big brother. He struggled to keep focused as I addressed him.

"Under the laws of this ship, decreed by you, its quartermaster, you must surrender Sandy to me."

I needed to get his crew on my side to increase the pressure.

"For the love of Nboquishakuana, do you yield?"

I stumbled with its name but made the 'N' silent and gave the word a threatening delivery that giving it the gravitas of a vengeful god.

Ryan sensed the instability of his crew as they huddled together at the sound of Bo-Q's name. One wrong move and they would be pulling my brother apart like tourists do salt water taffy on the boardwalk.

LeBouche was not so easily swayed. He was with Ryan.

"There shall be no quarter", the head of the captain hissed as he inched closer to his fallen body.

Ryan rubbed his hook as if it were a genie bottle, hoping a way out would be his wish answered. Then he raised an eyebrow maniacally at me.

"Point taken my captive, if our challenge, our wager is indeed complete, I would gladly hand over Miss Coppertone here, but alas..." He glanced back at LeBouche's spider head for approval. ".. the game have just begun, yo!"

He tried his hardest to look menacing but even wielding an arm outfitted with a deadly weapon sutured to it, he possessed all the threat of a trick-or-treater ghost costumed with fitted sheets.

Ryan wanted me to back down, to reaffirm his station on the ghost ship. If I agreed, then perhaps, he would back down. After all, we were brothers; we shared the same blood, *good* blood. It must have been tearing him up inside as much as I. From the first time he burst in my bedroom to put my head in a full nelson to demonstrate a new wrestling move only to come out of the skirmish with a bloody nose, my brother knew that I would not back down.

'*Its OK, stand down Ty.*' thought-spoke Sandy.

'*Sorry I'm not there, dude.*' added Bess.

"Do your worst." I challenged my brother.

'*that will be just about enough that Tyler Jamison Byrne... time out for the both of you!*' my mother yelled in my head.

LeBouche gurgled to Ryan, another wave crashing against the side of the ship.

"What are you waiting for, quartermaster? Pronounce sentence! We have much bigger fish to fry" LeBouche's neck tendrils clawed the deck, causing his head to maneuver sideways in a crablike motion through the foam.

'*Stand tall mate! I see a lot of your father in ya,*' Billybones thought-spoke.

My brother heard nothing but waves and 'cusser squabble but I heard the pirate's every word.

Hanging high in the gibbot cage, Billybones looked a little grey around the gills. Perhaps he didn't want to take this particular nugget to his watery grave.

'*You knew my...*'

'*Reginald! This is not the time nor the place...*' my mother scolded.

'*If not now when missy, now may be all we be havin'.*'

The inner dialogue rambled on; one voice stepping over another, the buzz of a crowded room filling my head. Ryan, deaf to the din, just stared back at me, still waiting for me to back down.

"Uncle?", he pleaded, whispering so no mooncussers could hear.

I raised my cutlass to meet his hook. The groans shorten to gasps throughout his crew.

"Bring it on bro." I replied, just soft enough for him to hear. I then addressed the rest of his fearful crew,

"May the wrath of Nboquishakuana be upon you."

Ryan's hook met my steel.

"Wheel ball!"

Each mooncusser and bygone alike exchanged glances with their glowing sockets wincing in confusion.

"Sacrableau!" yelled LeBouche. "Keel Hawl! Keel Hawl!" The captain's word refocused the mooncussers fear. They stood tall, back in formation in response to the damning words of my fate.

"Dang it, my bad captain. Keel hawl... keel hollah."

Ryan made a second attempt to flex his piratitude, excuse me, privateeritude. "Keel hawl the scallywag, yo!"

This was not a dress rehearsal like in the Anchor. It was going to be a long night, hopefully long enough for my crew to come to my rescue. If not, it would be my last.

My fate seemed appropriate to my inflated pirate ego. You might remember that the keel hawler is pirate torture of the highest echelon. Ropes were tied to each of my arms and legs. The wheels of the ship's triple purchase, a boxed series of pulleys that were thread with the restraints whirred until they met resistance... me. The rigging was drawn tight pulling my limps in four opposing directions until I looked like the international symbol for man that NASA sent up to the stars for the unknown to decipher. My joints sang a wordless song, a sea shanty of soulful anguish.

If the mooncussers kept up the pressure I would soon be the victim to a simple drawn and quartered, where my body would tear in fourths. Instead each rope travelled overboard, down past the devil and then went underwater where they strapped the encrusted belly of the beast, from stem to stern, back up to the main deck, and onto the other side. It would be a journey no man would want to live through.

While the undead crew strewn me up for a good hawling, I just stared at my brother, not for mercy, but for him to back down. His eyes stared back one word and one word only, uncle.

I would not say it.

"Don' give'm th' satisfaction. If we die this dee, we do it side by side, heads held high, mate," Billybones called down. It was as if he read the thoughts I didn't broadcast.

"Been here once before, yer blood by me side. Long as I breathe the salt of summer, history shall not be repeated here."

LeBouche finally traversed across the deck to his torso. It fused itself together at a grotesque angle, giving his stature a Quasimodo hunch. The tentacles beneath his head wove into his neck like a giant squid feeding on the fallen.

My body craved asylum but my mind would not concede defeat.

"A tip of my head to you sir, Bon voyage!"

"Yeah, Bon Voyageee, bro" With a flourish of his hook, Ryan the quartermaster gave the signal to start my torture. The sound of the ropes ratcheting up wheel wells clacked in counterpoint with the ocean against the hull. My body was starting to drag, face down, across the deck towards the severed figurehead at the bow of the ship.

The ropes pulled me up against the railings that crowned the bow of the ship. My body moved in fits and starts, first the taut ropes dragged me forward, then would go slack, followed by another tug. I flexed my back rigid against the tension that wanted to snap my spine backwards. I switched my gaze from my brother, to Sandy, through a smokescreen of pain.

'Focus on a single point of light... breath through the pain, as if through a straw...'

With another tug my body was pulled half overboard, my heels to the heavens, my bandana'd head inching closer to the salty void. Again, the slack. I was suspended in mid-air, dangling upside down over the ocean.

The ocean was devoid of any underwater predators thanks to Bess and the power of Bo-Q. Still, peril still waited underneath the waves. Countless barnacles eagerly awaited me, itching to give me razor sharp kisses. Tangles of seaweed that had failed many times in my short life to drag me down to Davey Jone's locker were at the ready for a more successful snatching. Every childhood fear was coming home to roost.

Each groan of the mooncussers as they reeled in the tethers brought me closer to a watery grave. My shirt tore from my bloodied chest as it scraped down the hull past the devil. Paint chips fell away and shards of wooden splinters pierced through me like needles through a sampler.

I fought back the pain, blowing harder through the imaginary straw leading to Sandy's beacon. The hair on my head became slick, soaked by the lap of the waves. I increased my breathing, in and out...in...out... deeper, deeper; preparing to fill my lungs with all the air in the night sky. In an instant my world would be just darkness and brine.

'Uncle.' I thought-spoke.

'Yes, baby... uncle.' My mother replied in a coo of resolution.

'Uncle, you got that right,' Billybones confirmed.

"Uncle?"

There was another tug and ocean swallowed. I held my breath, eyes wide open. I finally understood the meaning of the word that refused to pass my lips.

Uncle.

Chapter 19

MAELSTROM

They say things come in threes, whoever *they* are; death, luck and miracles are no exception. I suspect it's all a matter of perspective. In my eyes, it was nonsense, as illogical as back breaking cracks in a sidewalk. As the evening progressed, the words never rang more true. A religious man might say we beheld miracles that night. If we did, we hit heaven's trifecta. All would agree on this, the successive events were epic in scope and their count was three.

Expecting the unexpected makes the unexpected expected. I don't know where I read that from, pages of a famous philosopher's wool-gatherings or from the inside of a fortune cookie. If you embraced that convoluted phrase, you could never be taken by surprise, you'd always ready for whatever may come. As LeBouche's minions bound my hands and feet, I had no option but to surrender to the moment, accepting the phrase as gospel.

This might all sound like high falutin' thinking for a fourteen year old boy, but when you are seconds from having your young life flushed down the drain like a floater goldfish, you build a life's philosophy in a blink of a saltwater-stung eye. This motto proved was shelter against a sky gone green; a shabby attempt at best but tacked together with enough nails to weather the storm. So went my faith in what is good.

A choir of 'cussers grunted in unison. Ropes ratcheted, capstans strained. I'm bathed in indigo, moonbeams reflecting from bubbles rising all around; luckily none had yet escaped my lips. I was submerged head first into the ocean with the clock ticking.

In all the hoopla of plank-walking and keel-hawling, and the revelation that Billybones was my father's brother, I needed a moment to breath, to take it all in. My Dad existed solely in one of my few crystal memories, an out-of-focus snapshot taken dockside at the marina when he was scarcely older than me. I needed a breath of clarity. Instead, my lungs stung with possibly my last.

With another groaned chorus from the crew working my tethers I slid further down the hull. My body soon would be appetizers for the hungry barnacles coating the bottom of the hull. The bubbles swarming around me dissipated, replaced by liquid silence. Even the waves crashing against the ship overhead were just whispered rumors.

The ropes, pulled taut, strained every joint. My body cried uncle since my lips could not, would not, even on dry land.

Then it came, the rustling. It was a sound I was all too familiar with, the soundtrack of many nights of sweat-stained sheets. Its voice, leafy and wet, rose from the deep. I felt the flutter of seaweed on my back as Lebouche's men on topside moaned yet again, an echo already history by the time it reached my ears.

A forest of seaweed suddenly rushed between me and the unforgiving hull just as the knots around my wrist tightened, dragging me further down. I continued to nose dive past the splintered boards that struggled to stay attached to the hull. Long strands of green, the very sea snakes of underwater foliage I feared would one day drag me to my death, cradled my head. A large blanket of brown kelp slid its oily skin between me and the serrated teeth of the ship. A sheath of undulating sea life rescued my face from being shaved off. The ropes dragged me further across the bottom of the hull where barnacles waited.

I was just speaking of miracles right? Was it a fortunate coincidence of the ocean's tide, a pardon delivered at zero hour to spare my life? That would just be luck of the best kind. Now if Neptune himself sent an angel, that would be something else entirely, that would hint at the miraculous.

Face to face with my savior I panicked, a short burst of bubbles, my valuable oxygen, shooting from my mouth. Before me was a corpse, her face, a death mask bobbing in black only inches from my face.

We were both shrouded in darkness, her face a dull illumination, the palest of green, any lighter and it would be clam shell white. Her lips glowed chartreuse. They were full, not the chapped lips of a body pickled by the sea. Hair danced a ballet around her head, ends of the long tresses woven into the same tendrils of green seaweed that shrouded her body. Her eyelids were bruised a darker pitch of green, that of over-ripened fruit; so dark it hurt. Surely she was a victim of the same drowning vines that haunted my dreams.

Then the lids opened. An iridescent emerald lit the space between us. Their beauty literally took my breath away; another burst of air escaping my lungs. Her eyes were alive, a world in and of themselves. Fireflies of green flit and swirled in the amber of her pupils. Her iris focused in on me, contracting then expanding back to deep onyx saucers that took in the infinite sea around us.

The bottom of the ship tore at her hide as we continued to be dragged down and across the hull; I could not detect an iota of pain in her mystical pools. Her eyes were human, or were once human. They were eyes full of life's passion, not dead fish eyes, eyes that register nil even when wrestling on a line for life. I could see the reflection of my face in her pupils. Her iris again narrowed until I was the only thing in her world, just me, no place for pain.

Something slid up beside me as I lost myself in her eyes. I wore my skin tight. My inner pirate was replaced with the baby of my childhood fears. I cringed, my oldest nightmare, realized. Perhaps her captivating beauty was but a lure, iridescent tendrils on some hideous deep sea fish you only see on the pages of an encyclopedia, its prey, that's me, lured by the light unaware of the cavern of razor incisors closing in from behind. I was amazed how quickly my fearless façade could be unmasked. The face reflected in her eyes was out of both breath and courage.

My fear abated, what crept up my face was not grappling hooks, it was a caress. Like her face, her arms were fleshed out strands of seaweed and scale, an amalgamation of human and subterranean. Her pale fingers were long and delicate, tipped with dark nails manicured for danger. Between each finger was lace webbing that shrunk and expanded with the beat of her heart that I could feel between me and the hull. She brought her hand to my cheek as if patting a skittish animal. Her touch was smooth and surprisingly warm.

More bubbles streamed from my mouth as my lungs gave up the ghost. That was the fatal third and pin dots of white passed my eyes as my world shut down. My anchored body thrashed to no avail. Warm tendrils stroked the side of my face, calming the frightened colt within.

I looked deep into her universe for eyes. If this was the last frames of the documentary of my life, the film was *2001: A Space Odyssey* and not *Jaws*. Her clover lips parted. I awaited a voice to give me the last rites just as the final shot of *The Tyler Byrne Story* faded to black. Instead of a prayer for eternal peace, the dead girl under the waves gave me what I feared most that summer, more than pirates, more than the rape of my homeland, more than a watery grave.

Her lips were salty but not sea salty, they were *she* salty. I opened my mouth, welcoming seawater to fill my empty lungs. Instead I felt her breath give me life. Her warmth rushed through me as her lips went from a pucker to quivering surrender.

The mechanics of our kiss possessed all of the fumbling of strangers in the dark. I cautiously darted my tongue between her lips, exploring the contours of her mouth. I looked into the constellation deep in her eyes. Pulsars twinkled, falling stars shot across the emerald void in celebration. Then her eyes closed leaving us floating together in the dark. I could see motion behind the patina of the lids.

I mistakenly thought-spoke as I muttered the words, "*Ohh... my Sandy.*"

Everything stopped; retinal activity, reciprocal tongue-lashing, life saving air. I was left arm in arm with a cadaver, again, out of breath, soon to join her on the other side.

"*Hold on Ty, just a bit longer!*" Sandy thought back in spite of the threat of LeBouche's lash. She heard my words, not my every thought, every deed.

The eyelids of this dead girl, sea nymph, mermaid, whatever you want to call her, snapped open. The green glow returned, not the soft healing glow from the moment just passed, but a darker hue, spiked with jealousy. The activity in her eyes was more a swarm of disrupted wasps than galaxies of infinite heavens in orbit. She recoiled, pulled her lips from me and with them, my lifeline. I again began to lose consciousness... curtain... and scene.

In my darkening dream I was still in mid-kiss. First it was Sandy in my arms, then she transformed into my amorous abductor from the deep, then into my bedroom pillow. Then came darkness save for a single point of light below me, resting on the bottom of the sea. It was a gem mined from an oyster's gullet, a globe winking stray moonbeams back at me. It was the focus of my mantra.

'*a point of light... breathe through the straw... breathe.*'

And I was, breathing that is. I could feel myself being dragged further across the hull but there was no pain.

'*Breathe... focus on the pearl.*'

Pearl. She seemed far less of an apparition once she had been named. Pearl again had me in a lip lock. We were kissing if you consider otherworldly cardio pulmonary resuscitation a romantic concept. Her chest heaved more in desperation over losing me to death than with passion. My lungs filled with life. Our collective panic subsided as I took deep slow, breaths as if on land. I could breathe underwater through her. Now that is one heck of a first kiss.

Each time my ropes went slack we floated in each other's presence. When the cords constricted, we were thrust violently against one other. Pearl's eyes registered no pain; urgency, longing, bitterness, possibility, all resided deep in the pools of her soul, but no pain. A webbed hand against each side of my face maintained the life sustaining kiss during the tug of war of the rigging. I would not die that day, be it hell or high water.

Another jerk of the ropes and my body cleared the bottom of the keel and I began traversing the port side. My body was right side up inching towards the surface. Pearl held tight until the top of my head broke the surface of the water. I could feel my hair being tousled by the ocean gale.

Pearl released me with an exhale. Her lips softened, their corners turned up into a smile reserved for savoring sweets and kissing a newborn baby's toes. Her whisper of a finger lit on my numb bottom lip and closed my mouth before a wash of sea water could rush in. Then her celestial eyes closed again, darkness again swooped in. Only shards of moonlight separated us. She then turned the alabaster of her nubile body away from me as the ropes pulled me out of the ocean.

"Pearl," I thought-spoke without intention. No reply. Couldn't she here me call? I swore she heard Sandy's name. Perhaps she couldn't hear my thought-speak. It made sense. The Manifest could never taint something as pure as her.

To all who heard my utterance chime inside, Sandy included, the random word was the plea of a man holding on to the last threads of consciousness.

The ropes dug in again. When I opened my eyes I was hanging by my arms off of the port bow. I could hear the 'cusser grunts, smell their past deeds and feel the pain they dealt me.

Twisting my head as far it would turn, I caught one last glimpse of my aquatic guardian angel. She was majestic. From this day forth she should be referred to as The Pearl, as in The Krakin, The Leviathan, and The Nboquishakwana for there was none other in the world like her.

There was a rush of bubbles as she started her descent. First I saw her tresses, golden highlights braided with seaweed alive on top of the white wash of surf. She arched her body to return to the depths, her body peaking up over the waves. From the front she was the beautiful, naked, dead girl but from the back she appeared as a massive bottom feeder, part plant life, part scaled beast. What appeared as a large blanket of kale was actually a hood of flesh that ran down her spine. Folds of the scaled skin stretched between her arms and her waist like fins. With her arms outstretched she had all the appearances of a great fish shadowing the ocean floor.

As she crested over the waves I saw that the whole of her back was shredded by the insatiable hunger of ship's hull. White flesh veined with salmon pink peeking through her wounds, all raw and crying out. She disappeared beneath the waves, a trail of red pooling in her eddy.

The ropes jerked again and my body reached the ship's railing. I was alive and relatively unscathed, all thanks to The Pearl. I owed her my life.

"Thar he blows" LeBouche called out to his disenfranchised followers as the red markings on the trawler rigging crept over the rails. What he excepted was the tattered remains of humanity; personality erased, raw hamburger where once hung a face, a limp mass of flesh twitching involuntarily to pain who's volume knob had been turned up to eleven.

Save for the two weeping slashes across my chest inflicted by my brother Ryan, I was the same person they threw overboard. My pristine condition validated the suspicions that they were dealing with powers greater than those that cursed them into mooncussers.

LeBouche expected to reclaim the allegiance of his crew. Instead of a wave of finger pointing and guttural laughter, he witnessed a communal gasp.

I was dragged over the rail head first. I remained sprawled across the deck as I took an inventory of my aches and pains. Nothing broken, I flopped upright on legs no longer seaworthy. Average approach, muddy execution, the Russian judge gave me a 3.

Even LeBouche's vulture mascot turned on him. Its black tongue darted in and out in anticipation of a fresh kill. Denied its late night snack, it turned on his hunchbacked master. With a *bracaw*, it flew from its perch on the captain's shoulder leaving a white streak of turd across LeBouche's epaulets as it took flight. Such indignity would not be tolerated. Without a hint of emotion on his repositioned head LeBouche clutched his gun, engaged the flint lock and with a casual wave of his arm shot treason from the sky. His mascot's remains scattered across the deck like a forbidden toss of the bones.

A spattering of bygones released me from my shackles. The first flank of mooncussers had their flat blades at the ready in case I attempted anything. I instinctually grabbed at my sore wrists. They had gone beyond blister, as had my ankles, now crimson ghosts hiding beneath my skin. My touch, like the salty air, was fire to the touch.

My tethers had stretched out all my limbs. My ability to stand was tentative at best. I grasped the rail behind me with my sore arms so not to appear hobbled.

I needed to stand my ground, confirm the fear that grew in the mooncussers. I'm not sure it was defying death or no longer being in the suck-face-virgin club that made my inner pirate brandish his bravado. I raised the arm that wasn't keeping me upright and pointed at my captor. Pain shot throughout my body.

"*You, sir, are nothing to me*," I thought-spoke, saving *Him* the indignity of proclaiming my defiance in front of his crew. It was all posturing, a tactic he was well accustomed to. All of his power over the mooncussers was derived through posturing. Never trust a first impression Billybones once preached. Perspective can't be trusted. Half-standing in front of LeBouche those words rang true. What at first horrifies on closer inspection may by all gauze and stage blood, a weathered statue beckoning you into the Kooky Castle at the fair.

"No offense, but I have held up my part of the bet. Now, if it pleases you, as a nobleman and a privateer, I ask that you honor your word."

"It pleases me not a wit. Yes, you have proven yourself a worthy opponent, but... I have yet to test the fortitude of my quartermaster."

A grin smeared across LeBouche's powdered face.

"How do you think he will fare off the plank or a drag under the hull? Perhaps I have put my chips on the wrong meat bag, hmm??"

LeBouche knew that he had squandered my time changing ability too early in the game. It was now time to show his cards and the only royalty in his hand was a jester. He would never risk Ryan's life, his only remaining chance at the Wydah stash. He bet on my character, that I would never put my brother's life on the business end of my sword.

I peered out over the black seam of the horizon. A faint beacon shone through the weak threads of night. I needed to stall LeBouche a bit longer.

Sandy sensed LeBouche's desperation. She knew firsthand the short wick of his temper. Violence was his cure all and if she wasn't the victim, his wrath would be poured upon the Brothers Byrne. She kicked away some of the boney parrot remains that was once LeBouche's echo and backed her way into the captain's quarters, all the time maintaining a reverent curtsy.

When she returned to LeBouche's side, she cradled the antique fiddle I first saw in her holding quarters. The weathered wood seemed barely able to hold itself together against the tension of the tightened strings. In her other hand she held its bow which she rosined up as she knelt before her captor. She looked him up and down, giving him a coy smile and a bat of the eye to the younger man LeBouche was before he was cursed.

Mooncussers and bygones alike cringed at the sight of the instrument. They were used to the sound of a rutting cat spewing forth from its decrepit hollows. Sandy's bow floated down, horsehairs massaging the strings that had long ago forgotten song.

What filled the ears of all on deck was not a hellish caterwaul, but angels' breathe floating gently on spring morning dew. The sound that emoted from the weathered wood wove the most crystalline of memories to all who heard.

I think the composer was Debussy. It wasn't because I knew a shred about classical music, classic rock maybe, but nothing concerning the powdered wig set. To me the three Bs in music was The Beatles, The Band and the Boss.

On countless lazy days I did my best sloth impersonation sprawling across the porch swing at Sandy's cottage while she practiced the day away. As her arms sewn the air together, one note wove into another until all space was clothed in song. She gushed on and on about how, with Debussy, the beauty was all in the give and take of the major and minor chords. I nodded as if I understood and drifted away to the tug of war of happy and somber musical phrasings that became the soundtrack of my daydreams.

Whoever the author, the music or the memory, the notes soothed LeBough's savage brow. He looked down at Sandy, nodded approval then looked to Ryan walking cautiously towards him and further from his agitated crew who were temporarily subdued by the lilt of the strings.

The undead would have turned on my brother the instant they witnessed my death defying survival of the keel hawler save for one thing that kept them so subservient. I believe what the mooncussers wanted even more than treasure or a place to plunder was to pass on. Each atrocity committed was to avenge mortality lost. Unlike bygones and dammeds who each possess some semblance of humanity, and in that, the slightest potential for transcendence, mooncussers were far from human. Death had long been out of their grasp.

Billybones was right with his cryptic words at the Rusty Anchor. There are things far worse than death. Having caught more than an eyeful of these aberrations I learned not to fear death, but to fear never being able to die. I would opt for death with a final heartbeat. Immortality is for suckers. At least with death there is always the promise of bright lights up ahead.

Since mooncussers could never embrace death, then treasure would be their consolation prize. The only key on board that would fit that chest was my brother; any port in a storm. They, too, would never let any harm come to Ryan.

The minor chords slowly began to supersede the major, the lullaby slowly clouded over by a funeral dirge. As melody turned eulogy, it no longer consoled. The atmosphere turned to suspense. Sandy's tune sawed on like a music box winding down, each of the metal bars plucked, twisted with age, notes as sour as crab apples.

Among the bygones, shuffling between nervous 'cusser boots, I spied a familiar face. Bother was the first of the *good* pirates to board the death ship. Our bond on ol' Rusty had served me well. He mingled amongst the bygone troops, one by one rallying them to my cause. In a myriad of gurgles and belches only another bygone could decipher, he told tales of humans befriending bygones. He looked up at me, nodded and then stepped aside to reveal the latest recruit.

Jose looked like a new hatchling that had just fallen from its nest. He was still half dammed and half bygone but the latter was quickly winning over his constitution. His last meal, his own heart with a side order of hopes and dreams had given him little sustenance. Save for his head, his body had already shriveled to half its size. His sunken eyes were barely visible. His skin had turned to wet clay, his once warm hue of human skin, to ash. He was so fragile I feared that if a strong gale kicked in, he would blow into the wind like cremated remains. Lastly, the hole in his chest had scabbed over, now an embossed tattoo of his chosen fate.

As quickly as he revealed his newfound friend, Bother stepped back to keep Jose from LeBouche's sight line. He drew two of his willowy fingers to his glowing hollows where eyes should reside, then pointed his fingers out to sea, west, the direction of homeland shores, cowboys, white hats and men with no names.

Bother wove through the sea of rattling bones and blades. He was only waist high to the smallest mooncusser. It proved easy going; all bygones looked alike in a mooncusser's eyes. A mudhead was just a mudhead. You need to be human to see a shadow of yourself in them. There was Bother flexing his last stitch of humanity as he climbed the mizzenmast where Billybones was hung up to die.

Then came the chanting. It hung in the night air, but not at first. At first all the crew could hear was the sorrow filled strokes of fiddle strings at first.

Then there was of the Capt'n, his thought-voice rising over the lullaby.

"What do ya do wit a drunkin' sailor?"

Gatto, Big Red, and two stalwart tugboat men joined in.

"What do ya do wit a drunkin' sailor?"

Mooncussers had no voice nor could they hear voices in their skulls, the batteries in their psychic radio had long ago run dead. Perhaps they had been touched by *The Manifest* at one time, but they were no longer the souls that had done the touching. They heard not a peep.

The one exception to the mooncusser curse was LeBouche, who was prime time D.J. on Manifest radio. He was mooncusser through and through but his eternity was gilded, he could spy on our darkest of thoughts and could talk with a silver tongue. When he twisted time he must have made a deal with the devil before time twisted him.

Billybones himself was the first voice made real. He swallowed his pain and joined the quartet ; a foursome greatly in need of a barbershop.

"What do ya do wit a drunkin' sailor, early in th' mornin'?"

Sandy held a note on the violin just as Billybones finished the first verse. The music hung in mid air, dangling over a precipice of foreshadowing. Sandy's moon-eyed gaze shifted from LeBouche to me. Her smile was finally sincere. Vengeance rose resting on her sculpted eyebrow. She looked gleeful, her pirate rising.

During that musical coda, LeBouche heard the alarm; all hands on deck. He looked aft and fro for interlopers in his midst. There was just me and my ineffectual brother bowing before him. He tore at his recently moored head, pulling it off of his shoulders and raised it the length of his abnormally long arms. From that vantage point he could survey the nearing glow floating in the pitch.

Sandy sawed off three violent swipes at the strings, whipping the bow back and forth like the cat o nine tails that LeBouche had introduced her to. The staccato of the notes commanded the attention of LeBouche's nervous crew.

As the chorus started, Sandy's carved away at the notes the instrument was born to sing. The shanty scratched itself alive, the violin turned fiddle.

"Yo ho, up she rises, yo ho, up she rises, yo ho, up she rises, early in the mornin'!"

As the chorus repeated I joined in, not in a tired rasp as did Billybones, but a voice in full effect, a voice so loud, it shook the timbers and the mooncussers' confidence. On the third go around Sandy joined the chorus, all smiles. A fiery glint was in her eyes, the spirit the sadistic LeBouche had all but extinguished. Up she rises indeed!

I had learned from my dealings with Bother that bygones can't speak, but, unlike the Manifest-tainted, they could read the thoughts of those in their presence. That was how the mudheads in my bedroom measured what would scare me most. All they possessed was a backwards gargle that they had assembled into a rudimentary language no more advanced than the hand gestures of Bobo the chimp.

Bother tried his best at joining in. It was far from words but was right on the mark with its inflection and rhythm.

"What do ya do..."

Jose stepped up from the crowd to join in. He howled the verse, releasing his unfathomable rage. He had so recently turned that the guttural slosh that rose over his newly surfaced shark teeth still resembled English.

"What do ya do..."

One by one bygones joined in solidarity, a raucous celebration of mutiny.

"What do ya do..."

By the second chorus the bygones more accurately mimicked Jose's delivery and the haunting refrain rang in the ears of everyone and every *thing*.

The shanty was a diversion, a cloaking device for the communication of all good pirates in wait.

"What do ya do..." *'can you find cover Ty??'*

"What do ya do..." *'What can you possibly do against...* '

"What do ya do..." *'We be the very pirates they wish they were'*, Gatto chuckled, way too jovial for the confrontation in the offing. Ah Gatto! My compadre! My main man! How welcome was his voice. Even at the darkest of times I felt that everything would be fine with Gat watching my back.

"... early in the mornin'!"

Voices stumbled over one another as the shanty shadowed their words.

'Get Smythe!', 'Duck 'n cover!', ' Stop, drop and roll', 'Vamos comprende?' and Gatto's giddy call to battle, *'Its ninja time!!'*.

'Pirate time' I corrected him, a smile cutting through the pain as I forced my legs to run for cover.

LeBouche was cautious but confident, too busy accessing the external threat to pay mind to the cloaked communiqués laced between the rowdy shouting. His death ship had 34 cannons on each side and thrice as many mooncussers to dead-man them. Ol' Rusty had a sparse ten by side and only Billybones knew how many of them were merely ornamental and how many were operational.

"What do ya do..."

'If I take out Frenchie, there might be enough chaos on deck to give you a shot,' I thought back beneath the din. I dared not share with them that my legs and arms were for most purposes useless.

Flexing my muscles brought little motion and much pain. I was a rag doll dressed in pirate's clothes.

"What do ya do..."

'Take cover is all mate, we've been here before. We know how to handle the deathless,' Capt'n thought yelled back.

The bygones followed their new captain's orders and escorted me to the bunker that led below deck. Putting my faith in anyone but me, myself and I was humbling. All summer long it was Ty's world and you just lived in it. God forbid you threatened my doorstep. Now I was powerless with no choice but to go with the flow, ride the tide... choose your nautical reference.

Bother, the bygone scout of the good pirate crew, had already shimmied up the mizzenmast. Using his morphing body of sludge as a key, he was able to jerry rig the lock that held Billybones captive. Bother gurgled the shanty the whole time. The pirate looked down at his get-out-of-jail-free card with repugnant gratitude. Bother slid down the mast like melted ice cream, sprouted legs and wove his way through the wave of mooncussers. Billybones gingerly staggered down the mizzenmast following Bother's lead.

It was the oldest trick in the pirate book and LeBouche fell for it hook, line, and sinker. Perhaps it was his privateer naiveté still green to pirate trickery but one would think his severed neck should have been enough of a reminder not to take a pirate on his word.

LeBouche knew that the white flag he spied on the horizon was I lie. He knew not to trust the colours flown but with his command challenged, it was a lie he needed his crew to believe. It was just the lie he could get his minions to rally behind. He lowered his head back into the center of his lace collar. Sea strands and corded tendons quickly anchored it back in place, cleared his throat to share the lie with his crew.

LeBouche hollered his address over the looping shanty.

"Today you will once again taste victory. This is our legacy, why your allegiance is unwavering."

He looked down over his troubled underlings.

"Look at you! You be forged of tougher stuff than this. You shake in your boots over this, this charlatan? Ye of weak spirit, look to port. Breathers with far more to lose than you, cower in my wake. Alas, another conquest ne'er earned!"

As ol' Rusty neared LeBouche's ship, you could see with your naked eyes, its crew lined up on the starboard side. Heads were down, arms by their sides in surrender, a cast of characters making their final curtain call.

'Yo ho, up she rises!'

The chorus rang louder than ever though no lips moved. Between the drunken slur of the shanty's repetition came Capt'n's final warning.

'are ye set, matey?'

'Yo ho Capt'n Ready as I'll ever be!'

Bother, Jose and their converts gathered at my feet, melding into one another, hugging my legs. Now a bygone cast, they collectively shuffled me across the deck.

There was no way to get to the bunker without crossing directly in front of LeBouche. If ol' Rusty was preparing to attack, it was up to me to divert LeBouche's attention from the ship positioning to broadside.

"Benevolent sir, I underestimated your cunning. You are truly formidable and worthy adversary for any of the scourge of the sea, which, I will repeat for the record, I am not one of. I bow to you, my captain o' my captain"

I threw in the *o' captain* as a last second flourish. I had read it somewhere in my studies and it sounded all old school and groveling.

LeBouche may have been mock royalty with his antiquated letter of marquee and his fancy finery, but he wasn't stupid. It was apparent that he had been to university which is European for saying he was college bred. Losing one's head to a gentleman's betrayal also gives you a degree in the school of hard knocks. He was sure to know when he was being played.

"I pray you protest too much. You are quite a remarkable pirate, Tyler Byrne. Upon your passing I will have nothing but good words to share about you and your heroic fight to the finish...Indredible!"

The shanty was dissipated into lapping waves and 'cusser grumbles. Sandy, having finished her fiddle play, stood obediently beside LeBouche. She tapped the length of the bow against her palm in frustration. All the while, she stared at me, through me, her anger building. With all this buildup she must have expected me to rush to her rescue like Errol Flynn in a black and white swashbuckler. She didn't know how incapacitated I was. I attempted to bow at the feet of the monster that had enslaved her. Sorry about that Sandy, first things first.

I knew what LeBouche's ace card was. The latter side of his wager was for my brother to endure the same trials as me. First he would have to walk the plank and if he wasn't reduced to a buffet for the serpent and his legions, he would have to survive a good keel hawler without the aid of divine intervention. All LeBouche needed was to say the word and my brother would be chum.

LeBouche spied in my head all summer. He knew the measure of the man. I was elementally good, as well he may have been before Billybones took a little off the top. Would I sacrifice myself so that my brother could live? It would be a noble act to say yes, but my mind still would not say uncle.

My pirate soul made a good argument; let him go down with the tide. It wasn't his incessant noogie sessions that prompted this opinion. Blood is blood, sure enough, but my blood is *my* blood. I fought the pirate inside that LeBouche nurtured all summer. In spite of every fiber of my being pleading for self preservation, I made my decision. I would have to save my brother from himself.

"Let your vengeance be on me who has challenged you at every turn, not those would bend so easily to your will, captain. There be no lesson in it."

"I will not acquiesce to the noble intentions of a pirate's cabin boy. Fate be but a fickle thing and so am I. There can only be only one quartermaster."

My brother was not going to have his younger brother show him up. He must have thought, how bad could the challenge be if my twerp of a brother came through unscathed? My brother stepped up.

"I will take the challenge capitan! I will prove to you who is the true quartermaster is!"

LeBouche ignored my brother.

"I need a man like you, pirate Tyler, one that the Gods' favor. Have your brother try, then die. Then you can take your rightful position by my side. There's treasure on every horizon for the likes of us!"

"Ay, but haven't you made the right decision already? Who can bring you the war chest of the Wydah? Not I. Only quartermaster Ryan can give you the riches you so deserve."

"Do you have not eyes, boy? This, this fool will bring me providence?"

"He is compromised is all, clouded by the mire of grog he's been privy to since his induction.

I bowed with each embellishment.

Mire? Privy? My brother's neck was on the line, I'd try anything to dupe him.

Ryan was wasted and in the worst way, not just by spirits but in spirit. He had drowned the heavy weight of his quartermaster uniform and its entitlement in the wretched belly-wash stored in the bilge. Under the spell of demon liquor he wasn't a jovial chuckle-bucket nor a chug-'n-fall booze hound that his crew could laugh off as the green gills of a man without his sea legs. Drink gave him an unarmed sense of bravado. He aped control, each of his actions exaggerated, all the time lacking the confidence to back up his bravado.

Mooncussers, like men of the sea, can smell weakness as surely as they do fear. It stank higher than the collective history of evil reeking topside.

His thought process was just as dim. Lacking the understanding of the situation he found himself in, he was unable to differentiate between the rock and the hard place. There was no harder place on earth than the death ship that night and LeBouche was the rock that could pulverize his bones to sand. Then there was me, stuck in the middle.

"I await your decision. You are a kind and benevolent sentinel of the high seas. I have faith that you would never do anything to besmirch your stellar reputation. Whatever you decide, Your will shall be made flesh."

Benevolent? Besmirch? Heck, I was on a roll.

Bother's obedient bygones hovered about Sandy slowly ushering her safely back in the captain's quarters. LeBouche readied his spyglass to catch another glimpse of his latest conquest.

As LeBouche relished ol' Rusty's defeat, Billybones hobbled through the crowd of mooncussers, his squint challenging the amber sockets of any 'cusser who considered standing up to him. He managed to pocket a couple of stilettos as he passed the horde without protest. Jose led the way, marching Billybones toward the bunker as if under the Frenchman's orders.

LeBouche lowered his arm to address us.

"Enough with the pleasantries, we have not the time. Not plank, nor hawl, you two shall duel. The victor will rule by my side. The mademoiselle will adorn his right. Smthe will be free to pirate another day once the riches of the Wydah are secured. That is my sworn word."

LeBouche held back one of his giggling jags.

" The duel, however, shall not be to the death. The loser will be doomed to forever curse every moon that passes while he cannot, you have my word on that as well."

Ryan pulled the blade by his side from its sheath and brought its blade across the curve of his hook as if sharpening the edge. Cold steel sang.

"Let it be so, bro! It's go time."

My brother's fencing stance was feeble at best but at least his arms moved without compromise. Between Billybones and me, we may have had one good pirate between us.

LeBouche paid little attention to our exchange, instead continued to watch the white flag of surrender flap over deflated sails and heavy hearts. Through the corner of his eye he saw the freed Billybones approaching. He chuckled, finally getting the joke he was the brunt of centuries before,

"A tip o' th' hat... that was rich. Who's laughing now, Smythe?"

He clapped his hands twice making his decree a command.

"A duel it shall be! Make quick of it, there's company in the offing to be dealt with!"

Billybones slipped a short blade into my hands behind my back. All the weight was in its hilt. The blade was thin and arced forward able to cut air with little effort. I swallowed pain as I gave the blade a few swipes. Its ease of use would keep me in the game longer than expected.

I wasn't about to kill my brother even with the threat of 'cusserhood over my head. If my flesh didn't fail me, I would wear him down until he surrendered. Then it would Ryan and I against Frenchie; game, set, match.

Just as our blades were raised against one another, Sandy stormed out of from behind the billowing curtains, her reign of silence ended.

"Fools! Both of you! Do you believe a word this worm says? You'll all be undead by dawn if you play his game."

LeBouche brought his switch of nine tails to attention, cracking it against his thigh. Sandy stared into his smoldering eye sockets.

"Just try me, dead man!"

She stomped her way back into the captain's quarters, retreating not because she couldn't bear to see the two of us fight, but because she wasn't sure what the pirate vixen in her might do next.

The curtains flapped open again and she yelled at us.

"Don't think for a second that I'm part of the victor's purse. "You..."

Her pink tipped finger pointed at Ryan.

"... you...you're...you're unlovable! As for you..."

Her finger waved back and forth at me.

"... you are just... such a boy! What we have here is a sleeveless sweater Ty. I tried to warn you but do you listen.. no.."

She rambled on long after the drapes closed behind her. Sandy had damned me with the same epitaph as Billybones... boy.

I kept repeating to myself one of Billybones mottos, 'Men make decisions, men act on conviction and men are measured by their actions.' I drew my blade.

Ryan's hand trembled as Sandy's words drilled a wormhole in his pride. He called out to the girl behind the curtain

"Haw! What you know, ran-dee San-dee. Don't you want me bay-bee. Everyone wants me or wants to be me. I'm... I'm the man!"

Fueled more on self loathing than hatred, Ryan charged, practically tripping over his own shoes in the process. I knew the drill, drop to my knees, which my weak legs were want to do, then swipe at his hand, roll out to my right, and thrust my curved blade up, just below his breastplate. All his fight would topple to the deck boards. I could only hope that the wound would not be fatal.

Billybones whispered to me, but not in my head. His words were just for my ears.

"Bloody hell, y' can't be kill'n kin, matey. Ye be not a pirate, nor want t' be. The hat be too heavy."

Billybones stood before me. His cutlass fell at my feet. His weak arms clutched my shoulders, hoping they were still strong enough to put me in my place.

"Strike me for a lubber, but upon my soul, You both be the sires of better stock than this. Time would burn me thrice if I let ye shadow me steps."

With that I was back in my bedroom at the cottage, the promise of a peaceful summer night breathing through the window screen. Then Billybones face is before me, bigger than life, both eyes this time, blazing blue.

"So yer thought ya' mighta' *been* a pirate do ya lubby?"

My brother closed in on us and lunged. Billybones face grimaced, a spray of spittle accented his every word.

"Well *were* ya or *weren't* ya?"

There was the flash of chrome and a spray of crimson as Ryan's sword pierced through.

"Stranger things have happened... and will!"

The rapier's song played in my right ear, its warmth cutting air as all strength drained from Billybones grip. A lock of my hair fell to the floor between Billybones' body and my brother's freshly bloodied sword.

I close my eyes. When they open, I am back on the death ship, my mentor bleeding out at my feet, my brother standing bugged-eyed aghast, over his body.

LeBouche held his side as a stitch of laughter shook his bones. Sandy peeked out between the drapes, her eyes red and wet with tears. I dropped my sword as if its steel scalded my palm yet again. It took everything in me to suppress my inner pirate who so wanted to rush Ryan and gut him from nose to toe with one strike.

I left my brother standing there, overmatched and overwhelmed.

I, Tyler Byrne was not a pirate.

I looked to the western seam of darkness as the real pirates ship came into view, its white flag replaced with the jolliest of Rogers. The colours flapped angrily in the twilight sporting the traditional pirate moniker of crossed bones.

Instead of the typical grinning skull, the reaper lurking just below the surface of every God-fearing head, was a smiley face; a full moon cast over a field of black. Its eyes were black and lifeless. Its grin was thin and long, ear to ear if circles could hear. The line grew thicker where a bottom lip would hang revealing picket fence lines of teeth, its message clear.

Have a nice day... not!

Chapter 20

AVAST

*S*howtime.

The Gatto & the Capt'n's Crew Seaside Show-o-rama was about to commence on the port side. It opened without fanfare, just a firefly riding the tide of the ocean's swell. The hungry grin sprawled over their illuminated flag flapping wildly over the ship revealed ol' Rusty's true colors. The shanty was but a somber whisper of disembodied voices.

Cue the lights... curtain up.

"Gunners on the ready, leave nothing to chance!" LeBouche brayed. Recalling their place, the mooncussers lumbered to their appointed stations. Order and command was the tonic for the undead troops. They ran from motor control, not free will. Repetition and routine they understood. It went far in quelling superstition.

I left Billybones for dead, his life weeping across the deck. The man saved my life; I owed him more than that but it was every man for himself.

I grasped the rail leading down the hatch, strong enough to counter Bother's tugging. His fellow recruits joined in. I resisted the bygones good intentions and shook them off me. Bygones have no true substance. Their efforts resulted in the lot of them losing form and sluicing down the cascade of stairs. All that was left was a score of sausage fingers still clutching my pant leg, soon to crawl off like salt blind slugs.

There was no way that I was going to miss Gatto in his moment of glory. The cast of the main show assembled across the bow of Ol' Rusty save for the headliner, Gatto the deathless.

Drum roll... a moment held for dramatic effect, then Gatto made his entrance. His smile mirrored the ship's colours, Cheshire wide. A wreath of braided rope stained with tar created a makeshift wig framing Gatto's face. Each black dreadlock was woven with fireworks spitting sparkle and fire. Gatto's possessed expression beamed in the pre-dawn dark. Gatto's eyes were that of a mad man, not mad with an insanity imposed by time, but with a madness of imagination. It was a look all but the most fool hearty would stand clear of. Gatto was born for this.

Where Gatto was madcap, Capt'n Jack was the polar opposite, one cool customer. He stood, towering over all around him. His neck stretched out like a python overpowering a mongoose. An eye patch was slung over one eye, not to confirm his piratitude but to increase the accuracy of his already expert sniper skills. It wasn't a stretch to assume that he had done a stint in covert operations sometime in history. I never understood this term until I saw Capt'n in the zone that night, he was the master of all he surveyed.

Big Red followed his captain's studied nonchalance. Red always seemed to be holding back a canary-feathered grin. That night he sported his best smile yet as he flanked Jack. They had both survived 'Nam. Jack had a tour in Korea under his belt. In the time-bending times I was living in, they could have been gladiators in 1000 Year War.

The ladies on the ship were armed to the teeth. Somewhere between the fall of The Rusty Anchor and the launch of ol' Rusty, Bess and my mom had found common ground. They stood side by side, launching fountains of color into the night sky. Balls of color and spark that shot towards the heavens. Who would have thought of using Jack's arsenal of fireworks for the 3rd and a surplus of emergency flares to combat the mooncussers? Gatto, that's who.

"Smart kid, that swabbie," wheezed Billybones, lying motionless but still alive on the floor. Even at death's door he could appreciate a good comeuppance.

"Just watch'm scurry. They may be some mean scallywogs, but they spook easy."

Billybones spoke the truth. What we knew as roman candles was magic to a mooncusser. To them, the two spunky lasses were sorceresses summoning miniscule galaxies from their fingertips. Surely the phantom pirate ship shimmering on the far horizon was birthed from the same incantations that had cursed them into purgatory.

The mooncussers stood fear-struck by the enchantments unfurling before them. Mooncussers could taste fear, they feasted on it. The bitterness that stung their skulls that night was their own. They could even smell a hint of it on LeBouche. Their new quartermaster reeked worse of all.

Mooncussers can't die. They aren't dead, they are worse than dead. They have passed on but without a boarding pass to the afterlife, forever waiting on the docks for a ship to salvation that never arrives.

Our goal wasn't annihilation but incapacitation. Gatto and I learned firsthand on the killing fields of Lobster Cove that combating mooncussers only bought you time. It also sent a message loud and clear, 'don't mess with us, goons!'

So here's the question that haunted me. What's the point of fighting that which cannot be beaten? For privateer or a pirate, the living or the half-baked dead, it all comes down to fighting the good fight.

When being inundated with a plague of pirates from an era long past, you tend to forget that you are living on the cusp of a new millennium. A movie company even considered changing its name; the twentieth century was so yesterday. I was as guilty as the movie moguls. Whenever I struck out against Billybones or the mooncussers I always retaliated in kind; with a stick, stiletto, a flat blade of silver, perhaps the miracle of a flint lock pistol. Fighting them on their own terms seemed a noble act in my twisted mind. Only by beating them with the resources of yesteryear could I truly claim victory.

That night, with Sandy and the Manifest in LeBouche's possession, it was no longer about honor. It wasn't about winning or losing. It was survival, do or die.

Billybone's winked at me from across the deck.

'*don't take a blunderbuss to an AK 47 fight,*' he thought to me.

Capt'n had no such blinders on when he and his crew of motleys inched closer to aft of the death ship. Crewmates were just itching to break open the camouflage wooden crates at their feet.

Gatto's antics served as the diversion, dancing back and forth across the deck on fire. He lit cherry bombs, M80s and half-sticks and threw them overboard like a voodoo master summoning his pagan god. The mooncussers stopped in their tracks. If mooncussers could remember how to pray they would have been down on boney knees.

"Can't kill 'cussers but you sure 'nuff kin mess'm up darn good!" thought-grunted Big Red.

He pulled up an automatic weapon nearly as long as he was high. The spring loaded tripod assembled in the matter of seconds. Big Red was the gunner to end all gunners. He was a student of the state of the art of war, no cumbersome cannons and brass monkeys full of lead balls for him. His weapon of choice was lightweight and lethal. He maintained aim by wrestling the kickback with all the strength in his Popeye arms. The artillery snorted to life. An endless ribbon of bullets fed inside, a rain of shells spilling across the deck. This was artillery as opposed to a gun, quite like a ship is not a boat.

Bullets pierced the night. Steel on steel drown out the rocking of the tide. The flare's orbs bathed the mooncast in pulsating crimson. The light refracted on the bullets, a plague of gun metal locust closing in on their target.

The legion of mooncussers understood the language of gunfire and broke rank. Instead of prepping cannons for retaliation, they swarmed the two bunkers on deck seeking safety below. It was the only way off the top of the ship, save for diving into the unforgiving sea.

Can it truly be called mayhem when the casualties are already half-dead? If mooncussers felt no pain, could the massacre of LeBough's crew be considered a sin? Perhaps it was a half-sin, like a white-lie, a matter of interpretation.

The deck of the death ship was reduced to a bone yard. There was a slight delay from the report of the artillery and the bullet spray that swept the deck. Joints were torn asunder by metallic talons. Bones splintered, viscous of sinewy cords and eruptions of bilge spewed like geysers high into the air.

The first wave of fire was enough to break Ryan's stand-off. He fell to the floor and started crawling towards our shelter before any of the rounds could clip him. A few strays hit the metal sleeve of his hook as he dragged himself closer to the bunker. One ricochet braised his left cheek. He reached up, his hand brought down blood. He looked over at Billybones in a pool of his own blood, and, with his world painted red, Ryan lost it.

Another shot ricocheted off his hook, letting off a spark. I reached for my brother's hand, to pull him to safety. The metal rang like a bell as it dented. Ryan yelped he was through feigning courage.

I timed my attempts to save him between the light bursts on the deck of the pirate ship. I could see pin dots of fire from its starboard side, a racket echoed down the expanse of the ocean, a silent instant and then the world would tear. I pulled Ryan in between the successive bursts.

The few mooncussers who had not been reduced to marrow soup stormed the cannon deck below, two by two prepping the cannons. There were thirty-four cannons that peered out over the ocean in ol' Rusty's direction but only enough dead-man power to gunner ten.

I thought-warned the pirate crew of the incoming assault.

"Prepare for fire!"

Capt'n was way ahead of me. He had already maneuvered ol' Rusty towards the far back of LeBouche's port side, the ship's blind side to protect them from the cannon fodder. They were preparing for a textbook broadside as soon as LeBouche wasted lead, revealing just how much firepower he had at his disposal.

In the glow of the dissipating flare I saw my mother and Bess straddling the bowsprit, a large, pointed pole that reaches out over the bow of the ship. My mother was negotiating a large surface-to-air gun, rifle, missile launcher, whatever it's called; it was one mega-bazooka of a firearm. Bess had her back, helping her level the heavy artillery over my mother's shoulder. They hung over the nipping ocean awaiting Capt'n's command as if operating a heat-seeking weapon was as every day as skateboarding or baking cookies.

Capt'n gave the nod. Gatto got to yell the command.

"Fire!"

LeBouche gave his order at the same time, his cannons roared. The discharge of centuries old cannons is underground thunder. It gives your innards a good shakedown as you anticipate the destruction only a heartbeat away.

The death ship's rash of cannon fire all but missed ol' Rusty save for one, a ball shot from the gunner on the far aft, or back, of the death ship. Gatto once again caught in the line of fire. The projectile this time wasn't a bottle rocket on steroids; it was hell-cast lead on a firestorm of brimstone.

Just as the command left his lips, Gatto found himself riding the crest of a fireball, swinging on rigging that dangled from main mast. His laughing face was still animated with firework

light. I could hear him let out a mocking "Yo Ho Ho!" Clear across
the expanse of water between us".

LeBouche watched this devil imp, this Bluebeard in
miniature, bait him on. Gatto had LeBouche's full attention. He
didn't notice Bess loading the artillery strapped to my mother or the
snake of blue smoke that rocketed toward the mid-hull of his death
ship.

"All hands on deck, all hands on deck," Capt'n thought-
hollered to all of us who could hear. His urgency was directed for us
on the death ship.

"Move it, move it, move it!" I yelled. The troops of bygones
who had grown quite loyal in a short amount of time, followed my
order promptly, rushing across the top deck through the curdling
puddles of 'cusser remains that were already trying to reconfigure.

Sandy came out of hiding and ran out of the captain's
quarters.

LeBouche remained calm under fire.

"There will be no mutiny on my ship! Rank and file, Rank
and file!" Revolution thick in the air, then sauntered back to his
quarters. He needed something to regain the respect of his crew. He
returned with my backpack hat contained The Manifest, pulling it
out for all to behold. The book was jaw tight as it was raised high in
the air over the upper deck railing. It was LeBouche's trump card.
The fate of the world squirmed in his boney hand.

The bad book was more than a little pissed off. The Manifest
despised all but uninitiated innocents. His presence of LeBouche
repulsed The Manifest and it shook with revulsion. He had not only
tainted the pages ages ago but the resulting evil that trickled down
was far more damning than giving sight, healing the lame or killing

a kin. Fowl deeds hung thick around LeBouche. The curse upon the mooncussers stained his hands for all time.

The Manifest was a fish out of water, its cover twisted like fins, its thrashing pages, desperate gills. It knew what Sandy and I had come to realize; reality was hanging by a thread. One more oafish alteration and any trace of our existence would be reduced to a pile of dust, discarded serifs and punctuation for the custodian of whatever life form would follow us, to sweep into a dustpan of irrelevance.

When on a ship, follow the rats lead. The impact of the blast rocked the death ship, hitting square above the devil. The section had already been severely compromised by the attack of The N-BoQ and the impromptu patchwork to the breech was nothing more than spackle.

First, there was the hiss of rodent panic, scores of bilge rats stormed the hatches, rushing up the stairs. Fear with fur bit and scurried between legs and mooncusser remnants. Sea water was next, right on their tails, rampaging through the galley, swallowing everything in its path.

The impact not only tore at the hull of the death ship, it knocked The Manifest from LeBough's hands. It fell down to the main deck before my mumbling brother. Its pages were momentarily exposed by the impact.

"Avast!" LeBouche called, pirate-speak for stop. Sandy stood behind him as he tried to catch the book in mid-air. Her arms were obediently behind her back but her smile was no longer an emotionless line of pink drawn across her face.

Sandy whispered a not so sweet something into LeBouche's ear.

"Fermez! Fermez votre bouche, LeBouche!"

I had to laugh. Like most kids my age learning a new language, the first and foremost thing I tried to learn was how to curse in that tongue. The first thing I learned was Sandy's epitaph to LeBouche; Fermez votre bouche, shut your mouth.

With The Manifest no longer in his possession I there was nothing to fear in LeBouche. I continued laughing as I pointed up at him and said the only other derogatory thing I had learned in French.

"Tu a bête et tres pain"

"You just said he's dumb and very bread" Sandy yelled down to me. It should have translated as, you are dumb and very painful.

"Fermez, mademoiselle," I joked back

Sandy kept repeating the word fermez over and over. I joined her chant, soon grotesquely aped by the army of bygones. As our voices shook the gibbot cage, Sandy raised her hands above her head to reveal her two knitting needles. Sandy embraced her inner pirate. Fire was in her eyes and revenge in her craw.

"Au revoir, LeBouche."

The two points of the large wood shafts harpooned LeBouche just below each of his ears driving straight through to the other side. They crossed below his skull like a Jolly Roger's bones, making it impossible for his head to remain attached to his body. It fell to the main deck, adjacent to The Manifest. It was within arm's reach but alas, his head had none.

Ryan stepped towards The Manifest and poked it with the business end of his hook. He then recoiled as if he had just poked road kill and wasn't sure if it would continue to lay there dead, its innards on display or would open its blood-bathed eyes, fueled on full blown rabies, and go for his throat.

The Manifest turned its rattle of alarm into an inviting purr, pages all a flutter. Ryan was welcomed at its footnotes. The fair, the snake, the silence, couldn't Ryan feel the danger crawling on his skin?

Ryan was maddness-maddened. Mad dogs and Frenchmen named LeBouche aren't born, they're made. Sure a cur can turn when its chemistry set is turned ravenous but in most cases madness is fallout from the past. Some people can shake off the dust of bad days gone down. Others are born with a dent already in their showroom bumpers, less able to fight against the rust of evil consequence. My brother came off the car lot of life, used. You could see it in his headlights, never a high beam, one light focused just shy of straight.

Though the book gnashed against the spine and glue that held it together, it had no teeth, no claws. The Manifest's only defense against us dim-witted mortals was our free will. Left to our own devices, we would slowly alter ourselves out of existence. Our deepest wants empowered it. The Manifest was just a portal to our own extinction and we were at the helm.

Ryan knelt before the book. It opened itself to him with a wet turning of its living pages. The words etched in their flesh pulsed with a heartbeat. He looked into the body of the book as if staring into the barrel of a gun.

LeBouche's head rest a couple of feet to his right. He continued spitting orders at Ryan. If the word Wydah was a swear he had Turret's. "Wydah, here and now!" "Wydah, you dimwitted dolt!" "Wydah, damn you!" "Wydah, Wydah Wydah!"

The words were gibberish in Ryan's ears. He heard 'treasure this' and 'treasure that' but when it came to history, like everything else taught in school, he gave a deaf ear. Ryan realized whatever LeBouche demanded of him would only come back to bite him. It wasn't quantum physics. He had a hook for a hand to remind him.

Ryan closed his eyes, trying to block out the insanity around him, trying to make the right decision.

"Just back away, bro," I wanted to tell him. I wanted to plead with him that no matter what he wrote, he would never change things for the better. He would never be richer, never find true love, never find our father save for a nameless marker in an overgrown graveyard. I wanted to tell him "Its O.K." but his ears would have just regarded me as a fourth period history lesson. Whatever I said would just push his hand quicker to the page. I couldn't allow my passion to give his ink muscle. I said nothing.

His eyes opened and his good hand reached for the quill that poked out of the meat of The Manifest. I remembered how a million thoughts and desires spiraled through my mind when I sat in his seat. Ryan was lost in the same mental spins, visions of vintage 'vettes and playmates without staples in their midsections. Ryan nervously tapped the quill against the half blank page where the calligraphy ended.

Jose, crouched beside Bother, watched his friend battle his devils. A howl grew deep inside of his dusty shell. Jose reached out his willowy arms towards Ryan as if by sheer will he could pull the quill from Ryan's hand, saving his friend from a similar damnation.

He stood as tall as his withered form allowed and opened his mouth, the howl's crescendo overshadowed LeBouche's tirade. As it rose in intensity, the starburst pattern calloused across his chest began to weep. What broke threw his skin wasn't the grey slurry that made up bygones, it was blood, old blood, a dark syrup, oil dark.

Time does not heal all wounds even when the fantastic intervenes. The outline of the incision carved for self-evisceration glistened red. The trivet that floated within his chest cavity quivered with each heavy breath. Jose must have resisted devouring his own heart completely for his dammed soul still held residence. Dammed had defeated bygone in the battle for Jose's soul. Saw teeth lined his gums, flashing white and serrated where a toothless bygone jowl should have grown. His fingernails followed fashion, splintered into pins. His eyes residing in the hollows of his face refused to be swallowed into the bygone deep. They flashed the anguish of insatiable hunger.

The dammed ran on all fours towards Ryan. I could continue to call him Jose but any resemblance to my brother's buddy had been faded green. Its gait was swift and predatory. The dammed's tongue flitted between shark teeth. Its end was forked, not by nature but by the razor sharpness of the teeth it brushed across as it tasted the fowl air.

The gait of the charging dammed resounded against the floorboards snapping Ryan from his daydreams. Ryan clutched the quill tight, drew it to his chest and protected it, hook poised before him. Ryan was not in the dammed's line of vision. The Manifest was also not the target of the enraged abomination.

The dammed passed by a teary-eyed Ryan and pounced. LeBouche's head was silenced in mid-Wydah. His claws wrapped around the circumference of LeBouche's head, effectively muzzling him. The head shook from side to side to no avail. It was silenced but the tainted could hear inside the voice of the pirate thief whimper what sounded like French prayers to an uncaring God. The dammed dragged LeBouche's head across the deck to the far corner where the stairwell rose to meet the captain's deck. Mooncussers and bygones both cleared away from the dammed's path.

Inside the hollow of the stairwell it crouched over its prey, turned its back to us as if ashamed of its primal urges and bowed its head as if saying grace. It then bore down with fierce intensity on what had sentenced it to purgatory. There was the sound of the first bite of a still green apple followed by more unsavory sounds. Pirate radio was off the air.

"Stop!" yelled Ryan, swiping his hook back and forth at his damned friend.

"Avast, yo!"

It was too late, LeBouche was gone, the mooncusser that could not die, torn from this plane by one more damned than he. Perhaps LeBouche was still doomed to live an eternity only now he had to sit it out in the gullet of a dammed.

Sandy rushed to me, huddled behind my shoulder blade, using my body to shield her from Manifest-wielding Ryan, the wild thing feeding, the ocean spewing from the bunkers, from a world gone mad. It felt good to have her by my side. She still smelt of lavender and sand dunes.

Ryan's eyes were saucers, his detachment was scary indeed. The imminent sinking of the death ship did little to shake him sane. The stern of the ship gradually tipped down towards the angry waves. The blackened windows of the Captain's cabin popped like firecrackers under the pressure of ocean waves insisting entrance.

The Manifest's pages heaved in and out in frustration. Ryan wasn't even focused on the book before him. He just stared at his hook, brushing the length of its curved steel with the feather of the quill as if massaging the outline of his phantom hand. His voice was in another place.

"What's the 411 to this 911? The moral of the story? You don't like where the story's going, change it. Me, I don't read much, keep it short and sweet, like Bazooka Joe comics and tweeter peeps. Me, I'm the A to Z of ADD. If I don't like a book, I close it 'n start a nudda, brotha."

While Ryan rambled on nonsensically, Gatto and his crew were in stealth mode, broadsiding the death ship. There was no need for an exchange of firepower. The remaining mooncussers lacked a leader and were lost. Our rescuers were able to lay down large planks between the decks and board the sinking ship undeterred. A flank of tug boat men sprinted across and secured the walkway. A surge of grappling hooks bit into the death's ship's rails, ropes drawn tight. 'Ol Rusty was docked securely to the death ship's starboard side.

The ship of the late Captain LeBouche was quickly taking on water. It would be a matter of minutes before it sank, another sunken remain of an indistinguishable age. Capt'n and Gatto came aboard in full stride. Behind them was a crew armed with the latest in military weaponry.

Gatto, however, chose period armaments, not 17th century pirate but 12th century samurai. He had constructed a metal breast plate of flattened tin cans and metal scraps that he had soldered together. It wasn't Kevlar, but would protect him against a mooncusser's blade. He also wore a pair of gloves with large cuffs usually used for fish wrangling or furnace stoking. A collection of rusty circular saw blades dangled from his belt by a loop of cable. They rattled a warning as he marched on board. One of the blades gilded with orange was loaded into what looked like the marriage of a club and a sling shot.

"That's my Gat" I said to Sandy.

"Gatto, our little pirate", Sandy agreed.

A mooncusser in the back of the mollified horde detected the uninvited boarding and instinctually went for its steel. Gatto swung his homemade weapon back over his head, then forward as if pitching a screwball. The blade gained rotation as his arm went up and shot off of the grooved stick with a whirr on the way down. It tore clear through its target before the mooncusser could even pull his sword from its sheath. Other mooncussers turned away from Gatto's crew their fellow mooncusser fell to the ground in pieces. It was a message sent, ninja style; a check no undead pirate would cash.

The lure of the Manifest was intoxicating. My brother, like the rest of us, was too weak to resist. He continued mumbling to himself.

"Not good, no no no... don't like this story. Too dark yo"

I stood still, waiting for my brother to snap out of it. He caught my concerned gaze from the corner of his bloodshot eyes and shot me an inebriated smile.

"You, you're the reason we're here, bro. You could'a made everything right... but nnooo. Now, it's mine turn."

I don't know if writing the words *and then I woke up to find it was all a dream'* would have done the trick. I don't know if anything would. In Ryan's delirium, one thought won out over babes, booze, bundles of Benjamins; he wanted off this crazy ride.

The quill went down. I jumped with feeble legs and fell where I stood, a foot short. I could see over his shoulder what he wrote. In the worst cursive and sixteen year old scribble were the words 'The End', capitol T, capitol E, not *an* end but *The* End. He closed his passage with a resounding period of finality that left a swollen birthmark deep in the page.

I thought The Manifest smiled, which is impossible for it had no face. It pages stretched, its spine curved upwards then it relaxed and reverted to a nothing out of the ordinary book.

Gatto, oblivious of the wheels Ryan had set in motion, marched victorious towards us. The mooncussers, with no more fight left in them, moved aside. My mom flanked Capt'n Jack, caught sight of Ryan before The Manifest and cried out.

"Oh Rybo, what have you gotten yourself into now?"

She knew damn well what.

In the distance twilight was snuffed out, the first shadows of azure smoldering on the eastern horizon.

There was a hush; all eyes looked to the skies. It all went black. Not dark, but black. Black black. If black is actually the combination of all colors and white, the absence of color, I would have to say the horizon went *white* black for it was a blanket of nothingness. Even a starless night hinted of eternity. What swallowed the horizon moving rapidly towards us was a void.

"Holy..."

"Exactly." Sandy interrupted, hushing my mouth. Now was not the time to besmirch the reverence of an almighty with a hankering for wrath.

The ocean swells that where crashing over the deck settled into a calm. We were in deep ocean without even a quiver of a wave.

Then the undercurrent shifted directions. The waves returned, the white caps returned, this time rushing in the opposite direction towards where there once was a horizon a moment before.

Gulls cried in anguish, their voices snubbed out by the onyx slab of nonexistence as it closed in. A cloud of monarch butterflies surrounded the ship. A million wing flaps clouding our vision. As soon as they came they were suctioned further from the distant coast towards oblivion.

Gatto was finally back by my side. He gave me an elbow to the side.

"I may be good at this whole saving the day thing, but a hero needs a villain, right? An arch nemesis, something... not nothing. What is this?"

He pointed out to The End before us. It was as formidable an adversary as any we had encountered that summer, well deserving the title, *The*.

Bess tagged along behind Gatto. She was Lady Liberty with a flare ablaze in one hand to ward off any stray mooncussers.

"Maybe there's a reset button"

Bess referred to the arcade games at the town fair Gatto learned how to jerry rig for free games by crossing some wires.

Ryan cowered, The Manifest clutched tight against his chest for protection. The book was but a fickle thing. It lured him in, had him do it's will, tainted his soul for all time. Now it found him as repugnant as the rest of us. It shook itself free from his grip and fell into the wet of the main deck. As The End bore down over us, The

Manifest stretched and strained as if it was reeling The End in. The cover opened and closed rapidly, fanning our demise.

Ryan started to laugh to a joke never said. He swung his hook high into the air, bringing its point down on the center of The Manifest's cover. The book, stitched together with the whims of countless victims, allowed the quill of the uninitiated to carve its flesh like butter but the forged steel of Ryan's hook was no contest for The Manifest's will. The sharp curve of the hook could not mare the leather.

Instead, the force of his attack twisted metal and tore at the cords that sutured the hook onto Ryan's arm. The fusion of tendon and seaweed unraveled as Ryan fell backwards. The cuff of the hook ripped from his arm. Inside was not the cauterized stump I expected, but a hand, emaciated, but still attached. It was abnormally white, ripe with infection, the fingers, five gentrified hooks of skin. Ryan crawled away, still laughing, wanting so to grab at his hand but knowing that the pain would be too great.

"Never send a pirate to do a ninja's job," said Gatto.

"Pirate, no ninja." I nodded very piratey.

Gatto bowed his acknowledgement in a ninjary way. I gave him a buddy back slap, and then tended to my brother.

Nothingness was closing in.

It was now time for the main event, Gatto vs. Manifest for all the marbles. There was a nervous tremor in Bess' voice we had never heard before.

"Be careful big guy. It knows how to mess with your head..."

"It's real good at it Gatto, its one bad, bad, son of a bitch of a book." Sandy added.

"Be a clean slate..." I said in all seriousness. "... shouldn't be hard for you"

Gatto freed another rusty ninja star of a blade from his belt and loaded it into his launcher. "Har, har. No worries! No three wishes were wasted, no Stay Puff Marshmallow Man..."

For Sandy, this was no time for levity.

"This isn't a genie Gatto, this is Pandora's box. You know what's in Pandora's box? You don't wanna know what's in Pandora's Box but you walk around all day and night and all you can think of is 'what the hell is in Pandora's box'. THAT'S what's in Pandora's Box."

"You've got to close the book, once and for all" Bess demanded.

"And do what! Put the words, *only kidding*' after the words, The End?" I snapped back.

"Got any duck tape, that should do the trick!" Gatto scoffed.

I noticed that the straps of his breastplate were constructed of it. It was common knowledge among most men that duck tape, not fate and destiny, held our world together. It was meant as a joke but was as viable an option as any.

Gatto stopped laughing, trying hard to get his game face on. Billybones commanded Capt'n from the waterlogged deck.

"Capt'n... Jack! Fetch me the recruits. Be quick about it. Prop me up and git me swallow while you're at it"

"Reg, yer life be on the floor, take it easy... all in time."

"Ay, the one thing we be short a. Go on." The Capt'n knew the true rank of the crew and complied with haste.

"It's in moments such as this I ask myself what would Kurosawa do?" said Gatto.

"You mean, what would Billybones do?" I corrected.

"Same diff."

Jack gathered the four of us to Billybones side. He'd heard our every word, three in the head, one out loud; Gatto hadn't been cursed with an inside voice, yet.

"I'd get my butt off the bench and give that hell spawn the old heave ho!" a frustrated Billybones winced.

His summer bred crew stood at attention over him.

"Ay, ay Billybo... I mean"

"yeah, yeah I know... Jack, draw me a tot, and blazes, leave the bottle. Gentleman, this be the hour."

I knew the answer. "There be no gentleman here."

Billybones nodded, I could dole it out as well as take it. He gave me a wink that looked more like a wince.

Sandy started rambling, "are you comfortable, I mean, of course not, but maybe, maybe I could..."

Billybones shooshed her silent with a smile akin to a wince.

Bess remained silent. If there was something she could do to help Billybones, she would be the first at his side. She had seen the pallor of Billybones before in the crystal memory of her mother's deathbed. It was the one memory that would not grow moss as much as she prayed it would.

"... and ladies. If I needed one thing to keep the sod under my feet, it would be the chance to see the likes a ya."

Billybones turned to Gatto. "Be I before a mirror, funhouse glass fer sure, but I know when I sees me own reflection." He couldn't give Gatto a better compliment. He tried puffing his metallic chest out proudly.

Billybones sat up to address Gatto up close and personal. I saw the water pooling at the small of Billybones back, it drifted in and around an island of red.

"Ye first mate got ya into this... had no choice really. In my day, I didn't hold up as well as he, his Dad felt the brunt of that. Now it's your time. Step up and own it. Are you man enough?"

Gatto was born ready. It he wasn't he had no choice. Destiny is dealt, not offered.

"I knew as much, good man, good man."

He started to draw another shot, dismissed with the tot and drew a long swig from the clay bottle beside him. He closed his eyes as the liquor burned his throat, pushing the pain down.

"Now get on with it ya bilge monkeys! Give'm hell."

We all harbor inner pirates, everyone but Gatto. He grew into quite the man of action during the past two months. His path was indeed a bushido, a ninja's code, never motivated by selfish motives.

Gatto cracked his neck, one side, then the other. Rocky was between rounds. Bess gave him a ten second neck massage in the corner of the ring. In the distance a Buoy bell panged more and more franticly and then was silenced, a disquiet that hurt the ears.

Hearing the last clang of the bell, Gatto entered the ring. He took two steps towards The Manifest. It stopped its conniption and came to rest in a wash of saliva and lost vowels. In a moist exhale the book opened before him.

Gatto looked down at the words 'The End', a fresh bruise on the page. The two words were devouring history. Any script before the words moved rapidly across the page to the left side of the two words only to be sheered from the flesh, falling to the deck in a cloud of letter ash. To the right side there was a blank canvas

What wishes stayed hidden in the dark recesses of Gatto's heart, we'll never know. There wasn't any pretense in the man, what you saw is what you got. His soul had skylights, nowhere for shadows to hide.

When I was in the author's chair, I was more interested in hypothetical angels on the head of a pin. Being a classic rock geek I considered what would happen to rock 'n roll if in 1959 Buddy Holly didn't die? Would there be no Beatles? If they didn't there would be no band called The Cyrkle for us to name ourselves after. If there was no rock n' roll as we know it, would Aerosmith be reduced to the obscure blues legends Bleeding Gums Tyler and Bottleneck Perry. Most importantly, if there was no Cyrkle, would we exist at all?

Gatto was more mature than me in many ways. He had his friends and little else mattered. That was all needed to be happy.

It would take something unknown to the rest of the Cyrkle to tempt him, a dark secret cowering behind his heart. If it was there, The Manifest would find it and use it against him.

Gatto reached down to the book and brought his gloved hand against its spine, rubbing its length, calming it still. Words still fell from it, lifeless but the fever pace of our existence being erased was quelled. Gatto then pulled off one of his gloves and reached with his bare hand for the quill still wet with crimson ink clotting on the hollow of the feather's point.

Gatto's face went white. If *white* black adequately described The End that was now starting to erase ol' Rusty from the world, then *black* white was the color of Gatto's face. He was flushed with a world of endless possibilities. He closed his eyes to cut through the blur, exhaling deep and slow.

"*Yes Gatto, breathe through the straw, single point of light... Pearl.*"

"*Got ya, Pallie!*" he replied, online.

When his eyes opened, his course was clear. Instead of bringing the feather down and signing our fate in blood, he snapped it in two. Crimson sprayed from the severed halves and sprayed the open pages. The parchment puckered trying to absorb the fresh ink sent to its pages, laid down without meaning.

Gatto towered over the book swinging his arm over his head, readying to smite evil. The centrifugal force put rusty wheels in motion. The circular blade whirred to life, building speed. Gatto planted the blade squarely between spine and page.

I will try to impart to you what happened next, though no words can do it justice.

Faith looks across the storm. I stood there frozen between the shroud of shadow and the clarity of the light. It was everything and nothing simultaneously. On the black tarp that threatened to engulf us we saw all of time projected before us. There were shadows of great flying beasts, their wingspan blotting out the sky. Beyond them, the metallic shimmer of silver ships sailing on rainbows of incandescence. Galleon ships littered the horizon while mountainous humps of serpent scale bore through the waves between them. Castles rose from the white caps and disappeared again with the crash of the waves. Volcanoes spewed islands that grew, wilted, and returned to the sea before us.

"Thunder!" said Billybones holding on to his last breath. He didn't mean God bowling in a thunderstorm. It was pirate-speak for living thunder, a god-sent force that bestows clarity and vigor.

Then there was the light, as absolute as the darkness that preceded it. It was *black* white, not unlike Gatto's face a moment before. It was a montage of past, present and future. It was Truth and in that glorious instant, we were blinded by more than we could ever comprehend.

"Thunder," I agreed.

I stumbled over to Gatto who was staring down at The Manifest as each page wasted away as if consumed by hellfire. Ashes swirled into black dust devils that rode the ocean gale.

Sandy and Bess gave Gatto a big hug as they joined him watching the book cease to be.

The first rays of dawn broke through the blinding everything. The ocean calmed as we were transported to a new day. The mooncussers exposed to the light faltered between gelled bones and streams of ink billowing in the wind.

Those who remained on the top deck did not look to the heavens they were banished from. They fixated on the raging ocean that was swallowing their ship. Beneath the reflection of the cinematic sky, a keyhole in time was closing.

Deep under the waves, the morning light caught a fountain of gold, a million stars twinkling in the deep. It was a rain of Spanish golden pieces of eight, treasure, not just any treasure, but the Wydah treasure, floating and spinning in the undercurrent. It returned to the banks of the New England shores that it had called home for so long, its history being rewritten before us.

With mooncussers, little thought goes into their actions. Like a dammed that chooses the bygone path, routine protected them from the pains of damnation. If mooncussers couldn't have salvation, then they better well have treasure. Every task performed by rote, every order barked by LeBouche obeyed was ultimately all about the big ca-ching.

And there it was, the Wydah treasure, beckoning them. One by one, the twenty odd mooncussers dove off of the sinking ship and swam deep into the briny deep. They swam further and further down, arms outstretched, reaching for the unattainable. Despite their pursuit the sinking coins remained just out of reach. Captain Bellamy's dowry, like redemption, out of the mooncusser's grasp.

As the coins submerged, down where daylight ended, they lost their luster. The sands of time closed in, settling over the horde, turning from sludge to stone. The mooncussers faded into sediment that separated them from their illusive treasure. The elongated bodies of the desperate were frozen in time, flies caught in amber, preserved for the offspring of the great treasure hunter Barry Clifford to unearth a lifetime away.

One day they would unearth the Wydah treasure coin by coin, cannon by cannonball from their fossilized prison. Their discovery would make the history books for the first time again.

What their findings wouldn't include, what couldn't be rationalized, was the legion of deformed skeletons, arms reaching towards the ocean's floor, suspended in the rock. They would assume drowning from a shipwreck, but why so deep? Why weren't they reaching for the surface? Nothing unearthed would tell of the greed that drove them down.

There was one thing every one of those future researchers would agree on. There was no way they would even consider releasing even one of the monstrosities from the oceanic sarcophagus. Some secrets are better left buried.

Dawn burnt into day. To the east, the horizon was ablaze with possibility. Gatto helped the girls onto ol' Rusty as the pirate ship gave its last gasp. Capt'n tended to Billybones body. My mother tended to Ryan's withered hand with a tear of her blouse, a little spit and a mother's love. I climbed up to the bow of the death ship, just over its decapitated figurehead and looked out over the ocean, squinting, searching..."

I looked at my friends, to the sea and back again. Sandy and Bess bookended Gatto; he proudly explained his new invention of weaponry. He was the hero, not me, I told you that from the start, and to the hero goes the spoils.

As if they had practiced it all summer, Bess and Sandy rose on their toes, ever so slightly, leaned in, and gave Gatto a kiss in stereo, one set of lips on each cheek. He flushed and reciprocated by giving them both rough and tumble hugs that promised horseplay to come. He was long past the phase of throwing rocks at girls but was still a year from being fearless about tonsil wrestling.

Was I jealous? Yeah a little bit, but having Gatto as a best bud was one heck of a consolation prize.

I looked back across the water for a sign amidst the miraculous.

With a wheeze for a voice Billybones called up to me.

"Never you mind. I don't need to read minds to know wha' cha thinkin'. Some faces launch ships, others lead to the reefs."

Billybones voice still had a bellow to it.

"Ya better come, mate" Capt'n advised.

My roost on the bow of the sinking ship now pointed skywards. I slid down the slanted deck until I hit the flooded boards where Billybones lay.

My mother removed the treasure map that once adorned Billybones arm from my brother's belt and joined me. Ryan followed behind her. She knelt down beside our one true captain and unfurled the dried skin ornamented with half-memories and placed it ever so softly where it once lived.

Once the swatch of skin returned to its proper place, the torn edges melded with his arm. The seams grew pink then reduced to a frame of scar tissue bordering Billybones' masterpiece. Then the design faded to nothing more than freckles and sunburn.

"Ye did good, ya old salt. Let's call it even. Say hello to Paddy for me." My mother wiped away a tear she would soon struggle to remember.

"There be no mistakes on earth, just confounded executions of will. Everything, everyone has purpose... even you kids."

Billybones smiled one last time, even as blood tried to muzzle his words.

"Yer Dad and I stood here, but we were no match. He was thick-headed brave, had what it would take, but I saw to it that he never got his shot. T'was pirate lust that killed ya pop, not a stroke of yer pen or yours truly. There be no more despicable a pirate than one who takes the life of the ones he loves. So beware Bellamy! Shiver ya timbers Bluebeard! They hold not a candle to the pirate you all see before ya."

He then reached out and grabbed Ryan and me by the scruff of our necks.

"From swabbies to captains, to quartermaster, ye dad, he'd be proud."

His glint of blue steel lingered.

"... aren't ya Paddy?"

His eyes then looked up into the cloudless blue morning. The blue in Billybones eyes paled, another legend lost.

I looked down; all I could see was a man strange to my eyes sprawled across my lap. He was not a pirate, not at that time anyways. He was Reginald Byrne, the owner of a curiosity shop. If you were to call him a pirate, he wasn't one to speak of. Now, Billybones... *he* was a pirate, no longer solely in my mind.

Billybones was gone, perhaps he never was.

Everyone returned to ol' Rusty, the death ship docked itself somewhere far below the waves. Mooncussers were already a fuzzy memory. Capt'n and his crew saw to Mr. Smythe's body, taking one of the ship's small jolly boats, manning it with a solitary mast that caught the bite of the wind with ease. They propped Smythe up, put LeBouche's naval captain's hat, plumage still attached, onto his head, and let the boat sail east and away; a Viking on his way to Valhalla.

Miracles come in threes but the Cyrkle chimed in at four at the end of the season. That was something to hold on to. The Cyrkle turned out to be better musketeers than pirates, more light than dark in our young souls. Some might say that Dumas' triumvirates were landlubber pirates and *The They* just might be right. The musketeers were as pirates as much as Robin Hood and his merry hooligans.

If they are all pirates then so were we, guilty as charged. When the dust clears and the bounty is divvied out, it all comes down to whose side you are rooting for weather you are considered a pirate or a patriot.

Before we left the sinking wreck I stowed away Bother and his dammed friend. Bother was loyal to both of us and I knew he would help me remember what time would want me to forget. Jose, the dammed, albeit a monster, was one of us.

I felt, in time, we would need him, or could save him, or he could save us... something without words. I made Bother promise to leave the Cove off season so that if he couldn't control the dammed's cravings, it wouldn't feed on the lifers in town. The unlikely couple made their way inland, visible only by me. I wondered if next summer I would have any recollection of them at all.

We returned to dry land, our summer homes in tatters. Lobster Cove smoldered as it had every sixty years or so for as long as history had been recorded. A new aerial photograph would soon join the rogue's gallery at Haddad Hall.

Everyone pitched in as if it was the price of living on the edge of the Earth. The townsfolk were already fuzzy on the cause of the devastation. They were more focused on the reconstruction.

"What's past is past, time to move on," one grey haired resident told a neighbor who helped her clear rubble from her front yard. Her house was a husk of its former self but her foundation stood strong. The Cove would bloom again like tigerlilys each summer.

It was the end of the season. We usually would say our goodbyes, promise to write knowing that there would be little communication until next summer.

Not this year. We needed to talk throughout the year, to remember what we could and paint in the details between. We needed to keep this summer crystal.

"I'll miss the old coot," shared Sandy. "but I've always had a thing for mature men."

She giggled for the first time since her abduction,

"He sure wasn't boring."

"He showed us what we made of. As Friedrich Nietzsche said, 'What doesn't kill you makes you stronger.'

"Nietzsche?" Sandy raised a perfectly plucked brow.

"She reads and can shred a mean half pipe, who knew." Gatto smiled.

"Thanks for believing guys... in me... in him."

My friends nodded like a row of bobble heads on the prize shelf of the impossible to win milk-bottle-throw at the fair.

My brother walked over to us and we opened our Cyrkle to him. He had a can of soda in his good hand, the other rested in a sling. "You talking 'bout Billybones?" We nodded expecting a razz,.

In true gangstah style, Ryan tipped his soda can, spilling some soda to the thirsty ground in reverence.

"To the homies and men named 'bones,"

He bowed his head, we followed suit. He then broke the moment before it grew too saccharine.

"Yo ho ho, yo!!"

Gatto and I exchanged sly salutations as Billybones would say, elbow to elbow one last time.

"You certainly gave us a pirate adventure Ty."

"No pirate, ninja."

Pirate ways were far behind us. Gatto got on his skateboard and like a cowboy on his trusty steed, headed into the sunset.

I took the long way home, which I recommend doing whenever you can. On the way, I caught sight of Bess attending to the unearthed grave sight of her beloved Nboquishakwana. History had restored her beloved pet back into a shoebox. Bess smoothed over the soil, made a cross out of two twigs and some sea grass and paid last respects for the second time. She sat Indian-style before the grave. I kept walking to let her put her pain to bed.

I head to the beachfront, taking my last beach walk of the season. I did it every year that I could remember. This year it was to say goodbye. There it was again, ringing in my ears, the call of the sea.

'Join us childe, be one of the stolen... something wild, something wonderful!'

Before I walked fully clothed into the sea without any intention of returning to dry land, I was interrupted by the trunk of my mother's Jeep slamming shut. I walked back to the cottage. My mother was waiting. She had seen that look before, that all-encompassing obsession. It was the lure that brought my dad to the sea, to her and to his demise. She was not about to lose another.

I helped my brother with his bags. He was downright thankful. The journey may fade away but what we shared made us stronger as friends and as family. Ryan asked my mom to tell us tales of our father on the way home. For the first time, she agreed. I wondered how much of the tales would be crystal and how many would be tall tales woven of green remnants. We didn't care; we still wanted to hear them, all of them.

"So we were up against the wall, seas were so rough they knocked the balls off of the brass monkey, which isn't as dirty as it sounds. It's where the cannonballs were stored for the gunner. I wasn't a gunner, yet, but your father was as crack of a gunner as you would ever come across. Billybones caught sight of a ship of fools through the blanket of fog that would put blinders on those less seasoned. "Stand for action. Run up the colours and Tally ho, let it be known that this day be their last!" Billybones called out over the mist, a ghost's voice in the enemy's ears, "I'll plunge you forthwith to the very deeps of hell if you do not stand down." Paddy, that's your dad, he took my hand and showed me how to light wick then back away before I need to count my digits. Ay, his smile could cut pea soup, I never felt more alive..."

We sat crammed into the back cab as she lost herself in memory. The tales weren't exactly coffee clutch chatter for the PTO but they were as clear as could be. We felt my dad sitting beside us as my mom continued with her tale of fabricated fiction. Somewhere, Billybones was listening in as well; good company.

Color returned to the cheeks of home, a bruised blue gilded with a tangerine rind. The clouds hinted at our latest stab at history, a puffy cotton ball of hope one second, then thinning out. Colors bled one into the other, an emerald arm of greed stretching down from on high to threaten a perfect day. Then there were the Jesus lights, as we would call them, shafts of ethereal gold cascading down from heaven. They beat rainbows hands down. Welcome back Lobster Cove.

Far out past the bobbers, past the jetty, past the mirage of distant shores, Pearl watched in awe of it all. Her world was the promise of things unattainable in this life. In our moments most crystalline, we catch but a glimpse of it in our rearview mirrors.

Somewhere Pearl basks on a rocky ledge that protrudes like a throne over the ocean's crest. The first hint of autumn nights to come, chills the air. I hear her sigh, I can hear her now and only her, the only voice left to echo in my bones. I recall her smile knowing she waits patiently for the promise of another summer's day. Over and over in my mind rolls the tide of a single thought, follow the mermaid, follow the mermaid."

The End

(no period)

Epilogue

DEAD MEN'S TALES

"Old and young, we are all on our last cruise."
- *Robert Louis Stevenson*

*I*n L. Frank Baum's classic book *The Wizard of Oz* and the subsequent film adaptation, the Good Witch says "There's no place like home." It was all *Technicolor* pretty and lollipop sweet. Pay no attention to the terrifying flying monkeys, falling houses and chicks painted green.

So goes life. Think of this as *Zen and the Art of Inner Pirate Maintenance*. Take it all in and go along for the ride with every thread of your being invested in the outcome. Go too slow and the fantastic in life fades. You see the boom mike hovering in shot over a little girl marked for tragedy and the shadow of a set worker dangling lifeless from a rope backstage between papier-mâché trees.

There is really only one pirate, time. It is the thief of that which we hold dear. As we grow older it takes our treasures, one memory at a time. Ah, but it can be beaten. Hold on to your few *green* memories that matter most. When you talk to the elderly, many stumble over the day to day but recall the highlights of their past vividly.

The trick is to tell the tale. The only thing that differentiates us from other animals is opposable thumbs, the ability to tell stories and free will. Don't twiddle away your legacy. May your will allow the tale of your life to be told with your every breath.

What I leave you with is this, once you find a home, be it where you sleep or where you summer with inseparable friends; live there. May you all find your Cyrkle. Soak up the sun while it shines and to quote the infamous commencement, "wear sunscreen". Hallmark cards speak the truth; home is where the heart is. Not located north of the rib cage, a waiting dinner for dammeds, but where passions lay. Oh... and stay out of the shadows no matter how much their inhabitants beckon you to their home.

Time is but a fleeting thing, feathers dancing in the faraway. It is a vision let loose, a gull riding the wrath of a Nor'easter, motionless in midair. The turbulence feeds its bliss.

The only way to beat this pirate of all pirates is to refute its very power over us. Cherish your past but live fearlessly in the present. Only then, like a sea breeze over a fading sunset, will life's beauty take you places your mind can only dream. Be in that moment always.

I wait for the day when I look out over the new day given and get it. After this summer I know more than most, but it comforts not. The only solace is my faith that our efforts, however feeble, matter in the grandiose scheme of things. The end to all tales is always the same. All will pass despite good intentions.

Do may be better than try, but try ain't bad when it's all you've got. In the end it's just the eternal battle between the devil and the deep blue me.

Made in United States
North Haven, CT
10 June 2023

37568690R10241